The Other Family

www.rbooks.co.uk

For more information on Joanna Trollope and her books,
see her website at www.joannatrollope.com

The Other Family

JOANNA TROLLOPE

Doubleday
LONDON · TORONTO · SYDNEY · AUCKLAND · JOHANNESBURG

TRANSWORLD PUBLISHERS
61–63 Uxbridge Road, London W5 5SA
A Random House Group Company

First published in Great Britain
in 2010 by Doubleday
an imprint of Transworld Publishers

A CIP catalogue record for this book
is available from the British Library.

ISBNs 9780385616140 (cased)
9780385616157 (tpb)

Addresses for Random House Group Ltd companies outside the UK
can be found at: www.randomhouse.co.uk
The Random House Group Reg. No. 954009

The Random House Group Limited supports The Forest Stewardship
Council (FSC), the leading international forest-certification organization.
All our titles that are printed on Greenpeace-approved FSC-certified
paper carry the FSC logo. Our paper procurement policy can
be found at www.rbooks.co.uk/environment

Typeset in 11½/15pt Sabon by
Kestrel Data, Exeter, Devon.
Printed and bound in the UK by
CPI Mackays, Chatham ME5 8TD

10 9

Mixed Sources
Product group from well-managed
forests and other controlled sources
www.fsc.org Cert no. TT-COC-2139
© 1996 Forest Stewardship Council
FSC

For Jason

CHAPTER ONE

Looking back, it astonished her that none of them had broken down in the hospital. Even Dilly, who could be relied on to burst into tears over a shed eyelash, had been completely mute. Chrissie supposed it was shock, literally, the sudden suspension of all natural reactions caused by trauma. And the trauma had actually begun before the consultant had even opened his mouth. They just knew, all four of them, from the way he looked at them, before he said a word. They knew he was going to say, 'I'm so very sorry but—' and then he did say it. He said it all the way through to the end, and they all stared at him, Chrissie and the three girls. And nobody uttered a cheep.

Chrissie didn't know how she had got them home. Even though Tamsin and Dilly could drive, it hadn't crossed her mind to hand either of them the car keys. Instead, she had climbed wordlessly into the driver's seat, and Tamsin had got in – unchallenged for once – beside her, and the two younger ones had slipped into the back and even put their seat belts on without being reminded. Unheard of, usually. And Chrissie had started the car and driven, upright behind the wheel as if she was trying to demonstrate good posture, up Highgate Hill and down the other side towards home, towards the house they had lived in since Amy was born, eighteen years ago.

Of course, there was no parking space directly outside the house. There seldom was in the evenings, after people got home from work.

Chrissie said, 'Oh bother,' in an overcontrolled, ladylike way, and Dilly said, from the back seat, 'There's a space over there, outside the Nelsons',' and then nobody spoke while Chrissie manoeuvred the car in, very badly, because they were all thinking how he would have been, had he been there, how he would have said, 'Ornamental objects shouldn't be asked to do parking. Gimme the keys,' and Chrissie would – well, might, anyway – have laughed and thrown the keys at him ineptly, proving his point, and he'd have inserted the car neatly into an impossible space in no time so that they could all please him by saying, 'Show-off,' in chorus. 'I make my living from showing off,' he'd say. 'And don't you forget it.'

They got out of the car and locked it and trooped across the road to their own front door. There were no lights on. It had been daylight when they left, and anyway they were panicking because of the ambulance coming, and his frightening pallor and evident pain, so nobody thought of the return, how the return might be. Certainly, nobody had dared to think that the return might be like this.

Chrissie opened the front door, while the girls huddled behind her in the porch as if it was bitterly cold and they were desperate to get into the warmth. It occurred to Chrissie, irrelevantly, that she should have swept the leaves out of the porch, that it badly needed redecorating, that it had needed redecorating for years and Richie had always said that his granny, in North Shields on Tyneside, had scrubbed her front doorstep daily – except for Sundays – on her hands and knees. Daily. With a brush and a galvanized bucket.

Chrissie took the keys out of the door, and dropped them.

Tamsin leaned over her mother's bent back and switched on the hall lights. Then they all pushed past and surged down the hall to the kitchen, and Chrissie straightened up, with the keys in her hand, and tried to put them into the door's inside lock and found she was shaking so badly that she had to hold her right wrist with her left hand, in order to be steady enough.

Then she walked down the hall, straight down, not looking in at the sitting room and certainly not in at his practice room, where the piano sat, and the dented piano stool, and the framed photographs and the music system and the racks and racks of CDs and the certificates and awards and battered stacks of old sheet music he would never throw away. She paused in the kitchen doorway. All the lights were on and so was the radio, at once, KISS FM or something, and the kettle was whining away and all three girls were scattered about, and they were all now crying and crying.

Later that night, Chrissie climbed into bed clutching a hot-water bottle and a packet of Nurofen Extra. She hadn't used a hot-water bottle for years. She had an electric blanket on her side of their great bed – Richie, being a Northerner, had despised electric blankets – but she had felt a great need that night to have something to hold in bed, something warm and tactile and simple, so she had dug about in the airing cupboard and found a hot-water bottle that had once been given to Dilly, blue rubber inside a nylon-fur cover fashioned to look like a Dalmatian, its caricatured spotted face closing down over the stopper in a padded mask.

One of the girls had put some tea by her bed. And a tumbler of what turned out to be whisky. She never drank whisky. Richie had liked whisky, but she always preferred vodka. Or champagne. Richie would have made them drink champagne that evening; he always said champagne was

9

grief medicine, temper medicine, disappointment medicine. But they couldn't do it. There was a bottle in the fridge – there was almost always a bottle in the fridge – and they took it out and looked at it and put it back again. They'd drunk tea, and more tea, and Amy had had some cereal, and Tamsin had gone to telephone her boyfriend – not very far away – and they could hear her saying the same things over and over again, and Dilly had tried to pick some dried blueberries out of Amy's cereal and Amy had slapped her and then Chrissie had broken down at last herself, utterly and totally, and shocked them all into another silence.

That shock, on top of the other unbearable shock, probably accounted for the whisky. And her bed being turned down, and the bedside lamp on, and the bathroom all lit and ready, with a towel on the stool. But there was still a second towel on the heated rail, the supersized towel he liked, and there were still six pillows on the bed, and his reading glasses were on top of the pile of books he never finished, and there were his slippers, and a half-drunk glass of water. Chrissie looked at the glass with a kind of terror. His mouth had been on that glass, last night. Last night only. And she was going to have to lie down beside it because nothing on earth could persuade her either to touch that glass or to let anyone else touch it.

'Mum?' Amy said from the doorway.

Chrissie turned. Amy was still dressed, in a minidress and jeans and ballet slippers so shallow they were like a narrow black border to her naked feet.

Chrissie said, gesturing at the bed, at the whisky, 'Thank you.'

'S'OK,' Amy said.

She had clamped some of her hair on top of her head with a red plastic clip and the rest hung unevenly round her face. Her face looked awful. Chrissie put her arms out.

'Come here.'

Amy came and stood awkwardly in Chrissie's embrace. It wasn't the right embrace, Chrissie knew, it wasn't relaxed enough, comforting enough. Richie had been the one who was good at comfort, at subduing resistant adolescent limbs and frames into affectionate acquiescence.

'Sorry,' Chrissie said into Amy's hair.

Amy sighed.

'What for?' she said. 'You didn't kill him. He just died.'

For being here, Chrissie wanted to say, for being here when he isn't.

'We just have to do it,' she said instead, 'hour by hour. We just have to get through.'

Amy shifted, half pulling away.

'I know.'

Chrissie looked at the Nurofen.

'Want something to relax you? Help you sleep?'

Amy grimaced. She shook her head.

Chrissie said, 'What are the others doing?'

'Dilly's got her door shut. Tam's talking to Robbie.'

'*Still?*'

'Still,' Amy said. She looked round the bedroom. Her glance plainly hurried over the slippers, the far pillows. 'I don't know what to do.'

'Nor me,' Chrissie said.

Amy began to cry again. Chrissie tightened the arm round her shoulders, and pressed Amy's head against her.

'I know, baby—'

'I can't *stand* it—'

'Do you,' Chrissie said, 'want to sleep with me?'

Amy stopped crying. She looked at the extra pillows. She shook her head, sniffing.

'Couldn't. Sorry.'

'Don't have to be sorry. Just a suggestion. We'll none of us sleep, wherever we are.'

'When I wake up next,' Amy said, 'there'll be a second before I remember. Won't there?'

Chrissie nodded. Amy disengaged herself and trailed towards the door. In the doorway she paused and took the red clip out of her hair and snapped it once or twice.

'At least,' she said, not turning, not looking at her mother, 'at least we've got his name still. At least we're all still Rossiters.' She gave a huge shuddering sigh. 'I'm going to play my flute.'

'Yes,' Chrissie said. 'Yes. You do that.'

Amy flicked a glance at her mother.

'Dad liked my flute,' she said.

Then she went slowly away down the landing, shuffling in her little slippers, and Chrissie heard her starting tiredly on the stairs that led to the second-floor conversion that she and Richie had decided on and designed so that Dilly and Amy could have bedrooms of their own.

She did sleep. She had thought she neither could nor should, but she fell into a heavy, brief slumber and woke two hours later in order to fall instead into a pit of grief so deep that there seemed neither point nor possibility of climbing out of it. She had no idea how long she wrestled down there, but at some moment she exchanged her embrace of the Dalmatian hot-water bottle for one of Richie's pillows, scented with the stuff he used on the grey streaks in his hair, and found herself crushing it, and groaning, and being suddenly and simultaneously aware that there were lines of incipient daylight above the curtain tracks, and that a bird or two was tuning up in the plane tree outside the window. She rolled over and turned on the light. It was six-thirteen. She was six hours and thirteen minutes, only, into the first day of this chapter of life which she had always dreaded and, consequently, had never permitted herself to picture.

'I'll be a hopeless widow,' she used to say to Richie, and, if he was paying attention, he'd say back, 'Well, I'm not giving you the chance to find out,' and then he'd sing her something, a line or two of some Tony Bennett or Jack Jones ballad, and deflect the moment. He'd always done that, defuse by singing. Once she thought it was wonderful. Recently, however, in the last year or two, she thought he found it easier to sing than to engage. Oh God, if only! If only he *had* engaged! If only he'd done even that!

She drew her left hand out from under the duvet, and looked at it. It was a well-kept, pretty hand, as befitted a well-kept, pretty woman. It bore a narrow white-gold plain band and a half-hoop of diamonds. The plain band was not new, in fact it was quite worn, having been on Chrissie's finger since shortly after Tamsin's birth. She remembered the occasion exactly, since she had bought it herself, in order to wear it in hospital, and put it on her own finger. The diamonds, however, were new. They were quite big, bigger than they possibly might have been had they been dug out of the faraway depths of South Africa. Instead, they had been made, ingeniously, in a small factory near Antwerp, by a process which simulated what nature might have managed over millennia, but in only three weeks. They were, Chrissie told Richie, known as industrial diamonds. He had looked at her hand, and then his attention went back to his piano and he played a few bars of Gershwin, and then he said, 'You wear them, sweetheart. If they make you happy.'

She said, 'You know what would make me happy.'

Richie went on playing.

She said, 'I have to be Mrs Rossiter, for the girls. I have to be Mrs Rossiter at school. I have to wear a wedding ring and be Mrs Rossiter.'

'OK,' Richie said softly. He began on some mounting chords. 'Course you do.'

'Richie—'

'Wear the diamonds,' Richie said. 'Wear them. Let me pay for them.'

But she hadn't. She told herself that it was principle, that a woman of independent mind could buy her own manifestations of the outward respectability required at the school gates, even in liberal-minded North London. For a week or two, she registered the glances cast at her sizeable diamonds – and the conclusions visibly drawn in consequence – with satisfaction and even tiny flashes of triumph. When Tamsin, who missed no detail of anyone's appearance, said, 'Oh my God, Mum, did Dad give you those?' she had managed a small, self-conscious smile that could easily have passed for coquettish self-satisfaction. But then heart quietly overcame head with its usual stealthy persistence, and the independence and the triumph faded before the miserable and energetic longing for her status as Mrs Rossiter to be a reality rather than a fantasy adorned with meaningless – and engineered – symbols.

It wasn't really just status either. She was Richie's manager, after all, the controller and keeper of his diary, his finances, his pragmatically necessary well-being. She had plenty of status, in the eyes of Richie's profession, as Christine Kelsey, the woman – girl, back then – who had persuaded Richie Rossiter that a bigger, younger audience awaited him outside the Northern circuit where he had thus far spent all his per-forming life. Richie only answered the telephone for pleasure and left all administration, and certainly anything techno-logical, to her. No, it wasn't really status, it really wasn't.

It was instead that hoary old, urgent old, irreplaceable old need for commitment. In twenty-three years together, Chrissie could not shift Richie one millimetre towards divorcing his wife, and marrying her. He wasn't Catholic, he wasn't in touch with his wife, he wasn't even much in touch with his son by that marriage. He was living in London, in apparent contentment, with a woman he had elected to leave his wife for, and the three daughters he had had by her and with whom he was plainly besotted, but he would make no move of any kind to transfer his legal position as head of his first family to head of his second.

For years, he said he would think about it, that he came from a place and a background where traditional codes of conduct were as fundamental to a person as their heartbeat, and therefore it would take him time. And Chrissie at first understood that and, a little later in this relationship, continued at least to try and understand it. But his efforts – such as they had ever really been – dwindled to invisibility over time, corresponding inevitably with a rise in Chrissie's anxiety and insistence. The more she asked – in a voice whose rigorously modulated control spoke volumes – the more he played his Gershwin. If she persisted, he switched to Rachmaninov, and played with his eyes closed. In the end – well, it now looked like the end – she had marched out and bought her industrial diamonds and, she now realized, surveying her left hand in the first dawn of her new widowhood, let him off the hook, by finding – as she so often did, good old Chrissie – a practical solution to living with his refusal.

She let her hand fall into the plumpness of the duvet. The girls were all Rossiter. Tamsin Rossiter, Delia Rossiter, Amy Rossiter. That was how they had all been registered at birth, with her agreement, encouragement even.

'It makes sense to have your name,' she'd said. 'After all, you're the well-known one. You're the one people will associate them with.'

She'd waited three times for him to say, 'Well, they're our children, pet, so I think you should join the Rossiter clan as well, don't you?' but he never did.

He accepted the girls as if it was entirely natural that they should be identified with him, and his pride and delight in them couldn't be faulted. Those friends from the North who had managed to accept Richie's transition to London and to Chrissie professed exaggerated amazement at his preparedness to share the chores of three babies in the space of five years: he was a traitor, they said loudly, glass in hand, jocular arm round Chrissie's shoulders, to the noble cause of unreconstructed Northern manhood. But none of them, however they might covertly stare at Chrissie's legs and breasts or overtly admire her cooking or her ability to get Richie gigs in legendarily impossible venues, ever urged him to marry her. Perhaps, Chrissie thought now, staring at the ceiling through which she hoped Dilly still slept, they thought he had.

After all, the girls did. Or, to put it another way, the girls had no reason to believe that he hadn't. They were all Rossiters, Chrissie signed herself Rossiter on all family-concerned occasions, and they knew her professional name was Kelsey just as they knew she was their father's manager. It wouldn't have occurred to them that their parents weren't married because the subject had simply never arisen. The disputes that arose between Richie and Chrissie were – it was the stuff of their family chronicle – because their father wanted to work less and play and sing more just for playing and singing's sake, and their mother, an acknowledged businesswoman, wanted to keep up the momentum. The girls, Chrissie knew, were inclined to side with their father. That was no surprise – he had traded, for decades, on getting women audiences to side with him. But – perhaps because of this, at least in part – the girls had found it hard to leave home. Tamsin had tried, and had come back again, and when she came home it was to her father that she had instinctively turned and it was her father who had made it plain that she was more than welcome.

Chrissie swallowed. She pictured Dilly through that ceiling, asleep in her severe cotton pyjamas in the resolute order of her bedroom. Thank heavens, today, that she was there. And thank heavens for Amy, in her equally determined chaos in the next room, and for Tamsin amid the ribbons and flowers and china-shoe collections down the landing. Thank heavens she hadn't prevailed, and achieved her aim of even attempted daughterly self-sufficiency before the girls reached the age of twenty. Richie had been right. He was wrong about a lot of things, but about his girls he had been right.

Chrissie began to cry again. She pulled her hand back in, under the duvet, and rolled on her side, where Richie's pillow awaited her in all its glorious, intimate, agonizing familiarity.

'Where's Mum?' Tamsin said.

She was standing in the kitchen doorway clutching a pink cotton kimono round her as if her stomach hurt. Dilly was sitting at the table, staring out of the window in front of her, and the tabletop was littered with screwed-up balls of tissue. Amy was down the far end of the kitchen by the sink, standing on one leg, her raised foot in her hand, apparently gazing out into the garden. Neither moved.

'Where's Mum?' Tamsin said again.

'Dunno,' Dilly said.

Amy said, without turning, 'Did you look in her room?'

'Door's shut.'

Amy let her foot go.

'Well then.'

Tamsin padded down the kitchen in her pink slippers.

'I couldn't sleep.'

'Nor me.'

She picked up the kettle and nudged Amy sideways so that she could fill it at the sink.

'I don't believe it's happened.'

'Nor me.'

'I can't—'

Cold water gushed into the kettle, bounced out and caught Amy's sleeve.

'Stupid cow!'

Tamsin took no notice. She carried the kettle back to its mooring.

'What are we gonna do?' Dilly said.

Tamsin switched the kettle on.

'Go back to the hospital. All the formalities—'

'How do you know?'

'It's what they said. Last night. They said it's too late now, but come back in the morning.'

'It's the morning now,' Amy said, still gazing into the garden.

Dilly half turned from the table.

'Will Mum know what to do?'

Tamsin took one mug out of a cupboard.

'Why should she?'

'Can I have some tea?' Amy said.

'What d'you mean, why should she?'

'Why should she,' Tamsin said, her voice breaking, 'know what you do when your husband dies?'

Amy cried out, 'Don't say that!'

Tamsin got out a second mug. Then, after a pause, a third.

She said, not looking at Amy, 'It's true, babe.'

'I don't want it to be!'

'None of us do,' Dilly said. She gathered all the tissue balls up in her hands and crushed them together. Then she stood up and crossed the kitchen and dumped them in the pedal bin. 'Is not being able to take it in worse than when you've taken it in?'

'It's all awful,' Amy said.

'Will Mum—' Dilly said, and stopped.

Tamsin was taking tea bags out of a caddy their father had brought down from Newcastle, a battered tin caddy with a crude portrait of Earl Grey stamped on all four sides. The caddy had always been an object of mild family derision, being so cosy, so evidently much used, so sturdily unsleek. Richie had loved it. He said it was like one he had grown up with, in the terraced house of his childhood in North Shields. He said it was honest, and he liked it filled with Yorkshire tea bags. Earl Grey tea – no disrespect to His Lordship – was for toffs and for women.

Tamsin's hand shook now, opening it.

'Will Mum what?'

'Well,' Dilly said. 'Well, *manage*.'

Tamsin closed the caddy and shut it quickly away in its cupboard.

'She's very practical. She'll manage.'

'But there's the other stuff—'

Amy turned from the sink.

'Dad won't be singing.'

'No.'

'If Dad isn't singing—'

Tamsin poured boiling water into the mugs in a wavering stream.

'Maybe she can manage other people—'

'Who can?' Chrissie asked from the doorway.

She was wearing Richie's navy-blue bathrobe and she had pulled her hair back into a tight ponytail. Dilly got up from the table to hug her and Amy came running down the kitchen to join in.

'We were just wondering,' Tamsin said unsteadily.

Chrissie said into Dilly's shoulder, 'Me too.' She looked at Amy. 'Did anyone sleep?'

'Not really.'

'She played her flute,' Dilly said between clenched teeth. 'She played and played her flute. I couldn't have slept even if I'd wanted to.'

'I didn't want to,' Tamsin said, 'because of having to wake up again.'

Chrissie said, 'Is that tea?'

'I'll make another one—'

Chrissie moved towards the table, still holding her daughters. They felt to her, at that moment, like her only support and sympathy yet at the same time like a burden of redoubled emotional intensity that she knew neither how to manage nor to put down. She subsided into a chair, and Tamsin put a mug of tea in front of her. She glanced up.

'Thank you. Toast?'

'Couldn't,' Dilly said.

'Could you try? Just a slice? It would help, it really would.'

Dilly shook her head. Amy opened the larder cupboard and rummaged about in it for a while. Then she took out a packet of chocolate digestive biscuits and put them on the table.

'I'm trying,' Dilly said tensely, 'not to eat chocolate.'

'You're a pain—'

'Shh,' Chrissie said. She took Dilly's nearest wrist. 'Shh. Shh.'

Dilly took her hand away and held it over her eyes.

'Dad ate those—'

'No, he didn't,' Amy said. 'No, he didn't. He ate those putrid ones with chocolate-cream stuff in, he—'

'Please,' Chrissie said. She picked up her mug. 'What were you saying when I came in?'

Tamsin put the remaining mugs on the table. She looked at her sisters. They were looking at the table.

She said, 'We were talking about you.'

Chrissie raised her head. 'And?' she said.

Tamsin sat down, pulling her kimono round her as if in the teeth of a gale.

Dilly took her hand away from her face. She said, 'It's just, well, will you – will we – be OK, will we manage, will we—'

There was a pause.

'I don't think,' Chrissie said, 'that we'll be OK for quite a long time. Do you? I don't think we can expect to be. There's so much to get used to that we don't really want – to get used to. Isn't there?' She stopped. She looked round the table. Amy had broken a biscuit into several pieces and was jigsawing them back together again. Chrissie said, 'But you know all that, don't you? You know all that as well as I do. You didn't mean that, did you, you didn't mean how are we going to manage emotionally, did you?'

'It seems,' Tamsin said, 'so rubbish to even think of any-thing else—'

'No,' Chrissie said, 'it's practical. We have to be practical. We have to live. We have to go on living. That's what Dad wanted. That's what Dad worked for.'

Amy began to cry quietly onto her broken biscuit.

Chrissie retrieved Dilly's hand and took Amy's nearest one. She said, looking at Tamsin, gripping the others, 'We'll be fine. Don't worry. We have the house. And there's more. And I'll go on working. You aren't to worry. Anyway, it isn't today's problem. Today just has to be got through, however we can manage it.'

Tamsin was moving her tea mug round in little circles with her right hand and pressing her left into her stomach. She said, 'We ought to tell people.'

'Yes,' Chrissie said, 'we should. We must make a list.'

Tamsin looked up.

'I might be moving in with Robbie.'

Dilly gave a small scream.

'Not now, darling,' Chrissie said tiredly.

'But I—'

'Shut it!' Amy said suddenly.

Tamsin shrugged.

'I just thought if we were making plans, making lists—'

Amy leaned across the table. She hissed, 'We were going to make a list of who to tell that Dad died last night. Not lists of who we were planning to shack up with.'

Chrissie got up from the table.

'And the registrar,' she said. She began to shuffle through the pile of papers by the telephone. 'And the undertaker. And I suppose the newspapers. Always better to tell them than have them guess.'

Tamsin sat up straighter. She said, 'What about Margaret?'

Chrissie stopped shuffling.

'Who?'

'Margaret,' Tamsin said.

Amy and Dilly looked at her.

'Tam—'

'Well,' Tamsin said, 'she ought to be told. She's got a right to know.'

Amy turned to look across the kitchen at Chrissie. Chrissie was holding a notebook and an absurd pen with a plume of shocking-pink marabou frothing out of the top.

'Mum?'

Chrissie nodded slowly.

'I know—'

'But Dad wouldn't want that!' Dilly said. 'Dad never spoke to her, right? She wasn't part of his life, was she, he wouldn't have wanted her to be part of – of—' She stopped. Then she said angrily, 'It's nothing to do with her.'

Amy stood up and drifted down the kitchen again. Chrissie

watched her, dark hair down her back, Richie's dark hair, Richie's dark Northern hair, only girl-version.

'Amy?'

Amy didn't turn.

'I shouldn't have mentioned her,' Tamsin said, 'I shouldn't. She's no part of this.'

'I hate her,' Dilly said.

Chrissie said, making an effort, 'You shouldn't. She couldn't help being part of his life before and she's never made any claim, any trouble.'

'But she's *there*,' Dilly said.

'And,' Amy said from the other end of the kitchen, 'she was his wife.'

'*Was*,' Tamsin said.

Chrissie held the notebook and the feathered pen hard against her. She said, 'I'm not sure I can quite ring her—'

'Nor me,' Dilly said.

Tamsin took a tiny mobile phone out of her kimono pocket and put it on the table.

'You can't really just *text* her—'

Chrissie made a sudden little fluttering gesture with the hand not holding the notebook. She said, 'I don't think I can quite do this, I can't manage—' She stopped, and put her hand over her mouth.

Tamsin jumped up.

'Mum—'

'I'm OK,' Chrissie said. 'Really I am. I'm fine. But I know you're right. I know we should tell Margaret—'

'And Scott,' Amy said.

Chrissie glanced at her.

'Of course. Scott. I forgot him, I forgot—'

Tamsin moved to put her arms round her mother.

'Damn,' Chrissie whispered against Tamsin. 'Damn. I don't—'

'You don't have to,' Tamsin said.

'I do. I do. I do have to tell Margaret and Scott that Dad has died.'

Nobody said anything. Dilly got up and collected the mugs on the table and put them in the dishwasher. Then she swept the biscuit crumbs and bits into her hand and put them in the bin, and the remaining packet in the cupboard. They watched her, all of them. They were used to watching Dilly, so orderly in her person and her habits, so chaotic in her reactions and responses. They waited while she found a cloth, wiped the table with it, rinsed it and hung it, neatly folded, over the mixer tap on the sink.

Chrissie said absently, approvingly, 'Thank you, darling.'

Dilly said furiously, 'It doesn't matter if bloody Margaret knows!'

Chrissie sighed. She withdrew a little from Tamsin.

'It does matter.'

'Dad wouldn't want it!'

'He would.'

'Well, do it then!' Dilly shouted.

Chrissie gave a little shiver.

'I'd give anything—'

'I'll stand beside you,' Tamsin said, 'while you ring.'

Chrissie gave her a small smile.

'Thank you—'

'Mum?'

Chrissie turned. Amy was leaning against the cupboard where the biscuits lived. She had her arms folded.

'Yes, darling.'

'I'll do it.'

'What—'

'I'll ring her,' Amy said. 'I'll ring Margaret.'

Chrissie put her arms out.

'You're lovely. You're a doll. But you don't have to, you don't know her—'

Amy shifted slightly.

'Makes it easier then, doesn't it?'

'But—'

'Look,' Amy said, 'I don't mind phones. I'm not scared of phones, me. I'll just dial her number and tell her who I am and what's happened and then I'll say goodbye.'

'What if she wants to come to the funeral?' Dilly said. 'What if she wants to come and make out he was—'

'Shut up,' Tamsin said.

She looked at her mother.

'Let her,' Tamsin said. 'Let her ring.'

'Really?'

'Yes,' Tamsin said. 'Let her do it like she said and then it'll be done. Two minutes and it'll be done.'

'And then?'

'There won't be an "and then".'

Amy peeled herself off the cupboard and stood up. She looked as she looked, Chrissie remembered, when she learned to dive, standing on the end of the springboard, full of excited, anxious tension. She winked at her mother, and she actually smiled.

'Watch me,' Amy said.

CHAPTER TWO

More than six decades of living by the sea had trained Margaret to know what the weather was doing, each morning, before she even drew back the curtains. Sometimes there was the subdued roaring that indicated wind and rain; sometimes there was a scattering of little sequins of light reflected across the ceiling from bright air and water, and sometimes there was the muffled stillness that meant fog.

There was fog today. When she looked out, she would see that the sea mist had rolled up the shallow cliffs, and filled the wide grassy oval in front of the crescent of houses in Percy Gardens, bumping itself softly against the buildings. There would be shreds and wisps of mist caught in the fancy ironwork of the narrow balcony outside her bedroom window, and in the crooked cherry tree in the front garden. There would be salty smears on the window glass and the cars parked along the crescent and on the front-door brass that needed, really, daily polishing. And there would be this eerie silence, a muted quality to all the usual morning noise of slammed front doors and car engines starting and the woman two doors down shouting at her dogs, who liked to start the day with a good bark.

Margaret got out of bed slowly and felt for her slippers

with her feet. They were good slippers: sheepskin, of enduring construction, as was her padded cotton dressing gown
patterned with roses and fastened with covered buttons, and
although the sight of herself as she passed the mirror on her
bedroom wall caused her to pull a face, she knew she looked
appropriate. Appropriate for a professional woman – not
yet retired – of sixty-six living in a house in Percy Gardens,
Tynemouth, with a double front door and a cat and a large
stand of plumed ornamental grasses outside the sitting-room
window.

She opened the curtains and surveyed the mist. It
was ragged and uneven, indicating that a rising wind or
strengthening sun would disperse it quite quickly. A seagull
– an immense seagull – was standing just below her, on the
roof of her car, no doubt intending, as seagulls seemed to
enjoy doing, to relieve itself copiously down the windscreen.
Margaret banged on the window. The seagull adjusted its
head to indicate that it had observed her and intended to
ignore her. Then it walked stiffly down the length of her car
roof, and turned its back.

Margaret went down the stairs to her kitchen. On
the table, wearing much the same expression of insolent
indifference as the seagull, sat a huge cat. Scott had brought
him home as a tiny, scrawny tabby kitten some eight years
before, having rescued him from a group of tormenting
children on the North Shields quayside, and he had grown,
steadily and inexorably, into a great square striped cat,
with disproportionately small ears and a tail as fat as a
cushion.

'I don't particularly like cats,' Margaret had said to Scott.
'Nor me,' he said.

They looked at the kitten. The kitten turned its head away
and began to wash. Margaret said, 'And I don't like surprises
either.'

'Mam,' Scott said, 'this'll stop being a surprise soon. You'll get used to it.'

She had. Just as she had got used to a lot of other things, she got used to the kitten. Indeed, she realized how used to the kitten she had become when she found herself explaining to him that one of the main things about life that he should realize was that it consisted of, in fact, getting used to a great many things that were the result of other people's choices, rather than one's own. For the first year, the kitten was simply called the kitten. Then, as his bulk and solidity began to take shape as he grew, Scott christened him Dawson, after the comedian.

Dawson put out a huge paw now, as Margaret passed him on her way to the kettle, and snagged her dressing gown with a deliberate claw.

'In a minute,' Margaret said.

Outside the kitchen window, the sea mist had been diluted by having to slide up over the roofs, and the air here merely had a vague bleary look. The little paved yard – a patio, her neighbours preferred to call it – that passed for a back garden simply gave up in this kind of weather. Everything hung damply and dankly, and blackened leaves plastered themselves against surfaces, like flattened slugs. Margaret's neighbour, on her left-hand side, had been infected by holidays in Spain, and had painted her patio white, inset with mosaic pictures made with chips of coloured glass and mirror, and hung wrought-iron baskets on the walls which were intended to spill avalanches of pink and orange bougainvillea. But bringing abroad back to Tynemouth was not Margaret's way. Abroad was abroad and the English North was the English North. What was unhappy growing beside the North Sea shouldn't, in her view, be required to try.

She made tea for herself, in a teapot, and shook a handful

of dried cat food into a plastic bowl from a box which declared the contents to be designed for senior cats with a weight problem. She put the bowl on the floor. Dawson thudded off the table, inspected his breakfast with contempt and sat down beside it, not looking at Margaret.

'You won't get anything else,' Margaret said. She poured out her tea. 'You can sit there all day.' She added milk. 'It'll do you no harm to fast for a day, anyhow.'

Dawson's thick tail twitched very slightly.

Margaret picked up her tea, preparatory to going upstairs. 'I'll leave you to think about it.'

Dawson regarded the wall straight ahead of him. Margaret went past him, making a small detour to beyond claw-reach – how extraordinary it was, the intimate knowledge two living organisms who shared a house had of one another – and climbed the stairs. They had recently been recarpeted, with a good-quality wool-twist carpet in pale grey. Scott had suggested sisal, or seagrass. Margaret said she wasn't a *bachelor* (she emphasized the word, as if to underline her opinion of Scott's abiding single state, at the age of thirty-seven) in a *loft*, in *Newcastle*, and that what was appropriate to Percy Gardens was a hard-wearing wool twist in a neutral colour. She was pleased with the result, pleased with the resilience provided by the thick foam-rubber underlay. A new carpet, she reflected, had the same effect on a house as mowing a lawn in regular stripes did on a garden.

Dressing was not a matter of indecision for Margaret. For the twenty-three years or so that she had been on her own, she had kept to a number of habits which she had first devised as a way of keeping the grief and shock of being deserted at bay. Because she had, after Richie's departure, gone on doing for other people what she had once done – and very successfully – for him, there was a requirement to dress with professional care on a daily basis. In the early days without him, there was also of course an obligation to display an energizing measure of bravado, a need to show the world that her spirit had not been crushed, even if her heart had temporarily been broken. She had, from a week or two after he left, decided each night what she would wear the next day, got it out of her wardrobe, inspected it for stains or fluff, and hung it up for the morning, like a quilt put out to air. Sometimes, in the morning, she would feel inexplicably reluctant about the previous night's choice, but she never changed her mind. If she did, she was afraid, in some mysterious superstitious part of her mind, that she would just go on changing and changing it until her bedroom was a chaos of discarded clothes, and she was a weeping, wild-haired wreck in the middle of it all.

Today her clothes were blue. Grey-blue. And then the pearls Richie had given her when Scott was born, which she wore almost every day, and the pearl earrings Scott had given her for her fiftieth birthday. He'd only been twenty-one then. He must have gone without a lot, to buy pearl earrings for her, and even now, when she considered what sort of sweet and clumsy atonement he was trying to make for his father's absence, she felt unsteady about her earrings. So she wore them daily, even when she wasn't wearing her necklace, as she wore the Cartier watch she had awarded herself when she was sixty. The watch had a tiny domed sapphire set into the knob that moved the hands. That sapphire was, for some reason, a source of great satisfaction to her.

Breakfast was equally not a matter for daily whim. Porridge in winter, muesli in summer, with a grated apple, more tea and a selection of vitamin capsules measured out into an eggcup Scott had had as a child for Easter one year, fashioned like a rabbit holding a small china basket. The rabbit's ears were chipped, and the basket was veined with cracks, but its familiarity made Margaret grateful to it in the same way that she was grateful to the Lloyd Loom laundry basket in her bathroom, inherited from her mother, and the gateleg table she and Richie had bought, after his first successful gig, their first piece of grown-up furniture, a portent of one day owning a house of their own instead of sharing someone else's.

When Scott came out to Tynemouth at weekends – not often, but he came – he'd bring Continental breakfast pastries from Newcastle, and Colombian coffee, and cranberry juice. Dawson, who appreciated a good croissant, became quite animated at these breakfasts, leaning against Scott's legs and purring sonorously. Today, he had ignored his breakfast. It was untouched and he had removed himself to his favourite daytime place, stretched along the back of the sofa in the bay window of the sitting room, to catch any eastern sun there might be, and also any passing incident. He would not, Margaret knew, involve himself in anything that required exertion, but equally, he liked to know what was going on.

Breakfast eaten, Margaret put her cereal bowl in the dishwasher, restored the rabbit to his shelf by the vitamin-supplement boxes, switched on the telephone answering machine and checked her bag and her briefcase for everything she would need during the day. In the hall, she paused in front of what Scott used to call the lipstick mirror. It reflected what it always reflected. Someone once – an ill-advised someone – had told her that she looked like the best kind of Tory supporter, groomed, capable, formidable. Margaret, born and bred a socialist in a cramped terraced cottage in North Shields, had been offended to her very marrow, and had said so. Her heroine, as she was growing up, had been Barbara Castle.

The seagull had evacuated itself thoroughly down the back window of Margaret's car. If a day in the office awaited her, she would walk along East Street, behind King Edward's

Bay, to Front Street, but if, as today, her diary included a meeting in Newcastle, then she would take the car. She put her briefcase on to the back seat, and climbed in behind the wheel. The seagull's souvenir would have to wait.

Her office – Margaret Rossiter Entertainment Agency – was located beside one of Tynemouth's many cafés, and above a hairdresser's. A narrow door from the street – painted dark-grey matt at Scott's insistence, and with brushed-aluminium door furniture instead of the brass she would have preferred – led into an equally narrow white-painted hallway lined with framed photographs of some of Margaret's clients and towards a staircase at the back. At the top of the staircase was a second door, and behind that the two rooms which had paid for Scott's final years of education and training as well as providing Margaret's living for over two decades and a part-time living for Glenda, who did the correspondence, invoicing and books, and whose husband was disabled after an accident at the Swan Hunter shipyard when he was only twenty-seven.

It was the disablement that had swayed Margaret when hiring Glenda. It had swayed her because her own father had been disabled, and his injury had unquestionably darkened her childhood. He'd been chief engineer on a trawler, the *Ben Torc*, registered to North Shields, a trawler belonging to Richard Irvine and Sons, who'd owned almost two hundred trawlers and herring drifters when Margaret was a child and she could remember them, jammed up together against the Fish Quay in North Shields, tight as sardines in a can. And then her father – Darky, his mates called him, on account of his swarthy skin – had lost an arm in an engine accident, which was never described to Margaret, and was transferred to work in the Shields Ice and Cold Storage Company canning herrings, and, at the same time, had taken to frequenting a local shebeen called the Cabbage Patch. The rows at home were terrible. There wasn't space in that house for living, let alone for screaming. Margaret and her sister fled out or upstairs when the screaming began. They didn't discuss it, ever, but there was a mute and common consent that the rows were unbearable and that their mother was more than capable of looking after herself, especially if her opponent had only one arm and was unsteady on his feet. As a girl and a young woman, their mother had worked as a herring filleter, and both her daughters were filled with a determination not to follow her. The determination in Margaret's sister was so strong that she went to Canada when she was sixteen, and never came back, leaving Margaret and her mother to deal with life in North Shields, and the increasing wreck of Darky Ramsey and his appetite for what he infuriatingly referred to as 'liquid laughter'.

Glenda's husband didn't drink. He was a quiet, careful man in a wheelchair who spent his days mending things and regimenting things and analysing his household's meagre cash flow with a calculator. He dealt with his disability by the obsessive control of detail, and Margaret, in robust disregard of regulations, paid Glenda some of her wages in cash, so that not every penny went home to be scrutinized and allotted under Barry's ferocious micromanagement. If it wasn't for Margaret, Glenda said, she'd never get a haircut or new underwear or presents for the grandchildren. Glenda had become a grandmother before she was forty.

She was at her desk before Margaret. It wasn't what Margaret liked, but she understood that to be in first was a mark of Glenda's dedication to her boss and to the business. She was working, Margaret could see, on the month-end spreadsheets, which she would then want to explain, despite the fact that the way they were laid out made them absolutely intelligible without a word being said.

'You look nice,' Glenda said.

She said this most mornings and probably, Margaret believed, meant it. It was something that somehow had to be got over with, a ritual that must not be allowed to set her teeth on edge merely because she knew it was, inevitably, coming.

'Thank you, dear,' Margaret said.

She put her bag on the floor, and her briefcase on the desk. The windows were screened with vertical venetian blinds, and Margaret went across the room, behind Glenda, to open the slats and let in more of the unenthusiastic morning light.

'I thought the bus would be late,' Glenda said. 'What with the fog. But it wasn't. It was almost early. I had to run, you should have seen me, running down North King Street. No wonder I look a mess, all that running.'

She paused, waiting for reassurance.

Margaret, trained by Dawson in the art of sidestepping the obvious, said as if Glenda hadn't spoken, 'Glenda, dear. Has Bernie Harrison called?'

'Not yet,' Glenda said. She put her hand to her hair and tucked a frond or two behind her ear. 'Do I look a mess?'

Margaret glanced at her.

'No, dear. You look exactly the same as usual.'

Inside her handbag, her mobile began to ring. As she reached inside to find it, the telephone on Glenda's desk began to ring as well.

'Margaret Rossiter,' she said into her mobile.

'Margaret Rossiter Agency,' Glenda said simultaneously into the landline phone.

'Yes, dear,' Margaret said to Bernie Harrison's secretary. 'No, dear. No, I can't change today's meeting. We have to decide today because—'

'I'm sorry?' Glenda said.

'It's very rare to be offered the Sage as a venue,' Margaret said, 'and if you'll forgive me, dear, I shouldn't be discussing this with you, I should be speaking to Mr Harrison. Could you put him on?'

'Mrs Rossiter is on the other line,' Glenda said.

Margaret walked towards the window. She looked out into the street. Bernie Harrison's mother had worked in Welch's sweet factory, and now he drove a Jaguar and had a flat in Monte Carlo.

'Now, Bernie—'

'What sort of important?' Glenda said. 'Could I ask her to call you back?'

'Well,' Margaret said, 'if you can't make later, you'd better climb into that vulgar jalopy of yours and come and see me now.'

Glenda inserted herself between Margaret and the window. She mouthed, 'Something important,' stretching her mouth like a cartoon fish.

'One moment, Bernie,' Margaret said. She took the phone away from her ear. 'What now?' she said to Glenda.

'A girl,' Glenda said, 'a girl on the phone. She says it's important. She says she must speak to you.'

Something chilly slid down Margaret's spine.

'What girl?'

'She says,' Glenda said, 'she says her name's Amy. She says you'll know—'

Margaret gave Glenda a little dismissive nod. She put her phone back against her ear.

'Bernie. I'll call you back in fifteen minutes. You just tell your client that even Josh Groban would jump at the chance to sing at the Sage.'

She flipped her phone shut and held out her hand. Glenda put the landline receiver into it.

'Are you all right?' Glenda said.

Margaret turned her back. She said into the phone, 'Yes? Margaret Rossiter speaking.'

There was a fractional pause, and then Amy said, 'It's Amy.'

'Amy,' Margaret said.

'Yes. Amy Rossiter.'

'Is—' Margaret said, and stopped.

'No,' Amy said. Her voice was faint and unsteady. 'I tried your home number but you'd gone. That's why I'm – well, that's why I'm ringing now, because you ought to know, I'm ringing to tell you about – about Dad.'

'What—'

'He died,' Amy said simply.

'Died?' Margaret said. Her voice was incredulous.

'He had a heart attack. He was rushed to hospital. And he died, in the hospital.'

Margaret felt behind her for the edge of Glenda's desk, and leaned against it.

'He – he *died*?'

'Yes,' Amy said. 'Last night.' Her voice broke. 'He just died.'

Margaret closed her eyes. She heard herself say, 'Well, dear, thank you for telling me,' as if someone else was speaking, and then she said, in quite a different voice, a much wilder voice, 'What a shock, I can't believe it, I don't – I can't –' and Glenda came round from behind her desk and put a hand on her arm.

'I've got to go,' Amy said from London.

'Can – can you tell me any more?'

'There isn't anything,' Amy said, and then, with a kind of angry misery, 'Isn't that enough?'

'Yes,' Margaret said. 'Yes—'

'We thought,' Amy said, more in control now, 'we thought you should know. So I've told you. So Mum doesn't have to.'

Margaret said nothing. She stood, leaning against Glenda's desk with her eyes closed and the phone to her ear.

'Bye,' Amy said, and the line went dead.

Glenda transferred her hand from Margaret's arm to the telephone and took it gently out of her grasp, and returned it to its base.

Margaret opened her eyes.

'Amy,' she said. 'Amy. Richie's daughter. Richie's third daughter.'

She turned and looked at Glenda.

'Richie's dead,' she said.

Scott couldn't remember when his mother had last been to his flat. He went out to Tynemouth once a month or so, and slept in his old bedroom – weird to sleep in a single bed again – but his mother almost never came to his flat, preferring to meet him, if she was in Newcastle, somewhere impersonal, like a hotel. Despite her manifest opinion of the contemporary decor of his flat, she had found a hotel, down on the quayside, opposite the Baltic, which was definitely not traditional in any way, and they would meet there sometimes in the bar on the first floor, looking out over the river, and she would drink gin and tonic and look about her with approval. She liked the trouble girls took with their appearances now, she said, as well as the fashion for men having haircuts.

'In the 1970s,' she said to Scott, 'your father looked a complete nightmare. Purple bell-bottoms and hair to his shoulders.'

When she had rung earlier that day, Scott had just been coming out of the Law Courts, quite close to that hotel, after seeing a barrister about a complicated case of VAT fraud. The fraud had been perpetrated by someone who had once had business dealings with his mother, so that seeing her name on his speed dial made Scott think that she was apprehensive about being caught up in the case, and was ringing for reassurance. But she had sounded strangely quiet and distracted, and had merely said, over and over, 'I'd like to see you, dear. Today if you can make it. I'd like to see you at home.'

It was no good saying, 'What about?' because she didn't seem able to tell him.

'I'm not ill, dear,' she said, 'if that's what you're thinking. I'm not ill.'

So here he was leaving the office early – always difficult – and walking fast along the river westwards, and then turning off after the Tyne Bridge and climbing steeply up between old buildings and new office blocks to the Clavering Building where he had bought, two years ago, and for what his mother considered an exorbitant price, a studio flat with a view across the raised railway line to the old keep and the top of the Tyne Bridge arch and the distant shine of the Sage Centre, in Gateshead.

She was waiting in the central hall by the lifts. The Clavering Building had once been a vast Victorian factory, and the developers had been careful to leave an edgy industrial feel behind them, exposed bricks and metal pillars and girders painted black, and quantities of the heavily engineered nuts and bolts that gave the place its air of having had a much more muscular past than its present.

Margaret came forward and kissed Scott's cheek. She was very pale.

'You OK, Mam?'

'Yes, pet,' she said. She sounded suddenly more Geordie, as she was apt to do when tired. She gestured at the lift. 'Let's go up. I'll tell you when we're alone.'

Scott leaned forward to summon the lift.

'I wasn't expecting you, Mam. I think my bed isn't made—'

'Couldn't matter,' Margaret said. 'Couldn't matter.'

He followed her into the lift.

He said, 'Mam, could you—' and she turned and touched him on the chest and said, 'In a minute, pet,' and then she looked past him, at the steel wall of the lift, and there was nothing for it but to wait.

His flat consisted of one longish central room, wooden-floored, and held up by black iron pillars, with a kitchen at one end and a small bleak bedroom at the other. There was almost no furniture, beyond a metal table, a few chairs, a television and the Yamaha keyboard that Margaret had given Scott when he was twenty-one. He had left the blinds up – the view was too good to hide – and several beer bottles on the table, and a DVD he would have preferred his mother not to know he possessed lying on the crushed cushions of his big black sofa. But Margaret did not appear to notice the bottles or the cover of the DVD, nor that the sofa was scattered with crisp crumbs. She walked into the flat, turned, waited for Scott to close his front door, and then she said, with an effort at steadiness, 'Scott dear, it's about your father.'

Scott put his keys down on the nearest kitchen counter.

'Dad.'

'Yes, pet,' Margaret said. She came across the space between them and put her hands on his upper arms. 'Your – well, Amy rang me this morning. Amy Rossiter. She rang to tell me that your father had a severe heart attack last night, and he was rushed into hospital and he died there. Your father died last night.'

Scott gazed at her. He swallowed. He felt a lump in his throat of something intractable – could it be tears? – which would certainly prevent him from talking and might even prevent him from breathing. His father had left them when he, Scott, was fourteen. He had, up to then, felt a strangled but intense adoration for his father, especially at those rare but treasured times when his father sat down at the piano with him, and listened and watched while he played. Of course, Richie could never listen or watch for long, he had to join in and then take over, but when he was beside him on the piano stool, Scott had been what he later believed to be as close to joy as an adolescent could get. In retrospect, Scott could not bear to think about that joy. It got engulfed by grief and fury and blind incomprehension. He blinked now, several times, hard. Then he swallowed again, and the lump dispersed sufficiently to allow him to speak.

'Died,' Scott said.

'Yes, pet.'

Scott removed himself gently from his mother's grasp.

'Amy rang you?'

'She said,' Margaret said, 'she was ringing so that her mother wouldn't have to.'

'Charming.'

'Well, it's brave,' Margaret said, 'if you think about it. She'll still be well in her teens.'

Scott took a step back. He shook his head.

'So he's dead.'

'Yes.'

He shot a glance at his mother.

'Are you OK?'

She said, 'Well, I've got through today and got what I wanted out of Bernie Harrison, so I suppose – well, I suppose the news isn't going to kill me.'

Scott moved forward and put his arms round his mother.

'Sorry, Mam.'

'Sorry?' she said. 'What's there for *you* to be sorry for?'

He said awkwardly, 'Well, it can't happen now, can it, I mean, he can't—'

'I never hoped that,' Margaret said. 'Never.' Her voice rose. 'I never hoped that!'

Scott gave her a brief squeeze. She had never been helpful to hold.

'OK, Mam.'

'I'm telling you, Scott, I never hoped he'd come back to me.'

Scott let her go. He gestured.

'Drink?'

Margaret glanced at the table.

'I'm not drinking beer—'

'I've got brandy,' Scott said. 'I bought some brandy for a recipe and never used it. Let me get you a brandy.'

'Thank you,' Margaret said.

'Sit down, Mam.'

Margaret went slowly across to the black sofa. She picked up the DVD, regarded the cover unseeingly, and put it down on the coffee table among the scattered magazines and newspaper supplements. Then she sat down and leaned back into the huge canvas cushions and stared up into the gaunt and carefully restored rafters of the ceiling. She was suddenly and overwhelmingly very, very tired.

Scott came down the room from the kitchen end. He was carrying a beer bottle and a tumbler of brown liquid.

'Sorry,' he said, 'I don't run to brandy balloons.'

She turned her head slowly to look at him. Not as handsome as Richie, not as head-turning, but it was a better face, a less conscious face, and he'd got his father's hair. Looking at him, she felt a rush of emotion, a rush of something that could end in tears if she'd been a crying woman. She patted the sofa next to her.

'I'd drink it out of a jam jar,' she said.

Scott sat down next to her. He held out the brandy.

'Mam?'

'Yes, pet,' she said, heaving herself up to take the tumbler out of his hand.

'Mam,' Scott said, staring straight ahead, 'Mam, do you think we should go to the funeral?'

CHAPTER THREE

The church, Chrissie thought, looked more suitable for a wedding than a funeral. The Funfair Club, the disabled children's charity that so many in Richie's profession supported, had said that they would like to give the flowers for his funeral, and the result was that every Gothic column of the church was smothered in pyramids of cream and pink and yellow. The secretary of the Funfair Club had said that they wanted to do Richie proud, that he'd been such a valuable member for so long, so enthusiastic, such a supporter, and it hadn't occurred to Chrissie to ask what, exactly, doing Richie proud might entail florally. There must have been thousands of pounds' worth piled up against the pillars, roses and lilies and inescapable chrysanthemums exuding good intentions, and no taste. Chrissie glanced along her pew. At least she and the girls were doing Richie proud in the taste department.

They were all in black. Narrow black, with high heels. Tamsin and Dilly had pinned their hair up under glamorous little hats, and Amy's was down her back under a black velvet band. Chrissie had added long black gloves to her own outfit, and a small veil. She was wearing her industrial diamonds, and diamond studs in her ears. She would have been much happier to have been wearing them among a few simple architectural vases of madonna lilies.

The church was packed. Chrissie was aware, as she came up the aisle with the girls, that faces were turning towards her, and that there was a palpable wave of warmth and sympathy towards her, which made her feel, suddenly, very vulnerable and visible, despite the veil and the heels and the diamonds. If so many people were that sorry for you, then you were judged to have lost something insupportably enormous, and that consciousness added an unexpected layer of obligation to everything she was feeling already. She went up the aisle with her head up, and the girls just behind her, and, until she was safely in the front pew, did not allow her eyes to rest on the pale oblong of Richie's coffin ahead of her. Its presence, its known but unseen contents, required her to keep her imagination in as profound a state of inertia as she could possibly muster.

The girls, she was proud to see, were not crying. Not even Dilly. Tamsin's Robbie – in a suit, his soberly cherished workwear – was standing in the pew behind her in an attitude of contained tension, as if poised to catch her should she buckle under the emotion of the occasion. Amy had her head bent, and she was scowling slightly, but she was dry-eyed. Chrissie had heard her playing her flute late into the small hours the night before, the solo pieces she used to play to Richie's accompanying piano arrangements, Messiaen's 'Le Merle Noir', Debussy, and Jacob's 'Pied Piper'. Neither of the others was particularly musical, although Tamsin could sing. She sang, Richie used to tell her, like a young Nancy Sinatra.

Chrissie made herself look directly at the coffin. There was an arrangement of white jasmine on it, twisted and shaped to resemble a treble clef. It was what the girls had wanted. She drew off her gloves and laid them along the prayer-book

44

ledge of the pew. Then she picked up her service sheet and, as she did so, the diamonds on her left hand caught the sunlight slanting in through the east window and shot out brilliant unearthly rainbow rays.

At the back of the church, on the left rather than the right-hand side, Scott stood crammed against his mother. He couldn't believe how full the church was, nor what a ritzy congregation it was, with its air of barely suppressed flamboyance. They had arrived far too early, and had waited nervously on the gravelled space outside, carefully not asking one another how they felt, how they would arrange themselves if – when – they came face to face with Richie's other family.

Margaret had been doubtful about coming. She had wanted to, longed to, Scott could see that, but she had not wanted to be in a situation, or indeed to put anyone else in a situation – where old primitive energies might rise up and turn a ritual into a riot.

'I want,' Margaret said, 'to remember him as he was.' And then, a few minutes later, she said, 'I want to say goodbye to him.'

In the end, Scott had decided for her. It wasn't in his nature to insist, to be forceful, but it struck him that her regrets, her remorse, might insinuate themselves quietly and destructively into both their futures if she did not go to the funeral, and so he had said, in the voice he used for clients who wanted to have their cake and eat it, 'We're going.'

'We can't,' Margaret said. She was in an armchair in her sitting room and Dawson was heavily in her lap. 'I can't be there with them.'

'You can,' Scott said. He'd opened a bottle of wine to encourage them both. 'You can. You should.'

'But—'

'We're going,' Scott said.

'But—'

'We'll get the early train, do it, and be home for dinner.'

Margaret put her hand on Dawson's head. He flattened his little ears to the point where he looked as if he didn't have any, and was just an overblown example of a species of giant fur toad.

'Thank you, pet,' Margaret said.

So here they were, Margaret in black, he in his best dark work suit, hair gelled, sober tie, uncomfortably damp palms, in a North London church packed with showbiz people, looking at a pale-wood coffin with brass handles – and his father inside. It occurred to him that he, as his father's only son, and his mother, as his father's wife, had more right to be there than anyone, more natural right. This was not the first time this primordial assertiveness had occurred to him, either. It had happened a few days earlier after the announcement of Richie's death had appeared in the local press, following a gauche little visit to Margaret, in her office, by a journalist too young to know anything of significance about Richie Rossiter, and impelled him, boldly using the landline phone at the office, to ring the house in Highgate and inform them – no arguing – that he and his mother were coming to Richie's funeral. He was braced to speak to Chrissie, or to one of those girls who were, improbably, his half-sisters, but he got an answering machine instead, and a young, disorganized voice – not Chrissie's – asking him to leave his name and number and a message.

'It's Scott Rossiter speaking,' Scott said. 'I'm ringing to tell you that my mother and I will be coming to the service on Friday, and returning North immediately afterwards.'

He'd paused then, wondering how to end the message. Should he say, 'I thought you should know'? In the end, he said nothing, merely put the phone down, feeling that he had started that small enterprise better than he'd finished it. When he told Margaret what he'd done she said, 'Well, pet, better that way,' and he'd felt slightly cheated out of congratulation. But in the train, Margaret had rewarded him. She'd looked up from disapproving of her railway cardboard cup of tea and said, 'I couldn't do this on my own, Scott. And I couldn't do it if they didn't know, either.'

He looked down at her now. She wasn't a small woman, but he was considerably taller than she was, taller, he knew, than his father had been. Heaven knows what was going on behind her resolute expression. She had felt about his father in a way that he was certain he had never yet felt about anybody, to a degree that, when his father left her, he managed at the same time to take the colour out of all other men for her. They'd met at junior school, in North Shields, their childhoods permeated with the same fish and ships and fierce local loyalty to North Tyneside. They were married in 1963, when his father was twenty-two, in the middle of the big freeze, when the old ferryboat, the *Northumbrian*, had to navigate its way across the Tyne among great chunks of ice floating in the river. A photograph taken on their wedding day, an unofficial photograph, showed them standing, hand tightly in hand, he in an Italian suit, she plainly frozen to death in a minidress and coat and white knee boots, watching people stream off the ferryboat from South Shields, housewives, shipyard workers, carts of rag-and-bone men, brewers' drays, and none of those people were aware of the newly married couple, isolated on the edge of their own great adventure, gazing at them in the bitter wind.

Scott blinked. He hadn't looked at that picture for twenty-five years; hadn't wanted to. He wished he hadn't remembered it now. He stared ahead. At the front of the church, and to the right, he could see over the heads of the congregation to the front pew. Four women in black, three

47

hatted. Two blondes, one medium brown, one dark, with no hat. Well, that was them, then. The four women who had enveloped the last third of his father's life as completely as if they'd always been there, and he and his mother had never existed. It was hard, really, to know who to be angriest with.

He bent towards Margaret. She was glaring at her service sheet.

'OK?' he said.

'There's nothing here,' Margaret said in a fierce whisper, 'that he'd have wanted. *Nothing.*'

Amy had seen him as she came into church. She wasn't looking for him, she'd just had her head up because a whole ten days since Dad's death of people being so, so sorry for her, for them all, had made her feel that one more dollop of sympathy and she'd be sick, so she'd resolved to look as if sympathy was the last thing she wanted, and head them off that way. She'd almost stalked up the aisle, behind her mother, behind her sisters and their hats, and although she looked resolutely ahead, she'd caught him in her peripheral vision for the simple reason that, although he was taller and slighter, he looked exactly like Dad, same nose, same jawline, hair growing exactly the same way. And, disconcertingly, his looking like Dad didn't fill her with immediate outrage. It was weird, but it was comforting too. It was quite hard, in fact, to walk on up the aisle and not to stop, for a long, hungry stare.

She'd known he'd be there, after all. It was Amy who'd picked up the message on the answering machine and re-layed it to her mother. Whether Chrissie told the others, Amy didn't know, and didn't ask. As the youngest, Amy had been good at reticence from an early age, having learned that silent observation often yielded her more useful information than yammering on all the time, like her sisters did, Tamsin instructing and Dilly wailing to be included.

'He said,' Amy told her mother, 'that they'd come to the service and go away straight afterwards.'

'I see,' Chrissie said. She was at her computer, looking at something that seemed to be an invoice. 'I shan't seat them. I shan't give them special places.'

'OK,' Amy said.

'I can't stop them. But I didn't ask them—'

'You don't have to do anything,' Amy said. 'Their choice. You don't have to do a thing.'

Chrissie had looked so tired. She'd looked quite unlike herself since Dad died, as if some inner light had been switched off somewhere. But today – well, today she looked amazing. Amazing. Tam and Dilly did, too. Amy gave her head a tiny toss in order to shake her hair smoothly down her back. She hadn't looked past Scott Rossiter in any detail, but she'd had a fleeting impression, one of those vivid nanoseconds of observation that sometimes tell you more than gazing at something for ages. She'd glimpsed *her.* And she looked like a granny.

Amy took a deep breath and glanced along the pew. Dad would have adored seeing them like that, sleek and styled and polished. She picked up her service sheet, almost ready to smile. There was – and it was a triumphant little realization – no comparison. None at all.

The gravelled space in front of the church was full, afterwards, of people standing about in the chilly sunshine, talking with the kind of animation born of social awkwardness. Scott wanted to steer Margaret through the throng, quite rapidly, and out into South Grove, towards Highgate Hill and down to the safe anonymity of the tube station. He'd already planned to buy her a gin and tonic at King's Cross, and another on the train, and then take her out to dinner when they got home and send her back to Tynemouth in a taxi. But she was standing there staring, holding her bag over her arm like the Queen, her gloved hands folded in front of her. He put a hand under her elbow.

'Come on, Mam, h'way—'

'Don't you h'way me,' Margaret said. She twitched her elbow out of his grasp. 'I can't go till he's gone.'

Scott followed the direction of her gaze. The undertakers, treading softly in their black orthopaedic shoes, were sliding Richie's coffin into the gleaming black body of the hearse. The starry white flowers on top of the coffin, oddly ethereal and girlish, were ruffled by the wind, and those four women were standing in a row in front of them, watching.

'There's nothing to see—'

'That's not the point,' Margaret said. She began to move forwards, through the crowd.

'Mam—' Scott said, in pursuit. 'Mam. It's going – he's – it's going to the crematorium—'

'I know,' Margaret said. She was dangerously close to those four black backs. 'I know. But I can't go until he's gone.'

Scott was uncomfortably aware that people were staring at them, that some people, anyway, were remarking on how like Richie he looked. He took Margaret's arm again, more firmly.

'Mam—'

'It isn't right,' she said. 'It isn't respectful. I came to say goodbye.'

'Margaret,' someone said.

They both turned. A heavily set man in a dark suit and a lavish black-satin tie was standing very close to them. He bent forward.

'Margaret,' he said, 'Jim Rutherford.' He kissed her cheek.

'My God,' Margaret said, 'Jim Rutherford—'

He put large, flexible hands on her shoulders.

'I wondered if you'd come. I thought about ringing you.'

'Of course I came.'

'Now I see you,' Jim Rutherford said, 'I remember that I shouldn't have wondered any such thing.' He glanced at Scott. 'This your boy?'

Scott nodded. The undertakers had arranged the coffin and the flowers and were closing the doors of the hearse.

'You won't remember me,' Jim Rutherford said. 'Last time I saw you, you were only a nipper. Your dad and I ran you out down Tynemouth harbour wall. It was blowing fit to have your head off. You in the music business too?'

Scott shook his head.

'I'm a lawyer—'

Jim Rutherford smiled.

'As sensible as your mother, then.' He looked down at Margaret again. 'You bearing up then? You doing all right?'

'Yes,' Margaret said, 'and why wouldn't I?'

Jim Rutherford bent, and kissed her cheek again, and said, 'Glad to see you, Margaret, very glad to see you,' and as he straightened up the hearse slid away with Richie's coffin in it and a sudden respectful silence fell upon the crowd like a blanket. Then Jim Rutherford stepped back, and Scott tightened his grip on his mother and the line of four black backs in front of them broke up, and swung round, and Chrissie and Margaret found themselves face to face, six feet apart, in an unexpected, unrehearsed moment of supreme drama.

Nobody said anything. The six of them confronted one another in a ring of startled spectators. A few interminable seconds passed and then Chrissie, like someone caught in the slow inexorable motion of an automatic revolving door, turned smoothly away and began to walk with purpose towards the road. Released from the intense potency of the moment, her daughters turned too, less smoothly, and went after her, hurrying to catch up, to touch her, to reconnect.

Margaret simply stood there, her arm in Scott's grasp. People were looking at them now, looking and glancing, covert little snatches of reaction floating about like conversation heard down a stairwell. Scott cleared his throat. Margaret was not the only one in need of a gin and tonic.

'Mam—'

She was still gazing at the spot where Chrissie had stood only seconds before.

'Well,' Margaret said. 'Well. You never get what you expect. Do you?'

Chrissie had bought smoked salmon, and early strawberries flown in from Spain, and put two bottles of champagne in the fridge before they left for the church. She knew she wouldn't be able to eat or drink at the reception after she and the girls went to the crematorium, and she knew that if they didn't have something basic to focus on, like food and drink, when they got home, they were in for an evening as bad as – or perhaps in some ways almost worse than – the one on which Richie had died. The service had been bearable – just – but the crematorium had hardly been bearable at all, and Dilly had given a little scream when the coffin had, by virtue of some heartless modern mechanism, simply and silently sunk down on its plinth into a depth where no one's imagination could bear to follow it. As with the drive back from the hospital the night Richie died, Chrissie wasn't sure how she had got herself and the girls out of the crematorium and into the gleaming hired Lexus and back to confront all those hugs and smiles and champagne-flavoured offers of support, not to mention journalists and photographers asking her how she felt, wanting to take pictures of the girls in tears, asking them all to pose together, draped over one another in a stagy symphony of grief and loss.

Friends had suggested that they come back with them, that the late afternoon and evening would be better, easier, if the intensity of the four of them was diluted by other people, people who might, Chrissie's friend Sue hinted, be able to remind them that Richie, of all people, believed life was for living and would be urging them to get on with it.

'Tomorrow, maybe,' Chrissie said. There was something about Sue's smiling energetic desire to drive them forward out of the darkness and towards something more socially amenable that almost offended her. 'It's only been ten days. We'll get there, but we'll have to do it at our own pace. And I don't think, tonight, I could quite face—'

'OK, sweets,' Sue said. She'd put her arms round Chrissie, the way people perpetually did in television soap operas. 'You do what you need to do. But I'm there when you need me. I'll call in the morning.'

'Why didn't you let her come?' Dilly said later. She'd been strangely cheered by the sight of an ex-boyfriend, hovering at the edge of the reception, a boyfriend whom Richie had deemed a talented guitarist and who had abandoned Dilly for a scruffy little scrap of a girl with a cannabis habit and a deep smoky singing voice like the early queens of American blues. Yet here Craig was, at Richie's funeral, and when Dilly said to him, sniffing, 'Dad thought a lot of you, you little toerag,' Craig said, 'I didn't come just for him,' and that remark had given a sudden lift to spirits that Dilly had, only seconds before, believed would never rise again. So, a while later, she had felt a dawning renewal of her appetite for social life.

'Why didn't you let Sue come?' Dilly said. 'We could have

had her and Fran and Kevin and the kids. Couldn't we? It would have been a laugh.' She stopped. 'If you see what I mean.'

Chrissie had kicked off her shoes. They all had. They had kept their funeral hair and make-up, but in Amy's case put jeans back on. But their high-heeled shoes were all scattered across the sitting-room rug, and Chrissie was lying along the sofa, with her champagne glass, and her eyes closed.

'I couldn't manage any more today,' Chrissie said. 'I couldn't even manage Sue.'

'We've got to break out, though,' Dilly said. 'We've got to start—' She stopped again. Craig had retaken her mobile number. His had never been erased from her own phone. The promise this represented was compensation for restraining an inclination to provoke. She said with warmth, 'We did it, though.'

'We did,' Chrissie said. She rolled her head sideways on the sofa cushions and surveyed them. 'You all were so great. Dad would have been so proud of you.'

'That's what Robbie said,' Tamsin said. Robbie had been right behind her at the reception, had wanted to come to the crematorium to support her, had wanted to be there, that night, opening the bottles and filling the glasses. But she'd said no. Then she told her mother and sisters that she'd said no. Then she said that Robbie was quite hurt, because his being hurt was evidence of his devotion and even on an occasion like this, she didn't want anyone to be under any illusion about *that*.

'Nice boy,' Chrissie said absently. 'And Craig. Craig's a nice boy.'

'Dad liked Craig,' Dilly said.

Tamsin waited a second, and then she said, with precision, 'Dad liked Robbie.'

'He liked everyone,' Chrissie said. Tears began to leak down her face again. 'He liked everyone. And they loved him back.'

There was a pause, another exhausted, wound-up pause.

And then Amy said, 'Did you see him?'

'Who?'

'You know,' Amy said. 'Him. Scott.'

Chrissie turned her face towards the back of the sofa.

'Hardly. I was trying not to look.'

'He looked just like Dad,' Amy said.

'Amy!' Tamsin said reprovingly.

'Well, he did,' Amy said. 'You saw.'

Dilly said, with some venom, 'I saw *her*.'

'Shush,' Chrissie said.

Amy leaned out of her armchair to inspect something on one bare foot.

'She's old,' she said.

Tamsin said, 'Well, she must be Dad's age—'

'She looks it—'

'She was staring at us—'

'So was he—'

'They shouldn't have come —'

'She had this gross coat on—'

'What was she trying to prove?'

'Dad wouldn't have wanted her there—'

'He looked really awkward—'

'Dad never talked about her—'

'Or him—'

'Jesus,' Amy said suddenly.

'What?'

Amy sat up straight. She said, 'He's Dad's kid. How would we feel if Dad never talked about us?'

'Whose side are you on?' Dilly demanded.

'I just thought,' Amy said, 'I just suddenly thought—'

Tamsin got out of her chair and picked up the champagne bottle.

'He's got his mother,' Tamsin said.

She went round the circle, filling glasses.

'He's got his mother,' she said again firmly. 'And we've got ours.'

Chrissie smiled at her weakly.

'And now,' Tamsin said, 'I'm just going to call Robbie.'

Alone in her bedroom in Tynemouth, Margaret had the sensation of being so tired that she wondered if she was ill. It had, of course, been a long, long day, full of physical and emotional exertions of peculiarly demanding kinds, and she had had two double gins and two glasses of red wine in the course of the late afternoon and evening, but the thing that was exacerbating the fatigue, and making it agitating rather than obliterating, was trying to digest everything she had seen and done, to fit into her mind all those powerful jumbled images and impressions and believe, at the end, that she was back in the security of the familiar.

Dawson had been familiar, at least. He was not naturally affectionate or empathetic, but some instinct had urged him to sit in the hall and wait for her, and, when he heard her key in the lock past midnight, to pad down to the front door to welcome her and press himself inconveniently against her legs while she took off her coat. She had bent down, and heaved him up into her arms, and put her face into his rumbling, purring side for a few moments, and then she had put him down on the floor again, and he had gone to position himself, meaningfully, next to his empty dish.

'You'll have to wait for another day to dawn,' Margaret said to him. 'Just as I will.'

Her bedroom felt chilly and uninviting. She went through her rituals of closing and switching and turning down, and ran a bath with some of the rose oil – too sweet, if the truth be told – that Glenda had given her last Christmas. There was nothing much she could do about the kaleidoscope inside her head, except wait for it to stop swirling about in chaos and resolve itself into some kind of manageable order, but that was no reason to abandon the habits that had grown up round her, not because of lack of energy or enterprise, but because they suited her, and she functioned best within them.

A bath, an application of this and that to her face, a prolonged session with the immense variety of toothbrushes the fierce young hygienist at her dentist now insisted on, a vigorous hairbrush, a well-laundered white cotton nightdress with picot edging – they all added up to something that, some days, Margaret looked forward to almost from the moment she woke in the morning. Tonight, they all seemed completely pointless, but they must be done. At the very least, they represented life when it was normal, the life that she had worked out, and worked on, to deliver her some value out of what was left on offer.

She sat down in her petticoat in front of her dressing-table mirror. She took out Scott's pearl earrings and unfastened Richie's pearl necklace, and laid them both in the Minton dish, where they had spent most of their nights for as long as she could remember. Then she took off the small garnet ring from her right hand – it had belonged to Richie's mother, a gentle and affectionate woman who had been a great relief to Margaret after the abrasiveness of her childhood – and put it in the dish beside the pearls.

She looked at her left hand. She still wore her wedding ring. When she and Richie were married, the fashion had been for wide, flat wedding rings, as if cut from a length of metal tubing, but neither of them had liked that. Instead, they'd gone into Newcastle and found a small, old-fashioned jeweller and bought a thin, gold, D-shaped band, which had been on Margaret's wedding finger for forty-five years.

Perhaps she should, now, take it off. Whatever her quick denial, Scott had been painfully accurate in supposing that a tiny hope of Richie's return had gone on glowing in her, a night light in a coal mine. She'd never had the smallest reason, the smallest sign, that a corresponding intention lingered in Richie – except that he had never divorced her. He had talked about it, to start with, and there'd been lawyers' letters, and assessments of assets, but she, while never being uncooperative, had also never gone out of her way to move things along. And gradually, they had stopped moving. Richie acquired one new baby, then two, and she waited for what seemed to her the inevitable consequent request for a divorce so that he could marry these babies' mother. But it never came. A third baby arrived, and still it never came. Margaret realized, gradually and with little gleams of hope that she told herself were ridiculous but simultaneously had no wish to quell, that it probably never would.

But now was different. Today, with all its demands and complexities, had drawn a thick black line under twenty-three years of wondering and dreaming and hoping. Those three good-looking girls, that pretty, grieving, angry woman – the sight of them had brought Margaret to her senses. It might have been a consolation to go on wearing her wedding ring. She might have persuaded herself that she was legally entitled still to wear her wedding ring. But the Richie she had seen go off in his coffin today had transferred himself from belonging to her to belonging to that family in London, and that had to be recognized. In Margaret's view, once something was acknowledged, it should be accepted, right away. It was over. She took hold of her wedding ring with her right hand, eased it with difficulty over the joints of her wedding finger, and dropped it, with finality, into the Minton dish.

CHAPTER FOUR

Mark Leverton had followed his father into the family practice almost without thinking. His grandfather, Manny Leverton, had started his small solicitor's practice – 'Wills and probate a speciality' – in modest offices at the eastern end of West End Lane soon after the Second World War. In due course, a brother had joined him, and a nephew, and then his own son Francis, and the modest offices had spread down West End Lane to engulf a corner site on the Finchley Road, red brick with a handsome but sober white portal, and a business which now encompassed advice on civil partnership and inheritance-tax planning. Manny's photograph – black-and-white, the subject dressed in a three-piece suit with a watch chain – hung above the reception desk. There were twelve partners in the offices above, nine of them Levertons. Mark, who had idly, as a teenager, thought that he might do something creative in the media, found himself going from school to law college in a single seamless movement, propelled by his purposeful family, and was now in possession of an office of his own, sandwiched between two cousins, with a large modern desk adorned, among other things, with a photograph of a wife and two little sons, whom he was delighted to have but could not quite – again – recall having stirred himself much to acquire.

His father, Francis, had decided early on that Mark should specialize in that area of the law on which the firm had first concentrated: wills and probate. The boy might not be blazingly ambitious, but he was clever enough, and thorough, and his amiable manner would be invaluable in an area prone to intense disputatiousness among the clients. Mark would not mind detail, or shouting, or repetition. Mark would be good at reasoning and smoothing without identifying too much with any particular cause or person. Mark was the man, Francis considered, best able to deal with warring and divided families.

'Tell them,' Francis said to Mark when Mark joined Leverton's, 'tell them to assume nothing. That's the golden rule for inheritance, especially. Assume *nothing.*'

He gave Mark a quotation from Andrew Carnegie, carefully written out in copperplate, which Mark had framed and hung on his office wall. It was headed 'The Carnegie Conjecture': 'The parent who leaves his son enormous wealth generally deadens the talents and energies of the son, and tempts him to lead a less useful and less worthy life than he otherwise would.'

Mark's father Francis believed in Andrew Carnegie.

'Establishing yourself is difficult,' he told Mark. 'It ought to be difficult. It won't satisfy you if it isn't difficult. You've got to call people who don't want to talk to you. You've got to get on with it when you've got a hangover and you're bored stiff. Work delivers more than money ever will – you remember that when you're talking to people scrapping over a few thousand quid.'

Mark did remember it. He remembered too a study on happiness he'd read which concluded that Masai herdsmen and people on the Fortune 400 list were about as happy as each other. He remembered it when Richie Rossiter – whom his mother thought the world of – came to see him out of the blue and was very clear about making a will that superseded any will that he, or he and Mrs Rossiter, had previously made. He did not think that Richie Rossiter was in the habit of precision about any area of life that didn't concern music, but on that occasion he had been both decided and well prepared. The will had been drawn up as he had requested, he had come into the office to sign it, and the document had then been filed, along with twenty years of Rossiter papers, against such time – 'Shan't need this for decades, Mark' – as Richie should die.

And now, only a year later, he was dead. Suddenly, unexpectedly, felled by a heart attack that rumour was saying was probably genetically accountable. Richie Rossiter was dead, the Rossiter files had been opened, and Mark Leverton had, in his diary for that Wednesday, an eleven o'clock appointment with Richie Rossiter's widow.

Tamsin said that she would go with her mother to see Mr Leverton.

Chrissie looked round the table. You couldn't really call it a breakfast table since there was no social coherence to it, and everybody was eating and drinking different things, some of them – like the pizza crusts on Amy's plate – not conventionally appropriate to breakfast.

Chrissie said, 'I hoped you'd all come.'

'To the *solicitor's*?' Amy said, as if an outing to a slaughter-house was being suggested.

'Actually,' Dilly said, 'I'm a bit busy—'

Chrissie leaned forward.

'We should do this together. We should do all these things that concern Dad together.'

Dilly's mobile was lying on the table next to a banana skin. She gave it a little spin.

'Actually—'

'She's seeing Craig,' Amy announced to the table.

'Not till tonight,' Tamsin said.

Amy leaned forward too.

'But there's so much to do before tonight,' Amy said with exaggerated breathlessness. 'Isn't there, Dill? All the waxing and stuff. All the hair straightening. All the—'

Dilly picked up the banana skin and threw it at her sister.

'Shut up!'

Amy ducked.

'We don't say shut up in this house—'

The banana skin hit the wall and slid down to lodge limply in the radiator.

'Be quiet!' Chrissie said loudly.

They all looked at her.

'It won't take long,' Chrissie said. 'It's merely a formality. I know exactly what's in that will because Dad and I agreed it together. But it would be nice if we could all four go together to see Mr Leverton and hear him tell us, even if I know what he'll say.'

Amy squirmed.

'Why?'

'Because it's a kind of little ceremony,' Chrissie said. 'Because it's a formal ritual thing we do together for Dad.'

Dilly picked up her phone and peered closely at it.

'Sorry, Mum.'

'You're pathetic,' Tamsin said.

'I just can't,' Dilly said, her hair falling in curtains round her face and phone. 'I just can't do any more.'

'Usually you can't bear to be left out,' Chrissie said.

'Craig isn't usually,' Amy said.

Chrissie looked at her.

'What about you?'

'Sorry,' Amy said.

'It'll take half an hour—'

Amy put her hands flat on the table and pushed herself to her feet.

'Sorry,' she said again, 'but I don't want to think about wills. I don't want to think about money and stuff. It just seems – kind of grotesque.'

'*Grotesque?*' Tamsin said.

Amy picked the banana skin off the radiator and dropped it on the table.

She said, 'Doesn't matter—'

'It does matter,' Chrissie said. 'What do you mean, that hearing what's in the will is grotesque?'

'Well,' Amy said, shuffling, 'sort of wrong, then.'

'*Wrong?*' Tamsin said, with the same emphasis.

'Yes,' Amy said, 'because it isn't just us. Is it?'

Chrissie put her head in her hands.

'What isn't just us?'

'Well,' Amy said, 'this will. It's for us. It's what Dad wanted for us. But – well, he had a whole sort of life before us and what – what about them?'

Tamsin threw her head back and stared at the ceiling.

'I do not believe this.'

'Amy,' Chrissie said, 'are you saying that – that the – people in Newcastle should be included too?'

Amy nodded.

'Sort of,' she said. 'Maybe not included but kind of, well, kind of remembered?' There was a short pause, then Amy said firmly, 'Anyway, she doesn't live in Newcastle, she lives in Tynemouth.'

'Amy,' Chrissie said again. She looked directly at her. 'Amy. It doesn't matter where she lives, what matters is that she's out of the picture. All that was sorted long ago. A house, a sum of money, everything. It was a clean break, no coming back for more, no questioning of decisions made. It was conclusively agreed and it was absolutely fair. Do you hear me? Absolutely fair.'

Amy pulled out a long strand of hair and examined the ends.

'OK.'

'Do you understand me?'

'Yup.'

'And believe me?'

'Yup,' Amy said.

'Good.'

Chrissie got up briskly and crossed the kitchen to assemble the components for making coffee. With her back to her daughters, she said, 'However, Amy, I'm not sure I want you to come now. You may say you believe me, but what you said just now, the implied accusation in what you said just now, has made me feel that I'd rather you didn't come with me to see Mr Leverton. You may all be thinking how much you've suffered in the last couple of weeks, but perhaps it wouldn't do you any harm to think about me, not just what I've been through, but what I've got to go through in the future, without Dad.' Her voice shook. She stopped, and spooned coffee, slightly unsteadily, into the cafetière. 'If you can't support me wholeheartedly,' Chrissie said, 'I'd really rather go on my own.'

There was silence. It was broken after a few seconds by Dilly dropping her phone. Tamsin bent to pick it up, and tossed it at her sister.

She said to Chrissie's back, 'I'd like to come with you, Mum, please.'

Chrissie turned round. Dilly was looking at her phone and Amy was staring out of the window.

'Thank you, Tamsin,' Chrissie said with dignity. 'Thank you. Then it will just be you and me.'

Mark Leverton had arranged his office so that, when occasion demanded, he could sit beside his desk, rather than behind it, in order not to create too formal a distance between himself and those he was talking to. He seated Chrissie and Tamsin in padded upright chairs with wooden arms – upholstered easy chairs did not seem suitable for discussion about, or after, death – put the papers on one side of his desk, and then positioned himself on a chair next to them. He usually worked in his shirt sleeves, but he had put his jacket back on for the meeting, shooting his cuffs just enough to show off the silver Tiffany cufflinks that his wife had given him for their seventh wedding anniversary.

'Just to remind you,' she'd said, 'that an itch is not on your agenda.'

Chrissie hardly took him in, except to notice that he was neat and dark and vaguely familiar, and was wearing a wedding ring. She too was wearing a wedding ring, but with an unwelcome self-consciousness, which she was sure never needed to cross Mr Leverton's mind. There was nothing illegal in sitting in his office being called Mrs Rossiter and wearing a wedding ring, because she and Richie had agreed, and signed, everything together, and she wasn't doing anything furtive, or anything that Richie had not been party to; or anything that deprived someone of something they ought to have had, had she not been there. But sitting in that office, apparently composed and confident, in her well-cut trouser suit, with her well-cut hair tied back, and her expensive bag on the floor beside her well-shod feet, she felt, to her surprise and dismay, knocked almost sideways by an unexpected spurt of pure fury at Richie, for refusing to marry her and thus landing her in a situation where the unlovely choice was between pretence and potential humiliation.

Mark Leverton smiled at Tamsin. She was very pretty, with her mother's features and a smooth curtain of brown hair held off her face with a tortoiseshell clip. He smiled at her, not so much because she was young and pretty but more because she looked so much less tense than her mother and not as if she'd rather be anywhere else in the world than sitting in his office.

'I am so sorry,' Mark said. 'So very sorry, about Mr Rossiter.'

His uncles, he knew, in the same situation, were still apt to say, 'May I offer my sincere condolences on your loss,' but that sounded ridiculous to Mark. It also sounded insincere, and Mark was sincere for the very simple reason that, now he had a family of his own as well as the one he had been born into, he could empathize – often painfully well – with what the bereaved people sitting in front of him were going through.

'Thank you,' Chrissie said. She looked down at her lap. Tamsin reached across and held her nearest wrist.

'OK, Mum?'

Chrissie nodded.

'I won't keep you long,' Mark said. 'It's very simple.' He bent forward slightly towards Chrissie, in order to be encouraging. 'You know, I think, Mrs Rossiter, how simple it is. Mr Rossiter's will is very familiar to you.'

Chrissie nodded again.

Mark drew the neat folder of papers close to him across his desk, and laid his hand flat on it.

'In fact,' Mark said, 'there are only a couple of small alterations since we revised the will together three years ago, as I'm sure you will remember.'

Chrissie's head snapped up.

'Alterations?'

Mark smiled at her. This was the moment he had been rehearsing, the moment when he had to reveal to her that Richie had been to see him the previous spring and had indicated – but not actually specified – that the visit was private.

'I don't believe in secrets,' Richie had said, 'but I do believe in privacy. We're all allowed our privacy, aren't we?'

'There were just two small matters,' Mark said now, in as gentle a voice as he could muster, 'that represented what you might call wishes. Mr Rossiter's wishes. Two little gifts he found he wanted to make, and he came here about a year ago to tell me about them. They don't affect the bulk of the estate. That will be yours, of course, the house and so on, after probate.'

Tamsin said faintly, 'What's probate?'

Mark smiled at her.

'It's the legal proving that someone's will actually is their will.'

Tamsin nodded. She looked at her mother. Chrissie was staring straight past Mark at a picture on the wall, a picture Mark's wife had chosen, a sub-Mondrian arrangement of black lines and squares of colour. Tamsin twisted in her chair, gripping her mother's wrist.

'Mum—'

'What gifts?' Chrissie said, almost with her teeth clenched.

Mark glanced at Tamsin. She was concentrating wholly on her mother.

He said, 'Please be assured, Mrs Rossiter, that you and your daughters remain the main and major beneficiaries in every respect.'

'What *gifts*?' Chrissie said again.

There was a small silence. Mark took up the folder, and

held it for a few seconds, as if assessing whether to open it and, as it were, release some genie, and then he put it down again, and said quietly, 'Mr Rossiter wished to leave two items to his first family in Newcastle.'

Chrissie gave a violent involuntary shudder. Tamsin shot out of her chair, and knelt on the carpet next to her mother.

'Mum, it's OK, it's OK—'

Chrissie took her wrist out of Tamsin's grip, and put her hand on Tamsin's shoulder.

'I'm fine.' She looked at Mark. 'What items?'

Mark put his elbows on his knees, linked his hands loosely and leaned forward.

'The piano,' he said, 'and his musical estate up to 1985.'

'The piano—'

'He wished,' Mark said, his voice full of the sympathy he truly felt and of which his father would doubtless have disapproved, 'to leave the piano to his former wife and his musical estate up to 1985 to his son.'

Chrissie said, 'The Steinway—'

'Yes.'

'Oh my God,' Tamsin said. She crumpled against her mother's chair. 'Oh my God—'

'I gather,' Mark said, 'that 1985 was the year in which Mr Rossiter came south to London. His son was then fourteen. I believe the current value of the Steinway is about twenty-two thousand pounds. And, of course, there's value to those early songs, the rights in those. I haven't established more than an estimate—' He stopped.

Tamsin began to cry. She leaned forward until her forehead was resting against Chrissie's thigh.

'Not the piano,' she said indistinctly. 'Not the piano. Not that—'

Chrissie stroked her hair. She looked down at her, almost

absently, as if she was thinking about something quite different. Then she looked back at Mark.

She said, quite steadily, 'Are you sure?'

He put his hand on the folder again, drew it towards him, opened it and held out the top sheet inside for her to see.

'Quite sure,' he said.

She stared at the piece of paper, but didn't seem to take it in. She was simply gazing, where instructed, her hand moving across and across on Tamsin's head.

'But that is all,' Mark Leverton said. 'That's the only difference. There are no complications, I'm delighted to say, and no inheritance tax is applicable, because a will was made and you are Mr Rossiter's widow.'

Chrissie withdrew her gaze very slowly from the sheet of paper and transferred it, equally slowly, to Mark's face. She stopped stroking.

She said, quite clearly, but from a long way away, as if waking from some kind of trance, 'But I'm not.'

The clock beside Amy's bed said, in oblong green digits, two forty-five a.m. Last time she had looked it had said one thirteen, and the time before that twelve thirty-seven, and in between those times, she had tried to read and tried to sleep and tried to talk to friends online and tried to play her flute and tried to want to go downstairs and make toast or hot chocolate. She had tried, and she had comprehensively failed. She had been in her room since just before eleven, and had been able to do nothing but agitate about in it since then, fiddling and fidgeting and feeling her mind skid away from yet more information it had no wish to acknowledge, let alone absorb. Who on earth, actually, could possibly have a mind that did not react violently to being told, in the space of fifteen minutes, that your father had left two crucial elements of his life and being to the family that preceded yours, that your parents had never, actually, got around to being married, and that your sisters had somehow known this all along, but had carelessly – or deliberately – omitted to include you in this knowledge?

'Oh, *Amy*,' Tamsin had said, in the exasperated tone of one forced to indulge the deliberate babyishness of a younger sibling, 'you *knew*. Of course you knew.'

'I didn't—'

'Well,' Dilly said, 'I can't think how you didn't know. It wasn't exactly a secret. What were you *doing*, not knowing?'

Amy glared at her.

'You tell me.'

'They were together for twenty-three years,' Tamsin said. 'Twenty-five, if you count from when they met. He was only married once – before, for twenty-two years. He was with Mum for longer.'

'How do you know?' Amy said stubbornly.

'Mum told me.'

'Why didn't she tell *me*?'

'I expect,' Dilly said, 'you didn't ask her.'

'Ask her now,' Tamsin said. 'Go on. Ask her.'

But Amy hadn't. In the turmoil of the evening, with supper hardly happening, and Robbie and Craig appearing and then disappearing, with Chrissie sitting silently on the piano stool in front of the closed piano – Amy didn't think she'd ever seen it closed before – and nobody, for some reason, telephoning, there hadn't been a moment when Amy, despite the turbulence of her feelings, could ask her mother a question. Well, not a question of that kind, anyway, not a question that inevitably led to so many other questions, none of them comfortable. But not asking the questions had left her mind and her stomach churning, and was propelling her in and out of her bed and round and round her bedroom as if driven by some arcane disorder that would not let her rest.

She looked at the clock again. Two forty-eight. She got out of bed for the fiftieth time, pulled on an old cardigan of her father's that she had appropriated from his cupboard in the week after his death, and opened her bedroom door. Across the tiny landing, with its sloping ceiling and ingenious Swedish skylight, Dilly's bedroom door was closed. Amy had heard her come upstairs, about midnight, still murmuring into her phone, and shut the door in the definitive way that indicated she would not be accommodating about being disturbed. Often, and especially if she had had a bad day at the college where she was training to be a beauty therapist, she left her door just open enough to indicate that even Amy's company was preferable, just now, to her own. But last night, the pitch of her voice, low and almost happy, on the telephone had made it plain that Amy was not to be included in anything that might be diverting or comforting. And now her door was firmly closed and the silence of sleep was unmistakable.

Amy crept downstairs. On the main landing, Tamsin's door was shut, and so was Chrissie's. In the family bathroom, someone had left the light on over the basin and it illuminated the glass shelf below, where Richie's toothbrushes used to stand, in a Mickey Mouse mug Amy had brought back for him from a trip with a friend's family to Euro Disney, when she was seven. Richie had always kept toothbrushes in the family bathroom, a hangover from the days when he made a game of tooth-brushing, when they were small. Neither the mug nor the brushes were there any more, just a hair scrunchie and a plastic brush and a bottle of something creamy and pale pink. Girly, Amy thought, girly stuff. What this house is full of.

She went on down to the ground floor, less carefully.

There was a light on there, too, the light in the tiny room, not much more than a cupboard, beside the front door, that Chrissie used as an office. Amy put her head in to find the light switch. The computer was on, as well as the light, and Chrissie, still dressed, was sitting in front of it, typing.

'Mum?'

Chrissie turned. She didn't seem surprised.

'Hello, darling.'

Amy leaned against the door frame.

'Can't sleep.'

'Nor me.'

'What're you doing?'

Chrissie turned back to the screen.

'Looking up inheritance tax.'

Amy pushed herself away from the doorpost.

'What's that?'

'It's a tax the government makes you pay if you are left money and property. If you are married to the person who dies, you don't have to pay any tax. If you aren't, the government lets you have a certain amount without taxing you, and then it taxes you on the rest.'

Amy leaned over Chrissie's shoulder.

'What?'

'In the eyes of the law,' Chrissie said, 'living with Dad for twenty-three years doesn't make me his wife.'

Amy felt suddenly tearful. She said childishly, '*Why* didn't you marry him?'

Chrissie said, looking at the screen, 'I can't talk about it now, Amy. I'm sorry, but I'm angry, and I'll say the wrong thing and then I'll wish I hadn't. We'll talk about it as soon as I can.'

'They knew,' Amy said. 'Why didn't I?'

'I don't know,' Chrissie said. 'You didn't ask. I wish you had. I wish I'd told you. I wish we'd all talked about it, all of us, with Dad. When Dad was still here. I wish it wasn't too late.'

Amy moved sideways and perched on the edge of the desk. She began to pluck at the strands of her hair.

'Did you want to?'

'Want to what?'

'Did you want to marry Dad?'

Chrissie gave a little sigh.

'Oh yes.'

'Why didn't you ask him?'

'Amy,' Chrissie said, 'I told you. I can't talk about it now. I'm wrestling with knowing that I'm what the law calls a cohabitee and therefore not entitled to the status and privileges, in a tax sense, of being a married woman, and that is *enough*. Just now, that is quite enough for me to cope with.'

'So I'm illegitimate.'

Chrissie didn't look at her.

'Don't be melodramatic. Nobody uses that word now. You were wanted and adored and you know who both your parents are and that's more than a lot of people can say. Society and the law often take a long time to catch up with how people behave.'

Amy said, into her handful of hair, 'Don't you care?'

Chrissie put a hand out and held the edge of Richie's old cardigan.

'Darling, I care so much about so much at the moment that I sometimes think I might just fall to pieces.'

'Don't,' Amy said suddenly.

'I won't. I can't. There's just so much—' She stopped. She took her hand away from the cardigan and put it briefly across her eyes. 'It's just such a lot to take in, Amy. Such a lot that's different, that – that's not what I thought it was, believed it was—' She stopped again.

Amy pushed her hair back over her shoulders. She said, as a statement, 'The piano.'

Chrissie looked down at her keyboard.

'It was his voice,' she said. 'It – the piano – was everything, really, not just his stage name but how he thought of himself, how he was. I can't believe he did that, I can't believe he wanted to do that and didn't tell me, left me to find out like that, just left me to find out. Too late, like everything else. And I'm picking up the pieces.' She glanced up at Amy and put her hand out again, to take Amy's this time. 'Sorry, darling. I shouldn't be talking to you like this. I shouldn't be thinking like this. It isn't fair. It isn't fair to you. Or me. It's classic three-in-the-morning thinking. Sorry. So sorry.'

Amy said slowly, 'Perhaps she won't want it—'

'What?'

'Perhaps she won't want the piano. Perhaps,' Amy said a little faster, 'perhaps she's angry with him too.'

Chrissie gave another sigh.

'I don't really want to know. I don't care what she feels, I don't want to have to consider her.'

'OK,' Amy said. She took her hand out of her mother's and folded her arms. 'OK. But I'm angry.'

Chrissie looked down at her keyboard.

'Are you listening?' Amy demanded.

'Of course—'

'I'm angry,' Amy said, almost shouting. 'I'm angry at you and I'm even angrier at him. How *could* he? Why did he treat me like a little kid, why did you both play your make-believe and think it wouldn't affect me? What were you thinking of?'

'I suppose we weren't really thinking—'

'How *dare* you,' Amy said, suddenly not shouting, but almost whispering. 'How *dare* you. How dare *he*.'

'Well,' Chrissie said slowly, 'if it's any consolation, I'm

paying for it now. Aren't I? No income from Dad, this tax, everything frozen till after probate—'

'This isn't about you.'

'No,' Chrissie said. 'Sorry. Sorry, darling. It's just that—'

'It's about me,' Amy said. 'And Tamsin, and Dilly. And him.'

'Dad?'

'No,' Amy said. She sighed. 'No. Not Dad. Not you or Dad. Not parents. It's about the children, isn't it? The three of us, and him. In Newcastle.' She bent towards her mother and hissed at her. 'Isn't it?'

CHAPTER FIVE

'Where will you put it?' Scott said.

Margaret was standing by the sofa in the bay window of her sitting room, gazing out across the undulating grass of Percy Gardens, towards the sea. The sea was dark today, despite a blue sky, dark and shiny, and from this distance, calm enough only to shimmer. A few hefty North Sea gulls were picking their way around the grass, and there was an old man going past, very slowly, with a stick in one hand and a plastic shopper in the other. Apart from them, there was no sign of life, no people, no shipping. Dawson, stretched along the back of the sofa, was sleeping the sleep of one who knows there is nothing worth staying awake for.

'Put what?' Margaret asked absently. She was in some kind of mild reverie. She'd been in it, Scott thought, all weekend, abstracted and peculiar, with a groove on her left hand where her wedding ring had been. When he'd asked her where it was, she'd looked at her hand as if it was nothing to do with her and said, 'Oh, that's nothing, pet. It was just time. Time to take it off.'

Scott said loudly, 'Where will you put the piano?'

Margaret turned round, without hurry. She looked at the room, at her sofa and chairs covered in linen union printed

76

with peonies, at her occasional tables and lamps, at her brass fire irons hanging on their little tripod in the fireplace, at the glass-fronted display cabinet full of the porcelain figures she used to collect, shepherdesses dreaming on picturesque tree stumps, Artful Dodger boys playing with spaniels.

'Well,' Margaret said, 'there isn't room in here.'

Scott sighed.

He said, 'There is if you move stuff.'

Margaret made a vague gesture. 'It would be so dominating—'

Scott put his hands in his jeans pockets, and hunched his shoulders. He studied the toes of his trainers. He counted, with effort, to twenty. He wanted to say, with some force, that having the Steinway back was not just important because of what it indicated about his father's abiding remembrance of them – after all – but also because it would mean that he, Scott, could play it. And that, if he played it in his mother's sitting room, his mother might remember, at long last, that he, Scott, could actually play. Rather well. It might make her stop insisting that Richie was unique, that nobody could play like he could, that Scott had singularly failed to inherit his talent as well as his looks. Scott didn't even think his mother knew that he still played, or recalled that the modest Yamaha keyboard was stored in the flat in Newcastle behind the black sofa, and not only did Scott play it, often, but he also played for friends, and the friends told him he was fantastic and he ought to do something about it. Scott knew he wasn't fantastic. He didn't want his mother to tell him he was fantastic: he just wanted her to acknowledge that he could play, and to be interested in his playing. He wanted his father's Steinway in his mother's sitting room so that sometimes, on these laborious weekends together, they could communicate, and probably more satisfactorily without words. He wanted to play the piano for her, his father's piano, so that in some obscure way they could be a family again.

Margaret turned round. She said, with more interest than she'd shown in the topic of the piano, 'And there's those songs.'

'Yes,' Scott said.

'That's a wonderful legacy,' Margaret said. 'It's a really wonderful legacy to have his songs. And they're worth something, I can tell you. The rights in those songs could be very useful to you. Maybe even get you out of that flat and into a house with a garden.'

Scott shifted his feet. He said tentatively, 'Maybe they mean more to you than to me.'

Margaret resumed her expression of gentle reminiscence.

'They mean a lot to me.'

'Mam—'

'"Chase The Dream",' Margaret said, not listening. '"Look My Way". "Moonlight And Memory". "Twosome, Threesome, Lonesome". He wrote that after you were born. He wrote that when I couldn't go to some gig he was doing because you weren't sleeping, and I was so tired I wasn't making any sense. He didn't like it when I wasn't there. He liked me to be there, to tell him what's what afterwards. He relied on my opinion.'

'OK,' Scott said. He felt obscurely embarrassed, as if he was witnessing some parental intimacy that was definitely not for outsiders' eyes. Wanting to have affirmation of family life was definitely not the same as being shown unwanted evidence of his mother's abiding romance with his father. His father's music was not, actually, much to his taste, and revelations of the autobiographical inspiration for some of it made him fidget. He'd been initially overwhelmed to hear he'd been left the early Richie Rossiter songbook, but when it came to absorbing the real nature of the material his awed gratitude had been replaced by something much more awkward, a sense that these often throbbingly emotional songs were not at all for him and especially not if they were based in any way on Richie's private life with Scott's mother. He'd wondered, briefly, if it was pathetically immature to feel this squeamish at thirty-seven, and decided that, even if it was, this reaction was the case, and he couldn't pretend otherwise. As to the money they represented, well, he couldn't take that. Money wasn't what he'd wanted from his father, and it was now definitively too late to have what he'd really wanted.

'Look,' he said to Margaret, 'I've spent all these years, since I was fourteen, trying to look after you because my dad wasn't here to do it, and I can't suddenly spin round and agree he's the greatest romantic hero just because he's dead.'

Margaret looked at him. She smiled. She said, 'Of course not, pet.'

'Mam,' Scott demanded, 'Mam, what's the *matter* with you?'

'Nothing.'

'It's not nothing. You're all vague and dreamy—'

'I'm relieved,' Margaret said.

'*Relieved?*'

'Oh yes.' She smiled at him again. 'I'm just so relieved we've been left these things. I hardly dared to hope he hadn't forgotten us. There were months, years, when I was sure he had and then I'd tell myself, well, he's never asked for a divorce, not even with all those babies, he's never asked, and I'd find the hope starting up again. I came back from that funeral thinking that at least I didn't have to keep hoping any more, hoping and not being certain, never being sure, and then this happens. Out of the blue, this happens. It hadn't crossed my mind, not for a second. I'd imagined a thousand daft things, but never this. He did remember us.

He remembered when he was well, when he still thought he'd got years to go, he thought about you and me, and he went to a lawyer to make sure we knew he'd thought about us. It's the knowing that's such a relief. I don't need to see the piano, you know, I don't need to *have* anything. I just needed to know. And now I do.'

Scott went over to the sofa and sat down on one end of it, putting his hand out to touch Dawson's solid and thickly furry side.

He said, almost shyly, 'I'm glad about that too. I really am. It's just – well, it's just that I don't think I'm the right person for the songbook.'

'Bit mushy for you,' Margaret said. 'People don't think about love like that now, do they? More's the pity. It was lovely, letting yourself go with the romance like that. But it's not the way you do things now, is it, it's not the way you express yourselves. Mind you, the *feeling*'s just the same, it's just how you express it that's different.'

'Yes,' Scott said. He pushed his fingers into Dawson's fur, and felt the purring start up, and watched the claws begin to emerge and retract involuntarily, sliding in and out of their sheaths, as instinctive a reaction as Scott's was to his father's songs. 'Mam—'

'Yes, pet.'

'Why,' Scott said, 'why don't you have the songbook? Those songs mean a lot to you, have a history for you—' He stopped. He could not, for some reason, look at her.

'They do,' Margaret said. 'They do.'

She came and sat the other end of the sofa, upright, as she always was, her hands loosely clasped in her lap.

'Well,' she said, 'why don't I have the songbook and the royalties, and you have the piano?'

'Really?'

'Why not?'

80

'Mam,' Scott said, 'a twenty-two-thousand-pound Steinway next to an Ikea sofa—'

'So?'

'Is that OK by you?'

'Very OK.'

Scott leaned forward and kissed her cheek.

'Thank you,' he said. 'Thank you.'

'Nothing to thank me for, pet.'

'What, a mere Steinway?'

Margaret said, not looking at him, 'Well, it's a wonderful instrument, of course it is, and it meant the world to him, but it had its problems.'

'Like what?'

She glanced up at him.

'We had to buy it on the never-never. Of course we did, back then. And I was the one with the steady wage. There was a lot of going without, to pay for that piano.'

'I see,' Scott said.

He glanced down at her bare left hand.

'Will you put your wedding ring back on?'

'No,' she said. She didn't even look at her hand. 'No, pet. No need.'

Sunday evenings, after visits to Tynemouth, had never been satisfactory. It was something about the change of gear from Margaret's house, and the sea, and, all too often, too much lunch, of the kind of food he didn't normally eat, at the Grand Hotel, that left him feeling as disorientated as if he'd got back to Newcastle from Outer Mongolia. In the past, he'd tried seeing friends, or even going to a movie, but the intense temporary sense of unreality prevented him from being satisfied with either, and he now resorted to drifting about the flat, desultorily trying to create some order in honour of a new working week, clearing up dirty mugs and plates and glasses, straightening his bed (what for – when he was about to get into it again any minute?), finding a clean shirt for the morning, buffing up his black shoes with a handy gym towel. The friends he had who had live-in girlfriends complained mildly about the apparently compulsory domesticity of Sunday evenings and, although there were many poignant times when Scott remembered past girlfriends with inaccurate lonely yearning, he was mostly glad to be able to amble alone and haphazardly through this strange slice of life between time off and time on again.

And in any case, this particular evening was different. This particular evening required not just some energizing planning, but some actual shoving around of furniture. The black sofa needed to be pushed down towards the kitchen end, leaving a swathe of dusty, crumby detritus which had collected comfortably underneath it, as well as the coffee table, in order to leave a space big enough, at the window end of the flat, to house the Steinway grand in all its glory. The Yamaha keyboard could go into his bedroom, after all, where it would prove a useful clothes-parking place, the table and chairs (metal, cool to look at, unwelcome to sit on) could be rearranged on the wall opposite the sofa, never mind it was all a bit crowded, and then, when he came in, in the future, he could look down the length of the room to his spectacular view of the Tyne Bridge, and there the Steinway would be, gleaming and glossy, and full of the double resonance of its own voice and his father's. It was, for once, an exciting use of a Sunday evening, inspiring him not only to move everything around, but also to clean up the mess on the floor, throw away months' worth of old papers and magazines, and bang clouds of dust out of his sofa cushions. The results of his efforts were very pleasing indeed and gave him an irrational but gratifying sense that his life, from now on, would somehow be very different, and inclusive of a new, important, if as yet entirely undefined, dimension.

He dumped a stout row of black bin bags by the front door, to go down in the morning, and went off, whistling, to have a shower. Showered, and wrapped in a towel, he cleaned wedges of curious rubbery grey scum out of the plugs and the shower tray, poured bleach lavishly down the lavatory, and shined up the mirrors with handfuls of toilet paper. Because of the splashing and the whistling, he only heard the telephone in time to race out of the bathroom and seize it at the moment when his voicemail cut in.

'Hello?' Scott said.

'Hi,' his own voice said to him. 'Scott here—'

'Hello?' Scott said again over it. 'Hello? I'm here. I'm home.'

There was a silence.

'I'm here,' Scott said again. 'Who is it?'

'Amy,' Amy said.

'Amy—'

'Yes,' Amy said. 'You know.'

'Gosh,' Scott said. With his free hand, he tucked the towel more firmly round his waist. It didn't feel quite decent, somehow, to be talking to Amy, wearing only a bath towel.

'Is – it OK?' Amy said.

'OK what?'

'OK to talk to you.'

'Sure it is,' Scott said. 'I was just a bit surprised.'

'Me too. I mean, I'm surprised I've done it. That I've rung you.'

'Where are you?'

'I'm in my bedroom. At home. I'm on my phone, in my bedroom.'

Scott walked, with his phone, to the window with the view.

'I'm looking at the Tyne Bridge,' he said.

'What's the Tyne Bridge?'

'Don't you know?'

'If I knew,' Amy said, her voice becoming more confident, 'I wouldn't ask you, would I?'

'S'pose not,' Scott said. 'Well, it's a great massive thing, iron and stuff, over the Tyne. The railway goes over it. I can see the trains from my window.'

'Oh,' Amy said.

There was a pause. After letting it hang for some seconds, and wondering if he could actually hear her breathing, or whether he just thought he could, Scott said, 'Did you want something?'

'I don't know,' Amy said uncertainly.

Scott decided to grasp the nettle. He stood straighter and looked sternly at his view.

'Is it about the piano?'

'No,' Amy said.

'Well,' Scott said, 'that's something.'

'Yes.'

'Was it a dare?'

'What—'

'Did you,' Scott asked, 'dare yourself to ring me?'

There was another little pause and then Amy said, 'Maybe.'

'Did you think I'd refuse to speak to you?'

'No.'

'I might have. We didn't exactly get a welcome, Mam and me.'

'No,' Amy said again. 'What did you expect?'

'OK,' Scott said. 'OK.' He tried to picture her in detail. Tallish, slim, long dark hair down her back. But he couldn't

84

remember her face, only that when he and Margaret confronted the four of them outside the church she was the only one who hadn't looked daggers.

She said, 'I'm supposed to be revising. I'm always supposed to be revising.'

'A levels?'

'Don't mention them.'

He turned his back to the window and regarded the swept space where the piano would stand.

He said, 'You play an instrument?'

'Flute,' she said.

He looked at the ceiling.

'Nice,' he said.

'And you?'

'Piano,' he said. 'Not well.'

'Then you—'

'Yes,' he said. He let his gaze drop back to the floor. 'Yes, I'll play it here.'

She said, 'I'd better go—'

'Someone come in?'

'No, I just think—'

'Why did you ring, Amy?' Scott said. 'Why did you ring me?'

'I was thinking,' Amy said, 'about Dad. My dad.'

'Our dad. Was that why?'

'Do you miss him?'

'I don't know,' Scott said. 'I hardly saw him after I was fourteen.'

'Yeah,' Amy said, very quietly.

'Well, is that why you rang? Because he was my dad too and you knew he didn't see me?'

'Are you angry about that?'

There was a silence.

'Sorry,' Amy said. 'I shouldn't have asked that.'

'The answer's yes,' Scott said.

Amy said softly, 'Me too. About other things.'

'I've never said it out loud,' Scott said. 'Not for twenty-odd years. I've just let it stew around in my head.'

'Yes,' Amy said in a whisper.

'And then you ask me—'

Amy said, more clearly, 'I don't know why I rang. I just thought I would. It was in my mind and it was bugging me, so I did.'

'Will it bug you again?'

'You could ring me,' Amy said. 'It doesn't have to be me. You could phone.'

'I don't think so—'

'I'm going,' Amy said. 'I'm going to ring off.'

'Cheers,' Scott said. He waited. Amy said nothing. Then he heard her phone go dead. 'Bye,' Scott said, with exaggerated emphasis, into the ether. 'Bye. Thanks for calling.'

He threw his phone across the space of the floor on to the sofa, and put his hands into his still-damp hair, ruffling it up into spikes. What had all that been about?

Amy got down on to the floor and crouched there, holding her knees, pushing her eye sockets against them. She stayed there for some time, just breathing and waiting for the bones of her skull to press against the bones of her kneecaps until they were more painful than merely uncomfortable, and then she unrolled herself slowly and stood up and stretched until her fingertips touched the sloping ceiling above her bed. She had taped a big picture of Duffy up there, wearing a red-and-black jumper and a lot of eye make-up, posed against a brick wall and looking pretty panicky. It was a look that Amy could often identify with.

She bent to pick up her phone from the carpet, and put it in her jeans pocket, leaving the charm she had attached to it – a blue glitter dolphin – hanging outside so that she could tweak the phone out in an instant when it began to vibrate. She always had her phone on vibrate. Her sisters, of course, had loud ring tones but Amy preferred the near secrecy of vibrate, just as she preferred to let most family things drift her way, being ever observant but seldom demanding. It was only things that really mattered that got Amy into demand mode, that turned her into someone she wasn't all that pleased to be, someone who snooped, someone who went through drawers and checked e-mail inboxes and eavesdropped. Someone who opened her dead father's piano stool – something that had never even remotely occurred to her to do, all the eighteen years of her life – and found inside all sorts of old stuff; stuff relating to a place and a time which had nothing to do with the dad who was part of Amy's life, nothing to do with anything familiar to her either.

There was quite a lot of sheet music in there, battered copies of songs from musicals, *Show Boat*, and *Guys and Dolls*, and *Carousel*. There were football programmes from St James' Park, dated in the 1970s. There was a postcard of something called St Andrew's Churchyard and on the back someone had written in a handwriting that wasn't Richie's, 'Fifteen witches buried here!' and a date, 27 July 1963. There was a brochure for the Grand Hotel, Tynemouth, and a small wooden coat of arms, gold keys crossed on a red background, below a gilded helmet and a little ship, above a motto, '*Moribus Civilis*', and on the back of the shield was a grubby white label on which – her father's hand this time – was written 'Scott – 1983'. And there was a photograph. It was in an envelope but both the envelope and the photograph looked as if they'd been much handled. It showed a young mother, and a baby, quite a big baby, almost a toddler. The young mother had her hair in a curled pageboy, and a plainly home-made frock, and a hat like a halo. The baby was in hand-knitted shorts and an Eton-collared jersey and little socks and bar shoes.

Amy had been alone in the house when she opened the piano stool. Chrissie had gone to see the bank manager, Tamsin was at work, on reception at an estate agent's in the High Street, Dilly was at college. Amy was supposed to be upstairs, working. The period of grace she had been given on account of Richie dying had, quite suddenly, seemed to end. Chrissie had begun, with something approaching shrillness, to insist on Amy's catching up with the revision she'd missed in the last few weeks, the revision it was absolutely imperative she complete, before the school term began. She found revision so hard to approach that some days it was almost impossible. The music was OK. Even music theory was OK. But when it came to English and Spanish, her concentration seemed to fragment and scatter like little bobbles of mercury skittering away across a sheet of glass. She'd made herself sit there, in front of her *Hamlet* quotations, for almost an hour, and then she'd gone downstairs, to make, oh, coffee or toast or powdered soup in a mug, and drifted into Richie's piano room on a melancholy whim, to touch the keys, pressing them down very slowly, without a sound, and found herself on the floor, opening the worn padded seat of the piano stool.

There was a tie folded on top of all the papers. It was a terylene tie, navy blue with maroon-and-cream stripes. It was creased and had lost its label. It was definitely a tie that pre-dated Chrissie, Amy thought. Chrissie would never have countenanced Richie wearing a tie that wasn't pure silk, and French or Italian. But there was something about this old, worn, cheap tie that made Amy put it down beside her with respect, an eloquent something. It was almost as eloquent, in fact, as the photograph, which was right at the bottom of the piano stool, under everything else, gritty with dust. When Amy put everything back into the piano stool, very methodically, in the order in which she had taken everything out and with the tie neatly folded on top, she put the photograph in its envelope in the back pocket of her jeans. Then she took it out again, laid it on top of the tie, closed the piano stool, walked out of the room, paused, walked back in, opened the piano stool, extracted the envelope, put it back in her jeans pocket and went swiftly and stealthily up the stairs to her room like a burglar, even though she was the only person in the house. Once in her room, she slipped the envelope behind the Duffy poster. Then she went across to her laptop, and connected to Google Earth.

She had, she realized, no idea where Newcastle was, in any detail. Up north somewhere, like Manchester or Leeds, lost in that hilly other world that started after Birmingham and stretched vaguely up the map until it got to Scotland, but she had no precise idea of which side of up north it was, or whether it was in the middle or on the sea. It was surprisingly astonishing, then, to see the city swim up into view under the satellite's scrutiny, swelling out from the curving ribbon of the River Tyne, with a great space of sea to one side and crumpled hills scattered on the other. She moved on, over Tynemouth and Gateshead and North Shields, past bridges and monuments, along streets and alleys tipping down to the river, to the sea, and then into information about the area's history and music and decayed industries and revived nightlife. She was so absorbed in what she was doing that when she heard the front door slam, she'd given a little gasp, and hastily switched the screen back to *Hamlet*, back to those quotations that seemed to be, however passionately she chanted them, so dead on the page. '"It is not madness I have uttered",' she was saying, her eyes closed on an inward vision of Newcastle. '"Bring me to the test",' when Chrissie came into the room and asked her if she'd like a mug of tea.

That had been three days ago. Since Thursday, she had

gone back, half a dozen times, to look at Newcastle, and, almost as often, had slipped the photograph from behind Duffy's poster, and gazed at it again, almost greedily. Richie and his mother. Richie in 1942, perhaps, in a photographer's studio in North Shields, or maybe at home, although it seemed odd, even for 1942, to wear a hat at home. There was no background much to the picture, just the table Richie was sitting on, and a straight fall of thin curtain behind him and his mother, no other piece of furniture, no pictures or flowers. Just that proud young mother, in a frock she'd possibly made herself, and that baby, who would grow up to have his own babies. Four of them. Tamsin, Dilly, herself – and Scott. Scott, who still lived roughly where Richie had grown up and who was going to have the piano. Scott, who had come to the funeral, and looked like some weird echo of Dad. Scott, who had stood, almost defensively, at his mother's elbow but who had, at the same time, regarded his three half-sisters, that split second they were facing each other, with more interest than hostility. It was three days of this, three days of Newcastle and her father and her father as a baby and Scott, that finally got to her. She was lying on her bed, one of her Spanish set texts – Lorca – propped up on her stomach, when the impulse came to her, cramping up her nerve ends until she seized her phone and dialled Scott's number and waited, rigid with panic and thrill, for him to answer.

And then, of course, she didn't know what to say. When he asked her why she'd rung, she couldn't tell him. He sounded quite relaxed, though there'd been wary moments, and she discovered she wanted him to go on talking, wanted him to somehow take the conversation over and guide her, help her, suggest something she might do next. But of course he hadn't. He had let her drift on, waiting to see what she was after, and, as she hardly knew that herself, she'd lost her nerve, as suddenly as it had spurred her to act, and she'd ended the call, before she knew she was doing it, before she meant to.

She glanced at the radio clock beside her bed: seven forty-eight. Downstairs, someone might be making their traditional Sunday-night scrambled eggs, the eggs that were the only cooking Richie had ever done, and that not often. Food, Amy thought, would at least be distracting, would stop her thinking and wondering for a while, would clear Scott's irritating, endearing Geordie voice out of her ears. She touched the dolphin charm hanging out of her pocket to reassure herself that the phone was still there, and went out of her bedroom, and downstairs.

Only Tamsin was in the kitchen. She was wearing a white velour tracksuit, and had a dark-blue towel wrapped round her head like a turban. She was sitting at the kitchen table, painting her nails with clear varnish in long, slow, careful strokes. She glanced up as Amy came in.

'Where's Mum?'

'Out,' Tamsin said. 'I sent her out to have a drink with the Nelsons. Anything to get her away from the computer.'

'And Dilly?'

'Guess.'

Amy opened the fridge.

'Want something?'

Tamsin shook her head carefully, so as not to dislodge the towel.

Amy took out a plastic box of pieces of cheese and a tomato and a caramel yoghurt, and put them on the table.

'You been working?' Tamsin said.

'Uh-huh.'

'All this time?'

Amy began to rummage in a cupboard.

'It's so boring—'

'You'll break Mum's heart if you screw these exams up.'

91

Amy dumped a collection of cracker packets on the table, beside the cheese box.

'Don't say that!'

'Well,' Tamsin said, splaying the fingers of one hand and surveying them. 'You're the bright one. Dad always said that. I'm practical, Dilly's decorative and daft, and you're bright.'

Amy sat down at the table, holding a knife.

'Get a plate,' Tamsin said.

'I'm just going,' Amy said, 'to put bits of cheese, Madam Fusspot, on crackers and eat them. I don't need a plate.'

'Get a plate,' Tamsin said again.

Amy got up, sighing, and went to retrieve a plate from the cupboard, banging the door.

'Tam—'

'What?'

'Tam, d'you ever think about when Dad was little? What his life was, when he was little?'

Tamsin looked at her other hand.

'No.'

Amy took out a small block of cheese and put it on the plate. Then she hacked an irregular chunk from one end.

'I do.'

Tamsin shot her a glance.

'What d'you mean?'

'Well,' Amy said, 'we don't know anything about where he grew up, do we, we never went there, he never talked about it.'

'He didn't think about it,' Tamsin said. 'It was over.'

Amy balanced her cheese on a biscuit.

'How do you know?'

'We'd have known if he thought about it,' Tamsin said. 'But he didn't. He didn't want to know about it any more. He had a new life.'

Amy bit into her cheese. The biscuit broke and fragments scattered across the table.

Through her mouthful, she said indistinctly, 'I do.'

Tamsin stopped painting. She glared at her sister.

'*What?*'

Amy swallowed the cheese.

'I want to know about where Dad was born. I want to know about his life there.'

'You can't,' Tamsin said flatly.

'Why can't I?'

'You'd upset Mum.'

'Why would I, I'm only wanting to know where Dad—'

'You know why.'

Amy said nothing. She gathered up several pieces of biscuit, and pressed them into the remaining cheese.

She said, looking at the food in her hand, 'They didn't *ask* for the piano.'

Tamsin leaned forward. The towel turban made her face look older, more severe.

She said, 'Mum has enough to cope with. She's not in a good place. She needs us to be right behind her, not siding with people who've taken things they've no right to.'

'I'm not siding,' Amy said stubbornly. 'And they haven't *taken* anything.'

Tamsin slammed her hands down on the table. She almost shouted, 'Whose side are you on?'

Amy put another bite of cheese and cracker into her mouth.

'Everybody's,' she said.

CHAPTER SIX

Chrissie's friend Sue was sitting on the edge of Chrissie's big bed, gazing at the line of fitted cupboards across the room. Behind her, balanced unsteadily on the duvet, was a tray bearing the things she'd brought from the delicatessen – a bottle of Prosecco, some big green olives, a small whole salami in a netting tube – and two glasses, plates, and a knife. The door to the bathroom was closed. Behind it, Chrissie was doing God knows what. Sue crossed her legs and leaned back on her hands. Chrissie had said, a few days ago, that she couldn't face sorting out Richie's clothes alone, so Sue had said not to worry, I'll come, I'll bring a bottle, we'll have a party, and here she was, as good as her word, all alone on Chrissie's bed while Chrissie was locked in the bathroom.

Sue turned very slowly to look at the bedside tables behind her. On Richie's side of the bed there was just a pile of books and an old-fashioned alarm clock on legs with a metal bell on top. On Chrissie's side, there were books, and bottles of water and hand cream, and nail files, and scrunchies, and a notebook, and pens, and a small stuffed panda with a red felt heart stitched on his chest, and a photograph of Ritchie framed in black bamboo. It showed him leaning forward, smiling. He was wearing a blue shirt, open at the neck, and the cuffs were nonchalantly unbuttoned as was his habit, showing his strong wrists, and hands. You could see a watch on one wrist, but his hands were ringless.

Sue knew that women had swooned over Richie. Thousands and thousands of women had found his dark, solid, almost Latin looks devastatingly attractive. Sue herself wasn't one of them. She found his looks dated, old-fashioned. The men she found attractive were definitely more dangerous. 'Give me a skinny rock god any day,' she'd say to Chrissie, as if to reassure her that she, Sue, had no designs on a man whose fan mail still arrived in sacks, rather than by e-mail. 'Give me a really bad boy, any day.' Chrissie had laughed. It was easy, then, to laugh at the idea of not being helplessly susceptible to Richie Rossiter. She could laugh because she felt – you could see it – completely secure.

'It's amazing,' she'd say sometimes. 'It's amazing watching him flirt with three thousand women from the stage, and then switch it off like a light the moment he's back in the wings.'

'Lucky for you—'

'Very lucky for me,' Chrissie would say soberly. 'So lucky. He's a family man.'

'Rather than first a romantic?'

A tiny shadow would flit across Chrissie's face. She'd touch her earrings, or a bracelet, as if to indicate that these had been presents from Richie, sentimental offerings, and she'd say evasively, 'Oh, I wouldn't say that—'

Sue pulled the tray towards her across the duvet, and put her hand on the neck of the bottle of Prosecco.

'I'm opening it!' she called.

There was a pause. Sue wedged the bottle between her knees and began to peel off the foil and wire round the cork. The bathroom door opened.

'Sorry,' Chrissie said.

Sue looked up.

'Have you been crying?'

'No,' Chrissie said. 'Wondering if I might be sick, but not crying.'

'You need some time.'

'Maybe,' Chrissie said.

Sue eased the cork out deftly, and filled a glass with care. She held it out to Chrissie.

'Open those doors,' Sue said.

Holding the glass away from her as if to steady it that way, Chrissie crossed the room and, with her free hand, opened the two right-hand pairs of cupboard doors. On one side in two rows, one above the other, hung jackets and trousers, and on the other, a row of shirts on hangers above shelves of sweaters and T-shirts, all folded with precision.

'Heavens,' Sue said, 'looks like the menswear floor in John Lewis.' She averted her gaze from the pale-blue linen jackets and looked resolutely at the floor of the left-hand wardrobe. It contained brown and black shoes, all on shoe trees.

'Who kept it like that?' Sue said.

Chrissie was standing to one side as if it was rude to stand directly in front of a shrine.

'I did.'

'Blimey,' Sue said, 'care to come and blow fairy dust into my cupboards? You can't see for chaos. I'm the original makeover mess-up.'

'He liked clothes,' Chrissie said. 'But he liked me to buy them.'

'Liked, or let you?'

Chrissie took a tiny sip of her wine.

'Liked. He'd never shop on his own. He said he didn't trust his taste. We had a nickname for it, NC for Northern Circuit. He'd pick something up and hold it out to me and say, "Too NC?" Satin lapels and pointed shoes. That kind of thing.'

Sue said, 'There's never been anything smarter than a T-shirt in my house—'

Chrissie said abruptly, desperately, 'I can't touch these.'

Sue slid off the bed. She went over to Chrissie and put an arm round her.

'It's OK, Chris—'

'If I touch them,' Chrissie said, 'I'll smell his smell. Touching them will sort of release that. I can't—'

'You don't have to,' Sue said.

'But I've got to—'

'No,' Sue said, 'you don't have to do anything you don't want to.'

'Damn,' Chrissie said, looking at the white carpet. 'Look. I've spilled it—'

'White wine,' Sue said. 'Won't show. Go and sit on the bed.'

'But—'

'Go and sit on the bed.'

Chrissie was shaking.

'You came here to help me sort his clothes—'

'It doesn't matter. I came here as your mate, not as a second-hand clothes dealer. Go and sit on that bed before I push you there.'

She took her arm away from Chrissie's shoulders.

'I thought I could do it—'

'Look,' Sue said, 'it doesn't *matter*. This is a rite of passage. There's no dress rehearsal for rites of passage, you can't practise for widowhood. I'm going to shut these doors.'

Chrissie crept away from the cupboards and sat on her own side of the bed, facing away from the cupboards. Sue shut the doors decisively, and then she came to sit down next to Chrissie.

'Drink.'

'I—'

'Drink. Big swallow.'

Chrissie took an obedient gulp. She said, 'I'm in such a mess.'

'I don't wonder.'

'I don't know what to think, now. I don't know what he really felt, any more. I don't know what we're going to do.'

Sue put a hand on Chrissie's, urging her glass towards her mouth.

Chrissie said, 'He had bookings up to May next year. I've had to cancel them. They would have brought in almost forty thousand. There's fan mail like you can't believe. I should think every middle-aged woman in the North of England has written to say they can't believe he's dead. I'm left with a house and not enough savings and three daughters and an inheritance tax bill and the realization that he's left his piano and a good part of his creative output to the life he had before he even met me. And I can't even ask him what the hell he thought he was playing at, I can't ask him if he meant what he used to say to me, what he used to say to the girls, I can't even ask him, Sue, if he actually really loved me.'

Sue picked up the Prosecco bottle and refilled Chrissie's glass.

'Course he loved you.'

'But not enough to marry me.'

'Love,' Sue said firmly, 'is not necessarily about marriage.'

Chrissie took another gulp.

'Where Richie came from, it is. Where Richie came from, you had to make love *respectable*. He was always telling me that. Why didn't he get a divorce? Because where he came from, the way *he* was brought up, divorce was very difficult, divorce was frowned on, his fans would not have liked it if he had been divorced.'

Sue waited a moment, and then she said, 'None of that antediluvian claptrap means he didn't love you.'

Chrissie was staring straight ahead.

'But not enough to leave me his piano. His piano and a tea caddy were about the only things he brought with him when he came south. He bought that piano when he was thirty-five, with the royalties from "Moonlight and Memory", it was the absolutely most precious thing he had and, if any of us inadvertently put a glass or a mug down on it, he'd go berserk. Not leaving me the piano is like saying sorry, I tolerated you all these years because I fancied you once and then there were the girls so I was trapped and couldn't get away, but actually, all the time, my heart, my real heart, was somewhere else, where it had been all the time since I was a little kid at school, and I can't pretend any more so I'm leaving her the piano and not you. *You* can have the things anyone could give you, like a house and a car and an inadequate life-insurance policy and a load of memories which turn out to be rubbish because I didn't, I'm afraid, actually mean any of it.'

She stopped. Tears were pouring down her face. Sue moved closer, putting an arm round her again, holding out a clump of tissues.

'That's right, Chrissie, that's right. You let it out, you let it right out—'

'I don't know whether I'm sadder or angrier,' Chrissie said, taking the tissues but letting the tears run. 'I don't know if I'm so bloody furious or so bloody heart-broken that I can't see straight. Maybe it's both. I want him back, I want him back so badly I could scream. And I want to *kill* him.'

Sue pulled more tissues out of the box by the bed and mopped at Chrissie's face.

'I'm frightened,' Chrissie said, her voice uneven now because of the crying. 'I'm frightened of what's going to happen, how I'm going to make a living, what I'm going to do about the girls. I'm frightened about the future and I'm frightened about the past because it looks like it wasn't what I thought it was, that I've spent twenty years and more believing what I wanted to believe and not seeing the truth. I'm frightened that all the efficiency and competence and administration I thought was keeping us going and getting us somewhere was like just trying to mend a house with wallpaper. I—'

'Now stop it,' Sue said kindly. 'Time to *stop.*'

Chrissie gave an immense sniff and blotted her eyes with the tissues in her hand.

'Sorry.'

'It's understandable, but going on and on like this will just make you feel like shit.'

'I feel like shit anyway.'

'There are degrees of shittiness—'

'I just don't,' Chrissie said, 'know what to do.'

Sue prised the damp tissues out of her hands.

'Get up and go into that bathroom and wash your face and have a good scream and come downstairs. You've said it all, you've got it all out, but it doesn't help getting it all out over and over. I'm going downstairs. I'll be waiting for you downstairs.' She stood up, and bent for the tray. 'It's murder when people die while you've still got stuff to say to them, murder. Drives you crazy. But you mustn't let it. See you downstairs.'

In the kitchen, Dilly was sitting at the table with her laptop and a notebook and a large volume on anatomy open beside them. Sue put the tray down on the table next to her and glanced at it.

'What on earth's that?'

'The lymphatic system,' Dilly said.

She was wearing spotless white jeans and a pale-grey

T-shirt and her fair hair hung down her back in a tidy pigtail, fastened with a cluster of crystals on an elasticized loop.

'Why,' Sue said, 'do you need to know about the lymphatic system for Brazilian waxes?'

Dilly frowned at the screen.

'It's for facials. You have to know how the lymphatic system drains, for facials.'

'Yuck,' Sue said. She began taking things off the tray and putting them on the table. She had known Dilly since she was a tiny girl, since Amy was a baby, and Tamsin was going to nursery school at a termly price, Richie used to say, that would have covered a whole education in the North when he was a boy; Tamsin had a tabard for her nursery school, pink cotton with a flower appliqué. Sue Bennett's children had gone to nursery school in whichever T-shirt was cleanest. She sat down beside Dilly.

'You know what your mum and I've been doing—'

Dilly stared harder at the screen.

'Didn't really want to think about it.'

'No. You wouldn't.'

'It's too soon,' Dilly said.

'Well,' Sue said, 'that's exactly how Mum felt. When it came to it.'

Dilly turned to look at her.

'So it's – it's all still there?'

'Not a sock moved.'

'What a relief,' Dilly said. She looked back at the screen. 'Is she OK?'

'I was going to ask you that.'

'None of us are,' Dilly said. 'You're OK for a bit and then it suddenly hits you. And it's awful.'

'Has she,' Sue said casually, moving the olives and salami about on the table, 'has she talked to you?'

Dilly stopped swivelling the mouse panel on her laptop.

'About what?'

'About what's on her mind. About what's happened, since your dad died.'

Dilly said flatly, 'You mean the piano.'

'Yes.'

'She hasn't said much. But you can see.'

'Yes.'

'I don't get it,' Dilly said. 'I don't get why he'd do a thing like that.'

'I don't think you should read too much into it.'

Dilly turned to look directly at her. Her skin, at these close quarters, Sue observed, was absolutely flawless, almost like a baby's.

'What d'you mean?'

'What I mean,' Sue said, 'is that you shouldn't let yourselves think that just because he left the piano to her he was in love with her all along.'

Dilly made a small grimace.

'You should see her—'

'I did, briefly. At the funeral.'

'Well—'

'No competition for your mum.'

'But then he goes and leaves her the *piano*!'

Sue said carefully, 'That may have nothing whatsoever to do with love.'

'What then?'

'Well, it could be nostalgia. Or Northern solidarity. Or guilt. Or all three.'

Dilly leaned her elbows on the table and balanced her forehead in the palms of her hands.

'None of that means anything to us.'

'Well, think about it. Think about it and try and see it as something other than just a bloody great rejection. And while you're at it, stop behaving as if it's all the fault of that poor cow in Newcastle. What did she do, except get left to bring a child up on her own? She's never made trouble, never asked for anything. Has she? You're all letting yourselves down if you blame *her* for what your father did. You hear me?'

Dilly's phone began to play the theme tune from *The Magic Roundabout*. She pounced on it at once and peered at the screen. And then, without looking at Sue, she got up, saying, 'Hi, big guy,' happily into it, and walked away down the kitchen to the far window.

'You're a rude little cow,' Sue said equably, to her back.

In the doorway, Chrissie said, 'Do I look as grim as I feel?'

Sue turned.

'No,' she said, 'you just look as if you've been crying because you're extremely sad.'

'And mad,' Chrissie said.

Sue got up to find clean wine glasses.

'Mad's OK. Mad gives you energy. It's hate you want to avoid.'

Chrissie said nothing. She glanced at Dilly, smiling into her phone at the far end of the kitchen. Then she sat down in the chair Dilly had vacated, and picked up an olive. Sue put a fresh glass of Prosecco down in front of her.

'Drink up.'

'Thing is,' Chrissie said, staring at the olive in her hand, 'thing is, Sue, that I do hate her. I've never met her, and I hate her. I know it wasn't her that prevented Richie from marrying me but I can't seem to leave her out of it. Maybe it's easy to hate her. Maybe I'm just doing what's easy. All I know is that I hate her.' She put the olive in her mouth. 'I do.'

In her office in Front Street, Tynemouth, Margaret was alone. Useful and faithful though Glenda was, there was always a small relief in Margaret when five o'clock came and she could say, 'Now come on, Glenda, you've done all I've asked you and more, and Barry's been on his own long enough, don't you think?' and Glenda would gather up her jacket and scarf and inevitable collection of supermarket bags and, always with a look of regret at the comforting anonymity of the computer screen, say a complicated goodnight and disappear down the steep stairs to the street. When the outside door slammed behind her, Margaret would let out a breath and feel the office relax around her, as if it was taking its shoes off. Then, she would sit down in Glenda's swivel chair, bought especially to support her back, whose condition was an abiding consideration in their relationship, and go through everything, on screen and on paper, that Glenda had done that day.

On the top of Glenda's in-tray lay the estimates she had obtained for the transport of Richie's piano from North London to Newcastle. It was going to be a very expensive business, in view of the quality and the weight and the distance. Margaret looked at the top sheet, on which Glenda had pencilled, 'This firm specializes in the moving of concert pianos.' It was the highest estimate, of course, but probably the one she would accept, and pay, in order that Scott could benefit from something that represented a joint parental concern after over twenty years of only having hers.

She had discovered, over the last week or so, that her initial euphoria at being left the piano had subsided into something both more manageable and more familiar to her, a state of quiet satisfaction and comfortable relief. It was a relief and satisfaction to know Richie had remembered her, and so meaningfully; and it was a relief she didn't have to house the piano and look at it every day. It was a satisfaction that Scott wanted it and would play it and a relief that he would not be haunted by the memory of its purchase and arrival, more than thirty years ago, when Margaret had had every reason to believe that a shining future awaited her in every area of her life – a rising husband, a small son, the increasing exercise of her own managerial skills.

As it turned out, it had been the last two that had saved her. Scott, though he had inherited more of her unobtrusive competence than his father's flair, had been a good son to her. She wished he were more ambitious, just as she wished he was married, with a family, and a decent house near her and the sea, rather than living his indeterminate bachelor existence in that uncomfortable flat in the city, but that didn't make him other than a good son to her, affectionate and mostly conscientious, with a respect for her and her achievements that she often saw lacking in her friends' children.

And of course, those achievements had been a life saver. It wasn't a big business, Margaret Rossiter Entertainment, never would be, she didn't want it to be, but it was enough to maintain her and Glenda, to provide moderate holidays and to keep her involved in a world in which she had a small but distinct significance, the world of singers and musicians, of stand-up comics and performance poets, who still managed to make a living in the clubs and hotels and pubs and concert halls of the circuit she had known all her life. There was, she sometimes reflected with satisfaction, not a venue or a person connected with the minor entertainment industry in the North-East whom she did not know. By the same token, there was hardly anyone who did not know who Margaret Rossiter was.

She looked again at the estimate. She would probably, she told herself again, accept it. Then she would ask Scott to telephone the family in Highgate to make arrangements for the piano's packing up, and removal. It was not that she shrank from ringing herself, she told herself firmly, but rather that if Scott were to ring one of the girls, it would be lower-key, less of a drama. She closed her eyes for a moment.

A drama. Watching the Steinway being loaded into a crate, swaddled in blankets or bubble wrap or whatever, and taken away couldn't possibly be other than a drama. If she were Chrissie, Margaret thought, she'd be sure to be out of the house.

She had sometimes tried to visualize that house. There had been years – long years – when she had studiously avoided pictures in minor celebrity columns and magazines of Richie and Chrissie together, he so dark, she so blonde, so very blonde, and young, and dressed in clothes that appeared to have needed her to be sewn into them. But the house was another matter. The house was where Richie lived, and Margaret was occasionally tormented by the need to know how much it resembled – or differed from – that first house in Tynemouth of which they had been so proud, and from which Scott had been able to walk when – an even greater source of pride – he had gained a place at the King's School. She thought the North London house must be quite a big one, to house three children and a grand piano, and she knew that part of London was famed for its hills, so perhaps the garden sloped, and there were views from the top windows, views to the City perhaps, or out to Essex, unlike the view she had now, the view she had chosen almost as proof of her own achievements, out to sea.

Margaret swivelled Glenda's chair towards the window, and adjusted the venetian blinds – Glenda liked to work with them almost closed, in an atmosphere of elaborate and pointless secrecy – so that she could see down into the street. There was much activity down there, of the kind induced by imminent shop-closing. There were the usual groups of teenagers in their uniforms of clothing and attitude, and children and dogs and people pushing buggies and walking frames adapted as shopping baskets. All those people, Margaret thought, her hands lying on the arms of Glenda's chair, have stories that are just as important to them as mine is to me. All those people have to do the big things like dying just as they have to do the little things like buying tea bags. There'll be women down there whose men have pushed off and broken their hearts, and some of them will have got over it, and some of them won't, and I just wonder if that Chrissie, in London, is going to be one of the ones that doesn't, because a will is the last act of generosity or vengeance that we have left to us, even after death, and I bet she wasn't expecting Richie's will to turn out like that, I bet it didn't cross her mind that he even remembered he'd had a life before her. And the odd thing is, Margaret reflected, gripping the chair arms now, that it doesn't give me any pleasure, not a scrap, not even the smallest shred of I-told-you-so gratification, to think that I've got what she assumed would be hers. I've spent years – *wasted* years – on longing and jealousy, and now that I've got the proof I wanted, I'm glad to have it, but I'm sorry for that girl. I really am, I'm sorry for her and it's a weight off my mind I hardly knew was on it, I'd got so used to having it there. It's such a relief not to have to hate her any more, though I never liked that word hate, never really owned up to using it. And now I don't have to. It doesn't even figure any more.

She leaned back, and closed her eyes. Behind her lids, she conjured up that row of four women outside the church in Highgate, standing on the gravel square, facing her and Scott like an army drawn up in battle lines. It had only been seconds that they stood like that, but those seconds were enough for Margaret to take in the finish on Chrissie, the metropolitan polish, and to see that those three girls, Richie's three daughters, his second family, were very young. One of them, the one who had the courage and the spirit to ring Margaret and tell her of Richie's death, had looked not much more than a child, with her hair held back by a velvet band and falling down her back like Alice in Wonderland's. Long hair, almost to her waist. Involuntarily, Margaret thought what a pleasure it would be to brush such hair, long smooth strokes down the silky strands, rhythmic, intimate, maternal.

Her eyes flew open. What on earth was she thinking of? What in heaven's name was she doing, dreaming of brushing the hair of Richie's daughter by a woman who had every reason now to despair of him, and, however unfairly, to detest her? She stood up unsteadily. This would never do. She picked up a plastic cup with half an inch of water in the bottom that Glenda had left on her desk and swallowed it. Then she put the cup in the overflowing bin by Glenda's desk – an office-cleaning firm of dubious efficiency only came in two evenings a week – and moved purposefully around the room, ordering papers, switching off screens, switching on answering machines. Then she went into the tiny cloakroom beside the door and washed her hands vigorously, and arranged her hair and applied her lipstick without needing to look in the mirror. Only as she was leaving did she give it a glance.

'Pull yourself together,' she said out loud to her reflection. 'Act your age.'

'You're an attractive woman,' Bernie Harrison had said to her a few days earlier, over a vodka and tonic to celebrate a good booking at the Theatre Royal in Newcastle. 'You're an attractive woman, for your age.'

'And you,' she'd said briskly, 'are showing *your* age, talking like that.'

'I'm flattering you, Margaret.'

'Patronizing, more like—'

He'd leaned forward, and tapped her knee.

'Ritchie knew which side his bread was buttered. He knew right up to the end. Didn't he?'

And she, instead of agreeing with him as she had intended, instead of saying you can't believe how it feels, after all these years of wondering and worrying, to know, to actually *know*, had found herself saying instead, 'Well, it's nice to have the piano. But it's a dead thing, isn't it?'

Bernie had eyed her.

'Dead?'

'Yes,' she said. She picked up her drink and took the size of swallow her sweet little mother-in-law would have considered vulgar. 'Dead. She may be breaking her heart over that piano, but she's got her girls, hasn't she? She's still got those girls.'

CHAPTER SEVEN

Scott had a hangover. It was a peculiarly discouraging hangover because he had had neither the seductively reckless intention of getting drunk nor the reward of losing inhibition during the process, but had merely gone on accepting drinks and buying rounds, with a passive kind of aimlessness, until he found himself tottering unsteadily under the railway arch outside the Clavering Building and wondering why it was so difficult to extricate his keys from his pocket.

It was then, as he stood fumbling and cursing, that Donna had caught up with him. Two summers before, he'd had something going with Donna, who worked in the same law firm as he did and who thought his ability to play the piano was a very hot attribute indeed. They had spent a lot of nights and weekends together on the modern, black-framed bed in Scott's flat, and then Donna had begun to ask to meet Margaret, and to stock the fridge with probiotic yoghurts, and berries in plastic boxes, and to collect Scott's work suits from the dry cleaner's, and Scott had, in response, devised ways of avoiding her in the office and leaving clubs and pubs before she did. When she cornered him, and demanded to know what he was playing at, he said exactly what was in his mind, which was that sex was one thing, but love was quite another, and she should know that he thought sex with her was great. In revenge, she went out, immediately, with Colin from the family department, who was divorced and drove a BMW, and it didn't seem to strike her that Scott, after a pang or two of competitive sexual jealousy, hardly minded at all. There'd been Clare, from accounts, anyway, even if that only lasted six weeks, after she'd borrowed two hundred quid from him and never paid it back.

But recently, Donna had started to be very nice to Scott again. Not flirtatious nice, but just friendly and pleasant and cheerful, which made Scott look at her rather as he had first looked at her two years ago, and she had picked up these tentative signals in an instant, and had watched, and waited, and last night, at the end of one of those post-work office-colleague social sessions that seemed like a good idea at the time, she had followed him down the hill from the city centre to the Clavering Building, and slipped her hand into his trouser pocket from behind, and pulled his keys out with no trouble at all. And then she had taken him into his own building, and up to his own flat, and into his own bed, and he had felt, then, quite pleased to acquiesce, and, a bit later, for a short while, positive and energetic, and, later still, perfectly content to fall down, down into slumber with Donna against his back and her breath stroking between his shoulder blades in little warm puffs.

In the morning, she was gone. She had slipped out from beside him, smoothed the pillow she had lain on, dressed, and left. There was no evidence she had been there, no hairs in the basin, no damp towels. His toothbrush was dry. The only thing that proved to him that she had not been part of a giant alcoholic hallucination the night before – if pressed, Scott knew he probably couldn't even name the last club they had all been to – was that on the kitchen worktop was an empty tumbler and a foil square of Alka-Seltzer tablets. Scott ran water into the tumbler, and dropped two of the tablets into it, holding the glass away from him, eyes screwed shut, as if the fizzing of the tablets as they dissolved was too much for a head as tender as his to bear.

He drank. Then he held his breath. There were always a few seconds, with Alka-Seltzer, when you wondered whether you would throw it up as fast as you had swallowed it. Nothing happened. He ran another glass of water, and drank that. Then he bent and inserted his face sideways under the tap, and let the water splash across his eyes and ears and down his neck.

In the bathroom mirror, he looked at himself with revulsion. Being so dark meant a navy-blue chin most mornings. Today, his skin was yellowish grey and there were bruises around his eyes and he looked ill. Which he was. Poisoned. His liver must be in despair.

'You are,' he said to his reflection, 'too old for this. Any day now, you'll just be sad. Sad, sad, sad, sad.' He shut his eyes. This was the moment self-pity usually kicked in, the self-pity which had lain in wait for him ever since a history master at school – who had had his own reasons for ingratiating himself with the better-looking boys – had taken him aside, after Richie had left, and put an arm round his shoulders and said, in a voice intense with understanding sympathy, 'I am very, very sorry for you, my boy.' Scott had broken down. The history master had been very adept at comforting him, had made him feel there was no loss of manliness in weeping.

'Just not in front of your mother,' the history master said. 'She has enough to bear. Come to me, when things get too much. Come to me. It will be our secret.'

The word 'secret' had alarmed Scott. But the feeling of warmth, of understanding, remained. All his life since then,

Scott could summon up, at will, the adolescent desolation of that moment, and the permission he had been given – whatever the motive – to grieve for his loss, and for the loneliness it left him in. Now standing naked in his bathroom, feeling disgusting and disgusted in every atom of his maltreated body, he waited to be given the pardon of self-pity. But it wouldn't come.

'Fuck,' Scott said to the mirror.

He picked up the spray can of shaving foam, and pressed the nozzle. Nothing happened. He shook the can. It rattled emptily. He flung it furiously across the bathroom and it clattered into the shower tray. He picked an already used disposable razor out of the soap dish, and, with his other hand, attempted to lather a cake of soap onto his chin. He was two unsatisfactory stripes down the left-hand side when his phone rang.

Of course, he couldn't find it. Last night's clothes – his work suit, a shirt, socks, underpants – were in a shameful stew on the floor. From somewhere inside the mess, his phone was ringing. It would be Donna. Not content with the gentle hint of the Alka-Seltzer, she would be ringing to make sure he was awake and would not be late for work. She would also, no doubt, be after some little reference to last night, some little reassurance that he had wanted what had happened, that she had, somehow, reminded him of what he had been missing, that they might now— He found the phone, in the back pocket of his trousers, just as it stopped ringing. 'One missed call', said the screen. He pressed Select. 'Mam', the screen said helpfully.

Scott went back to the bathroom, and found a towel. He wound it round his waist, and then he took the phone into the sitting room, to look at the view rather than at his own dispiriting face. It was seven-forty in the morning. What could Margaret want, at seven-forty in the morning, unless she was ill? Scott dialled her number, and then stood, lean-ing against the windowsill, and looked at the rain outside, falling in soft, wet sheets through the girders of the Tyne Bridge and into the river below.

'Were you in the shower?' Margaret said.

'Sort of—'

'Sorry to ring so early, but I've got a long day—'

'Are you OK?' Scott said.

'Of course I am. Why wouldn't I be? I'm off to Durham in ten minutes.'

'Oh,' Scott said. If he didn't concentrate on focusing, he would see two Tyne Bridges, at least. He wondered if his mother had ever had a hangover.

'I wanted to catch you,' Margaret said, 'before you got to the office.'

'Are you OK?' Scott said again. He shut one eye.

'Perfectly fine,' Margaret said. 'Why d'you keep asking? I'm fine, and so is Dawson, and I'm about to drive to Durham to see a new club. I could do with more venues in Durham. Scott, dear—'

'Yes?' He closed both eyes.

'Scott, pet,' Margaret said. Her voice was warm and he could tell a request was coming. 'I want you to do something for me.'

'What—'

'It's for you, really. It's about the piano. I want you to make a call, about the piano.'

Scott opened his eyes and made himself focus sternly on a single bridge.

'Who to?' he said.

Tamsin worked in the oldest estate agency in Highgate village. There were a great many estate agencies up the hill, but the one where Tamsin worked prided itself on its antiquity, and the famous houses – famous both for their beauty and for the celebrity of their inhabitants – that had been bought and sold over the years through their good offices. Tamsin, after failing to get into art school and declining either the cookery course or IT skills course suggested to her, had found herself a job in the estate agency, with which she declared herself perfectly satisfied. It was, basically, a reception job with the added task of arranging all the appointments for viewings of the properties, and it was becoming plain to the five partners of the company that Tamsin possessed the kind of competent attention to detail, as well as an admirably together appearance, that made her, especially in the present perilous times, good value in every sense. Rather than promote her, or increase her pay, the partners tacitly decided that the initial tactic to prevent her beginning to think that she might be better off somewhere else was to flatter and thank her. Tamsin, deftly managing the office diary, and answering the telephone and enquiries in person, to perfection, was well aware that the smiling compliments that came her way on a daily basis were not without ulterior motive. In return, she declined to reassure the partners that, for the moment, aged twenty-one, with a boyfriend who was the definition of steady and the recent loss of her father and the effect of that loss on both her mother and sisters, she had no intention of going anywhere.

All the same, it was nice to be treated as valuable. It was nice to have the attention she paid to hair and clothes obviously appreciated. It was nice to know that, as far as representing the firm was concerned, she was giving a good impression. All these reassurances were contributing to Tamsin's sense that, amidst all the family grief and insecurity and anxiety, she was emerging as the one member of the family who could be relied on to think straight even in the midst of emotional turmoil. And so, returning home one evening from work, and walking into the empty kitchen to find Amy's phone jerking its little jewelled dolphin about and ringing, unattended, on the kitchen table, Tamsin did not hesitate to pick it up and, after a cursory glance revealed an unfamiliar number on the screen, say crisply into it, 'Amy's phone.'

There was silence at the other end.

'Hello?' Tamsin said, still using her office inflection. 'Hello? This is Amy's phone.'

She waited another second or two and then a voice, a man's voice with a distinct North-East accent, said, 'It's Scott here. I was hoping to speak to Amy.'

'Scott!' Tamsin said in her normal voice.

'Yes—'

'Why are you ringing? Why are you ringing Amy?'

'Because,' Scott said, 'she's the only one I've spoken to.'

'When?'

'When what—'

'When,' Tamsin demanded, 'did you speak to her?'

'Look,' Scott said, more belligerently, 'I'm not bothering her. And I'm not saying anything that might get her into trouble. I rang her because we've spoken and I've got her number. Who are you, anyway?'

'Tamsin,' Tamsin said frostily.

'Ah. Tamsin.'

'And what did you want to say to Amy?'

There was a sigh the other end of the line.

'I didn't want to say anything to Amy. In particular. I just wanted to ask one of you something, and Amy was the one I'd spoken to.'

Tamsin found she was standing at her full height, as if she was in court, giving evidence.

'What did you want to ask?'

'Well,' Scott said, 'I want to ask when it would be convenient to collect the piano.'

'*What?*'

'When would it be—'

'I heard you!' Tamsin shrieked.

There was a scuffle behind her. Amy appeared, holding out her hand for the phone.

'Gimme—'

'How *dare* you,' Tamsin said to Scott. 'Have you got absolutely *no* sensitivity? How—'

'Give me that!' Amy said, trying to reach her phone. 'What are you doing on my phone? I'd only gone to the loo. Give it—'

'Take it,' Tamsin said furiously. She flung it across the table, where it skidded to the far side and fell down beside the radiator. Amy darted after it.

'Who is it?'

'That man,' Tamsin said between clenched teeth. 'That *man*. From Newcastle—'

Amy was under the table. Tamsin bent down so that she could see her.

'What's he doing, ringing you? What've you been up to?'

Amy retrieved her phone and held it to her ear.

'Hello? Are you still there?'

'Are you OK?' Scott said. 'Is that Amy?'

'I'm fine,' Amy said. 'I'm under the kitchen table.'

Tamsin straightened up. She thumped hard on the table above Amy's head.

'What was that?' Scott said.

'My sister—'

'Don't talk to him!' Tamsin shouted. 'Don't have anything to do with him!'

Amy took the phone away from her ear. She shouted back, 'We're not all witches like you!' and then she said to Scott, 'Why are you ringing?'

'Sorry if it's not very tactful,' Scott said, 'but I was wondering when it'd be OK to collect the piano.'

'Oh.'

'Have I rung at a bad time?'

'It's all pretty bad just now.'

'Look, forget it. Sorry. Leave it. I'll ring another time. In a few weeks. It was just my mam—' He stopped.

Amy watched Tamsin's legs move very slowly towards the door.

Scott said, 'Are you really OK?'

'Yes.'

'Are you still under the table?'

'Yes.'

'Look,' Scott said, 'I'll ring off now. You've got my number. You ring me when things have calmed down a bit.'

Amy said, clearly so that Tamsin could hear, 'It's your piano, you know.'

Tamsin's legs stopped moving.

'No hurry,' Scott said. 'I'll leave it to you. OK? You ring me when you can.'

'Cheers,' Amy said. She clicked the call to end. Then she sat crouched and still under the table.

Tamsin came back and bent down again.

'What are you playing at, you disloyal little beast?'

'Nothing,' Amy said.

'I heard you,' Tamsin said, 'I heard you. Talking to him all nice as pie. I *heard* you.'

'He said to leave it. He said he didn't mean to upset anyone. He said he'd leave it till we're ready.'

'We'll *never* be ready.'

'We've got to be,' Amy said. 'We've got to, one day. It's *their* piano.'

Tamsin straightened up again.

'Come out of there.'

Amy crawled slowly out from under the table, and stood up. She was wearing a green sweatshirt and cut-off jeans, since her school did not require uniform in the sixth form.

'You wait,' Tamsin said. 'You just wait until Mum hears about this.'

Amy raised her chin, just a little.

'OK,' she said.

Donna, having left Scott in bed that morning with what she felt was admirable sophistication, found that she couldn't concentrate at work. It seemed that the price of being mature enough to leave a sleeping lover without a word of affection from him was that the maturity was only temporary, and the need to be reassured came back later, in double measure, as a result of being initially repressed. So, after two hours of fiddling about pointlessly at her computer, Donna made a plausible excuse to her nearest colleague, and headed for what she hoped would be the reward for her early-morning restraint.

Scott shared a room at work with two others. The room was at the back of the building – only the senior partners' and the boardroom looked out on the river – and they need-ed to have the lights on, even in summer, on account of the new building behind it being constructed so close that Scott and his colleagues could see if the people working across the way were playing games on their computers. They had been provided with blinds, heavy vertical panels of translu-cent plastic, but by tacit agreement the three of them found it more amusing to have the blinds at their widest setting, giving a clear view into the opposite office. In any case, there were some good-looking girls in the opposite office, and, for Scott's gay colleague, Henry, there was a particular guy, who, Henry knew, just knew, was aware of being watched and liked it.

When Donna came into the office, it was empty. She had checked that both Henry and Adrian were at the Law Courts that morning, and she had reckoned on finding Scott alone. She had spent ten minutes in front of the mirror in the Ladies on her floor, and was planning to breeze in, kiss Scott's cheek, wink, say something like, 'Just fabulous,' and then swing out again, leaving a seductive and tantalizing breath of Trésor on the air, which would drive him to seek her out later in the day and hint that she might like to cook him supper.

But Scott's chair was empty. His jacket was not even on the back of it. But his screen was on, and his mobile – not one she recognized – was lying in the chaos of papers across his desk. There was also a tall takeaway cup – cold, when she touched it – and a half-eaten Snickers bar, the wrapper peeled roughly back like a banana skin. Donna sat down in his chair. The document on his screen showed a series of mathematical calculations, one column entirely in red, and was no doubt something to do with one of the VAT cases in which he was becoming something of a specialist. If Scott had taken his jacket, he'd gone to do more than have a pee, but if he hadn't taken his phone then he hadn't left the building. Donna sighed. If he came back and found her in his chair, he would be able to assume the initiative in any future development between them, and that was absolutely not what Donna wanted. From past experience, Donna knew that, if Scott had the initiative, he just left it lying about without using it until it ran out of its vital initial energy, and simply expired. She lifted one leg and flexed her foot. What a waste of spending all morning in four-inch heels it might turn out to be.

On the desk in front of her, Scott's phone beeped twice and jerked itself sideways. Donna leaned forward so that she could see the screen.

'One message received', the screen said.

Donna hesitated. She glanced at the doorway. Then she stretched her arm out and touched Select.

'Amy', said the message box.

Donna uncrossed her legs and sat straighter. She touched again.

'Sorry about that,' Amy had written.

Donna peered at the screen. That was all there was. 'Sorry about that.' No signing off, no x's, no initial. She scrolled down. Nothing but a mobile number and the time of the message. Sorry about what? Donna put the phone down. She stood up. She felt, abruptly, sick and angry and guilty. She also felt consumed by disappointment, waves of it, rolling and crashing over her in just the way they had when Scott had told her that she was a fantastic fuck but that didn't mean he loved her, because he didn't.

She walked – with difficulty, her knees seeming to have locked rigid with shock – to the window. Ten feet and two windows away, a girl in a short skirt and knee boots was perched on the edge of a man's desk, and he was leaning back in his chair with his fingers interlaced behind his head, and they clearly were not talking about the cost of insurance of cars with two-litre engines. Donna felt hot tears spring up and flood her eyes. She swallowed hard and tossed her hair back. No crying, she told herself. No crying and no softness over what her Irish father would have called feckin' Scott Rossiter.

'Oh, hi,' Scott said from the doorway.

Donna whirled round. He was in his suit, but looking slightly dishevelled, and he had a plastic cup of water in each hand. Donna glared at him.

'Who is Amy?' she demanded.

'Look,' Scott said later, stretched on his sofa and replete with a Thai green curry Donna had made with real lemon grass and kaffir lime leaves purchased in her lunch hour, despite the four-inch heels. 'Look. That was great, last night was great, but I am completely bushed and you've got to go now.'

Donna had kicked her shoes off. She had removed the jacket of her work suit and replaced it with a little wrap cardigan that tied meaningfully under her bosom, of which she was proud. She looked at the remaining wine in her glass.

'I'm not suggesting a repeat of last night,' Donna said.

Scott repressed a groan.

'But it's nice,' Donna said, still looking at the wine and not at Scott, 'to have a bit of support at family times like this. Nice for you.'

Scott said nothing.

'It's a comfort,' Donna said. 'It's a comfort not to be alone.'

Scott closed his eyes. Then he made a huge effort and swung himself upright. He looked directly at Donna.

'I want to be alone,' Scott said.

Donna regarded her wine in silence.

'You're right, it is a family time,' Scott said. 'But it's my family and my difficulties, and you don't know any of them.'

Donna let a small pause fall, and then she said, 'But I could.'

Scott stood up. His clothes were deeply rumpled.

'No.'

Donna leaned forward very slowly and put her wine glass down among the dirty plates on the coffee table.

She said, 'I thought you said Amy was just your kid half-sister.'

'She is.'

'Who you've seen but never spoken to except on the phone.'

'Correct.'

'Then why are you making such a big deal about this piano and Amy and everyone? Why do you have to do anything about her or anyone else, except your mother? Why don't you want me to help you?'

'Because,' Scott said, looking down at her, 'it's none of your business.'

'Thank you!' Donna cried. She waved wildly at the curry plates. 'After all I've—'

'I didn't *ask* you to!' Scott shouted. 'I didn't ask you to snoop round my office and check my phone! I didn't ask you to be a shoulder to cry on because I don't want one, I don't need one, I never have, my family is my business and always has been and I'll deal with it my way and on my own as I always have!'

Donna leaned out of her chair and found her shoes. She put them on and stood up, with difficulty.

She said, 'I think it's disgusting, getting fixated on an eighteen-year-old, especially if she's your half-sister.'

'I'm not fixated,' Scott said, 'I'm just trying to get this bloody piano to Newcastle. And before you start spreading the news that I'm some sort of perv, let me tell you something, something that's none of your bloody business, but I'll tell you to stop you making mucky trouble. When my father left, Donna, there was no one to comfort me. Yes, there was my mother but she was in her own bad place and, anyway, she wasn't a child like me, his child, I was on my own there. And all I'm trying to do now, Donna, is to help Amy a bit because I know what it's like. I'm trying to do for her just a little of what no one did for me. OK? Get it?'

Donna turned to look at him. Her eyes were huge.

'I just *love* it,' she said softly, 'when you play the piano.'

Scott closed his eyes. He clenched his fists. He heard Donna's heels approaching, not quite steadily, across the wooden floor, and then felt her wine- and food-scented lips on his cheek for what was plainly intended to be a significant number of seconds. Then the lips were removed, and the heels tapped unevenly away across the floor, paused to open the door, tapped outside and let the door bang behind them. Scott let out a long, noisy breath and opened his eyes. Then he fell back on to the sofa and lay there, gazing at the girders of the ceiling and resolutely refusing to let his brain change out of neutral. His phone beeped. He picked it up and eyed the inbox warily. Donna. She could hardly have left the building.

'Grow up Scottie. U R 37 not 7. Little girls not the answer.'

He deleted the message and struggled to sit up. The mess on the table revolted him, the mess of the last twenty-four hours revolted him, the mess he still seemed brilliant at getting himself into revolted him beyond anything. He looked at his phone again and retrieved Amy's message. She'd said once that she played the flute. Scott got up and went to the window and looked at his view, glittering under a night sky. He stared out into the darkness, at the lines of light the cars made, at the dramatic glow of the Tyne Bridge. There was something very – well, *clean* was the word that came to mind, about picturing his half-sister – yes, she was his half-sister – with her hair down her back, playing her flute. He closed his eyes again, and rested his mind on this mental image, with relief.

'I think,' Chrissie said, 'that we need to talk.'

She closed Amy's bedroom door behind her. Amy was on her bed, propped up against the headboard, with her flute in her hands. She hadn't been playing anything in particular, just fiddling about with a few pop tunes, but it had been absorbing enough to prevent her from hearing Chrissie coming up the stairs, and when the handle of the door turned she'd given a little jump, and her flute had knocked against her teeth.

'Ow,' Amy said, rubbing.

Chrissie took no notice. She turned Amy's desk chair round so that it was facing the bed, and sat down in it. She was wearing camel-coloured trousers and a camel-coloured sweater and a rope of pearls. She looked extremely considered and absolutely exhausted.

'Now,' Chrissie said, 'what is going on?'

Amy polished her flute on her T-shirt sleeve.

'Nothing.'

Chrissie looked up at the skylight.

'Tamsin tells me you spoke to Scott about moving the piano to Newcastle.'

'Sort of,' Amy said.

'He rang you.'

'Yes,' Amy said.

'How,' Chrissie said, 'did he know your number?'

Amy put the flute down beside her, and laid her hands flat on the duvet. She looked directly at Chrissie.

'Because I rang him once.'

'And why did you do that?'

Amy thought for a moment. She was conscious of a dangerous energy beginning to surge up inside her, an energy compounded of apprehension at Chrissie's imminent anger and distress, and excitement at defending her own position.

She said slowly, 'It was an impulse.'

'Inspired by what?'

'Newcastle,' Amy said truthfully.

'*Newcastle?*'

'I Googled it.' She got off the bed and reached up to slide the envelope from behind the Duffy poster. 'And I also found this.'

Chrissie took the envelope and opened it. Amy watched her. Chrissie glanced at the photograph, and then held it and the envelope out to Amy.

'Please put that away.'

'It's Dad!' Amy said.

'I know it's Dad.'

'But—'

'Look,' Chrissie said, suddenly agitated. 'Look. I know he came from Newcastle. I know he was born on North Tyneside. I know his parents struggled for money and his mother adored him. I know all that. But I can't bear to know it. After everything that's happened, after everything he's done and we've discovered, all his life in the North, all his loyalties in the North just seem like a betrayal to me. Perhaps you can't feel it because he never let you down, but, Amy, having you talk to that man, having you making plans with that man, and without telling me, just makes me feel worse, it makes me feel that I can't trust you, that you're taking sides with people whose existence has made my life so difficult for so long and stopped me having what I really wanted, what I should have had, I should, I *should*.'

Amy sat down on the edge of the bed and held the photograph between her hands.

'I wasn't making plans.'

'But you were, about the piano, Tamsin—'

'Tamsin answered my phone,' Amy said. 'I was in the loo, and she answered my phone.'

Chrissie began to wind her pearls in and out of her fingers.

'Did you hear a word I've just said?'

Amy nodded.

'Do you have any *idea* of what I've been through?'

Amy looked up.

'Of course.'

'Then how *can* you? How *can* you talk to that man about the piano behind my back?'

'He's not that man,' Amy said, 'he's Dad's son. He's our half-brother.'

'Don't you care at *all*?'

'Of course.'

'You said that already.'

'Mum,' Amy said, suddenly allowing the dangerous energy to spurt out like hot liquid, 'Mum, it's not all about you, it's not all about Tam or Dilly, or me, either, it's about other people too, who never did you any harm except by existing, which they couldn't help, and who didn't ask for the piano or expect the piano, they just politely wondered when it would suit *you* to have them arrange for it to go. Don't take your anger at Dad out on them, it isn't fair, it isn't OK, it isn't *like* you.'

'Amy!'

Amy slid the photograph back into the envelope.

'How dare you,' Chrissie said. 'How dare you speak to me like that?'

Amy's head drooped. She felt the energy drain away and be replaced by a tremendous desire to cry. She put the back of her hand up against her mouth and pressed. She was not going to cry in front of her mother.

Chrissie stood up.

'I want you to think about what I've just said to you. I want you to think about family loyalty. I want you to use your emotional intelligence and *feel* the shock this has all been.'

She moved to the door and put her hand on the knob.

'Amy?'

'Yes.'

'Will you?'

Amy nodded. Chrissie turned the doorknob and went out

127

into the little landing outside, not closing the door behind her. Amy waited a few moments and then she tipped backwards on to her bed, and rolled towards the wall, her knees drawn up, the photograph in its envelope held against her chest. Only then, as quietly as she could, did she allow herself to cry.

CHAPTER EIGHT

Bernie Harrison liked quality in a restaurant. He liked stiff white tablecloths, and heavy cutlery and his fish to be filleted with a flourish at the table, and presented to him complete with a half-lemon neatly wrapped in muslin. He liked carpets, and thick curtains, and properly dressed waiters who said things like 'Mr Harrison, Chef has some guinea fowl he'd very much like to offer you today.' Booking a table at his favourite restaurant in the centre of the city, he specified a particular table for two, and was not in the least pleased to be told that that table had already been reserved.

'Then unreserve it,' Bernie said to the young woman – Dutch? Scandinavian? Eastern European? – on the other end of the line.

'I'm afraid I can't do that, Mr Harrison.'

Bernie glared ahead of him. He usually had his personal assistant telephone restaurants for him, but he found he did not particularly want Moira to know that he was giving Margaret Rossiter dinner. Moira had been the late Mrs Harrison's choice of assistant for Bernie – personable without being seductive, middle-aged and capable, with enough of her own family and life to prevent her from becoming needy – and she had been silently but eloquently intolerant of Bernie's entertaining any woman alone since his wife's death five years before. Admittedly, Bernie's taste, in the immediate aftermath of Renée's death, had run to the extremely obvious, but Margaret Rossiter was of the calibre of lady dinner companion that Moira considered to have the potential to be a real threat. Margaret Rossiter would be a catch, even for a man like Bernie.

'I've eaten at La Réserve, young lady,' Bernie said, 'since before you were born. I want table six, in the alcove, and a bottle of Laurent-Perrier on ice, by eight o'clock tomorrow night, and no more bloody nonsense. *If* you please.'

Then he put the phone down. Stupid girl. Not only did he want to give Margaret Rossiter a good time, he wanted her to see that he was a man of consequence who was acknowledged as such, in places where you paid London prices. He put his hands flat either side of his head and smoothed his thick iron-grey hair back. Renée had hated to see him do that. Touching your hair in public, she said, was common.

Margaret had reacted to his invitation to dinner without surprise.

'Well, that's nice of you, Bernie, but what are you after?'

'Your company, my dear.'

'I don't like flattery, Bernie.'

He beamed into the telephone.

'I'll come clean. We've done a few good deals just now, and I'll admit I couldn't have got the Sage gig without you. I think you've had a rough time just recently with Richie going and all that upset. We get along fine and I'd like to buy you dinner.'

'Thank you, Bernie.'

'I'll send a car for you.'

'You won't,' Margaret said. 'There's a perfectly good taxi service in Tynemouth.'

'If you insist.'

'I do.'

Bernie beamed again.

'Till Wednesday.'

Renée Harrison had not cared for Margaret Rossiter. Renée had been much better-looking than Margaret, much better-groomed, with a more sophisticated taste in food and friends and travel. She had also come from a professional family in Harrogate, and she preferred not to remember that Margaret and Bernie had been at King Edward School in North Shields together, in Miss Grey's class, and that Bernie's father had been a fisherman and Bernie's mother had worked in Welch's sweet factory. This unease was confounded by Bernie's chosen career, which, although it paid for the house in Gosforth and the cruises and the golf membership and the wardrobes of superior clothes, was not one that Renée would have chosen, even if she did occasionally get to shake the hand of the likes of Dame Shirley Bassey. To all but her most intimate and trustworthy friends, Renée had referred to Bernie as an impresario.

There had been times when Bernie had believed her. He had produced the odd thing, after all, the odd one-off, showy thing, and he had been an angel a few times for friends with favours to call in, who were taking a bit of a risk on a rising unknown, or a rival, or a comeback star. But mostly he knew he was an agent, a hugely successful, extremely hard-headed agent, with an unrivalled spread of contacts and a greater range of artists on his books than anyone else in the North-East. He was, professionally, in a different league from Margaret Rossiter, and the fact that she not only didn't seem to care but also declined to acknowledge the difference was both an irritation and a challenge. He looked forward to their dinner. She was, after all, officially a widow now and that new state of affairs must – surely it must – create in her just a little of that attractive vulnerability which was both to his taste and to his purpose.

Dawson had roused himself from his slumber along the back of the sofa to inspect Margaret briefly before she went out.

She stood in the doorway of the sitting room and said to him, 'Will I do?'

Dawson considered.

'Scott would say lilac was a Queen Mother colour,' Margaret said.

Dawson yawned.

'I won't be late,' Margaret said. 'I've got my pearls on, so there's nothing to pinch, except you, and nobody but me would want you.'

Dawson shut his eyes again. Margaret switched off all the lights but one lamp and let herself out of the front door. The taxi driver, she noted, did not get out of his cab and open the door for her. He looked no more than twenty. He had the radio on at full volume. Football commentary.

'Passenger on board,' Margaret said loudly.

He glanced at her in his rear-view mirror.

'What?'

'I'm here,' Margaret said. 'I'm in the car. You have re-sumed work.'

He turned the volume down a very little.

'We're playing at home!' he said, as if that justified every-thing.

'And we'd better win,' Margaret said. 'I don't want us slipping back to the second division. You won't remember it, but in the early 1990s, we were nowhere. I remember the Gallowgate end at St James' Park almost empty. Now turn that off, and concentrate on driving me.'

He glanced at her again. His gaze was startled. Then

reluctantly he turned the radio off and pulled away from the kerb.

'You remind me,' he said conversationally, 'of my nan.'

'The taxi driver,' Margaret said, a bit later, to Bernie Harrison, settled in the alcove table with a glass of Laurent-Perrier in front of her, and a napkin across her knees as stiff with starch as if it had been plasticized, 'told me I reminded him of his grandmother.'

Bernie raised his glass.

'Did you tell him to turn his radio off?'

'Certainly I did.'

'Well,' Bernie said, 'you'll *be* a grandmother one day. More than I'll ever be.'

Margaret gave him a quick glance. Renée Harrison had never looked like a childbearing woman, but then you could never tell, you could never dismiss a childless woman as not having wanted children. And Bernie had wanted them all right; Bernie hadn't wanted to put another child through a single childhood like his own.

'You'd have made a wonderful father.'

'I would. I envy you that boy.'

A waiter put a huge, plum-coloured, tasselled menu into Margaret's hands.

'That boy,' she said, 'will be thirty-eight on his next birthday. Thirty-eight. No wife, no children, not even a girlfriend at the moment. And don't say there's plenty of time yet, because there isn't. He's getting set in his ways and they're not good ways.'

Bernie indicated something to the waiter from the wine list.

'A Pouilly-Fumé, Margaret?'

She looked up from the menu.

'I haven't had that for years—'

'Then you shall have it tonight.'

She looked round.

'I haven't been anywhere like this for years, either.'

'Traditional French,' Bernie said with satisfaction. 'Plenty of cream and butter. None of this fusion and foam twaddle. I recommend the fish.'

'The sole,' Margaret said. She put the menu down. 'I can say this to you, Bernie, because I've known you almost as long as I've known myself, but Scott worries me.'

Bernie indicated that she should drink her champagne.

'In what way?'

'Well,' Margaret said, 'he's aimless. He's drifting about when he's not at work, his flat looks as if it belongs to a student and he doesn't seem to know where he's going. He's too old not to know where he's going.'

'We'll start with the *coquilles Saint-Jacques*,' Bernie said to the waiter, 'and then the lady will have the sole and I'll have the turbot. You'll take the sole off the bone.' He held his menu out, and then he said to Margaret, 'Vegetables? I never do.'

'Spinach,' she said. 'Spinach, please. Just steamed.'

'Drink up,' Bernie said, 'drink up. Plenty of young men nowadays are like Scott. I see it all the time. One good thing about the music industry is that they don't differentiate between work and play, they just live music all the time.'

Margaret drank some champagne.

'His work I'm not worried about. He does his work. It's the rest of his life that bothers me. He doesn't have a *focus*.'

Bernie put his glass down and looked at her.

'Do you?'

'Do I what?'

'Do you have a focus?'

'Well,' Margaret said, 'I have a structure—'

'We all have that.'

'I have my work and my home and my son—'

'Yes?'

'But to be honest with you, Bernie,' Margaret said, putting her own glass down firmly, 'I've felt a bit adrift since Richie went, I've felt that I've lost a dimension somehow, that some kind of power supply's been shut off.'

'Ah,' Bernie said.

'What's "Ah"?'

'Well, I wondered.'

Margaret folded her hands in the space between the parallel lines of the cutlery.

'And what did you wonder?'

'I wondered,' Bernie said, leaning forward and laying one heavy hand on the cloth not very far away from Margaret's folded ones, 'I wondered how his death had affected you.'

'What did you feel after Renée?'

He smiled down at the tablecloth.

'Devastated and liberated.'

'Well, there you are,' Margaret said, 'and add to that the sense that you've got nothing to prove any more, so the savour goes out of a lot of it. I'm not a bravely achieving abandoned woman any more, I'm just a working widow, and I don't, if I'm honest, feel the same energy. I'm *doing* as much, but I'm driving myself. I can't quite remember what it's all for. And when I look at him, I wonder if Scott—'

'I don't want to talk about Scott,' Bernie said. 'I want to talk about us.'

Margaret drew herself up.

'No sentimental nonsense, please, Bernie.'

He winked.

'Wouldn't dream of it.'

Margaret gave a mild snort.

'You were a pest when you were nine and you have every potential to be a bigger pest now. You and Eric Garnside

135

and Ray Venterman—' She paused. Better not to bring up Richie's name.

'Both dead,' Bernie said.

'We were different ends of the school,' Margaret said, as if he hadn't spoken. 'Boys and girls. And you boys lay in wait for us after school, you and Doug Bainbridge—'

'I want to talk business,' Bernie said.

Two huge white plates bearing scallop shells topped with potato purée piped in intricate squiggles were put simultaneously in front of them.

'Business?' Margaret said.

'Yes,' Bernie said.

He indicated that a waiter should pour the wine, and picked up his immense napkin prior to tucking it in over his expensive silk tie. Then, unbidden, an image of Renée rose in his mind. She was wearing black and diamonds and her hair was newly done. She said sharply, 'Don't behave like a lout, Bernard.' Bernie lowered his napkin again to his knees.

'You can wear it on your head, for all I care,' Margaret said.

He smiled at her. There was an element in her that was entirely unchanged from the lippy nine-year-old in Miss Grey's class in King Edward School.

'Margaret,' he said, 'listen carefully. I have a very attractive proposition for you.'

They were all sitting, at Chrissie's request, round the kitchen table. She had opened a bottle of wine but nobody except her was drinking it. Dilly and Tamsin had bottles of mineral water with sports caps in front of them and Amy was drinking Diet Coke out of the can in a way Chrissie deplored.

'Please get a glass, Amy.'

'I've nearly finished it—'

Chrissie said again, very slowly, 'Please get a glass when I ask you to.'

Amy got up and lounged across the kitchen towards the relevant cupboard. Chrissie watched her, and her sisters regarded their water bottles. Amy drifted back with a glass in her hand and set it on the table. She upended the can and a few drops of dark brown liquid fell into the tumbler.

'Sit down, please,' Chrissie said. Her voice was not quite steady.

Tamsin glanced at her.

'It's OK, Mum.' She looked at Amy. 'Do not be such a *pain.*'

Amy sat down, and drained her tumbler.

Dilly said, 'I hope you aren't going to tell us something else horrible.'

Chrissie looked down at the pile of papers in front of her.

'I want a discussion. A family discussion. To help me come to a few decisions.'

Tamsin arranged herself to look alert and businesslike.

'Is it about money?'

'Basically,' Chrissie said, 'yes.'

Dilly said, 'You mean there isn't any.'

'No,' Chrissie said deliberately. 'No. There is some. But not as much as there was. Not as much as we're used to having. We are all going to have to think differently about money.'

Nobody said anything.

'We lived, you see,' Chrissie said, 'on Dad's performing. Because I managed him, there was no percentage payable to anyone else, but he was the only person I managed. I do not, you see, have other performers to fall back on. There was only Dad.'

They were all looking at her.

'And,' Chrissie went on, her eyes fixed on a spot on the tabletop beyond her papers, 'Dad was not making the money he had made in the past, when – when he died. He was always in work, I saw to that, but his CD sales had declined and been subject to the inevitable piracy, and his appearances didn't – well, he didn't command the highest fees any more, in fact he hadn't made very much at all in the last few years, which is why I was urging him to take everything that was offered, everything I could find, and of course now I feel very bad about that, and I worry that I was driving him too hard and, even though I'm so upset about what he did with his will, I can't get it out of my mind that I might have somehow—' She stopped, with a little gasp, and put her hand over her eyes.

Dilly took hold of her other forearm, still lying on the table.

'You didn't do anything wrong, Mum. He'd got a family to support.'

'He loved performing,' Tamsin said. 'Never happier.'

'He didn't love it like he used to,' Chrissie said, still not looking up. 'He wanted, really, just to have fun, sort of – sort of *talk* to it. I think he'd rather have talked to the piano than to anyone, I think that was the language that really suited him.'

Amy knocked her Coke can against the glass to make a point of extracting the last drops.

'Well,' she said, 'the piano was what he grew up with. Wasn't it? The piano was what he played all the time he was a teenager. It was a kind of friend. He'd had it all his life. Hadn't he?'

Tamsin glared at her sister.

'Thank you for that, Amy.'

Amy looked up.

'It's true.'

'What's true?'

'That the piano was part of his life from when he was

little and all through his life till Mum met him and you can't pretend that bit of his life didn't exist because it did and it mattered to him.'

Dilly looked at Chrissie.

'Mum. Tell her where to get off.'

Chrissie was still looking at the tabletop. She said, 'I'm not sure why Amy wants to be hurtful but as she does seem to want to be, I am, for the moment, ignoring her until she can behave with more sensitivity. But Dad's past is not what we are talking about now. What we are talking about now is that without Dad here to perform we are virtually without an income.'

Dilly leaned forward.

'Let's just sell the piano!'

Chrissie shot Amy a ferocious silencing glance, and then she said, 'Don't be silly. It isn't ours to sell.'

Tamsin looked round the kitchen with an appraising and professional eye.

'It's not a good time for the housing market, of course, but we could sell this. A good family house in this postcode would always—'

'Where would we live?' Amy said, her eyes wide.

'In a flat, maybe—'

'I don't want to go to a different school—'

'You won't be going to *any* school after the summer, you dork. You'll have finished with school—'

'That,' Chrissie said, 'was the conclusion I had come to. That we must face selling this house.'

Nobody said anything.

'Yes,' Chrissie said, 'we must sell the house and I must find work. I have already approached several agencies.'

They looked at her.

'What do you mean?'

'I have approached a few agencies asking if, given my

contacts, they would consider taking me on to represent people on their books who maybe they don't have time for.'

Dilly said, 'You mean you'd manage other *people*.'

'Yes.'

'But you can't—'

'I have to,' Chrissie said. 'What else do you suggest?'

Tamsin took a neat swallow of her water.

'I'm sure I could negotiate a good selling commission—'

'Thank you, darling.'

'And as,' Tamsin said deliberately, 'I shall probably be moving out soon to live with Robbie, you won't need more than a three-bedroom flat. Will you?'

Chrissie gave a little gasp.

'Mum,' Tamsin said, 'I did warn you, I warned you just after Dad—'

Chrissie held a hand up.

'I know—'

Dilly said, shooting a glance at Amy, 'I'm not sharing a room with *her*.'

'Dilly,' Chrissie said, 'I would so like this conversation to be about what we can contribute, and accommodate our-selves to, and not about what we refuse to do.'

Dilly put her chin up.

'I'll have finished my course this summer. I can get a job then. Soon it'll only be Amy you have to worry about.'

They all turned to look at Amy. She had pushed the ring pull off her drinks can down on to her finger, and was now trying to work it off again, over her knuckle. She flicked a look at her mother.

'If I'm here,' she said.

Alone in her bedroom, Chrissie lay with the curtains pulled, and her eyes shut. Even with the door closed, she thought she could hear the faint strains of Amy's flute, and the rise and fall of Dilly's voice on the telephone. Tamsin, she knew, had gone back to work, with the brisk step of someone with a place to go to, and a purpose to fulfil. Tamsin might be acting as if she was an equity partner in the estate agency, rather than its lowliest and least professionally defined employee, but at this alarming and dispiriting moment Chrissie felt nothing but gratitude for her show of resolution.

Dilly, Chrissie told herself, was plainly frightened. Doted on by her father for her blondeness and her dependency, she could not now be expected to cope at once with a life without that reliable cushion of indulgence to buffer her frequent inability to face things or endure things. Chrissie had noticed that Dilly's room, always as orderly as her reactions were chaotic, was ferociously neat just now, as if the confusion and uncertainty created by Richie's death could only be endured by exercising a meticulous control of areas where Dilly felt she had power, in the polished regiments of bottles and jars on her speckless make-up shelves, and the precise piles of fastidiously folded clothes and the paired-up shoes in her cupboards. Chrissie felt a need, a wish, to forgive Dilly her distinct unhelpfulness in planning their future. Dilly was the one who looked most like her. Dilly was the one who, for all her talents in various specific areas, had the fewest obvious intellectual gifts. Dilly was the one who, by tacit agreement between her parents, had always needed the most protection and the least demands made. 'Decorative and daft,' Richie said, both of her and to her, holding her chin in his hand, kissing the end of her nose. It was to be hoped, Chrissie thought now, lying in the centre of the great bed (only four pillows now – she had tried just two, and they had looked not just forlorn but somehow defeated), that Craig was sufficiently drawn to Dilly's looks and girlishness not to become bored and take his own good looks on to try their languid luck somewhere else. Craig's appearance at Richie's funeral had been one of the few bright moments in that dark day.

As, it had to be admitted, had Tamsin's Robbie's sturdy support been. Robbie was not what Chrissie – and, she secretly suspected, Tamsin – would call exciting. Robbie was solid in both person and personality; he was capable and competent, and if in conversation presented with a concept rather than a fact, looked distinctly alarmed. He worked for a removals company, being the man in a suit who went round to assess the nature and quantity of goods to be packed, so specialized in a soothing manner and a steady, uneventful speaking voice. He plainly found Tamsin fascinating. When they lived together – Chrissie found herself tearful at the prospect, although only days before Richie's death, she had been contemplating the possibility with a satisfaction close to relief – Robbie would quietly take on all the heavier domestic chores as only appropriate to a man sharing his life with a woman. There would, in Robbie's mind, be areas of their life together where he would never dream of trespassing, just as there would be roles he would assume as natural to his gender and everything that implied. That Tamsin might become exasperated by this ponderous respectfulness was something Chrissie had once mischievously imagined, but which she now rejected out of hand. In their present circumstances, Robbie looked set to become the man in Chrissie's life as well as in Tamsin's, who could be relied upon in all domestic crises, large and small. Robbie represented, to her surprise, a patch of solid ground in all the current marshes and quicksands, where she could set her foot. She bit her lip. How absurd, how ridiculous, how evident of her present state of mind that the thought of Robbie, in his high-street suit with his clipboard and his impassive voice, should bring tears to her eyes.

As Amy did. Only, the tears that Amy caused were angry

and hot and painful. Amy had succeeded in wrong-footing Chrissie in every way, in provoking in her mother all the unworthy demons of jealousy and self-pity and mistrust. Amy was dealing with her father's death by imagining him, Chrissie supposed, when he was deathless, when he had been as young as she was now, a teenager on Tyneside with a singing voice and an aptitude for the piano, in a community whose focus was entirely taken up by life in the shipyards and on the herring drifters. And in imagining her father as a boy, as a young man, Amy's imagination had also latched on to that other young man, on to Richie's son, who looked, albeit in a weaker version, so disturbingly like his father, and presumably sounded like him too, the Richie whom she, Chrissie, had first gone round to see at the stage door of the Theatre Royal in Newcastle to tell him that she not only thought his performance wonderful but that she was sure there were hundreds of thousands of women in the South of England who would think so too.

Perhaps, Chrissie thought, opening her eyes, and straining her gaze up towards the shadowy ceiling, perhaps that is all Amy is doing. Perhaps she is just trying to recapture her father through that – that man. Perhaps she is trying to bring her father back by hiding his baby picture, by going on about Newcastle, by playing, over and over, all the pieces they played together. Perhaps she doesn't have the faintest idea how much pain she is inflicting, how disloyal and callous she seems. Or perhaps I – Chrissie felt the tears start again, spilling in a warm stream out of the sides of her eyes and down her face into her hair – perhaps I am the one in the wrong; I am the one too insecure and jealous and vengeful to let her seek solace in a way that suits her but is so painful for me.

Chrissie rolled on to her side, careless of her clothes in a way that Richie, she thought now angrily, would have probably rejoiced to see. She could picture herself at that stage door, dressed like a pretty urban hippy, in 1983, pink suede boots and a floating print frock and her hair in long curls caught up with a slide decorated with a dragonfly. He'd looked at her as if she'd been offered to him on a plate, the perfect little pudding complete with a silver spoon. He'd said, 'I've never sung south of Birmingham, pet,' and then he'd laughed and she'd looked at his teeth and his skin and his thick hair and she'd thought, 'I don't care if he's over forty, he's gorgeous,' and two weeks later he'd taken her to bed in a hotel with brocade curtains and fringed lampshades and they'd drunk champagne in a shared bath later and he'd told her he didn't make a habit of this, that he was a family man, but, by heck, she was worth making an exception for. And on the train back to London, a heart pendant from Richie on a chain round her neck, she'd told herself that she'd found a man and a cause, a lover and a life's work. She would bring him south, she would marry him, she would make him a Southern star.

On the table at her side of the bed, the phone began to ring. She waited for a moment, waited for Amy or Dilly to stop what they were doing and pounce on it, but they didn't. She rolled back across the bed and picked up the handset.

'Hello?'

'Well,' Sue said, the other end, 'I don't like the sound of *you*. What are you doing?'

Chrissie swallowed.

'Lying on my bed and remembering—'

'And snivelling.'

'That too.'

'Remembering when he was hot and you were hotter and the future was bright with promise?'

'Yes.'

'Right,' said Sue. 'Stop right now.'

Chrissie gave a shaky little laugh.

'You be thankful,' Sue said, 'that you didn't get lumbered with a decrepit old granddad to nurse. When men stop being hot, nobody looks colder.'

Chrissie struggled to sit up.

'You're a good friend.'

'So, what's happening?'

'Today,' Chrissie said, 'a very unsatisfactory family conversation about the future.'

'Such as?'

'Nobody seems to care much about what I do or what happens to me because they all have plans for their own futures.'

'Surely you exaggerate—'

'Only a bit.'

'OK,' Sue said, 'come right round here, and we'll discuss your future and drink green apple Martinis.'

'What?'

'I have no idea either,' Sue said, 'but they've just been demonstrated on the telly. That illegally gorgeous Nigella woman. Get off that bed and get in your car.'

'Thank you,' Chrissie said fervently.

'If nothing else,' Sue said, 'my children will make you feel really grateful for yours.'

Chrissie put the phone down and swung her legs off the bed. A tiny movement by the bedroom door caught her eye, the door handle turning fractionally and silently. Then it was still, and the sound of light, quick feet went down the landing.

'Amy?' Chrissie called.

There was no reply. Chrissie went over to the door and opened it. There was no one there, but the air on the landing had an unmistakably disturbed quality. Chrissie listened. No sound. No flute, no voice on the telephone. She shut the door again, very carefully, and turned on all her bedroom lights.

Then she went into her bathroom and turned on all the lights there too. She looked at herself steadily in the mirror. Maybe Sue had something. Maybe whatever had propelled her twenty-three-year-old self round to the stage door of the Theatre Royal in Newcastle in 1983 was still in there somewhere, under all the layers superimposed by the years, by the children, by Richie.

She leaned forward and inspected herself closely.

'Go, girlfriend,' Sue would say.

CHAPTER NINE

Amy should have been in school. Her school, named for the American educator William Ellery Channing, and founded in 1885, was tolerant of the relaxed rules for the sixth form, but, all the same, Amy should have been in a Spanish literature class, and not in a tea shop in Highgate village, just up the hill from her school, sitting under a chandelier composed of glass cups and saucers, and eating a slice of home-made carrot cake with her cappuccino. On the table in front of her, as well as the cake and the coffee, was a copy of Lorca's *Poeta en Nueva York*, published posthumously, after he had been killed by the Nationalists in the Spanish Civil War at the age of thirty-eight. The young man, newly graduated and teaching Amy's A level Spanish literature class, had told her to forget poetic comparisons between Lorca and John Keats, both dead before they were forty.

'You don't,' he said, 'want to fall into cliché. Do you?'

Amy had been offended. Out of her whole family, she was, in her own view, the least clichéd by a million miles. Her father had liked that quality in her, had urged her to believe in her difference, in her independence of thought, had encouraged her to play the flute rather than the piano or the guitar, as soon as her teeth and jaw were strong enough, and to use the flute to play whatever she wanted on it. She had, by the same token, chosen to concentrate on Lorca's poetry, not his plays, and she wasn't going to be told by some big-head Cambridge graduate that her ideas about Lorca were banal merely because someone else might have thought of them before.

'If the idea's new to me,' Amy had said to Mr Ferguson, 'then it's new. OK?'

She had stalked out of the classroom, and now she was sitting in the tea shop, with Lorca's poems in front of her, and the local paper in one hand and the cake in the other. The local paper was folded to the small-ads page.

'Lindy Hop, swing dancing,' said the ad which had caught her eye. 'Beginners 6–7 p.m. Improvers 7–8 p.m. £1. Movers and Shakers Studio, Highgate Road.'

Below it was an ad from the South Place Ethical Society, a talk: 'British Democracy Works'. Then, below that, the Heath and Hampstead Society, a walk, 'Flora of the Heath', led by Sir Roland Philpott, tickets £2. And below that again, an ad for an active meditation drop-in, at Primrose Hill Community Centre, once a week on Thursday evenings.

If you didn't have a life, Amy thought, if you didn't have school and work and friends and a family, you could still fill your days with stuff, you could still put things in your diary, you could still tell yourself that there was a reason not just to stay in bed with your head under the duvet, breathing your own bedfug and wondering if you'd just vanished, just got rubbed out like a mistake made in pencil.

She put the paper down and picked up her coffee cup. It was very pretty, decorated with posies of flowers linked by ribbons. So it ought to be, at that price. Tamsin had lectured Amy on extravagance at breakfast, had told her that she couldn't just waltz around letting money leak out of her pockets like she used to. That the least they could do for Chrissie was not to worry her about money. That it was perfectly possible to hand-wash most stuff, not take it to the dry-cleaner's. The effect of this lecture had been to send Amy upstairs to put on her only cashmere jersey (a present from Richie), and to find the nicest, least economical place in Highgate to spend the hour when Mr Ferguson would be expounding on Lorca to Chloë and Yasmin and the others who were doing A level Spanish and who – pathetically, in Amy's view – thought he was wonderful.

In any case, being out of the house and alone gave her space to think, a space less encumbered by longing, as she so often did in her own bedroom, to go downstairs as she used to and find her father at the piano, absorbed but never too absorbed to say, 'That you, pet? Come on in. Come in, and listen to this.' He'd let all of them interrupt him, always, but the others didn't want to join in the music quite the way that Amy did. Tamsin loved being accompanied while she sang – there was a family video film of her singing 'These Boots Are Made For Walking' to an enthusiastic audience at her seventh birthday party – but neither she nor Dilly liked, as Amy did, to slip on to the edge of the piano stool beside him, and watch what he did with his hands, where he put his fingers on the notes, how lightly or heavily he touched them, how his feet on the pedals seemed to know exactly what to do by instinct. His hands had been beautifully kept – 'Pianist's hands,' he'd say – long-fingered and broad in the palm, with knuckles so flexible they felt almost rubbery when she kneaded them, as he let her do.

For her part, she thought, scooping the last of the foam out of the bottom of her coffee cup with her forefinger – 'Use your *spoon*,' she could hear Chrissie saying – she would like the piano out of the house as soon as possible. It was increasingly awful having it there, like some sad old dog who doesn't understand that its master is never coming home again. It would be easier, Amy was sure, when it wasn't sitting there, closed and unplayed, a constant and haunting reminder of what had been, and wasn't any more, and never, ever would be again. Quite apart from the fact that it ought to be in Newcastle now because that was what Dad had asked for, it simply ought not to be sitting mournfully in his practice room, making them all feel terrible every time they passed the open door – about one hundred times a day, by Amy's calculation.

She looked at her Lorca, and sighed. The piano was only one thing that was putting her at cross purposes with her family just now, that was making her behave in a way that she was ashamed of, like listening at Chrissie's bedroom door and hearing her tell Sue that her three daughters were too selfishly concerned with their own futures in these new, unwanted circumstances to concern themselves with hers. Hearing her say that had made Amy feel more frustrated than furious, more despairing of Chrissie's inability to see what seemed to Amy both transparently clear and manifestly right and fair. It was no good, Amy thought, no *good*, blaming the people in Dad's previous life, or Dad for having *had* a previous life, for the utter, angry misery and shock of finding yourself facing the future without him.

Amy knew that Chrissie thought her being interested in the Newcastle family was Amy's way of somehow bringing her father back to life, or cheating his deadness by finding intimate connections of his who were still very much alive. But Amy, overwhelmed with grief as she was at some point in every day still, had no illusions about how dead Richie was. Rather, what she had discovered – to her amazement – since his death was how alive *she* was, not just in straightforward, physical, physiological ways, but in terms of the richness and diversity of her heritage, which gave her the sense that she had more dimensions than she had ever imagined. She was Amy, living with her family in North London, with a considerable talent for the flute, and an agile (her mother would say frequently perverse) mind, and she was now also Amy with this alluring and almost exotic North-Eastern legacy, this background of hills and sea and ships and fish, this weird and wonderful dialect, this intense sense of place and community, which had produced a boy as shaped by but as simultaneously alien to that background as she felt herself to be to hers. She couldn't think quite how – if ever – she could explain this to Chrissie, but the eager interest in the Newcastle family was not really about them, or even about Dad. It was about *her*. And, at such a time, and after such a shock, it really was not on, in any way, to do more than hint that your attitudes and opinions were rather about yourself than about your dead father or the family he had belonged to before he belonged to yours.

She pulled the Lorca towards her and opened it randomly. She gazed at the page without taking it in. She felt dreadful about Chrissie, dreadful about her palpable apprehension at the future and revulsion for the present. But she couldn't help her by pretending to feel and be something other than she felt and was. She couldn't want to keep the piano or hate the Newcastle family just to make Chrissie feel temporarily better. Nor could she, just now, think of a way to explain to Chrissie without angering and hurting her further that, if Chrissie tried to refuse her the freedom to go and explore her newly realized amplitude, then she was going to just *take* the freedom anyway. What form that taking would assume she couldn't yet visualize, but take it she would.

Amy sighed. She shoved the book and the newspaper into her schoolbook bag, and stood up. The coffee and cake came to almost four pounds; four pounds, it occurred to her, that she really ought to be saving towards whatever future this freedom urge resolved itself into. Oh well, she thought, today is today and the carrot cake has given me enough energy to face Mr Ferguson as he comes out of class.

She put a crumpled five-pound note on the table and weighted it with her coffee cup, and then she sauntered out into the street, her book bag over her shoulder like a pedlar's pack.

Sitting inoffensively at her desk in the office on Front Street in Tynemouth, Glenda wanted to tell Margaret that whatever she had on her mind – and Glenda wished Margaret to know that she was extremely sympathetic to all burdens on Margaret's mind – there was no reason to snap at her. She had merely asked, out of manners, really, if Margaret had enjoyed her evening with Mr Harrison, and Margaret had responded – with a sharpness of tone that Glenda thought was quite uncalled for – that fancy French food was not for her and that Bernie Harrison took way too much for granted.

Glenda swallowed once or twice. She drank from the plastic cup of water – she would much rather have had tea – which Margaret told her she should drink because everyone in Scott's office in Newcastle had this fetish about drinking water all day long.

Then she raised her chin a fraction and said, 'Did he make a pass at you, then?'

Margaret, reading glasses on, staring at her screen, gave a small snort.

'He did not.'

Glenda wondered for a second if Margaret was in fact slightly disappointed that Mr Harrison hadn't tried anything on. Then she remembered that they had known each other since primary school, and that Margaret never made a particular sartorial effort if she had a meeting with him, and dismissed disappointment as an idea.

Instead, she took another sip of water and said, 'Oh,' and then, after a few more seconds, 'Good. I suppose—' and then, a bit later and defensively, 'I wasn't prying—'

Margaret said nothing. She went on typing rapidly – Glenda knew she was writing a difficult e-mail to a young comedian whose act Margaret considered better suited to the South than the North-East – with her mouth set in a line that indicated, Glenda imagined, that her teeth were clenched. Glenda was familiar with clenched teeth. Living with Barry's methods of enduring his disability had resulted in so much teeth-clenching on her part that her dentist said she must do exercises to relax her jaw, otherwise she would grind her teeth to stumps and have a permanent headache. She opened her mouth slightly now, to free up her teeth and jaw, and tried not to remember that Barry had managed to start the day in as disagreeable a mood as Margaret now seemed to be in, and that neither of them appeared to be aware that the person who was really suffering was her.

Margaret stopped typing. She took off her reading glasses, put them back on again, and reread what she had written.

'Doesn't matter how I put it,' she said to the screen. 'A no's a no, isn't it? He won't be fooled.'

Glenda drank more water. She would not speak until Margaret spoke to her, and pleasantly, as Margaret herself had taught her to do when answering the telephone to even the most irritating caller. It was hard to concentrate with a personality the size of Margaret's, in a manifestly bad mood, eight feet away, but she would try. She had commissions to work out – the clients Margaret had represented for over ten years paid two and a half per cent less than those she had had for only five years, and five per cent less than anyone taken on currently – and she would simply do those calculations methodically, and drink her water, until Margaret saw fit to behave in what Glenda had learned to call a civilized manner.

'Poor boy,' Margaret said. 'Refusal sent!' She glanced up. 'Coffee?'

Usually, she said, 'Coffee, dear?'

Glenda said, as she always said, 'I'd prefer tea, please.' Normally, after saying that, she added, 'But I'll get them,' but this morning she added nothing, and stayed where she was, looking at her screen.

Margaret didn't seem to notice. She went into the little cubbyhole that led to the lavatory and housed a shelf and an electric plug and a kettle. Glenda heard her fill the kettle at the lavatory basin, and then plug it in, and then she came back into the room and said, 'I've got Rosie Dawes coming at midday, and I'm giving lunch to Greg Barber and I'm going to hear these jazz girls tonight.'

Glenda nodded. She knew all that. She had entered all these appointments in the diary herself.

Margaret perched on the edge of Glenda's desk. Glenda didn't look at her.

'You know,' Margaret said, in a much less aggravated tone, 'there was a time when I was out five or six nights a week at some club or show or other. There was always a client to support or a potential client to watch. I used to keep Saturday and Sunday free if I could, in case Scott could manage to come home, but the rest of the time I was out, out, out. I never stayed till the end, mind. I'd stay long enough to get a good idea, and then I'd speak to the performer at the end of their first set, and say well done, dear, but I never stayed for the second set. I'd seen all I needed to see by then. I'd go home and make notes. Notes and notes. I don't do that now. I don't make notes on anyone. And I don't go and see many people now, do I?'

Glenda half rose and said, 'I'll get the kettle.'

'I was speaking to you,' Margaret said.

Glenda finished getting up. She said, 'I thought you were just thinking aloud.' She moved towards the cubbyhole.

'Maybe,' Margaret said. She didn't move from Glenda's desk. 'Maybe I was. Maybe I was thinking how things have changed, how I've changed, without really noticing it.'

Glenda made Margaret a cup of coffee with a disposable filter, and herself a powerfully strong cup of tea, squeezing the tea bag against the side of the cup to extract all the rich darkness. Then she carried both cups – mugs would have been so much more satisfactory but Margaret didn't like them – back to her desk, and held out the coffee to Margaret.

'Thank you, dear,' Margaret said absently.

Glenda sat down. This tea would be about her sixth cup of the day and she'd have had six more by bedtime. Nothing tasted quite as good as the first mouthful of the first brew – loose tea, in a pot – she made at six in the morning, before Barry was awake. She took a thankful swallow of tea, and put the cup back in its saucer.

Then, greatly daring, she said, 'So what did happen last night?'

Margaret turned her head to look out of the window. She said, 'Bernie Harrison asked me to go into partnership with him.'

She didn't sound very pleased. Glenda risked a long look at her averted face. Bernie Harrison agented three times the number of people that Margaret did, as well as handling a lot of Canadian and American and Australian business. Bernie Harrison had offices near Eldon Square, and a staff of five, some of whom were allowed their own – strictly regulated – expense accounts. Bernie Harrison drove a Jaguar and lived in a palace in Gosforth and had an overcoat – Glenda had hung it up for him several times when he came to see Margaret – that had to be cashmere. Why would someone like Margaret

Rossiter not leap at the chance to go into partnership with Bernie Harrison, especially at her age? Then a chilling little thought struck her.

'Would there be still a job for me?' Glenda said.

Margaret glanced back from the window.

'I turned him down.'

'Oh dear,' Glenda said.

Margaret got off the desk and stood looking down at her.

'My heart wasn't in it.'

'What d'you mean?'

'When he made his proposal,' Margaret said, 'I waited to feel thrilled, excited, full of ideas. I waited to feel like I've felt all my working life when there was a new challenge. But I didn't feel any of it. I just thought, It's too late, you stupid man, I'm too old, I'm too tired, I haven't got the bounce any more. And then,' Margaret said, walking to the window, 'I spent half the night awake worrying about why I didn't leap at the chance, and in a right old temper with myself for losing my oomph.'

Glenda leaned back in her chair.

'You aren't that old, you know.'

'I do know,' Margaret said. 'I'm behaving as if I'm fifteen years older than I am. And the thing that's really getting to me is that I *have* got energy, I have, it's just that I don't want to use it on the same old things.'

Glenda drank her tea. This was a profoundly unsettling conversation.

'What,' she said nervously, '*do* you want to use it on?'

Margaret turned.

'Don't know,' she said. 'Simply don't know. Stuck. That's the trouble. Restless and stuck. What a state to be in at sixty-six. All very well at thirty, but sixty-six!' She peered at Glenda. 'Was I a bit sharp with you this morning?'

*   *   *

Scott had arranged to meet Margaret in the pub close to the Clavering Building. It was more a hotel than a pub proper, with panelling inside, and a dignified air, and was not, therefore, a place Scott frequented much. When he got there – late, having run some of the way up the hill from work, after yet another bruising and unwanted encounter with Donna – Margaret was sitting with a gin and tonic in front of her, and a pint for him on the opposite side of the table, jabbing in a haphazard sort of way at her mobile phone. Scott bent to kiss her. He was aware of being breathless and sweaty, and his tie fell forward clumsily and got entangled with her reading glasses.

Margaret said, extricating herself, 'What's the dash, pet?' She put her phone down.

'I'm late—'

'You're always late,' Margaret said. 'I allow for you being late. Have you been running?'

Scott nodded. He collapsed into a chair and took a thirsty gulp of his beer.

'Magic—'

'The beer?'

'The beer.'

'You should have rung. There was no need to half kill yourself, running.'

'I needed to work something off,' Scott said.

'Oh?'

'A work thing.' He pulled a face. 'The consequence of me being wet and indecisive. A work thing.'

'I can't decide either,' Margaret said. She twisted her glass round in her fingers. 'That's why I wanted to see you.'

Scott grinned at her.

'This work thing,' he said, 'I *can* decide. I *do* decide. And then I just can't *do* it.'

Margaret lifted one eyebrow.

'A woman thing?'

'Maybe—'

'You want to tell me about it, pet?'

'I'd rather,' Scott said, 'hear what you want to talk about.'

Margaret picked up her glass and put it down again.

She said, 'I had dinner with Bernie Harrison. In all the years I've known him, coming up sixty years, that would be, he's never asked me to have dinner. Drinks, yes, even a lunchtime sandwich, but never dinner. And dinner is different, so I wondered what he was after—'

'I can guess,' Scott said, grinning again.

'No, pet. No, it wasn't. Bernie prides himself on being a ladies' man, but ladies' men like Bernie don't like risking a failure, so I knew I was safe there. No. What he wanted was quite different. He wanted to offer me a partnership in his business.'

Scott banged down his beer glass.

'Mam, that's fantastic!'

'Yes,' Margaret said carefully, 'yes, it was. It is. But I said no.'

'You *what*?'

'I said no, pet.'

'Mam,' Scott said, craning forward, 'what's the *matter* with you?'

She took a very small sip of her drink.

'I don't know, pet. That's why I thought I'd better talk to you. I've been worrying about you being aimless and unfocused, and then I get the offer of a lifetime at *my* age, and I find I'm just as aimless and unfocused as you are. I turned Bernie down because, as I said to poor old Glenda, whose head I bit off for no fault of her own, my heart just wasn't in it. I thought, How lovely, but I couldn't feel it. I couldn't feel I could match either his expectations or my own, so I turned him down. And I've been, as my father used to say, like a man with a hatful of bees ever since. I don't expect you to come up with any solutions, but you had to know. You had to know that your stupid old mother just blew it, and she can't for the life of herself think why.'

Scott put a hand across the table and took one of Margaret's.

'D'you think it's Dad?'

'Could be. There's no practice for these things, after all. Could be shock and grief. But it's been weeks now, we've had weeks to get used to the idea.'

'It's unsettled still, though,' Scott said. He squeezed Margaret's hand and let it go. 'All that antagonism from London, and no sign of the piano.'

'Do you really think the piano will make a difference?'

Scott shrugged.

'Having it *sorted* will make a difference.'

'But it isn't going to change our lives. We know what we needed to know, and that's a relief, even if I can't understand why the relief hasn't let me go, hasn't liberated me to get *on* with things, instead of having to prove things all the time, like I used to.'

'Mam, I'm sure you could change your mind—'

'Yes, I could. I'm certain I could. But I can't. I *want* to, but I can't. I can't see the point of changing anything, but I don't feel very keen about just chugging along with nothing unchanged either. I am *not* impressed with myself.'

'Join the club,' Scott said.

Margaret eyed him.

'Who is she?'

'A colleague. A work colleague. I let her get the wrong idea and now she won't let go of it. She's a nice girl, but I don't feel anything for her.' He paused, and then he said with emphasis, '*Anything.*'

'Then you must make that plain.'

'Oh, I do. Over and over, I do.'

'There's none so deaf as those that won't hear—'

'Mam,' Scott said suddenly.

'Yes, pet?'

'Mam, can I say something to you?'

Margaret sat up straighter.

'I'm braced for it, pet. I deserve it—'

'No,' Scott said, 'not about that. Not about Bernie. It's just I wanted to ask you something because I'd like to know I'm not the only one, that I'm not a freak like Donna says I am, that I'm not unnatural or pervy or weird or anything, but do you just feel sometimes, when it comes to other people, that you are just – just *empty*? And at the same time you have a hunch, which won't go away, that there is someone or something out there that might just fill you up?'

CHAPTER TEN

Since the evening of the green-apple Martinis – not an evening to be remembered without wincing, on several fronts – Chrissie had been much on Sue's mind. Chrissie had always been such a contrast to Sue, so organized in her life and her person, so apparently able to make decisions and steer her life and her family in a way that was invisible to them but satisfactory to her, so very much an example of that exasperating breed of women who, when interviewed in their flawless homes about their ability not to go mad running four or five people's lives as well as their own, plus a job, smiled serenely and said it was really just a matter of making lists.

Sue had never made a list in her life. There was a large old blackboard nailed to the wall in her kitchen on which the members of the household – Sue, her partner Kevin, Sue's sister Fran, who was an intermittent lodger, and three children – were supposed to write food and domestic items that needed replacing. But nobody did. The blackboard was used for games of hangman, and writing rude poems, and drawing body parts as a challenge to Sue to demand to know who drew them, and then forbid it. But Sue wasn't interested in challenges about which child was responsible for a row of caricature penises drawn in mauve chalk. Sue, just now, was interested in why her friend Chrissie seemed to have disintegrated since Richie's death, and be unable to access any of the admirable managerial and practical qualities that she had manifested when he was alive. It shocked Sue that Richie's clothes still hung in the bedroom cupboards and that the only change to their bedroom had been the removal of two pillows from the bed. It shocked her even more that his piano still sat in the room where he had practised, hours every day, which now was in grave danger of becoming the most lifeless and pointless kind of shrine.

'I wouldn't be surprised,' Sue said to Kevin, 'if she wasn't hunting for hairs in his comb.'

Kevin, who was twelve years younger than Sue, and worked for a high-class local plumber, was reading the evening paper.

He said, without looking up, 'Wouldn't you do that for me?'

Sue looked at him. Kevin had had a shaved head ever since she met him.

'Very funny. But Chrissie isn't funny. She might be grief-stricken but I think she's more loss-stricken. The structure of her life was founded on that bloody man, and that's gone now he's gone.'

Kevin said, staring at the sports page, 'What a wanker.'

'She loved him,' Sue said.

Kevin shrugged.

'Kev,' Sue said, 'Kev. Are you listening to me? You like Chrissie.'

Kevin shook the paper slightly.

'Fit bird.'

'You like her. When I suggest seeing her, you don't behave like I've asked you to have tea with the Queen, like you do with Verna or Danielle.'

Kevin made a face. Sue leaned across the table and twitched the paper out of his hands. He didn't move, merely sat there with his hands out, as they had been while holding the paper.

'Listen to me, tosser boy.'

'On message,' Kevin said.

'Chrissie is stuck. Chrissie is lost. Chrissie is consumed by a sense of betrayal and a hopeless rage and jealousy about that lot up in Newcastle. Chrissie needs to move forward because there's no money coming in and those useless little madams, her daughters – sorry, I exclude Amy, on a good day – aren't going to lift a spoiled finger to help her or change their ways. Chrissie is in some bad place with the door locked and what I would like to do, Kev, is find the key.'

Kevin gazed at her. Sue waited. Years ago, when they had first met, Kevin sitting gazing, apparently blankly, at her had driven her wild. She'd shrieked at him, certain his mind had slipped back to its comfort zones of football and sex and boiler systems. But over time she had learned that not only did Kevin not think like her, he also manifested his thinking quite differently. Quite often, when he was just sitting there, ostensibly gormlessly, his mind was like rats in a cage, zooming up and down and round and about, seeking an answer. If Sue waited long enough, she had discovered, Kevin would say something that not only astounded and delighted her with its astuteness but also proved that, while absorbed in the newspaper or the television, he had missed not a nuance or a syllable of what had been going on around him.

'I learned deadpan as a kid,' he once said to Sue. 'It was best, really. Saved getting clobbered all the time.'

Kevin leaned forward. Very gently, he took his newspaper back. Then he said, 'Get that piano out of the house.'

*   *   *

The house was quiet. Amy was at school, Tamsin was at work and Chrissie, in a grey-flannel trouser suit, had gone into town, to an address off the Tottenham Court Road, for an interview.

'I don't hold out much hope,' Chrissie said to Dilly before she left. She had her handbag on the kitchen table and was checking its contents. Dilly had her laptop open. She preferred working in the kitchen because that left her bedroom pristine and undisturbed. It also meant that, if there were any distractions going on, she wouldn't miss them. Next to her laptop lay a manual on hair-removal techniques. The screen on her laptop showed her Facebook account.

'Why'd you say that?'

'It just doesn't feel right,' Chrissie said. 'It doesn't feel *me*. I didn't like the tone of the woman I spoke to.'

Dilly was looking at the screen. Her friend Zena had posted a series of pictures of her trip to Paris. They were so boring that Dilly couldn't think why she'd bothered.

'Why're you going then?'

'Because I have to,' Chrissie said. 'Because I *have* to find something that will bring some money in. We're not on the wire, but we're close.'

Dilly gave a little shiver. It was frightening when Chrissie talked like this, and she'd talked like this a lot recently. Dilly didn't want to be unsympathetic, but she couldn't see what was so very different about the way they'd lived since Richie died, apart from his glaring absence. Chrissie wore the same clothes; the fridge was full of the same food; they all took showers and baths and spent hours on the computer and switched the lights and the television on, just as they always had. Tamsin had made a bit of a speech about economy the other day, but then she swished off to work in a pair of shoes Dilly swore she'd never seen before, and for shoes Dilly had a memory like a card index. It wasn't so much that Dilly was afraid of economizing, afraid of making changes, but more that she was made fearful by the uncertainty, by these vague and awful threats of an impending doom, which was never quite specified and whose arrival, though certain, was vague as to timing.

'Mum,' Dilly said, turning away from yet another of Zena's art shots of the Eiffel Tower, 'Mum, we'll all get on our bikes when you tell us what's happening and how we can help.'

Chrissie picked up her handbag and blew Dilly a kiss.

'I'll tell you that, poppet, as soon as I even begin to know myself.'

When she had gone, Dilly was very miserable. Even the thought of texting Craig, of seeing Craig on Friday, didn't have its usual diverting capacity. She logged off Facebook with an effort of will and glanced at her manual. The next section was on sugaring and threading. Threading was really difficult. The Asian girls on Dilly's course said that in their community the threading technique was passed down from mother to daughter, so they'd known how to do it since they were tiny, a sort of beauty routine cat's cradle. Dilly looked up, tapping a pencil against her teeth. Anxiety was an almost perpetual waking state now, and it made her fidgety and unhappy, unable to distract herself as she usually could with a phone call or a coffee or a bit of eBay browsing. She would have liked to cry. Crying had always been Dilly's first resort when confronted by the smallest hiccup in life, but one of the many miseries of the present time was that she couldn't seem to cry with any ease at all over little things. Crying seemed to have taken itself into another league altogether, and involved huge, wrenching sobbing sessions when she suddenly, all over again, had to confront the fact that Richie was no longer there.

Her phone, lying on the table beyond her laptop, began to

ring. She picked it up and looked at the screen. It was bound to be Craig. It was, instead, a number she didn't recognize. She put the phone to her ear.

'Hello?' she said cautiously.

'Dilly?' Sue said.

'Oh. Sue—'

'Got a minute?'

'Well, I—'

'Home alone, are you? I need to see you for a moment.'

'Me?'

'Dilly,' Sue said, 'I'm ringing you, aren't I?'

'I'm – I'm working—'

'No, you're not,' Sue said. 'You're doing your nails and comparing boyfriends on Facebook. I'm coming round.'

'Mum isn't here—'

'Exactly. I'm coming round to see you.'

Dilly said warily, 'Are you going to tick me off?'

'Why would I?'

'You just sounded a bit – forceful—'

'Not forceful,' Sue said, 'decided. That's why I'm coming round. I've decided something and I want your help.'

Dilly said, 'Why don't you ask Tamsin whatever it is?'

'Too bossy.'

'Amy—'

'Too young.'

'OK,' Dilly said doubtfully.

'Don't move. I'll be ten minutes. Put the kettle on.'

Dilly roused herself. She said abruptly, 'What's it about?'

'Tell you when I get there.'

'No,' Dilly said, 'no. No games. Tell me now.'

'No.'

'Then I won't open the door to you.'

'You're an evil little witch, aren't you—'

'Tell me!'

There was a short pause, and then Sue said, 'It's about the piano.'

Bernie Harrison asked Scott Rossiter to meet him in his offices. He had thought of suggesting a drink together, but he wanted the occasion to be more businesslike than convivial, and he wanted Scott's full attention. So he thought, on reflection, that to meet in his offices would not only achieve both those things but would also impress upon Scott the size and significance of the Bernie Harrison Agency.

He had known Scott almost all his life. He remembered him as a small boy at home in one of the plain-brick, metal-windowed council houses on the Chirton Estate in North Shields, when Richie and Margaret were still sharing with Richie's parents. Richie's parents had been living in the house since Richie was five, being categorized as 'homeless' after the Second World War, which then meant being a married couple still forced to live with their parents. And then, a generation later, it had happened to Richie and Margaret, before Richie's career struck gold, and while he was still taking low-key dates in obscure venues, and she was a junior secretary in a North Shields legal firm, and Scott was a toddler, cared for in the daytime by his sweet and ineffectual grandmother. After that, of course, it all changed. After that, after Richie's 'discovery' on a talent show for Yorkshire Television, it was very different. The house on the Chirton Estate was abandoned for a little terraced house in Tynemouth and then a semi-detached, much larger house, with a sizeable garden, and when Scott left primary school he left the state system too and gained a place, a fee-paying place, at the King's School in Tynemouth. Richie and Margaret had almost died of pride when Scott got into the King's School.

Bernie held out a big hand.

'Scott, my lad.'

Scott took his hand.

'Mr Harrison.'

'Bernie, please—'

Scott shook his head. 'Couldn't, Mr Harrison. Sorry.'

Bernie motioned to a leather wing chair.

'Good to see you. Sit yourself down.'

'Isn't that your chair?'

Bernie winked.

'They are *all* my chairs, Scott.'

Scott gave a half-smile, and subsided into the chair. He had a pretty good idea why Bernie had asked to see him, and an even better idea of what he was going to say in reply. He had not told Margaret he had been summoned, but he was going to tell her about the meeting when it was over. He was feeling fond and protective of Margaret at the moment. When, the other night, he'd asked her if she ever felt like he did that there might be someone or something out there that could spring him from the trap of his sense of obstructing himself from moving forward, she'd said, 'Oh, pet, you know, you always hope and hope it'll be someone else who does the trick, but in the end it comes down to you yourself, and the sad fact is that some of us can and some of us can't,' and then she'd taken his hand and said again, 'Some of us just can't,' and he'd had a sudden lightning glimpse of how she'd looked at his age, younger even, when there seemed to be everything to live for, and nothing to dread. He looked now at Bernie Harrison.

'I shouldn't be too long, Mr Harrison.'

'Me neither,' Bernie said firmly.

He balanced himself against the edge of the desk and held the rim either side of him. 'It's your mother, Scott.'

'Yes,' Scott said. He looked at Bernie's shoes. They were expensive, black calf slip-ons, with tassels. The fabric of his suit trousers looked classy too, with a rich, soft sheen to it, and his shirt had French cuffs and links the size of gobstoppers.

'Did she tell you,' Bernie said, 'about my proposal?'

'Yes,' Scott said. 'The other night.'

'So she also will have told you that she declined my offer.'

'Yes.'

Bernie cleared his throat.

'Can you enlighten me as to why she'd turn me down?'

'I wouldn't try,' Scott said.

'OK, OK. I'm not asking you to betray any confidences. I'm just seeking a few assurances. Is it – is it me?'

'You?'

'Well,' Bernie said, 'does she think that if she worked with me I'd make a nuisance of myself? Your mother's a good-looking woman.'

Scott smiled at him.

'No, Mr Harrison, I don't think that was the problem.'

Bernie flicked him a look.

'Sure?'

'Pretty sure.'

There was a small silence, tinged with disappointment. Then Bernie said robustly, 'Well, she can't have doubts about her *own* abilities, can she? It may be small, but that's a cracking little business she has.'

'No,' Scott said, 'I don't think the possibility of inadequacy crossed her mind. Quite rightly.'

'Oh,' Bernie said with energy, 'quite rightly, I agree. Well, if it's not me and it's not her, what is it?'

Scott said carefully, 'Sometimes you find you just don't want to do something, however great the offer is.'

Bernie regarded him.

'But that's not like your mother.'

Scott shrugged.

169

Bernie said, 'Has she been affected by your father's death? I mean, badly affected?'

Scott looked out of the window. He said, 'It's something to come to terms with. Obviously.'

'You're not helping me much, young man.'

Scott looked back. He said, 'I can't answer your question because I don't know much more than you do. She was very pleased and very flattered by your offer, but she doesn't want to accept it. Maybe she doesn't know why any more than we do.'

Bernie shook his head. He stood up and put his hands in his trouser pockets, and jangled his keys and his change.

'I'm baffled.'

He shook his head again, as if to clear a buzzing in his ears.

'It isn't me, and it isn't her, and it isn't your dad's death—'

'Or it's all three of them.'

'Maybe.'

'But it won't be *personal*, if you see what I mean. Mam's not like that. She won't have said no for any reason that isn't straight, she wouldn't do it just to spite you or something like that.'

Bernie shook his keys again.

'That's one of the reasons I asked her. Because she's so straight, and everyone knows that. I want her reputation as much as I want her expertise and her input and her presence.'

Scott made to get up.

'If it's OK by you, Mr Harrison—'

Bernie looked at him again. He took his hands out of his pockets and jabbed a forefinger towards Scott.

'If this is how it is, my lad, I'm not giving up. If it was a concrete reason, I'm not saying I wouldn't have another go, but I'd respect it. But as it's all this vague, don't-know, wishy-washy stuff, I'm going to keep trying. And I'd be grateful if you'd put in a word for me with her now and then. I want to keep the pot boiling.'

Scott said, standing now, 'I'm happy to see you today, Mr Harrison, but this is between you and my mother. Whatever I think may be good for her is really neither here nor there. It's what she thinks is good herself that counts, and she's had years of practice deciding that. I'd like to see her here, Mr Harrison, but only if that's what she really wants.'

Bernie looked at him in silence for a few moments. Then he touched Scott's arm.

'Anyone tell you how like your dad you are, to look at?'

Threading his way through the ambling crowds in the Eldon Square shopping centre, Scott felt his phone vibrating in his top pocket. He paused to take it out and put it to his ear.

'Hello?'

A female voice with a slight London accent said, 'That Scott?'

Scott moved into a quieter spot in the doorway of a children's clothes shop.

'Who is this?'

'My name's Sue,' Sue said. 'I'm a friend of your stepmother's.'

'My—'

'Of Chrissie's,' Sue said. 'Of your father's wife.'

Scott shut his eyes briefly. This was no moment to say forcibly to a stranger on the telephone that his father had only ever had one wife, and it wasn't Chrissie.

'You still there?' Sue said.

'Yes—'

'Well, I just rang—'

'How did you get my number?'

171

There was a short pause, and then Sue said, 'Amy's phone.'

'Amy knows you are ringing? Why aren't I talking to Amy?'

'Amy doesn't know,' Sue said.

'Then—'

'Dilly took the number from Amy's phone,' Sue said. 'Dilly is Amy's sister.'

'I know that.'

'Well,' Sue said with irritation, 'how I got your number is neither here nor there—'

'It is.'

'It's *why* I'm ringing that matters. And you'll be pleased when you hear.'

Scott waited. A lump of indignation at Amy's phone being investigated behind her back sat in his throat like a walnut.

'Listen,' Sue said.

'I am—'

'The piano is fixed.'

'What?'

'The piano. Your piano. With Dilly's help, we're getting it shifted. I think it'll be next week. You should have your piano by the end of next week. I'll let you know the exact timing when I've got firm dates from the removal company.'

Scott said, 'Does Amy know? Does – does her mother know?'

'Look,' Sue said, suddenly furious, '*look*, you ungrateful oaf, *none* of that is any of your business. No, they don't know, nobody knows but Dilly and me, but that's none of your business either. Your business is to thank me for extricating your sodding piano and arranging for it to come north. All I need from you is thanks and a delivery address. The rest is none of your business. You have no idea what it's like down here.'

Scott swallowed. He said, with evident self-control, 'I told Amy the piano could wait until – until it was OK for them to let it go.'

'They won't even *begin* to be OK until the piano has *gone*. Trust me. Cruel to be kind, maybe, but the piano has to go.'

'I don't like it being a secret—'

Sue yelled, 'It has nothing to *do* with what you like or don't like!'

Scott held his phone a little way from his ear. He wanted to explain that he didn't, for reasons he couldn't quite articulate, wish to do anything remotely underhand as far as Amy was concerned, but he had no wish to open himself up, in any way, to this assertive woman.

Sue said, slightly less vehemently, 'Don't go and bugger this plan up now by refusing the piano.'

'I wouldn't do that—'

'You're doing Chrissie a favour, removing the piano. You're doing them all a favour. None of them can move on one inch until that piano is out of the house and they aren't passing it every five minutes.'

Scott put the phone back against his ear.

'OK,' he said. 'Thank you.'

'That's more like it,' Sue said. 'Jeez, what a family. I thought mine was a byword for dysfunction but the Rossiters run us a close second. Text me your address and I'll let you know the delivery date.'

'OK.'

'Is it too much to ask,' Sue demanded, 'that you say, "Thank you so much, stranger lady, for restoring my birthright to me"?'

Scott considered. Who knew if this woman was a miracle-worker or a meddler? He remembered that she had called him an oaf. A peculiarly Southern insult somehow.

'Yes,' Scott said decidedly, and flipped his phone shut.

That night, instead of slamming a curry or chilli con carne into the microwave, Scott cooked dinner. He paused in the little Asian supermarket on his way home and bought an array of vegetables, including pak choi, and a packet of chicken-breast strips, and a box of jasmine rice, and when he got home he made himself a stir-fry.

He put the stir-fry on a proper dinner plate, instead of eating it out of the pan, and put the plate on his table with a knife and a fork and three carefully torn-off sheets of kitchen paper as a napkin. Then he stuck a candle-end in an empty bottle of Old Speckled Hen, and put a disc in the CD player, a disc of his father playing Rachmaninov, a disc that had never sold in anything like the numbers that his covers of Tony Bennett songs had. Then he sat down, and ate his dinner in as measured a way as he could, and reflected with something approaching pride on having stood up to Bernie Harrison, not allowed himself to be grateful to that rude cow from London, and succeeded, at last, in taking Donna out for a coffee – not the drink she would have preferred – and telling her that he was very sorry but she was mistaken and nothing she could do was going to make him change his mind.

He had feared she might cry. There were long moments while she stared down into her skinny decaff latte with an extra shot, and he had been afraid that she was going to opt for tears rather than fury. But to her credit, she had neither wept nor shouted. In fact she'd said, after swallowing hard several times, 'Well, Scottie, I'll be thirty-six next October, so you can't blame me for trying,' and he'd squeezed her hand briefly and said, 'I don't. I just don't want you to waste any more time or effort on *me*.'

She looked at him. She said, with a gallant attempt at a smile, 'Rather have a piano than a relationship, would you?'

He said, 'At least you know where you are with a piano,' and they'd grinned weakly at each other, and then she bent to pick up her bag and stood up and said she was off to see the girls from work to drown her sorrows. Or, as it was only Wednesday, to half drown them anyway. She bent and gave his cheek a quick brush with her own.

'It was nice being wanted for my body—'

'Great body,' Scott said politely.

Then she had clicked out of the coffee bar on her heels and he had gone to the Asian supermarket and bought the ingredients for a proper meal. Which he had now prepared, and cooked, and eaten. And washed up. He put the kettle on, to make a coffee, and then he strolled down the length of his flat and contemplated the space he had cleared – but not swept, recently – where the piano would sit.

It was very, very wonderful to think that, within ten days, it would be sitting there, huge and shining and impregnated with memories and possibilities. Now that it was actually on its way, Scott could permit himself to acknowledge how much he wanted it, how hard it had been to say that they should not let it go until they were ready to let it go. It had been hard, but it had been worth it, both because it gave Scott the sense of having behaved honourably in an awkward situation and because the joy of knowing it would soon be on its way north was so very intense by contrast.

The joy was, Scott thought, an unexpected bonus. It gave him an energy of pleasure that he couldn't remember feeling about anything much for a very long time. The only element that tempered it – and Scott had not allowed himself to consider this fully till now – was that a deception was being practised on Amy, and on her mother and older sister, in order that he might have the Steinway sitting where he was standing now, with the night view of the bridge, and the Gateshead shore shimmering away beyond, outside the uncurtained window.

Scott moved over to the window and leaned his forehead against the cold glass. He supposed that part of him felt that Amy's mother and sister could look out for themselves. He had, after all, had no contact with them except cold looks at the funeral and an unpleasant brief telephone exchange with Tamsin. But Amy herself was another matter. Amy had had the guts to ring him, had spoken to him as if the bond between them didn't just exist but should be respected and, for God's sake, she was only eighteen, she was only a kid, but she had shown an independence of mind that would do credit to someone twice her age.

Scott took his phone out of his trouser pocket, and tossed it once or twice in his hand. If he rang her, and told her about Sue's call, she might well flip and refuse to let him have the piano. He looked, for a long time, at the dusty space where the piano was going to sit. He walked across it, and then back again. He weighed his desire for it to be there against his peace of mind. He flipped his phone open, and dialled Amy's number.

Her phone rang four times, then five, then six. Then her voice said hurriedly, 'This is Amy's phone. I'll call you back,' and stopped, as if she had meant to leave more message, and suddenly couldn't think what more to say.

Scott looked out at his view.

'Amy,' he said, 'it's Scott. I'm calling on Wednesday night. It's about the piano. There's something we should talk about. Could you call me when you get this? Any time. I mean, *any* time.'

She rang back at ten past two in the morning. She sounded odd, but she said that was because she was under the duvet. Apart from being a bit muffled, her tone was normal, even neutral.

She said, 'What is it? About the piano?'

Scott, lying back on his pillow, his eyes still closed from the deep sleep he'd been in, told her briefly about Sue's call.

'Oh,' Amy said.

'Look,' Scott said, 'it doesn't have to happen, not if you—'

'It does have to happen. It's not that—'

'Not what?'

'It's not you having the piano—'

'Oh,' Scott said.

Amy said, 'I'm glad.'

'Are you?'

'Oh yes,' she said.

He waited for her to ask if she'd woken him, but she didn't. Instead, she said, 'I won't let my phone out of my sight now.'

'No.'

There was a silence. He longed to say more but couldn't initiate it.

Then she said, 'Night-night. Thanks for telling me,' and the line went dead. Scott looked at the clock beside his bed. Two-thirteen and he was awake now. Wide awake.

CHAPTER ELEVEN

Tamsin was keeping her eyes and ears open. It was completely obvious, from the agents who were being summoned into the partners' rooms and coming out looking as if they'd been hit with a bucket, that a fair number of redundancies were going on. There had been a confidential memo sent round saying that the present economic climate and resulting effect on the housing market meant that there inevitably had to be a certain amount of restructuring within the company, but that for the sake of all those concerned the partners requested that all members of staff should behave with as much discretion as possible. Which meant, Tamsin knew, that none of them were supposed to gossip when people were got rid of. And people *were* being. People were going out of the building by the back door, carrying boxes and bin bags, with the contents of their desks in them, and a lot of company cars were beginning to sit idle, day after day, in the company car park.

Tamsin had said to Robbie that the fact that she wasn't paid much more than the minimum wage might work either way. The partners might think she was extremely expendable, or they might think that she was very good value. Robbie said he thought the latter would be the case and that she should work on that assumption anyway, so Tamsin was going into work having made an extra effort with her appearance every day, and was conducting herself with increased alertness and alacrity as well as a wide and confident smile every time she encountered a partner. If she *was* made redundant, she reckoned, she'd make sure she left with a glowing recommendation.

The reception desk, Tamsin decided, was where she was going to make her mark. It didn't take much to realize that the first face of a business that a customer saw was also the one that made the significant first impression. So Tamsin was making an extra effort to greet everyone, including the least prepossessing of the courier delivery boys, with a wide smile and an air of being completely impervious to any possibility of suffering in the current crisis. It was annoying, therefore, to turn from a switchboard complication to greet a new arrival and find that she was wasting warmth and charm on her sister Amy.

'What are you doing here? Why aren't you in school?'

'Revision period,' Amy said. She was wearing jeans and a black hooded sweatshirt and chequerboard sneakers.

'I'm working,' Tamsin said. 'Can't you see?'

Amy leaned forward.

'I've got to talk to you—'

'About what?'

Amy glanced round. The office was open-plan, and several people were plainly not as absorbed by what was on their screens as they were pretending to be.

'Can't tell you here.'

'Amy,' Tamsin said again, 'I'm working. You shouldn't be here.'

'Ten minutes,' Amy said. 'Tell them it's family stuff. It *is* family stuff.'

Tamsin hesitated. There was her natural curiosity and, in

addition, there was the aggravation of not knowing something that, by rights, she should both have known and have known first.

She said, 'I'll ask Denise.'

Amy nodded. She watched Tamsin go across to talk to a girl with dark hair in a short glossy bob. The girl was typing. She neither looked up nor stopped typing when Tamsin bent over her, but she nodded, and then she stood up and followed Tamsin back to the reception desk.

'This is my sister Amy,' Tamsin said.

'Hi,' Amy said.

Denise looked at Amy. Then she said to Tamsin, 'Fifteen minutes, max. I've got a client at twelve and he's my only client all bloody day.'

On the pavement outside, Amy said, 'Is she always like that?'

'Everyone's worried,' Tamsin said. 'Everyone's wondering who's next.'

'Are you?'

'No,' Tamsin said.

'Really?'

'I'm cheap,' Tamsin said, 'I'm good. It'd be a false economy to lose me. Now, what is all this?'

There was a sharp wind blowing up the hill. Amy pulled her sleeves down over her knuckles and hunched her shoulders.

'Can we get a coffee?'

'No,' Tamsin said. 'Tell me whatever it is and go back to school.'

Amy said unhappily, 'You won't like this—'

'What won't I like?'

'I thought I wouldn't tell you. I thought I wouldn't say. But I think not telling you is worse than telling you. I don't know—'

'What, Amy?'

Amy looked at the pavement.

'The piano's going.'

'It—'

'Next Thursday. It's booked.'

'Does Mum—'

'No,' Amy said. She flicked a glance up at her sister. 'No. That's the point. Sue's done it. Sue's organized it with Dilly while Mum's out, next Thursday. The removal people will just come and take it.'

Tamsin said nothing. Her mind raced about for a few seconds, wondering what aspect of this new situation she was most upset about. Then she said furiously, 'How do you know? Did Sue tell you?'

'No,' Amy said.

'Dilly?'

'No,' Amy said.

'Then—'

Amy sighed. She said reluctantly, 'It was him.'

'What him?'

'You know,' Amy said. She stretched her sleeves down further. 'Him. In Newcastle.'

'*What?*'

'He rang me. Sue had rung him to ask for his address. Dilly got his number off my phone. He rang because he thought it shouldn't be behind our backs—'

Tamsin snorted.

'It was *nice* of him!' Amy cried. 'It was nice of him to warn us!'

Tamsin seemed to collect herself. She leaned forward and gripped Amy's shoulders.

'Let me get this straight. You are telling me that Sue, with Dilly's connivance, has arranged for the piano to be taken away next Thursday while Mum is out of the house?'

'Yes.'

'And you only know about it because Newcastle Man rang you?'

'He's called Scott,' Amy said.

Tamsin let go of her sister's shoulders.

'I'm not sure who I'm going to kill first—'

'It's good the piano's going,' Amy said. 'It's *good*. It'll be better for Mum. It'll be better for all of us—'

Tamsin wasn't listening. She was looking away from Amy, eyes narrowed.

'I think,' she said, 'I'll start with Dilly.'

Chrissie had not been thinking straight. She'd begun at Bond Street Station, intending to take the Central Line to Tottenham Court Road and then change to the Northern Line to travel north. But for some reason, she had drifted down the escalator to the Jubilee Line, going northwards, and sat blankly on the train for a number of stops until the sight of the station name, West Hampstead, jolted her back into realizing that she was miles further west than she had intended to be. She got out of the train in the kind of fluster she used to watch, sometimes, in middle-aged and elderly women with a slightly contemptuous pity, and made her way up into the open air and West End Lane, thankful that no one she knew had seen her.

Only once she was out of the station did it occur to her that she should have crossed the road and taken the overland train to Gospel Oak. But somehow, she couldn't face retracing her steps. She stood in the light late-afternoon drizzle for a few moments, just breathing, and then she set off northwards, towards the fire station where West End Lane turned sharp right before it joined the Finchley Road, and she felt she was back in the main swim of things and might find a cup of coffee.

At the junction of West End Lane and the Finchley Road, something struck her as familiar. The building she was beside, the red-brick building with a portal and an air of solidity, was of course her solicitor's building, the offices of Leverton and Company, where there had been that dreadful interview with Mark Leverton in which she had had to confess that she and Richie had never been married and, inevitably, convey that this situation had persisted despite her earnest and growing wish to the contrary. At the end of the interview, when Tamsin had preceded her out of the door of Mark Leverton's office, he had said to Chrissie, in a low and urgent voice that she was sure came from a human rather than professional impulse, 'If there's anything I can do to help—' She had smiled at him with real gratitude. She had thanked him warmly and, she hoped, conveyed that, touched though she was, she had always been a coping woman and intended to continue to cope. But now, weeks later, standing on the damp pavement outside the building, and disproportionately shaken by having made such a muddle of her journey home, Chrissie felt that not only was coping something she no longer felt like doing but also it was, for the moment at least, something she simply could not do. She pressed the bell marked 'Reception' and was admitted to the building.

The receptionist said that she thought Mr Mark was still there, but as it was twenty past five, and a Friday, he might well have already left for family dinner.

'Could you try?' Chrissie said.

She crossed the reception area and sat down in a grey tweed armchair. On the low table in front of her was a neat fan of legal pamphlets and a copy of the business section of a national newspaper. She stared at it unseeingly, until the receptionist came over and said that Mr Mark was on his way down. She said it in a tone that made Chrissie feel that

Mr Mark should not have had his good nature presumed upon.

'Thank you,' Chrissie said.

The receptionist's heels clacked back behind her desk. Five minutes passed. Then ten. A small panic rose up in Chrissie, a panic that caused her to demand of herself what she thought she was doing, what on earth should she say to Mark Leverton, and then he was beside her, in a tidy fawn raincoat over his business suit and he was bending over her and saying, 'Mrs Rossiter?' in the tones you might expect from a doctor.

She looked up at him.

'I'm so sorry—'

He put a hand under her elbow to help her to her feet.

'Are you unwell?'

'No,' she said. 'No. I'm fine. I – I – this is just an impulse, you know. I found myself outside and I just thought—'

He began to steer her towards the door. He said, 'Goodnight, Teresa,' to the receptionist, and leaned forward to push the door open to allow Chrissie to go through ahead of him.

'I'm due home soon,' he said to Chrissie, 'it being a Friday. But there's time for a coffee first. It looks to me as if you could do with a coffee.'

'I'm sorry, so sorry—'

'Please don't apologize.'

'But you're a solicitor, you're not a doctor or a therapist—'

'I think,' Mark Leverton said, holding Chrissie's elbow, 'we'll just pop in here. I often get a lunchtime sandwich here. It's run by a nice Italian family—'

The café was warm and bright. Mark sat Chrissie in a plastic chair by a wall and said he was just going to call his wife, and tell her that he'd be half an hour later than he'd said.

'Oh, please—' Chrissie said. She could feel a pain beginning under her breastbone at the thought of Mrs Leverton and her children, and maybe her brothers and sisters and parents, sitting down to the reassuring candlelit ritual of a Jewish Friday night. 'Please don't be late on my account!'

Mark said something briefly into his phone, and then he made a dismissive, friendly little hand gesture in Chrissie's direction, and went over to the glassed-in counter of Italian sandwich fillings and ordered two coffees.

'Cappuccino?' he said to Chrissie.

'Americano, please—'

'One of each,' Mark Leverton said, and then he came back to the table where Chrissie sat, and slipped off his raincoat and dropped it over an empty chair.

'I'm so sorry,' Chrissie said again. 'This isn't like me. I don't know what I'm thinking of, bothering you like this—'

'It's not a bother.'

'And it isn't,' Chrissie said unsteadily, 'as if I can afford to pay you for even ten minutes of your time—'

'We're not ogres,' Mark said. He was smiling. 'We don't charge just for picking up the phone. You wouldn't have come to find me if you didn't need help now, would you?'

The coffee was put down in front of them. Mark looked at his cappuccino.

'Europeans would never drink it like this after mid-morning. But I love it. It's my little vice. Ever since I gave up chocolate.' He grinned at Chrissie. 'I was a real shocker with chocolate. A bar of Galaxy a day. And I mean a *big* bar.'

She smiled back faintly. 'I wish chocolate was the answer—'

He dipped his spoon into the cushion of foam on top of his coffee cup.

'D'you want to tell me, Mrs Rossiter, or would you like me to guess?'

'I'm not Mrs Rossiter, Mr Leverton.'

'I'm Mark. And you are, in my mind and for all practical purposes, Mrs Rossiter. OK?'

Chrissie nodded.

'And I'm guessing that the shocks of the last couple of months have now segued into anxiety about the future.'

Chrissie nodded again. She said, 'Got it in one,' to her coffee cup. Then she glanced up and she said, 'I can't believe I was so stupid. I can't believe I let us rely so heavily, in such an undiversified way, on his earning power. I can't believe I didn't see how that earning power was diminishing, because even if he still had a huge fan base it was very much women of a certain age, and getting good gigs was harder and harder and no one seems able to stop the rip-offs and illegal downloading of CDs. I can't believe I didn't see that I'd put all my eggs in one basket and that basket turned out to be – to be—' She stopped, took a breath, and then she said, 'You don't want to hear all that.'

'It's background,' he said.

She took a swallow of coffee. She said simply, 'And now I can't get work.'

'Ah.'

'I've been to seven interviews. It's a waste of time. Everybody seems to want to be an agent, so there's an infinite supply of cheap young people they can train up like they want to. They don't want someone like me who managed just one talent for twenty years. They say come in and we'll talk and then they take one look at me and you can see them thinking, Oh, she's too old, too set in her ways, won't be able to adapt to our client list, and so we exchange pleasantries – or veiled unpleasantries – for twenty minutes or so, and then I get up and go and you can hear the sighs of relief even before the door is shut behind me.'

Mark Leverton put his hands flat on the table either side of his coffee cup.

'Two things.' He grinned again. 'And I won't charge you for either.'

Chrissie tried a smile.

'First,' he said, 'sell your house. Really sell it. Don't just play with the idea. Put it on the market and take whatever you can for it.'

She quivered very slightly.

'Second,' he said, 'change your thinking. Put agenting, managing, whatever, behind you.'

'But I—'

'My father says,' Mark said, reaching for his raincoat, 'that there's always work for those prepared to do it.' He winked at her. 'I mean, d'you think I'd *choose* to do what I do?'

'If you tell your mother,' Sue said to the assembled Rossiter girls, 'you are all three going to wish you had never been born.'

Tamsin was standing. She had been standing throughout this conversation in order to assert herself and to make it very plain to Sue that her interference – even if it was for everyone's good, especially Chrissie's – was completely out of order, on principle. Dilly, looking mulish, was sitting by the kitchen table and Amy was staring out of the window at the slab of darkening sky between their house and the next one with an expression that indicated to Sue that her mind was absolutely somewhere else.

'Did you hear me?'

Tamsin said nothing, elaborately.

Amy turned her head. She said, 'Why would we?'

'Because,' Sue said mercilessly, 'you're all in the habit of running to Mummy about everything.'

'No,' Amy said, 'we ran to Dad.'

Dilly put her hand over her eyes.

Tamsin said grandly, 'I have no objection to being spared the sight of the piano all the time—'

'Oh, *good*.'

'But I really, really object to its going to those people in Newcastle. I hate that.'

'Me too,' Dilly said.

Amy opened her mouth.

'Shush,' Sue said to her loudly. She folded her arms. 'You have no choice. You know that.'

Dilly said, 'Twenty-two thousand—'

'Shut it, Dill. Never mind all those royalties on the music—'

'The good news is,' Sue said loudly, 'that once the piano is gone you need have no further dealings with Newcastle ever again. You can put all that behind you. You need have no further contact. You can forget they even exist.'

'Thank goodness—'

'They've poisoned us,' Dilly said.

There was a short, angry silence and then Amy said, 'No, they haven't.'

Tamsin glared at her.

'You wouldn't know loyalty if it bit you on the nose—'

'And you—' Amy began. There was the sound of a key in the lock of the front door, and then it opened, paused, and slammed shut.

They froze. Chrissie's heels came down the hall and she opened the kitchen door. She looked terrible, weary and washed out. She blinked at the four of them.

'What's going on? What are you doing?'

Sue made an odd little gesture.

'Plotting, babe.'

'Plotting?' Chrissie went over to the table and put her bag down. 'What are you plotting?'

'Well,' Sue said slowly, fixing each girl's gaze in turn, 'we were plotting what to do about all those clothes upstairs. How to help you. How to find a suitable home for a cupboardful of terrible tuxedos.' She paused. Then she said, 'Weren't we, girls?'

Amy lay on her bed, her phone with the dolphin tag in her hand. Nobody had rung her all evening. Nobody had rung her yesterday either. Her friends weren't ringing because she, Amy, couldn't join in the required hysteria about the imminent exams. She'd wanted to, she'd tried to, goodness knows she was nervous enough about them, but somehow they couldn't get to her the way the other stuff did, they couldn't seem, as they plainly seemed to all her friends as well as to a lot of the staff at school, like the only thing in the world that mattered, or would ever matter. They loomed ahead of her in a menacing and unavoidable way that she really hated, but they still couldn't compare with everything else, not least because, if she made her mind stop jumping about and settle down, she could tell herself that the exams would be over in four weeks and Richie's death wouldn't. Ever.

Amy had tried explaining this to friends at school and they had nodded and been sweet and hugged her, but you could see that, in their heart of hearts, in their secret deep selves, they couldn't imagine what it was like to have your father die, because all their fathers were alive, very much so, and mostly a pain because they either didn't live with their mothers any more for one reason or another, or were insanely restrictive about boys and alcohol and, like, *freedom*, for goodness' sake. A dead father wasn't even a romantic concept to them, it was too way out even for fantasy, it was something you hurried over with squeezes and sad eyes and whispered 'Poor babe' before you went back to the familiar mutual agonizing over revision and personal stupidity and boredom and the shackles of adult expectation. Amy couldn't see that these exams might literally spell the end of the *world*, because lousy grades meant no uni, and if there wasn't uni, your father – oh God, Amy, *so* sorry, so *sorry*, Amy – would yell that he'd been right all along about wasting money educating a girl and then your mother— No wonder, Amy thought, they aren't ringing me. I can see it matters, of course I can, but I can't, can't see that it matters all that *much*.

She sighed and reached out to drop the phone on the rug by her bed. It had been another exhausting evening in a long, long sequence of exhausting evenings. She didn't know if Chrissie had believed Sue or not, but they had all trooped up to Chrissie's bedroom, and just opened the cupboards, and looked miserably at Richie's clothes, all dead too now, except for his shoes, which remained painfully alive – and then Dilly had fled from the room, and Tamsin had put an arm round Chrissie and Chrissie had said faintly, 'I still can't do it. I know you mean well, but I can't. Even if I know it will make me feel better, I can't.'

Then she'd gone to have a shower, and Tamsin and Sue and Amy had gone back down to the kitchen, and even Sue had been uncharacteristically subdued, and had almost said sorry for interfering in a family matter, and then she'd muttered something about getting something in for her and Kev's supper and Tamsin had said sharply, 'He'll faint. When did you last get him supper?' and Sue had gone off leaving a jangled atmosphere behind her and nothing, Amy felt, that she and Tamsin could say to each other made anything any better. Tamsin went off to ring Robbie, and Amy looked, rather hopelessly, in the fridge to see what they might have to eat so that Chrissie could come down to a laid table and pans on the hob, but there was nothing there that looked like a real meal to Amy, so she got out cheese and hummus and made a salad, and when Chrissie came down she said tiredly, 'Oh, lovely of you, sweets, but I'm just going to have a mug of soup.'

She'd taken the soup into the sitting room, to drink it in front of the television, and Amy asked Dilly and Tamsin if they wanted supper and they said no in a way that really meant, 'I don't want *that* supper.' So Amy picked wedges of avocado out of the salad she'd made, and collected a satsuma and a bag of crisps and a foil-wrapped chocolate biscuit and went up to her bedroom, and realized with despair that she didn't even feel like playing her flute.

So, here she was on her bed, with her stomach uncomfortably full of ill-assorted things eaten far too fast, and a silent telephone. She wondered if this acute kind of loneliness was part of grief, that the stark fact of being left behind by her father translated into a keen sensation of solitariness, of being, somehow, an outcast. It was all made worse, too, by feeling that she hardly belonged in her own family just now, either. They were, certainly, haphazardly united by the anger of grief so common at a sudden death, but beyond that she couldn't meet them, couldn't make enemies out of Scott and Margaret, couldn't blame them because it was easier to blame them than blame Richie.

Amy sighed, shudderingly. It was perfectly plain that neither she nor the rest of her family could change their profound convictions about justice and injustice, and if sticking to her guns meant that her sisters would scarcely speak to her, she would just have to bear that, however hard it was. And it was hard. It was hard and it was wretchedly alone. She sighed again, and then, with an effort, swung herself upright and off her bed until she was standing on the rug by her telephone.

She looked across the little room. Her laptop was, as usual, on. She crossed the room and sat down in front of it and put her hands on the keys. No point looking at Facebook. Her Facebook account would be as empty of life as her telephone. Maybe a little swoop over Newcastle on Google Earth would make her feel better, maybe she could divert herself by remembering that, even if Richie was dead, what he had left her, deep in her, by virtue of where he had come from was still very much alive. She leaned forward and tapped the keys. It was worth a try.

CHAPTER TWELVE

The carton of sheet music sat on the floor, in Margaret's sitting room. Scott had sent it over in a taxi. Dawson had investigated it in a leisurely way, and had tried sitting on it, but had then retreated to his usual place along the back of the sofa, which was, after all, cushioned, and got the morning sun. Margaret had opened the carton with a kitchen knife, kneeling on the carpet. Then she had turned back the flaps and there, on top, was the familiar – oh, so familiar – cover of 'Chase The Dream', with Richie's blurred photograph on the front against a background of a geometric pattern, printed in aquamarine, with the song's title in black across the top, italic script, and Richie's name at the bottom.

She lifted it out. You didn't get proper, printed, published song sheets like that any more. Everything was virtual, digitalized, ephemeral. You couldn't hold a song in your hands, not unless it was by Sondheim or someone and worth publishing in huge numbers. But Richie's songs, in the early days, came out as sheets at the same time that they came out as records. In that carton lay something that was far more valuable to Margaret than the copyright, which was a stack of these battered paper copies, all the songs that Richie had written in the golden decade before he'd believed – Margaret would never say 'been persuaded': it took two to tango, every time – that going to London would fire him off into some career stratosphere. Those years, the Tynemouth houses, Scott's school success, had produced songs that were right for Richie and, crucially, right for their times. And those songs lay, in their faded physical form, on her sitting-room carpet. It wasn't a carpet Richie had ever trodden on – he had never been to Percy Gardens – but the furniture mostly dated from their time together, and the songs were the essence of those times.

'You might have liked him,' Margaret said to Dawson. 'Except he wouldn't have liked you much. He preferred dogs to cats.'

Dawson yawned.

'It's something to leave behind, isn't it, a box of songs? It's quite something. It's more than I'll do. It's certainly more than you'll do. Though I expect I'll get a little pang when I pass your dish on the floor, after you've gone.'

Dawson closed his eyes. Margaret closed hers too, and sang the first lines of 'Chase The Dream'.

'"When the clouds gather, when the day darkens, when hope's small candle flickers and dies—"'

Dawson flattened his little ears. Margaret opened her eyes.

'"That's when I want you, that's when I need you, that's when I find the dream in your eyes."' She stopped. She said to Dawson, 'Bit soppy for you?' She looked down at the sheet in her hand. 'Never too soppy for me. I can picture him writing it, picking out the melody with his left hand and singing snatches of the words and scribbling them down. It was lovely. They were lovely times. You must be very careful, you know, not to let good memories get poisoned by what comes later.'

She put the song sheet back in the carton and got stiffly to her feet. Better not to remember what those months and years had been like, after Richie left. Better not to recall how desperate she had been, both emotionally and practically, how unreachable poor Scott had been, mute with rage and misery, and twitching himself away from her hands. Better, always, to focus on what saved you, saved you from bitterness and nothingness. She glanced at Dawson.

'We'll have some nice times, with those songs. I'll sing and you can turn your back on me, and then we'll both be happy. I just hope the piano makes Scott a bit happy too, poor boy.'

Scott had asked Margaret to come and see the piano *in situ*. She had bought champagne to take with her and, for some reason which wasn't quite clear to her although the impulse had been strong, flowers. She knew she couldn't put flowers on the piano – Richie had been adamant that nothing should ever, ever be put on the piano – but they could sit on the windowsill near by, and lend an air of celebration as well as compensating for the fact that Scott seemed to feel no need for either blinds or curtains.

She'd gone up in the lift of the Clavering Building with an armful of flowers and the champagne ready-chilled in an insulated bag, and Scott had been on the landing to meet her, looking animated and more than respectable in the trousers from his work suit and a white shirt open at the neck. He'd stepped forward, smiling but not saying anything, and he'd kissed her, and taken the champagne and the flowers, and then he'd gone ahead of her into the flat and just stood there, beaming, so that she could look past him and see the Steinway, shining and solid, sitting there with the view beyond it as if it had never been away.

'Oh, pet,' Margaret said.

'It looks fine,' Scott said, 'doesn't it?'

She nodded.

'It looks—' She stopped. Then she said, 'Have you played it?'

'Oh yes. It needs a tune, after the journey. But I've played it all right.'

Margaret moved down the room.

'What have you played?'

'Bit of Cole Porter. Bit of Sondheim. Bit of Chopin—'

Margaret stopped in front of the piano.

'Chopin? That's ambitious—'

'I didn't,' Scott said, grinning, 'I didn't say I played it well—'

He put the flowers down on the kitchen worktop. He lifted the insulated bag.

'I guess this is champagne?'

'Laurent-Perrier,' Margaret said.

'Wow—'

'Well, if it's good enough for Bernie Harrison, it's good enough for a Steinway, wouldn't you say?'

'Our Steinway.'

Margaret sat down gingerly on the piano stool.

'*Your* Steinway, pet.'

Scott extricated the bottle from the bag.

'I even have champagne flutes.'

'Impressive—'

'They came free with something.'

Margaret put a finger lightly on a white key.

'I'm getting the shivers—'

'Good shivers?' Scott said. He was almost laughing, twisting the cork out of the bottle and letting the champagne foam out and down the sides, over his hand.

'Just shivers,' Margaret said, 'just echoes. Just the past jumping up again like it wasn't over.'

Scott poured champagne into his flutes. He carried them down the room to the piano.

'Don't put them down!' Margaret said sharply.

'Wouldn't dream of it,' Scott said. He handed her a glass. 'What shall we toast?'

Margaret looked doubtful.

'Dad?' Scott said.

'Don't think so, pet.'

'Us? Each other?'

Margaret eyed him.

'That wouldn't suit us either, dear.'

'OK,' Scott said, 'the piano itself, music, the future—'

Margaret gave a little snort.

'Don't get carried away—'

'I feel carried away. I am carried away. I want to be carried away.'

Margaret looked up at him. She took a sip of her champagne without toasting anything.

She said, 'Talking of carried, who paid for the carriage? Who paid for this to come up here?'

Scott hesitated. He looked fixedly at his drink. Then he said, 'I did.'

There was a silence. Margaret looked at him steadily. She took another sip of her drink.

'Why did you do that?'

'I wanted to,' Scott said. 'I needed to.'

'How did you arrange it?'

'Doesn't matter.'

'Who did you speak to?'

'Mam,' Scott said, 'it doesn't matter. It's done, it's sorted and I've got the piano. I couldn't bear to be obliged to them.'

'No,' Margaret said, 'I see that.' She paused, and then she said quietly, 'I wonder how it was, for her, when it went.'

197

Scott moved round behind the piano and leaned against the windowsill, his back to the view.

He said, 'She wasn't there.'

Margaret looked up sharply.

'What?'

'She wasn't there. It went while she was out. They arranged it that way on purpose. She'd gone out with a friend.'

'How do you know all this?'

Scott took a big swallow of champagne.

'Amy told me.'

'Amy—'

'I rang her.'

'Again?'

'Yes,' Scott said, 'I rang her to check she was OK about the piano, that she didn't think I was party to some kind of plot. I rang her to say I wanted to pay for the carriage.' He grinned at his drink. 'She said she thought they'd expect me to do that anyway.'

Margaret gave a second small snort.

'She said she hoped I'd really play it,' Scott said. 'She said she hoped it'd bring me luck. She said—' Scott stopped.

Margaret waited, holding her glass, the finger of her other hand still lightly poised on the piano key.

'What?'

'She said,' Scott said with emphasis, 'she said that one day she hoped she'd hear me play it. She wants, one day, to hear me play the piano. She said so.'

Margaret's finger went down on the middle C.

'And,' Scott said, 'I told her I hoped so too. I told her I'd like her to hear me play. I'd like it.'

'I see.'

Scott put his champagne glass down on the windowsill.

'Move over,' he said to his mother.

'What?'

198

'Move over,' Scott said. 'Make room for me.'

'What are you doing—'

'I'm going to play,' Scott said. 'I'm going to play Dad's piano and you're going to listen to me.'

Margaret moved to the right-hand edge of the piano stool. She felt as she used to feel at the beginning of one of Richie's concerts.

'What are you going to play?'

Scott settled himself. She watched him flex his right foot above the pedals, settle his hands lightly on the keys.

'Gershwin,' he said, '"Rhapsody In Blue". And you can cry if you want to.'

Margaret's throat was full.

'Wouldn't dream of it,' she said.

The door of Richie's practice room was shut. While he was alive, it had never been completely closed except on very rare occasions, because he liked to feel that his playing belonged to all of them, to the whole house; so much so that Chrissie had had to organize insulation for the party wall with the neighbouring house, and have ugly soundproofing tiles fixed to the ceiling. But now the door was firmly shut so that none of them, Chrissie said, would have to see the sharp dents in the carpet where the little wheels on the piano's legs had dug almost through to the canvas.

'It's worse than his shoes,' Chrissie said.

There was a silence when she said this. All the girls felt a different kind of relief once the piano had gone, but it wasn't, plainly, going to be possible to admit to it. Tamsin felt relieved because she might now be able to implement a few plans for the future; Dilly felt relieved because her own part in an alarming plot was over, and Amy felt relieved that justice had been done, and the piano was at last where it was supposed to be.

'I wouldn't expect,' Chrissie said, 'any of you to feel like I do.'

When she had come home, after her expedition with Sue, which had produced nothing except an abortive conversation about what work avenues Chrissie might explore next, she had found Tamsin and Dilly waiting tensely in the kitchen with the kettle on, and the corkscrew ready (which would she be in the mood for?) and Amy sitting cross-legged on the empty space of dented carpet where the piano had once been.

'I didn't want,' Amy had said unhappily, 'for there to be nothing here when you came back.'

Chrissie had been quite silent. She stood in the door-way of the practice room holding her bag and her keys, and she looked at Amy, and then she looked all round the room, very slowly, as if she was checking to see what else was missing, and then she said, 'Did Sue know too?'

Amy nodded.

'Get up,' Chrissie said.

Amy got to her feet. Chrissie stepped forward and took her arm and pulled her out into the hall. Then she closed the door of the practice room, and propelled Amy down the hall to the kitchen.

Tamsin and Dilly were both there, both standing. Even Tamsin looked slightly scared. She opened her mouth to say, 'Glass of wine, Mum?' but nothing happened.

Chrissie let go of Amy and put her bag and her keys on the table. Then she said, 'I suppose this is the same impulse that makes you want me to clear out his clothes.'

'We want to *help*,' Tamsin said bravely.

'Yourselves, maybe,' Chrissie said. She sounded bitter.

Dilly said, on a wail, 'I didn't want it to go!'

'You can't do someone's grieving for them,' Chrissie said.

'You can't move someone on at the pace that suits you, not them.'

Amy cleared her throat. She said, 'But if we're going to live together, we count as much as you do. We can't be held back just because you won't move on.'

Tamsin gave a little gasp. Chrissie looked at Amy.

'Is that how you see it?'

'It's how it is,' Amy said. 'I knew you'd take it hard, that's why I sat there. But you could think why we did it, you could try and think sometimes.'

'You have a nerve,' Chrissie said.

Amy said rudely, 'Someone needs nerve round here.'

Chrissie stepped forward with sudden speed, reached out, and slapped her. She used her right hand, and the big ring she was wearing on her third finger caught Amy's cheekbone and left an instant small welt, a little scarlet bar under Amy's left eye. Then Chrissie burst into tears.

Nobody moved. There was a singing silence except for Chrissie's crying. Then Tamsin darted forward and pushed Amy down the kitchen to the sink and turned the cold tap on.

'Ice is better,' Dilly said faintly. She moved towards the fridge and then Chrissie sprang after her, pushing her out of the way, and clawing to get ice cubes. She ran unsteadily, still sobbing and sniffing, down the kitchen, bundling ice cubes clumsily into a disposable cloth. She held it unsteadily against Amy's face.

'Sorry, oh sorry, so sorry, darling, so—'

'It's OK,' Amy said. She stared ahead, not at her mother.

'It's a big deal, the piano,' Tamsin said. She still had an arm round Amy. Amy took the bundle of ice cubes in her own hand, and pressed it to her cheekbone.

'I should never—' Chrissie said, 'I'm so sorry, I'm—'

'We shouldn't have done it!' Dilly cried.

Tamsin glared at her.

'Sue—' Dilly said.

'Don't blame Sue,' Chrissie said. She drooped against the kitchen unit. 'Don't blame anyone.'

'It was Kevin's idea,' Tamsin said.

'What would he know—'

Nobody reacted. Chrissie gave a huge sigh and tore off a length of kitchen paper to blow her nose.

'So it'll be another bill—'

'No,' Amy said. She was still staring ahead, holding the ice cubes to her face. 'No, no bill. He paid for it.'

Chrissie didn't look at her.

'I won't ask how you know.'

Amy removed herself from Tamsin's arm.

'I'm going up to my room.'

Chrissie said, 'I'll find you some arnica.'

'I don't want any arnica.'

'Amy, *please*, let me—'

'I don't want any arnica,' Amy said. 'And I don't want you to say anything else.'

'I'll make some tea,' Dilly said.

Chrissie nodded slowly. She put out a hand to detain Amy, but Amy ducked round it and went down the kitchen, and through the hall, and then they could hear her feet thudding on the stairs.

'What *have* I done?' Chrissie said.

There was another silence. Dilly picked up the kettle, preparatory to filling it. Tamsin took her phone out of her pocket.

'I think,' she said, 'I'll just ring Robbie.'

Later, Dilly took a tray up to Amy's room. She had been in the kitchen on her own for what felt like a lifetime, since Tamsin had gone to meet Robbie and Chrissie had shut herself in the sitting room with her phone and the television. Dilly had heard her on the phone for quite a long time, going on and on about something, probably to Sue, and then she'd come out and made a cup of coffee, and dropped a kiss on Dilly's head, and gone back to the sitting room without speaking. Dilly hadn't dared to speak herself. All the time Chrissie was making coffee she had stared at her laptop screen, stared and stared without really seeing anything, and when Chrissie had kissed her, she hadn't known what to do and had heard herself give a little startled bleat that could have meant anything. And then the sitting-room door had closed again, very firmly, and she could hear the *EastEnders* theme tune, and she thought that she simply had to be with someone else, and not alone in the kitchen with Chrissie shut away and the practice room shut away and this terrible sense that everything was now in free fall.

So she put random things on a tray, pieces of fruit, and pots of this and that, and some sliced bread still in its bag, and added a carton of juice and some glasses, and tiptoed stealthily past the sitting-room door and up the stairs to the top floor.

Amy was playing her flute. It was something Dilly recognized and couldn't name, something she knew Amy had learned from her James Galway CD. Amy was playing it well, Dilly could tell that, playing it with absorption and concentration. Dilly put the tray down on the landing and opened her own door. In a drawer in her desk was a box of chocolate-covered almonds a girl on her course had given her in order to stop her eating them herself. Dilly took them out of the drawer and added them to the tray. The addition went a little way towards Dilly's incoherent but definite feeling that she wanted to do something to assuage the slap.

Amy finished playing her piece. Dilly counted to ten. Then she knocked on Amy's door.

'Yes?' Amy said. She did not sound helpful.

Dilly opened the door and stooped to pick up the tray.

'What's that?' Amy said.

'Supper. Kind of.'

'Did Mum send you?'

'No,' Dilly said. 'Would she have sent all this?'

Amy looked at the tray.

'Thanks, Dill.'

'I couldn't stand it down there,' Dilly said. She peered at Amy. 'How's your face?'

'The ice did it. Mostly. I don't want to talk about it.'

'Nor me,' Dilly said.

'I keep thinking,' Amy said, 'that it can't get worse, and then it does.'

Dilly put the tray down on the floor.

'Craig says—'

'Craig says—' Amy mimicked.

'If you're going to be a bitch,' Dilly said, 'I'm leaving.'

'Sorry—'

'Don't take it out on me. I brought you supper.'

'Sorry, Dill.'

Dilly knelt down beside the tray.

'I didn't bring any plates. I don't really want to go back down. And I forgot knives and stuff.'

Amy knelt too.

'Doesn't matter. What does Craig say?'

Dilly looked obstinate.

'Dill,' Amy said, 'please. What does Craig say?'

'That when people do your head in, mostly you can't do anything about it except put yourself out of their reach.'

Amy took a slice of bread out of the packet.

'What if you live in the same house as them?'

'He does,' Dilly said. 'He lives with his mum's boyfriend. He can't stand him. That's why he's out all the time.'

Amy sighed. She tore a strip off the bread slice and dipped it into a pot of salsa.

'It isn't that I can't stand Mum. It's that I can't get her to see that not everyone thinks like her.'

Dilly picked up a banana, and put it down again.

'I suppose no one else is in her position. I mean, I suppose she's responsible for us now. I can't wait for this course to be over so I can get a job.'

Amy said, with her mouth full, 'You are so lucky.'

'I'm scared,' Dilly said. She put a grape in her mouth. 'I want it to happen, but I don't know how I'm going to do it. I don't know how you do it, jobs and flats and things.'

'Won't Craig help?'

There was a short pause and then Dilly said, 'No.'

'Dill—'

'I'm trying,' Dilly said, 'not to need him. Not to – lean on him.'

'Dill, has he—'

'No,' Dilly said, 'he's still my boyfriend. But I know him better than I did. You can't make people what they aren't.'

'Oh God,' Amy said. She put her bread down and reached to take Dilly's arm. 'Are you OK?'

'No,' Dilly said, 'not about anything. But at least I'm not pretending.' She looked at Amy. 'I want Dad back.'

'Don't—'

'He'd know what to do.'

'No,' Amy said quietly, 'he wouldn't.' She removed her arm and picked up her bread. 'He'd know how to cheer us up, but he wouldn't know what to *do*. He relied on Mum for that, and now she doesn't know what to do. At least you know what you're going to do, even if it scares you.'

'Yes,' Dilly said. She picked up the banana again and a slice of bread and climbed off the floor and onto Amy's bed. She settled herself against the pillows. Amy watched while she carefully peeled the banana and rolled the slice of bread round it.

'Banana sandwich,' Dilly said.

'I've made up my mind,' Amy said.

Dilly took a bite.

'About what?'

'I'm not doing these frigging exams.'

'Amy!'

'I'm not. It's pointless. Music and Spanish and English lit. What's the use of any of it? It's just playing. I can't bear to be playing. I'm going to leave school and get a job and stop feeling so helpless.'

Dilly put her banana roll down.

'Amy, you *can't*. Mum'll *flip*.'

'She's flipped already.'

'No, I mean, seriously flip. It'll finish her. You're the cleverest. Dad always said so. Anyway, what about uni? You've always wanted to go to uni. Dad was thrilled you wanted to, he was really chuffed, wasn't he? He kept saying, over and over, that at least one of us took after Mum in the brains department.'

'Well,' Amy said, 'I'll use my brain differently. I'll get a job where they'll train me. I'll work for Marks & Spencer.'

'You are eighteen years old.'

'Loads of people leave school at sixteen. I don't want to go to uni.'

Dilly said severely, 'You don't know what you want.'

'I do!' Amy said fiercely. 'I do! I want all this to stop, I want all this drifting and not deciding and crying and being upset all the time to stop. I want to stop being treated like a child, I want to be in charge of my own life and make my own decisions. There is no use in doing A levels. A levels are for people who can afford to do them, and I can't any more.'

'You're overreacting,' Dilly said.

'*You're* a fine one to talk—'

'We haven't run out of money, we aren't desperate—'

'We soon will be,' Amy said.

Dilly looked up at the ceiling.

'Mum's going to sell the house.'

'I know.'

'There'll be some money when she sells the house.'

'She'll have to buy something else,' Amy said. 'She hasn't found a job yet. I don't think she's in a fit state to find a job.'

Dilly rolled on her side and looked at her sister.

'How will you tell her?'

'I don't know. I haven't thought that far. Don't say anything.'

'I won't—'

'Don't say anything to Tam, either.'

'Amy,' Dilly said, 'just think about it. Grade eight music. A level music. All that Spanish. Just throw it all over to wipe tables in a coffee place?'

Amy looked defiant. She reached out to pick up Dilly's banana roll, and took a bite. Round it, she said carelessly, 'Sounds OK to me.'

There was a muffled thud from downstairs, and then another. Dilly sat bolt upright.

'What's that?'

Amy put the banana down.

'Mum—'

They struggled to their feet and made for the door.

'Oh God—'

'I'll go first,' Amy said. 'Follow me. Come with me.'

It was quiet on the landing. Amy called, 'Mum?'

There was another thud, more muted. And then a small clatter.

'Mum?'

'I'm here,' Chrissie called.

They started down the stairs.

'Where—'

'Here,' she said. She sounded exhausted.

They reached the first-floor landing. Chrissie's bedroom door was open, and out of it spilled heaps and piles of clothes, still on their hangers, jackets and trousers and suits. Richie's clothes.

The girls stared.

'Mum, what are you doing?'

Chrissie was still in the clothes she had been wearing when she went out with Sue, still in her gold necklaces, still in her high-heeled boots. She had scraped her hair back into a ponytail and there were dark shadows under her eyes.

'What do you think I'm doing?'

'But—'

'I'm moving Dad's clothes out. I'm emptying the cupboards in my bedroom of Dad's clothes.'

'But not now, Mum, not tonight—'

'Why not tonight?'

'Because it's late, because you're tired, because we'll help you—'

Chrissie waved an arm towards the sliding heaps of clothes.

'I've done it. Can't you see? I've done it. You can help me take it all downstairs if you want to, but I've done it.'

They were silent. They stood, Dilly slightly behind Amy, and looked at the chaos of garments and hangers. Amy said brokenly, 'Oh Mum—'

Chrissie turned sharply to look at her.

'Well,' she demanded. 'Well? It's what you wanted, isn't it? It's what you wanted me to do?'

CHAPTER THIRTEEN

Beside the street-door release button in Margaret Rossiter's office in Front Street was a small screen which showed, in fish-eye distortion, the face of the person speaking into the intercom. Margaret had had the screen installed to reassure Glenda, who, in the early days of her employment at the agency, had been convinced that she might, inadvertently, let someone into the premises whom she did not recognize, and who had no business to be there. Even with the screen, Glenda was inclined, when alone in the office, to go down to the street door to let visitors in in person, rather than risk them coming in unsupervised, and failing to secure the door behind them. It also seemed to Glenda that the casualness of buzzing someone into a building electronically from the first floor was rude, especially when, to her considerable alarm, she saw that the face on the screen, his mouth looming cartoon-large, belonged to Bernie Harrison.

'One moment, Mr Harrison,' Glenda said, and fled downstairs to the street door, wishing that she had, at six-thirty that morning, obeyed a frivolous impulse to put on her new cardigan.

Bernie Harrison was smiling. He looked entirely unsurprised to see Glenda.

'Bet you didn't expect to see *me*?'

Glenda held the door a little wider. Bernie Harrison wore grey flannels and a soft tweed jacket and a tie. When she left home that morning, Barry was engaged in his usual angry independent battle to get dressed, in tracksuit bottoms and a sweatshirt and a fleece gilet, none of them in coordinating colours.

'No, Mr Harrison,' Glenda said.

'May I come in?'

Glenda stood back against the wall of the narrow hallway to let him pass.

'Mrs Rossiter isn't here—'

Bernie began to climb the stairs with a purposeful tread.

'Glenda, I know Mrs Rossiter isn't here. I know Mrs Rossiter has a meeting in the city this morning. I have come to see *you*.'

Glenda closed the street door in silence. Then she followed Bernie Harrison up the stairs and into the main office, where he was already standing, and looking about him with an air that Glenda felt was improperly assessing. She folded her hands in front of her.

'Can I get you anything, Mr Harrison? Tea? Or coffee?'

'Nothing, thank you.' He beamed at her. 'You don't think I should be here, Glenda, do you?'

She raised her chin a little. She said primly, 'I'm not in the habit of doing anything behind Mrs Rossiter's back.'

He laughed. Glenda did not join in. He crossed the room and sat down in the chair by the window that Margaret used when she had papers to read for a meeting, because the light was good.

'Won't you sit down?'

'No, thank you, Mr Harrison.'

'I shan't stay long,' Bernie said. 'I can see you won't let me stay long, anyway.' He leaned forward. 'I think you know pretty much everything that goes on in this office.'

Glenda said nothing. She stood where she had halted, a few feet inside the door, with her hands clasped in front of her.

'You will therefore know,' Bernie Harrison said, 'that I made Mrs Rossiter an offer recently.'

Glenda gave the most imperceptible of nods.

'Which she turned down.'

Glenda raised her chin a little further, so that she could look past Bernie Harrison and out through the venetian blinds to parallel slits of cloud-streaked sky above the roofs of the buildings opposite.

'Have you,' Bernie said, 'any idea why she turned me down?'

Glenda took a breath. Margaret would expect her to be discreet, but she would not expect her to be either dumb or insolent.

'I think it didn't suit her, Mr Harrison. I think what she has here suits her very well.'

'And does it suit you?'

Glenda said in a rush, 'I couldn't wish for better.'

'Are you sure?'

Glenda nodded vehemently.

'So you'd turn down more money and better working conditions and more variety and responsibility in your job?'

'I'd turn anything down,' Glenda said fiercely, 'that didn't involve working for Mrs Rossiter.'

Bernie spread his hands and put on an expression of mock amazement.

'Who said anything about not working for Mrs Rossiter?'

'Mr Harrison, you were hinting—'

'Glenda, whatever I was suggesting to you was in the context of still working for Mrs Rossiter.'

Glenda found that her hands had unclasped themselves and were now gripping her elbows, crossed over her body.

'I don't follow you—'

'Mrs Rossiter turned me down,' Bernie said, 'but that doesn't mean I accepted her refusal. I didn't. I don't. It makes every bit of sense for me to buy up this agency, making Mrs Rossiter my partner with you remaining as her assistant. I'm not giving up. I'm not a man to give up, especially when what I want happens to be good for all concerned into the bargain.'

'So—'

'So I came here to tell you that your job is safe as long as you want it. That your pay would go up – something of a rarity in these dark days, wouldn't you say? – and you'd work in proper offices in Eldon Square with enough colleagues to give you a better social working life.'

Glenda let go of her elbows.

'Couldn't you say all this in front of Mrs Rossiter?'

Bernie Harrison got to his feet.

'Not at the moment. She won't listen to me at the moment. But I think she will in time – I intend she will in time. And when she does—' He stopped and directed another smile right at Glenda, like a spotlight. 'I want you to remember this conversation.'

'Very well, Mr Harrison.'

'I'll see myself out, then.'

'No,' Glenda said, 'I'll see you out. That way, I can make sure the street door is really shut.'

Bernie leaned forward. He gave Glenda a wink.

'*Behind* me?' he said.

Margaret took the metro back to Tynemouth from Monument station. She had walked from her meeting to Monument through the Central Arcade because she always liked, for professional as well as sentimental reasons, to pause by J. G. Windows to check out the sheet music, and the instruments. The instruments never failed to excite her, never had, since that first day she and Richie had gone in as teenagers and had stood in front of the guitar that he longed for, and couldn't afford, and he'd said daft teenage things like, 'One day, I'll be able to afford all the guitars I want,' and she'd said, 'Course you will,' because when you're fifteen the promise of the future has as much reality as the present. Then there'd been a time when Richie had had his own section there, his own bin of sheet music, his racks of records, then tapes, then CDs. Even now, some of the assistants still knew her, even if now they knew her more because of her local clients than because of Richie. Going into J. G. Windows always gave Margaret a visceral jolt, as if reminding her of the fundamental reason that she did what she did instead of working, as she had for so many years, for a solicitor whose clients all lived within ten miles of his practice.

On her way out of the instrument department, she passed a tall, cylindrical glass display case. It was a case she had passed hundreds of times before but which was noticeable on this occasion because a mother and daughter were having an argument in front of it. The case was full of flutes, displayed upright, on perspex stands, and in the centre was a pink Yamaha flute with a price ticket attached to it which read '£469'.

'Then I won't frigging play at all!' The daughter was shouting.

Margaret looked at the mother. She did not appear to be the kind of mother to give in, or to be embarrassed by the ranting going on beside her.

'There's that new Trevor James,' the mother said, 'Three hundred and ninety-nine pounds. Or the Buffet at three hundred and forty-nine pounds. I'm not going above four hundred.'

The daughter collapsed against the display case. She said aggrievedly, 'I want a pink one.'

'Why?' Margaret said.

Neither mother nor daughter seemed at all disconcerted at the intervention. The daughter squirmed slightly.

'I like pink—'

'How old are you?'

'Twelve.'

'What grade?'

The daughter said nothing.

The mother said, 'Answer the lady, Lorraine.'

'Four,' Lorraine said sulkily.

'I've been in the music business,' Margaret said, 'for three times as long as you've been alive. And I can tell you that the Buffet is good value and all you need for grade four.'

'There,' the mother said.

'It's a lovely instrument, the flute,' Margaret said. 'You should be proud to play it. Not everyone can. You need a good sound, not a colour. It isn't a *handbag*.' She glanced at the mother. 'You stand firm, pet.'

The mother was looking back at the case of flutes.

'It's my life's work, trying to be firm,' she said.

Later, on the train, speeding home through Byker and Walker and Wallsend, Margaret thought about the episode with the flute, and how Scott would have told her that, even if she was the generation she was and proud to be a plain-speaking Northerner, she shouldn't have interfered. And thinking of Scott made her think, in turn, of the piano, and then the piano led to thoughts of the family who had had the piano and how they must be feeling, and of the girl in that family, that foreign London family, who played the flute and who had said to Scott – boldly, in Margaret's view

– that one day she would like to hear him play. That girl, that Amy, would be grade seven or eight by now, eight if she'd inherited anything of Richie's aptitude, she'd be playing the Bach Sonatas, and Vivaldi, she wouldn't be whining on about wanting a flute the colour of candyfloss. And yet it was good that Lorraine was playing anything at all, even if it was only because her mother made her, just as Margaret's mother, hardened by never knowing any indulgence in her own childhood, had made Margaret and her sister learn the survival skills that would mean they would never be doomed for lack of a basic competence. Margaret hadn't filleted a fish in years, but she could still do it, in her sleep.

At Tynemouth metro station, Margaret helped a girl, struggling with a baby in a buggy, out of the train. The girl was luscious, with long blonde hair pinned carelessly up and a T-shirt which read, 'Your boyfriend wants me.' The baby was neatly dressed and was clutching a plastic Spiderman and a packet of crisps.

'Ta,' the girl said. She slid a hand inside the neck of her T-shirt to adjust a bra strap, and Margaret, recalling the little episode by the case of flutes, refrained from saying that she'd have been happier to see the baby with a banana. When she was that girl's age, she thought, she and Richie were going to the Rex Cinema together, where what went on in the back row wasn't something you'd have told your mother about, but equally wasn't what would have resulted in a baby.

'You take care,' Margaret said.

The girl laughed. She had wonderful teeth too, as well as the skin and the hair. She couldn't have been much more than eighteen. She gestured at the baby.

'Bit late for that!'

At Porter's Coffee House at the back of the station, Margaret bought a cup of coffee, and took it to a table by the wall, below a poster advertising the Greek God Cabaret

Show, '£29 a head, girls' night out, to include hunky male hen party attendant and the country's most exciting drag queens'. She felt no disapproval. In North Shields, when she was growing up, there'd been ninety-six pubs within a single mile, and for every miner killed in the local coal mines, four fishermen were lost at sea. 'The sea has no conscience,' people used to say, in that world of her childhood when it seemed impossible that the seas would ever run out of fish and that women like Margaret's mother would look to a life other than that spent stooped on the windswept quays, gutting and salting the herrings and packing them into the wooden casks that Margaret still saw now, occasionally, in people's front gardens, planted up with lobelias. There was a statue of a fishwife in North Shields, outside the library, but Margaret didn't like it. It seemed to her folksy and patronizing. Her mother, she was sure, would have wanted to take an axe to it.

She finished her coffee and stood up. She was lucky to have Glenda in the office, she was lucky to have someone so reliable and conscientious who was not averse to detail and repetition. All the same she knew that, when she was out of the office, Glenda was waiting for her in a way she never felt that Dawson troubled to at home, and the knowledge chafed at her very slightly and drove her to linger on her way back in a manner her rational self could neither admire nor condone. If only, she thought suddenly and urgently, if only I had something new to go back to, something energetic, something that gave me a bit of a lift, if only Scott would do something like – like, find a girl and have a baby.

In the office, Glenda was standing by the open metal filing cabinet where the clients' contracts were kept, rifling through files.

'I was beginning to worry,' Glenda said. 'You said you'd be back by eleven-fifteen and it's after twelve.'

'I stopped for coffee,' Margaret said.

'I'd have made you coffee—'

Margaret took no notice. She moved behind her desk to look at her computer screen.

'Any calls?'

Glenda said nonchalantly, 'Mr Harrison came.'

'Did he now.'

'To see me.'

'Has he offered you a job?' Margaret said, still looking at her screen.

Glenda allowed a small offended silence to settle between them.

'Or did he,' Margaret said, 'encourage you to work on changing my mind?'

Glenda slammed the filing drawer shut.

'It's a good offer.'

Margaret looked up. She watched Glenda walk back to her desk, and sit down, and open the folder she had taken from the filing cabinet. Then she said, 'Do you want me to take it?'

Glenda said crossly, 'It's not up to me and well you know it.'

Margaret moved out from behind her desk and came to stand in the line of Glenda's vision.

'What is it, dear?'

Glenda shook her head and made an angry, incoherent little sound.

'What?' Margaret said.

Glenda said, still crossly, 'He unsettled me—'

'In what way?'

'Well,' Glenda said, 'while he was here, I just thought what cheek, coming here when he knew you were out, and chatting me up, telling me what I could have if we worked with him, the money and the chances and things, and then after he'd gone I just felt flat, I just felt he'd taken something away with him and I could have cried, really I could. The thing is—' She stopped.

'The thing is?'

'I don't want to moan,' Glenda said, 'you know I don't. You know how I feel about my family. The children are lovely. And Barry . . . well, Barry does his best, I don't know how I'd be, stuck in a wheelchair all my life. But after Mr Harrison had gone, I felt something had gone with him. I can't explain it, I just felt I'd let a chance go, and I wouldn't get it back again.'

Margaret waited a few seconds, and then she said, 'What chance?'

Glenda looked at the contract file on her desk.

'You'll think me silly—'

'I won't—'

'You—'

'What chance, Glenda?'

Glenda didn't raise her eyes. She said quietly, 'The chance for something to *happen*.'

Margaret said nothing. Then she came round Glenda's desk, and touched her shoulder briefly.

'Me too,' Margaret said.

Scott had started to ask people from work back to his flat, to hear him play the piano. Once a week or so, he'd say casually to Henry or Adrian, 'Fancy a singsong at mine Friday?' and the word would get round, and eight or ten people would gather in his flat and order in pizzas, and sometimes they'd sing – Henry did a brilliant version of Noël Coward – and sometimes Scott would play something classical, and they'd pile on the sofa or lie about on the floor and just listen, and after they'd gone, Scott would be conscious of having made a brief connection, through the music, which left him feeling curiously isolated and empty when it was over. And it was in one of those post-playing moods, closing the piano lid, picking up the pizza boxes, carrying the ashtrays – disdainfully – to the bin, that an impulse to ring Amy came upon him.

It was not a new impulse. He had, when the piano first arrived, thought he might ring to say that it was safely in Newcastle. Then he had thought that texting would be better – polite, but more casual. So he had composed a text, and deleted it, and then a second, less brief one, and deleted that, and realized that he would rather like to hear her vocal response to his description of where the piano now was. But his nerve had failed him. There was no real reason, if he was honest, to ring her – unless, of course, he admitted to the real reason, which was that he didn't want the piano's arrival in Newcastle to mean that there was no further excuse for them to be in touch with one another. She was only his half-sister, after all, and there wasn't any comfortable shared history between them, but even the scrappy communications that they'd had had given him a sense of how much better furnished he felt to know that there was a sister there – even, potentially, three sisters – and how very much he did not want to return to the state of being the only son of a single mother; he did not, emphatically, want his human landscape to shrink again.

He dialled Amy's number with quick, jabbing movements, not stopping to think what he was going to say. She didn't answer, and he listened to her rapid, awkward little message and then he said, with a flash of inspiration, 'Hi, it's Scott, just ringing to wish you luck,' and, as an afterthought, before this burst of courage failed him, 'Ring me.' Then he put his phone on the piano, and sat down on the stool and began to play the theme from *The Lion King*, which someone had asked for earlier that evening, and which was running in his head with an insistence that was, he knew, the mark of a successful show tune.

His phone rang. Amy.

'Amy,' he said.

'Hi.'

'Sorry to ring so late—'

'I wasn't asleep,' she said. 'I was doing stuff.'

'I'm sitting at the piano,' Scott said.

'Are you?'

He shifted the phone to his left ear and hunched his shoulder to hold it in place.

'Playing this.' He played a few bars. 'Recognize it?'

'*The Lion King*,' Amy said.

Scott was smiling. 'Yes. *The Lion King*. I rang to wish you luck.'

'What for?'

'Your exams. Aren't you about to start your exams?'

'No,' Amy said.

'Oh, I thought—'

'The exams are starting,' Amy said, 'but I'm not doing them.'

Scott waited. He took his right hand off the keyboard and retrieved his phone. Then he cleared his throat.

'Come again?'

'A levels start this week,' Amy said. 'Spanish literature and music theory. But I shan't be doing them.'

'Why not?'

There was a silence.

'Why not?' Scott said again.

'Because,' Amy said, 'I need to get a job.'

'Do you?'

'Yes,' she said. 'I've got to stop being a kid, a schoolgirl, I've got to get out there and do something and earn some money, because—' She stopped.

'Because?'

'Doesn't matter.'

'Maybe I can guess—'

'Because,' Amy said angrily, 'it's all in meltdown here, and I can't go on pretending anything is how it was and that I can be sort of protected from it. I've got to do something.'

'Like not sit your exams.'

'Yes.'

'Have you told your teachers?'

'I haven't told anyone,' Amy said, 'I just won't turn up. I'll pretend I'm going to school, but I won't. I'll be finding a job instead.'

'What kind of job?'

'Anything,' Amy said. 'Waiting tables, putting leaflets through letterboxes, I don't care.'

Scott stood up. He walked to the window and looked at his dark and glittering view.

'Amy?'

'Yes.'

'Are you listening to me?'

'Yes—'

'Do not,' Scott said, 'be so bloody stupid.'

'I didn't ask for your opinion—'

'This isn't an opinion,' Scott said. He found he had straightened his shoulders. 'This is an order. I am telling you not to be such a complete and utter idiot. I am telling you to get into that school and do those exams to the best of your ability and to do yourself and all of us proud. I am *telling* you.'

There was a pause, and then Amy said, 'Oh.'

'Did you hear me? Did you actually *hear* what I *said*?'

Amy made a small unintelligible noise.

'You're a clever girl,' Scott said. 'You're a talented girl. You are eighteen years old with your life before you, and you may *not* give up just because there are some short-term problems you don't like the look of. I won't have it. I won't *have* you throwing your chances away, wasting your opportunities. Is that clear?'

Amy said faintly, 'You've no right—'

'I have!' Scott shouted. 'I have! I'm your brother! I'm your *older brother.*'

'Wow,' Amy said. There was a hint of admiration in her voice.

'Any more of this,' Scott said, slightly more calmly, 'and I shall come down to London and frogmarch you into that school personally.'

'I haven't done enough revision—'

'Nobody's ever done enough revision.'

Amy sounded imminently tearful. She said, 'I can't change now, I've made up my mind, I can't—'

'Don't snivel,' Scott said. 'You can. You will.'

'There isn't enough money—'

'There isn't enough money for you to bugger up your own chances.'

Amy said in a whisper, sniffing, 'It's awful here.'

'And you think it's a good idea to make it worse?'

'I wouldn't—'

'You think your mother would thank you giving up your future for a minimum-wage job washing pots in a café?'

'She—'

'Don't be daft,' Scott said, interrupting. 'Don't fool yourself. Giving up's never the best way out of anything. I should know.'

'I wish I hadn't told you,' Amy said.

Scott laughed. 'Do you?'

'I'm scared—'

'Course you are. Exams are hideous.'

'I wish,' Amy said suddenly, 'I wish I had something to

look forward to, I wish it wasn't just all this unravelling, all this uncertainty.'

Scott's gaze was resting on the great gleaming curve of the Sage Centre, across the river, its shining flank visible through the girders of the Tyne Bridge. He said thoughtfully, 'I'll give you something.'

'What?'

'I'll give you something to look forward to. Well, maybe looking forward is a bit strong, but something to think about, something a bit different.'

'What?' Amy said again.

'When your exams are done,' Scott said, 'when you're in that time after exams and you're waiting for the results and trying not to think about them, why don't you come up here?'

'Come—'

'Yes,' Scott said. 'Pack your flute and I'll give you the train ticket, and you come to Newcastle. I'll show you where Dad lived, when he was a kid. I'll show you where he came from. Tell your mother, so it's all above board, and come up to Newcastle next month.'

There was a silence. Scott wondered if he could hear Amy breathing, or whether he just imagined he could. He pressed the phone to his ear and began to count. When he got to ten, he would say her name again. One, two, three, four—

'OK,' Amy said.

CHAPTER FOURTEEN

The flat was on the top two floors of a tall house close to Highgate School. The rooms were small, with thin walls and creaky floorboards, but there were spectacular views eastwards, over a dramatically sloping garden, and the rolling roofscape of London all the way to the hazy blue lines of Essex. The owner of the house, a television producer, lived half his life in Los Angeles, and wanted a tenant who would be there permanently, paying the mortgage and justifying the investment in a building whose owner only occupied it for half the year.

Sue had found the flat. Or rather, Sue's Kevin had found it while commissioning a new boiler his firm had put in for the owner. The owner happened to be there, a tall, bespectacled man with long grey hair, in a black T-shirt, and they had fallen into conversation while contemplating the boiler – 'These new systems mean you can control the therms on your rads from here,' Kevin explained – and the owner had mentioned that the top floors of the house were empty, and self-contained, and that he was looking for a tenant.

'As you're local,' he said to Kevin, making it sound like a social condition, rather than a category, 'you might know of someone.'

The rooms, apart from a cooker and a fridge and two aggressively modern chairs upholstered in leather, were empty. They were painted white and carpeted with narrow grey-and-black stripes, like the stripes of an expensive carrier bag. Chrissie looked round with the apprehension born of being confronted with something completely alien.

'I haven't lived in a flat since I met Richie—'

'Look,' Sue said, 'it's been weeks, months now. Richie didn't die yesterday. You are still waiting for probate. You can't do anything major till then but you *can* start moving yourself.'

She was not going to be roused. She had said to Kevin that morning, drinking tea in the kitchen while he packed his customary lunch of carbohydrate and sugar, that she'd accompany Chrissie to the flat in the spirit of friendship but that she was not, *not*, going to involve herself in anything emotional again. If Chrissie threw a fit and said she couldn't contemplate living anywhere like that, Sue would just let her throw it.

'I've done enough, and look where the last lot got me. I'll show her and that's that.'

Kevin came round the kitchen table, his canvas bag on his shoulder, and kissed her goodbye on the mouth. It was something she could always say for Kevin – he always kissed her hello and goodbye and he always kissed her on the mouth.

'Good luck,' he said.

'D'you think I shouldn't be bothering?'

He considered for a second, then he said, 'A mate's a mate,' and kissed her again, and she felt the brief glow of being approved of. Now, standing watching Chrissie trying to imagine herself in the flat's sitting room with its uncompromising decor and wonderful view, she tried to recall that sensation of doing the right – but still the sensible – thing.

'It's so different,' Chrissie said.

'Course it is.'

'I don't know about renting—'

Sue leaned against a wall and folded her arms. She said patiently, 'We discussed that.'

'I know—'

'We discussed releasing all the capital in the house, and using the interest from investing that, to rent for a year or so until you've got your breath back.'

'Tamsin says it's such a bad time to sell—'

Sue looked at the ceiling.

'It's going to be a bad time for a while. Waiting isn't going to help. And you can't afford to stay.'

Chrissie said nothing and then Sue said, in the same voice but a little slower, 'You can't afford to stay.'

Chrissie crossed the room to look out of the window. The house was on the edge of such a precipitous slope that it felt like being in a tower, with the ground falling away so steeply below her. It felt improbable, completely improbable, the idea of living here, coupled with the idea of *not* living in the house with her little office, and the sitting-room window that jammed no matter how often the cords and weights were adjusted, and her bedroom with its cupboards and adjacent bathroom, and intimate knowledge of the way the light came in round the curtains in the morning. The sense of alarming unreality that had possessed her, on and off but more on than off, since Richie died seemed to have found its physical embodiment in this flat, and the prospect of living here.

'Suppose,' she said, not turning, still gazing out eastwards, 'suppose I take it and find I can't stand it?'

Sue imagined Kevin listening to her. He'd be eating a cheese-and-pickle sandwich (white bread only) right now.

She said levelly, 'Then you move.'

'But—'

'You take it for six months, and if you can't stand it, you move.'

'It would just be me and Dilly and Amy.'

'Would it?'

Chrissie turned.

'Tamsin's been talking about moving in with Robbie for ages. Now she's going to do it. Robbie has a flat in Archway.' She smiled weakly. 'He's going to build a cupboard for her clothes. Sweet, really.'

'Yeah,' Sue said. Domestically considerate men, in her view, lacked sex appeal. She suppressed a small yawn. 'Tam's left before, though.'

'She came back—'

'As I recall it,' Sue said, 'Richie wanted her back and he got his way.'

'Maybe—'

'You didn't want her back, Chris,' Sue said. 'You thought it was time one of them showed a bit of independence. You thought Richie babied them.'

'He did,' Chrissie said fondly.

'And look what that's landed you with. It's good that Tamsin's making a move. Even if it would be better that she was doing it for herself rather than exchanging one support system for another.'

Chrissie said, nettled, 'And when did you last live on your own?'

Sue took her shoulder away from the wall, and hitched her bag higher.

'I was on my own for eight years before Kev. But that's not the point. The point is you and your future and what you can afford. You can't stay in the house – bad – but you can stay in Highgate – good. You can't have all your children here – bad – but you can have two out of three – good. You can't afford the house – bad – but you could afford this flat with ace views and a civilized landlord – good to very good. Shall we just start from there?'

Chrissie walked past her and began to climb the stairs to the top floor and the bedrooms.

'Dilly won't be with me long, she says—'

Sue sighed. She followed Chrissie up the stairs.

'There'll still be Amy—'

Chrissie was standing in the doorway of one of the bedrooms.

'This is pretty small for Amy.'

'It's as big as the bedroom she has now.'

'I don't think so.'

'I'm not arguing,' Sue said, 'I'm saving my energy to argue exclusively about the big stuff.'

Chrissie ran a hand down one wall, as if it were an animal.

'Amy's been so sweet—'

'Has she?'

'That day,' Chrissie said, 'that day when I completely lost it and chucked all his clothes on the landing, she was so sweet. Poor Dilly didn't know what to do, she just stood there, looking petrified, but Amy didn't seem scared, which was amazing when you think how I'd managed to scare myself.'

Sue came into the room.

'What did she do?'

'She gave me a hug,' Chrissie said, 'she hugged me. Then she pushed me back to the bed and told me just to stay there and then she picked up all the clothes, very calmly, hanger by hanger, and put them back in the cupboards, exactly where they'd been. And she made Dilly do it too. She sort of talked her through it and I just sat there and watched them until everything was back and the doors were shut. And then she took my hand and led me downstairs and made tea and toast and all the time she was just quietly talking, about nothing very much, as if I was a dog or something that had been frightened. It was amazing.'

'Well done Amy,' Sue said. She looked round the room. 'She'll probably be the same about this, you know. She'll probably be amazing about this too.'

Chrissie closed her eyes briefly.

'I just wish I could be too.'

'Well,' Sue said, 'you'll have to work at it.'

Chrissie turned to look at her.

'What's the *matter* with me?'

Sue shrugged. The morning had gone on long enough, as had going round in unproductive circles.

'Shock,' she said tiredly. 'Grief. Disappointment. Anger. To name but a few.'

Chrissie came to stand close to her.

'Sorry.'

'Please don't—'

'I hate not being able to decide, I'm used to being able to decide—'

Sue leaned towards her and gave her cheek a quick kiss.

'I'm going to leave you to do just that.'

'Please—'

She made for the door.

'You'll be better on your own. And I must run.'

Chrissie said nothing. She heard Sue's booted feet going rapidly and resolutely down the stairs, and then the sound of the flat's front door opening and shutting decisively. She went slowly over to the window and looked once more at the view. Their house had no view, only the prospect into the street one way and the garden – not of great interest to either her or Richie, ever – the other. She wasn't used to views. She gazed out at the improbable distances. She wasn't, she told herself, used to any of this. And that was the problem.

*   *   *

229

Amy had put flowers on the kitchen table. They weren't much, just the ones the guy with a stall by the tube station let her have, as the last, slightly squashed bunches in the bucket, for fifty pence. They were those Peruvian lily things, with spotted throats to their petals, which made them look slightly exotic, and they were a gloomy purplish red and the flower guy said give them some warm water and a bit of sugar, or an aspirin, and they'll perk up. Amy had dissolved a sugar cube in water in the blue jug with cream spots that she knew Chrissie liked, and stuck the lilies in there. They still looked sad, and sort of gawky, so she took them out again, and chopped off a length of stalk and picked off all the floppy leaves, and put them back again. They looked better, but still not right. Maybe flower arranging was like hair plaiting, something that some people could make look really cool without even trying, and other people just couldn't. Whatever, the table looked better for having flowers on it, and not just papers and jars of peanut butter and the cables for Dilly's laptop.

When Chrissie came in, she looked at the flowers, and the mugs Amy had put out, and the milk in a jug rather than in its carton and she said, 'What's all this about?'

Amy was filling the kettle. She said, without turning, 'Just felt like it.'

Chrissie put her bag on the kitchen worktop.

'How was today?'

'OK.'

'How was the exam?'

'Didn't have one today,' Amy said. She plugged in the kettle and switched it on. 'Music theory tomorrow. Revision today. Revision, revision, revision.'

Chrissie was looking through her post. She said absently, 'But worth it.'

Amy let a pause fall, and then she said, 'You?'

Chrissie glanced up.

'Me?'

'Your day OK?'

'I don't know. I really don't know—'

Amy took the Earl Grey tea caddy out of the cupboard.

'Another interview?'

'No,' Chrissie said. She put her letters down. 'No. A flat.'

'Oh,' Amy said.

Chrissie came to stand close to her. She watched her detach a couple of tea bags from the clump in the box and drop them into the teapot.

'I'm afraid,' Chrissie said, 'we can't stay here.'

'I know.'

'And I don't want to buy anything just now.'

'I know,' Amy said, 'I know all this. You've said so. We all know we can't stay here, we've known for ages.'

'I'm finding it hard, deciding—'

The kettle gave a small scream as it came to the boil, and switched itself off.

'Where's the flat?'

'Almost in the Village. Up by the school.'

'Cool—'

'It's a flat, Amy. A rented flat. The rooms are small and everything feels very thin and fragile. It's the top two floors of a house. You can see practically to the sea.'

Amy poured water on top of the tea bags.

'Did you take it?'

'Course not,' Chrissie said. She sounded faintly shocked. 'I wouldn't take it without you seeing it. You and Dilly.'

Amy opened her mouth to say, 'We'll be fine, we won't be there much anyway,' and thought better of it. Instead, she said, 'Did you like it?'

'Darling, at the moment, I don't know *what* I like.'

Amy carried the teapot across to the table. Maybe the

flowers were beginning to look a shade more energized by their sugar. She said, 'Sit down.'

'Thank you, darling.'

'Is it cheap?'

'Is what cheap?'

'The flat.'

'Not particularly,' Chrissie said, 'but if we sell this even halfway reasonably, that'll help.'

'Good, then.'

Chrissie looked at her. She was pouring tea. She had left her hair loose, and it had swung round her face, obscuring it.

'Aren't you interested?' Chrissie said.

Amy hooked one side of her hair behind an ear.

'Kind of.'

'Don't you care where we live? Doesn't your home matter to you?'

'Course—'

'It doesn't,' Chrissie said, 'sound much like it.'

'If you're OK with where we live,' Amy said, 'I'll be OK. So will Dill.'

'I'm not sure I can choose alone—'

'Why not?' Amy said. 'You always have.'

'Ouch—'

'Well, you have. You said, and then Dad and us did it.'

Chrissie picked up the milk jug.

'Maybe,' she said carefully, 'I'm trying not to be so bossy.'

Amy pushed a mug towards her.

'Does that mean we all get a bit of say-so?'

'Well, I'd like you to have an opinion about this flat—'

'I mean, about more than the flat. About what we want ourselves and stuff—'

'I – well, I suppose so.'

'Good,' Amy said with emphasis.

Chrissie looked sharply at her.

'What is all this about? What are you asking?'

Amy bent over her tea mug, cradling it between her palms.

'Well, I'm not exactly *asking*—' She stopped. Chrissie waited. Then Amy said, 'I've been asked to go up to Newcastle when the exams are over. I've been invited. To see where Dad grew up. And things.'

There was a silence. Chrissie picked up her mug, drank, and put it down again. She looked at the flowers. Then she looked at Amy.

'Who invited you?'

'Scott,' Amy said. She was sitting up very straight now, her hair tucked behind her ears.

'When did you speak to him?'

'He left a message,' Amy said, 'to wish me luck in the exams, and so I rang him back, and he was playing the piano and he said he'd send me the train ticket to come up to see the places Dad knew. And see the piano. Where it is now. And I said yes.'

'You said you would go—'

'Yes,' Amy said, 'I said yes, I'll come.'

Chrissie took another swallow of tea.

'This – is very hard.'

'I'm not going for ever. I'm going for a few days.'

'Where will you stay?'

Amy said, 'In his flat, I should think.'

'I don't think you *can* stay in his flat—'

'Where I stay,' Amy said, 'is a detail. The point is, I'm going. I'm going to Newcastle.'

'You realize—'

'*Yes*,' Amy said. She sounded as if she was reining in considerable impatience. 'Yes, I realize this is awful for you, but this has nothing to do with my loyalty to you, that's a given, that's there whatever happens, but I really, *really* want to see where Dad came from, where half of me comes from. Can't you just try and understand that?'

Chrissie closed her eyes.

'I am trying—'

'OK.'

'Those people—'

'Don't call them that,' Amy said sharply.

'You might like it up there—'

Amy sighed. She put a hand out and squeezed Chrissie's arm.

'Yes, I might. But I'm your daughter and I grew up *here*.'

Chrissie gave herself a shake.

'I know.' She glanced at Amy. 'I never thought you'd want to.'

'That's unfair—'

'Is it?'

'Yes,' Amy said, 'you know it is.'

'Darling, it's just that I—'

Amy put her hands over her ears.

'Sorry, Mum, but don't say it. Don't say it again. We know how it is for you. It isn't much of a picnic for us either.'

'No.'

'OK, then?'

'About Newcastle?'

'Yes.'

Chrissie said reluctantly, 'I suppose so.'

'Good,' Amy said. She picked up her tea mug. 'Because I'm going, anyway.'

Sitting on the tube on the way back from college, Dilly read Craig's text probably twenty-five times.

'Sorry babe,' it started, and then, without any punctuation, it went on, 'sorry cant do friday sorry cant do have a nice life,' and two kisses. Of course she knew, at about the second reading, what he was trying to say, trying to tell her, but it wasn't until she read it ten more times, scrolling endlessly back to the beginning, that she allowed herself to realize that she was, unceremoniously, being dumped. That Craig, lazy, undependable, fanciable Craig, was taking the ultimately cowardly way out of an unwanted situation and was telling her that their relationship, as far as he was concerned, was over – by text.

Once she had permitted full recognition of both his message and his conduct, Dilly waited to fall to pieces. After all, that is what she did when faced with something unwanted or unexpected, what she had always done, and even if this news was hardly unexpected, it was certainly not what she would have chosen. It was also outrageously humiliating. Dilly sat in her seat between a girl with her MP3 player plugged in and an old man in a fez reading an Arabic newspaper and waited for the full horror of what she had just read to sink right in and reduce her to tears. It didn't happen. She reread the text a few more times and waited a bit longer. Still, nothing happened. She glanced around her and saw that the world she would have assumed to look entirely distorted and unfamiliar through her own shock appeared perfectly normal. She looked down at her phone again. Perhaps she really was in shock, and in a few minutes or hours the reality of what had happened would kick in, and she could react as she usually did with all the attendant panic and sobbing.

She reached Archway station still in one piece, and got off the train. On the way up to the street, she found she had put her phone in her pocket, as if it was a perfectly ordinary day in which she had received perfectly ordinary messages. Once outside, she resisted buying a gossip magazine and a packet of M&Ms – economy, economy – and started to walk up the hill, past the hospital, past the entrance to Waterlow Park, where, on a bench soon after Richie died, Craig had presented her with a pretty – but cheap – bead bracelet, which was, she reflected, about the only thing he had ever given her, towards the estate agent's office where Tamsin worked.

It did not cross her mind that Tamsin might not be there and so she was not in the least surprised to find her behind the reception desk, hair in a neat knot behind her head, being busy in a way peculiar to herself. Dilly put her forearms on the high rim of the desk and leaned forward.

'Hi.'

Tamsin did not take off her telephone headphones. She flicked a glance sideways, towards the big modern clock on the wall.

'Not till half past five—'

Dilly took her phone out of her pocket and held it for Tamsin to see.

'Something to show you—'

'Not now.'

'Tam, it's *important*. It's Craig.'

Tamsin leaned forward.

'I don't care,' she said in a loud whisper, 'if it's Brad Pitt. I am not talking to you till half past five. Ten minutes. Go and sit down.'

Dilly sighed, and put the phone back in her pocket. She trailed across to a pair of red upholstered chairs by a glass table bearing brochures featuring photographs of houses with 'Sold! Sold!' excitably printed across them in scarlet. She sat down and looked about her. There were eight desks that she could see, two occupied, the rest suspiciously tidy. At one of the occupied desks, a young man in a sober suit and an exuberant tie was talking earnestly to a middle-aged couple, who looked as if they were having trouble believing anything he said. Every so often, they looked at each other, as if for reassurance, and when they did that, the young man leaned a little bit further forward and redoubled his exertions. Dilly wondered if the couple were thinking of buying a house or trying to sell one, and then she thought how completely useless Craig would have been in any situation like that, which led to a renewal of her amazement that she hadn't yet wanted to cry. She looked at the clock. Eight minutes left to go. Perhaps when she showed Craig's text to Tamsin she'd want to cry then; perhaps that would be when reality kicked in.

The middle-aged couple got up. The young man rose too and held out his hand to shake theirs in a way that forced them to take it in turn, whatever their inclination. Still talking, he escorted them across the room to the door, and ushered them out. On his way back to his desk, he said loudly to Tamsin, as he passed her, 'Waste of bloody time,' and Dilly heard her laugh. It was weird, hearing her laugh in a work situation. Or maybe it was just weird hearing her laugh at all. There hadn't been much laughing at home lately. Breda, from south of Dublin, on Dilly's course at college, said that there'd been so many jokes after her father died that they'd almost forgotten he wasn't there to share them. Dilly couldn't picture that. Richie had been the one for jokes in their house – too many jokes, Chrissie sometimes said – and when he died, the jokes seemed to die with him. Dilly had managed to laugh a bit with Craig when he fooled about, but that was relief mostly, relief at being with someone not connected to Richie's dying. Would it, she wondered, be a relief to cry now, or was it more of a relief not somehow seeming to want to?

At the two occupied desks, the computers were being shut down. Tamsin took her headphones off and began switching and stacking in a practised manner. A door to an office at the back opened to reveal a middle-aged man in rumpled

shirtsleeves holding a mug in one hand and a mobile telephone
to his ear with the other. He crossed the room, still talking
into his phone, paused by the reception desk to bend and say
something to Tamsin and put his mug down, and then he
retreated to his office at the back and closed the door. Dilly
got up and went over to her sister.

'Who was that?'

Tamsin said, with a hint of satisfaction, 'Mr Mundy.'

'Is he your boss?'

Tamsin looked round the room. The young man and a
middle-aged woman from an adjoining desk were deep in
conversation.

'Tell you later,' Tamsin said.

'What?'

'Shh,' Tamsin said. 'Good news.'

She stood up and smoothed her top down.

'I'll get my jacket.'

Out in the street, Dilly produced her phone again.

'Look at that!'

Tamsin stopped walking and took Dilly's phone.

'What's up?'

A woman banged into them from behind.

'Can't you look where you're bloody going?'

Tamsin took no notice. She stared at Dilly's phone for
several seconds and then she said, 'What a complete jerk.'

'He's dumping me,' Dilly said. 'Isn't he?'

Tamsin nodded slowly. Then she glanced up at Dilly.

'You OK?'

'Well,' Dilly said, 'I seem to be. I don't get it, but I don't
feel anything much yet.'

Tamsin gave a sniff.

'Of course, Robbie never liked him—'

'Dad did.'

'Dad liked anyone who was good company.'

She put an arm round Dilly.

'Poor babe. Poor you. You don't deserve this.'

Dilly said, her face awkwardly against her sister's, 'Should I do anything?'

'Heavens, no,' Tamsin said. 'Good riddance, I'd say. Don't you do a thing.' She took her face and arm away.

Dilly said, 'I don't even know if I'll miss him—'

'Good girl, Dill.'

'But I'll miss having a boyfriend.'

'There'll be others, Dill. There'll be real ones, like Robbie.'

Dilly gave her head a tiny toss.

'I don't want a boyfriend like Robbie.'

'Even when you're down,' Tamsin said sharply, 'you can be such a little cow.'

Dilly took her phone out of Tamsin's hand and began to walk away from her up the hill. Perhaps this was the time, the moment, for the tears to start. Perhaps now, with Tamsin's self-absorption making her such a very unsatisfactory confidante, the usual wave of self-pity would come sweeping in, and she could give in to it, give herself up to it, and arrive home in the state that would at least ensure Chrissie's full attention for a while. She tried visualizing her own situation, her humiliation, her looming loneliness, even the appalling prospect of inadvertently seeing Craig somewhere around, with someone else. She blinked. Her eyes were still dry.

Tamsin caught up with her.

'Dill—'

'What?'

'Sorry,' Tamsin said, 'this is so bad for you, so bad—'

'Yes,' Dilly said. They were negotiating the crossings at the top of Highgate village. 'Yes, it is.'

Tamsin took her arm.

'Will you tell Mum?'

Dilly was amazed.

'Of *course*!'

Tamsin held Dilly's arm a little tighter.

'I've got something to tell Mum too—'

Dilly tried to withdraw her arm.

'About Robbie?'

'Oh no,' Tamsin said. She was smiling. 'Not him. About my job. Mr Mundy told me my job is safe. Quite safe, he said. No more money just now, but more responsibility. He said the partners felt they were lucky to have me.'

Dilly twitched her arm free. She thought of her phone, and its message. She remembered Tamsin in her headphones, being all lah-di-dah and self-important.

She said nastily, 'He just meant cheap at the price,' and then she broke into a run, to get down the hill ahead of Tamsin, to get home first.

She found Chrissie and Amy in the kitchen, looking at pictures on Chrissie's digital camera. The atmosphere was a bit weird and there was a teapot on the table and a jug of sad purple flowers. They both glanced up when she came in, and she was conscious of being breathless and interestingly redolent of drama. She flung her bag on the floor and her sunglasses on the table.

'We were just,' Chrissie said, trying to avoid a reaction to Dilly's entrance, 'looking at pictures of a flat I saw.'

Dilly glanced at the camera. The room it showed could have been anywhere, white and empty with a dark carpet. She said, in a rush, 'You won't believe—'

'What?'

Dilly plunged her hand into her pocket and pulled out her phone, thrusting it at her mother. Chrissie peered at it.

'What does this mean?'

'You look!' Dilly shouted at Amy.

Amy bent over the phone.

'Oh my God—'

'*What?*' Chrissie said.

'Oh my God,' Amy said, 'the shit, the shit, how *could* he?' She launched herself at Dilly, wrapping her arms round her shoulders. Dilly closed her eyes.

'Please,' Chrissie said, '*what* is happening?'

'He's dumped me!' Dilly cried.

'He's—'

'Craig has dumped Dilly!' Amy said. 'He hasn't the nerve to do it to her face so he's sent her this pathetic text!'

Chrissie stood up. She moved to put her arms round Dilly too.

'Oh, darling—'

The front door slammed, and Tamsin appeared in the doorway.

'Don't you want to kill him?' Amy demanded.

'He's not worth it.'

'No, Dill, he's not worth it, he's not worth crying over, not for a second—'

'I'm not crying,' Dilly said.

Chrissie stepped back.

'Nor you are—'

'I want to,' Dilly said, 'I'm waiting to. But I'm not.' She glanced at Tamsin. 'Maybe it's having such a *fantastically* supportive sister.'

Tamsin put her handbag down on the table. It was a habit that had driven Richie wild – 'Put the bloody thing on the *floor*, where it *belongs*!' – but Tamsin had always insisted that her bag sat on the table or hung on a chair.

She said, with the air of being the one person, yet again, in full possession of themselves, 'I am entirely supportive, Dilly, in fact I think you are well rid of him. It's just that, in the present circumstances, it's more useful to focus on the positive and I had, actually, some positive news today because my job is safe. Mr Mundy has confirmed that I'm staying.'

'Oh good,' Chrissie said faintly.

Amy said nothing. She let go of Dilly, just retaining her nearest hand.

Chrissie said, with slightly more energy, 'Well done, darling.'

Tamsin inclined her head.

Dilly glanced at Amy. She said, 'Nothing to worry about any more, then.'

Amy gave her the smallest of winks.

Chrissie picked up the camera. She held it out. She said, half-laughing, 'What a day!'

They all three regarded her in silence.

'First, I may have found a flat!'

Silence.

'Two, Tamsin has her job confirmed!'

Silence.

'Three,' Chrissie said, subduing her artificially affirmative tone, 'Dilly is freed from someone who in no way deserves her—'

The silence was more awkward this time. Chrissie glanced quickly at Amy.

'And four—' She paused, and then she said to Amy, 'You tell them.'

Amy cleared her throat. She let go of Dilly's hand. She said, 'I'm going up to Newcastle for a few days,' and then she stopped, abruptly, as if she had intended to say more, but had thought better of it.

Dilly caught her breath. She looked from her mother to Tamsin and back again, waiting for the explosion. Chrissie was looking at her camera. Tamsin was looking at the floor. She turned her head slowly so that she could see Amy. Amy looked excited. Amy was excited about going to Newcastle, Chrissie was excited about a flat and Tamsin was excited about her job. As far as her family was concerned, Craig's cowardice and betrayal registered right, right down on the scale of things that mattered just now. Out of pure unadulterated temper at her family's failure to pay her the attention that was unquestionably her due, Dilly began to cry.

CHAPTER FIFTEEN

If Margaret was restless, Dawson reacted to her by being particularly inert. He would lengthen himself along the back of the sofa in the bay window of the sitting room and sink into an especially profound languor, only the minuscule movements of his little ears registering that he was aware of her fidgeting round him, endlessly going up and down the stairs, opening and shutting drawers in the kitchen, talking to herself as if she was the only living creature in the house. Only if it got past seven o'clock, and she seemed temporarily absorbed in some area of the house unrelated to his supper, would he lumber down from the cushions to the floor, and position himself somewhere that could not fail to remind her that she had forgotten to feed him. He was even prepared for her to fall over him, literally, if it served his purpose.

This particular evening, seven o'clock had come and gone – gone, it seemed to Dawson, a very long time ago. Margaret had been in the sitting room, then her bedroom, then back in the sitting room, then at her computer, but nowhere near the place where Dawson's box of special cat mix lived, alongside the little square tins of meat that Dawson would have liked every night, but which were only opened occasionally by some arbitrary timetable quite unfathomable to him. He had placed himself in her path at least three times, to no effect, and was now deciding that the last resort had been reached, the completely forbidden resort of vigorously clawing up the new carpet at a particularly vulnerable place where the top step of the stairs met the landing. Margaret shrieked. Dawson stopped clawing. He sat back on his huge haunches and regarded her with his enigmatic yellow gaze.

'You *wretched* cat!'

Dawson stared on, unblinking.

'I've a lot on my mind,' Margaret said furiously. 'Which I realize means nothing to you, since you have so little mind to have anything *on* in the first place.'

Unoffended, Dawson yawned slightly, but did not move.

'And it wouldn't do you any harm to feed off some of that blubber for once either.'

Dawson put out a broad paw, claws half extended, towards the carpet, where shreds of wool he had already raked up lay on the smoothly vacuumed surface.

'All *right*,' Margaret said. 'All *right*.'

He preceded her downstairs at a stately pace, his thick tail held aloft in a gesture of quiet triumph. In the kitchen, he seated himself again, in his accustomed mealtime spot, and waited. He considered a reproachful meow, and decided that it was hardly necessary. She was shaking a generous, impatient amount of his special mixture into his bowl, and it was better not to deflect her. As the bowl descended to the floor, he got to his feet, arched his back and soundlessly opened his little pink mouth.

'There,' Margaret said, 'there. You fat old menace.'

Dawson bent over his dish. He sniffed the contents and then, as if affronted by something quite out of the ordinary about the deeply familiar, turned and padded out of the kitchen. Margaret let out a little cry and kicked his bowl over. Cat biscuits scattered across the floor, far more of them than it seemed possible for one small dish to hold. Dawson appeared briefly back in the doorway, surveyed the scene, and withdrew. Margaret, using words she remembered from the men who frequented the Cabbage Patch in her childhood, went to fetch a dustpan and brush.

It took twenty minutes to sweep every last tiny biscuit, replenish Dawson's bowl and make and drink a steadying cup of tea. On occasions like this, Margaret was relieved to live alone, thankful that there were no witnesses to either her loss of self-possession or her subjection to a cat. Scott would, of course, have laughed at her, and his laughter would have aggravated the agitation she was feeling already on account of the fact that he, Scott, had taken it upon himself to ask this child of Richie's to Newcastle, and to assume, with a casualness no doubt typical of his generation but deeply improper to Margaret, that she, Amy, should stay with him in that unsatisfactory flat in the Clavering Building. When it had been first mooted, Margaret had felt that the plan was bold, but attractively so, with an edge of novelty to it that was very appealing. But when she had had time to consider it, to visualize how it would be to have Amy, Richie's last child, actually, physically there and requiring shelter and conversation and entertainment, she was inexorably over-taken by a profound inner turbulence, a feeling of extreme anxiety and uncertainty, made worse by the fact that Scott found her reaction only funny, and said so.

Attempts to analyse her feelings seemed to lead nowhere. It was as unreasonable to react as she was reacting as it was undeniable. If there was an analogy to her present state of mind, it was how she had felt in those early days of her relationship with Richie, when they were still at school, and later, in the first phase of his fame, when she could not see how the amount of attention he was getting from other girls and women could fail to turn his head. It hadn't, of course; miraculously he had seemed pleased and flattered but fundamentally unaffected for years and years, so that when Chrissie came on the scene Margaret had, for months, been able to dismiss her as yet another adorer who would eventually bounce off Richie's focused professional commitment like a moth off a hot lampshade. There'd been no blinding flash of realization that Chrissie was different, that Chrissie meant to stay, that there was steel inside that sugared-almond exterior. It was more that, as the weeks wore on, and Richie, ever pleasant, ever sliding evasively over anything that threatened to be problematical, grew equally ever more distant, Margaret had gradually realized she was up against something she had never needed to face before. She had, she remembered – and long before the energy of anger kicked in – been sick with fear, simply sick with it. And fear, in a less extreme form, was exactly what she was feeling now at the prospect of having Amy Rossiter to stay in Tynemouth.

Fear, of course, was best dealt with by doing something. Twenty-five years ago, she had confronted Richie and, by so doing, had exchanged the paralysis of fear for the vigour of fury. None of what had then followed had been what she wanted, but at least she had made sure that no one was going to see her as a sad little object of pity, an expendable and outgrown encumbrance tossed aside, as her mother would have said bitterly, like a shilling glove. From the moment she had acknowledged that Richie was indeed going south, and that he meant to start a new life, a new career and, she assumed, a new marriage, in London, she had exerted herself to be robust in the face of this rejection, to assert her validity independent of Richie and all that was attached to him. If anyone felt sorry for Margaret Rossiter she would be obliged, thank you very much, if they kept their pity to themselves.

Which was presumably why, when Glenda had said of Amy's visit, 'Oh, that's a lot to ask of you, isn't it? These young people, they just don't think, do they?' Margaret had reacted by saying stonily, her eyes on the papers she was holding, 'I can't see a problem, Glenda, and I'll thank you not to invent one.'

Glenda had shrugged. Living with Barry had made her an expert reader of nuances of bad temper, and even if she felt it was unfair to be exploited because of it she was confident that she was in no way responsible. She waited an hour, and then she said, conversationally, putting Margaret's coffee cup down on the desk beside her, 'Well, you could always have her to stay at yours.'

Margaret had grunted. She did not look at Glenda, and she did not acknowledge the coffee. If she confided in Glenda, she could not then expect Glenda not to respond in kind, and if the response was of exactly the right and practical sort that she should have thought of herself, then Glenda could hardly be blamed for it. But it was, somehow, difficult to admit to. It was easier, Margaret discovered, to put a box of cream cakes – Glenda's passion – on her desk wordlessly, later in the day, and then go home to telephone Scott, in privacy, and tell him that Amy should stay in Percy Gardens.

'Oh no, she doesn't,' Scott said pleasantly. He was at work still, which always gave him a gratifying sense of being able to master his mother.

'It's not suitable,' Margaret said. 'You may be related but she's only eighteen and you hardly know each other.'

'We know each other better than you and she do—'

'I'm not saying I'm comfortable,' Margaret said. 'I'm not saying I'm easy about her coming. But you've taken it into your head to ask her, and she's said yes, so there we are. But it doesn't look right, her staying with you.'

'*Look?*' Scott said.

'Very well, it *isn't* right. Not a man your age and a girl, like that.'

'I'm sleeping on the sofa,' Scott said. 'There's a bolt on the bathroom door. I'll sleep fully dressed if that makes you feel better.'

'I'm not arguing, Scott—'

'No,' he said, 'nor am I,' and then he said, 'Sorry, Mam, got to go,' and he'd rung off, leaving her standing in her sitting room, holding her phone while Dawson kept a barely discernible eye upon her from the back of the sofa.

Now, two hours later, tea drunk and any kind of supper a pointless prospect, Margaret felt no less wound up, an agitation increased by a strong and maddening sense that her own reactions were the cause, and also not immediately controllable. She did not want Amy in Newcastle – and she was coming. She did not want Amy to stay with Scott – and she was staying there. Margaret put her teacup down with a clatter and, impelled by a sudden impulse, went into the sitting room at speed to find the morocco-bound book in which she listed telephone numbers.

She dialled the number in London rapidly, and then stood, eyes closed, holding her breath, waiting for someone to pick up.

'Hello?' Chrissie said tiredly.

Margaret opened her mouth and paused. She wasn't sure, in that instant, that she had ever, in all those long and complicated years, spoken directly to Chrissie.

'Hello?' Chrissie said again, a little more warily.

'It's Margaret,' Margaret said.

There was a short silence.

'Margaret?'

'Margaret Rossiter,' Margaret said.

'Oh—'

'Am – am I disturbing you?'

'No,' Chrissie said.

'I wanted,' Margaret said, 'I just wanted—' She stopped.

'I don't think,' Chrissie said, 'that we have anything to say to one another. Do you?'

Margaret took a breath. She said, more firmly, 'This is about Amy.'

'Amy?' Chrissie said, her tone sharpening. 'What about Amy?'

'She's coming up to Newcastle—'

'I know that.'

'I wanted – well, I wanted to set your mind at rest. About where she'll be staying.'

There was another pause. It was extremely awkward, and seemed to go on for a long time, so long in fact that Margaret said, 'Can you hear me?'

'Yes.'

'Well,' Margaret said, 'I can imagine how you must be feeling—'

'I doubt it.'

'About Amy coming up here, and I just wanted to reassure you that she'll be staying with me.'

Chrissie gave a little bark of sardonic laughter. '*Reassure* me?'

'You'd rather that,' Margaret said, 'wouldn't you, than that she stays with my son Scott?'

'Oh my God,' Chrissie said.

'I think they were planning—'

'I don't want to know about it,' Chrissie said. 'I don't want to know anything about it.'

'I see,' Margaret said. She was beginning to feel less disconcerted, less wrong-footed. 'I see. But all the same, you'd like to know she'll be safe?'

Chrissie did not reply.

'You'd like to know,' Margaret said, 'that'll she'll be

safe in my guest bedroom while she's in Newcastle?'

'Yes,' Chrissie said stiffly.

Margaret smiled into the receiver.

'That's all I rang for.'

'Yes.'

'To reassure you. That's all I rang for. I'll say goodbye now.'

There was a further silence.

'Goodbye, then,' Margaret said, and returned the phone to its charger.

She looked round the room. Dawson was back in place along the sofa, his eyes almost closed. She felt exhilarated, triumphant, slightly daring. She had put herself back in a place of control, a place from which she could face and deal with things she had no wish to face and deal with. She glanced down at the phone again. Now to ring Scott.

Tamsin said that Mr Mundy himself was going to come and talk to Chrissie about the best way to market the house. She managed to say this in a way that made Chrissie feel both patronized and incompetent, and then she went on to say that she had found an agency called Flying Starts, which specialized in quality second-hand clothes for people involved in performing, in clubs or the theatre or on television, whom she had booked to come and see what might be suitable for their stock in Richie's wardrobe. Then, having delivered both these pieces of decisive information, she had retied her ponytail, picked up her handbag, and gone out to meet Robbie in order to choose doorknobs for the cupboard he was building for her clothes in his flat in Archway.

'I'd quite like glass,' Tamsin said, pulling her hair tight through its black elasticated band, 'as long as it isn't that old-style faceted-crystal stuff.'

Then she'd kissed her mother with the businesslike air of one who has calmly arranged all that needs to be arranged, and swung out of the house, letting the front door slam decisively behind her.

Chrissie picked up her tea mug and walked slowly down the hall from the kitchen. She paused in the doorway to Richie's practice room and surveyed the dented carpet and the crammed shelves and thought to herself that what had once looked like a wounded and violated place now looked merely lifeless and defeated. She went across to the shelves, and pulled out a CD at random, a CD of Tony Bennett's whose cover featured a photograph of him as quite a young man, a big-nosed, languid-looking young man in a suit and tie, sitting casually on the floor of a recording booth, eyes half closed and a score held loosely in one hand. Perhaps he'd been in his thirties then. She'd never known Richie in his thirties. In the 1960s, when the young Tony Bennett was first recording 'I Left My Heart In San Francisco', Richie was in his twenties still, and struggling. By the time Chrissie got to him, he was forty-two, and she was only twenty-three. The age gap had seemed so exciting then, so sexy, she had had such an awareness of herself as young and new and energizing. His being so much older had given her such a supreme sense of being alive. When he died, there were still nineteen years between them, but they were shorter years, somehow. He would, if he'd lived, have been seventy in three years. By which time she, Chrissie, would be fifty-one.

She sighed, and slid Tony Bennett back into his slot on the shelves. He'd been Richie's hero, not just for his singing voice but for his air of easy geniality. Were there times, in the Bennett household in California or wherever it was, when his nonchalant, good-natured charm drove everyone completely insane with irritation and the air was rent with shrieks and screams instead of 'Put On A Happy Face'? Were there times, too, when the very people who'd made the man the star, those thousands and thousands of devoted, emotional, possessive fans, were a scarcely bearable pressure on the man's family, exacerbated by the knowledge that without them the man would be nowhere? Chrissie turned and moved slowly out of the practice room and along to the little room beside the front door that served as her office.

The fans. Her inbox was full of them, hundreds and hundreds of e-mails commiserating and remembering and asking for some kind of memento, some little thing to establish a link, a significance. In the week or two after his death, she had faithfully answered a good many of them, impelled by a brief feeling of sisterhood, united in shock and loss and longing. But as the weeks passed, those feelings of intense empathy had cooled, and become tinged with a distaste that had now blossomed into a full-blown resentment. It was a resentment directed both at these pleading women and Richie, the cause of their neediness, who had whipped up this storm, and then conclusively removed himself, leaving her to confront and cope with what he had left behind.

She sat down in front of her screen. There were three hundred and seventy-four new e-mails from the website she had set up for Richie, and managed for Richie, and shielded Richie from. That was three hundred and seventy-four messages in the last two weeks, because she hadn't checked for a fortnight, hadn't felt she could bear to. Several, she noticed, were from the same person, the kind of people whose lives were lived almost entirely outside their own small reality, and who had no shame in badgering on and on and on until they got a response.

Well, Chrissie thought, there *was* no response. She'd mailed everyone whose address she had after he'd died, and again a few weeks later. There was no more to say, and that was that. Their idol was dead and they would all have to find what solace they could from his music, from what he had left behind. She, Chrissie, was not going to let anyone appoint her keeper of the flame, and to make that perfectly plain she was going to delete the lot of them. She moved the computer mouse slightly on the mouse mat the girls had given her, bearing a picture of their father at the piano, head thrown back, eyes closed, singing, and three clicks later it was done. All gone.

'You do what you have to do,' Sue had said exasperatedly to her the other day, fatigued by her indecisiveness. 'Don't keep asking me. Trust your instincts. You always have, so why change the habits of a lifetime at the very moment things are in free fall?'

Chrissie stood up. She would leave the computer on, and clear more stuff out of it later. She would clear and clear until she could stop seeing Richie only through this thicket of complication and rancour, and could remember something, some small thing, that was of consequence to her alone. Surely that was possible to do? Surely the last few months, and the disappointing years that had preceded them, couldn't entirely obliterate everything of strength and value that had gone before?

She drifted into the sitting room. The girls had virtually stopped using it, had taken to retreating to their rooms with their laptops, or, in Tamsin's case, to the growing alternative domestic allure of Robbie's flat and his appreciation of what he insisted on calling a woman's touch. Only her habitual chair looked inhabited, the cushions still dented from last night's television-watching, the magazines and files piled on the low table in front of it, a single empty wine glass balanced on a book. She would have to take it in hand, she would have to spruce and plump and polish, she would have to buy flowers and candles before the room could be shown to Mr Mundy. If she shrank from the idea of Mr Mundy's appraising eye swivelling round her sitting room, she shrank still more from attempting to tell Tamsin that she would allow it, but not yet. She couldn't keep saying 'Not yet', Sue had told her. Not yet, taken to extremes, was what landed people in places where they had no choices any more. Was that what she wanted? Was it? Did she really want to be the kind of person, in fact, who was unable to stand up to her late husband's first wife in a telephone call, as she was very much afraid she had been?

She put her tea mug down beside the wine glass and made a half-hearted attempt to straighten the cushions in her chair. Once, she'd have done it briskly, late at night, before they went up to bed, so that the sitting room – the whole house, in fact – looked alert and ready to wake up to. Now, although she was trying very hard not to let any standards actually slip, they were muted, they took more effort, there seemed less point in keeping the motor running. She wondered, vaguely, and apropos of nothing she had been preoccupied with before, if losing the business of running Richie had left as disorientating a blank in her life as his death itself had. Who was it, some government minister or someone, who'd said, 'Work is good for you'?

'Mum?' Dilly said from the doorway.

Chrissie gave a little jump.

'Heavens, I thought you were all out—'

'I was upstairs,' Dilly said. 'D'you want a coffee?'

'I've just had tea—'

Dilly looked around the room, as if she was remembering how it was.

'Bit sad in here—'

'I know. Where's Amy?'

Dilly shrugged.

'Dunno.'

'Tamsin's gone to Robbie's.'

'No change there, then—'

'Dilly—' Chrissie said.

Dilly stopped gazing round the room and looked at her mother.

'Dilly,' Chrissie said, 'will you come and look at the flat with me?'

Dilly said reluctantly, 'Why me?'

'Tamsin's usually at Robbie's. Amy's going – well, you know where Amy's going. And I don't want to do this alone, I don't, I really don't.'

She paused. Dilly had bent her head so that her pale hair had fallen forward to obscure her face.

'Please,' Chrissie said, 'please come with me. Please – help me?'

There was a long silence. Then Dilly tossed her hair back and began to smooth it into a bunch. She smiled at her mother wanly.

'Why not?'

Scott was humming. He'd put one volume of Rod Stewart's *American Songbook* into his CD player and he was singing along to it. He'd opened the windows in his flat and hung his stripped-off duvet over the sill, as he'd once seen done in a Swiss village, on the only school trip he'd ever been on, when they'd been supposed to ski, but he and his gang had gone tobogganing instead, on plastic sledges, on snow packed as hard as stone. The village had been half modern blocks of flats and half little chalets varnished the colour of caramel, with shutters and incredibly regimented log piles, and over the balconies of these chalets, in the bright, cold morning air, people hung quilts and bolsters, creating nursery-rhyme images of tidy housewifery and goose-feather beds. So now, in honour of Amy's coming, Scott was airing his own duvet in full optimistic view of the trains trundling over the Tyne Bridge.

Also in her honour, he had bought new bedlinen. It had taken him a whole Saturday morning to choose, wanting to make some effort but not too much, and he had come away with a set in grey-and-white striped cotton, which, he hoped, looked androgynous enough not to embarrass either of them. He had also bought new towels, and a bottle of pale-green liquid handwash and a raft of cans of Diet Coke. All the girls in his office drank Diet Coke when they were having a brief respite from coffee and alcohol. If Amy didn't drink it, the girls in the office would, after she'd gone, but at this moment Scott wasn't dwelling on after she'd gone. He was revelling instead in her coming.

His high spirits had even carried him clean through a potentially enraging call from his mother. She'd rung the evening after his bedlinen expedition to say, with undisguised triumph, that she had spoken to Amy's mother – '*What?*' Scott had shouted – and it was agreed that Amy should stay, in perfect propriety, in Percy Gardens.

'You *spoke* to her?'

'I did,' Margaret said. Her voice was full of satisfaction.

'Well,' Scott said, 'I have to hand it to you. I really do, Mother.'

'Thank you.'

'So, it's all arranged—'

'Yes,' Margaret said. 'I'm sorry to disappoint you, pet, but I'm sure you'll see it's for the best.'

'Well,' Scott said casually, 'it's not for long—'

'Four nights.'

'Oh no,' Scott said, 'just three.'

'You said four nights—'

'Did I? I don't think so. Don't want to overdo it, the first time.'

257

'Four nights,' Margaret said firmly. 'Thursday to Monday. Four nights.'

'We changed it,' Scott said.

'You changed it?'

'Yup,' he said. 'We changed it. I've sent her the tickets.'

'It's hardly,' Margaret said, 'worth her coming for three nights—'

'It's what she wanted.'

'I'm not at all sure—'

'It's arranged. It's done. It's sorted. You'll see her on Sunday. I'll bring her out to Tynemouth on Sunday.'

'Scott,' Margaret said. Her tone was suspicious. 'Scott. Are you telling me the truth?'

He looked down at the new bedlinen, lying pristine in its shining packets, on his black sofa. He smiled into the telephone.

'Course I am,' he said to Margaret. 'Course I am! Why would I lie to you about a thing like that?'

CHAPTER SIXTEEN

Francis Leverton approved of his daughter-in-law. Miriam was not only good-looking, and had produced two little boys in five years, but she was a woman of competence and flair who shared Francis's view that a great deal more might be made out of Mark than he might manage if left entirely to his own devices. They had never gone so far as to discuss Mark and his possibilities – and failings – openly, but a tacit understanding existed between them that sometimes the way forward for Mark had to be – tactfully, of course – pointed out to him; especially if it was a situation in which his natural warmth of heart might influence matters in a way not beneficial to either the firm or the family.

Such a situation had arisen over Chrissie Rossiter – or, as Francis Leverton firmly called her, Chrissie Kelsey. Richie Rossiter had been a fixture in Francis's household for years, on account of his wife and her sisters being ardent fans, and full of a proprietorial pride that he had lived in the same London postcode as they did. When Richie died, the Leverton family had been shocked and full of sympathy for the widow and her daughters, and then the subsequent revelation that Chrissie was in fact the mother of Richie's second family had slightly tempered the sympathy.

So when Mark arrived home, a little late, for Friday-night dinner and found his parents as well as his wife and her brother and his wife waiting for him, and explained why he had been delayed, his father had reacted by saying, in his measured, paternalistic way, that lawyers were not counsellors and that he, Mark, must endeavour not to confuse a natural human compassion with such professional help as was appropriate to give, and duly recompensed for. Francis then glanced at Miriam for support. Miriam, however, was not in the mood for complicity. She was preoccupied with the chicken she had prepared being up to her mother-in-law's exacting standards, and also, in this case, aware that one of the elements that made Mark, in her view, a much more satisfactory husband than her father-in-law would have been was both his warmth of heart and his preparedness to blur boundaries and challenge codes of conduct if the habits of a lifetime seemed to him to have become no more than habits. So she picked up her fork, and smiled at her father-in-law and said she was sure he was right but that there wasn't, was there, a universal solution to all the arbitrary human problems that Mark had to deal with every day.

Mark had been amazed. He was used to confronting Miriam and his father together, and to acknowledging, often reluctantly, that he might have – yet again – allowed his heart to rule his head. But here she was, at his own dining table, standing up for him, and to his own father. He shot her a look of pure gratitude, and adjusted his shirt cuffs so that she could see he was wearing the Tiffany links she had given him. She, in turn, smiled steadily at his father.

It was a long evening. Francis had needed to dominate the proceedings by way of recompense for Miriam's defection, and had prolonged the prayers and rituals to a stately degree. He had also talked at length – at great length – about the value of professional distance from personal dilemma, and Miriam's sister-in-law, who had grown up in a very liberal household where Friday nights were casually observed, if at all, grew visibly restive and began, with increasing obviousness, to attract her husband's attention.

'It's the babysitter—'

Miriam kissed her father-in-law very warmly as he was leaving, and squeezed his arm.

'Lovely dinner, dear,' her mother-in-law said, 'but I prefer not to put thyme with the chicken.'

In the kitchen, among the dirty plates and glasses, Mark put his arms round his wife.

'What was all that about?' he murmured into her hair.

She gave a little shrug.

'I just felt sorry for her. For Chrissie whatsit.'

'Not for me?'

'No,' she said, 'I'm on your side anyway, aren't I? Who's she got on her side, I wonder?'

Mark took his arms away. He said, 'Mum's hard on her, I think. Imagine Mum, who's got a mind and a temper of her own, ever getting my father to do one single thing he didn't want to do.'

'Exactly.'

'She was so pathetic,' Mark said, 'sitting there with her coffee. I mean she's a successful woman, she's a good-looking, capable woman, she kept that man making money for them all, all these years, and now the whole house of cards has just fallen in, and he even made sure she didn't get the piano. How can you not feel sorry for her?'

Miriam was stacking plates in the dishwasher.

'Nobody's asking you not to. I'm certainly not.'

'I told her to sell the house and get a job. Any job. Not necessarily anything to do with what she did before.'

'Well,' Miriam said, straightening up, 'that seems sensible.

261

Not hearts and flowers, just sensible.' Then she looked at him directly. 'And I don't see why you shouldn't help her, if anything comes your way with a job, I mean.'

'Really?'

'This is the modern world,' Miriam said. 'We do things differently now.' She leaned across and gave him a quick kiss. 'No disrespect to your father. Of course.'

Since that dinner, there'd been no word from Chrissie Kelsey. By making discreet enquiries, Mark learned that the house in Highgate was on the market, but that the proceeds which would remain after the mortgage was paid off would probably not be sufficient to buy anything else of any size, and that Chrissie was looking at flats to rent. She had not, as far as he could gather, found any work, and he conjectured that she must be living on whatever meagre bits and pieces of income and royalties remained from Richie's career, supplemented by credit. Mark did not like credit. In that, he was completely at one with his father.

He supposed that Chrissie's plight had caught his attention – as, to a lesser degree, it had caught Miriam's – because it was such a peculiarly modern dilemma. A working woman, a professionally working woman of over two decades' worth of experience, was the victim of a law that still required people to be married if the maximum amount of tax exemption was to be granted to them. As a lawyer, he saw the anomaly. As a man, he felt it keenly. It was no good talking darkly, as his mother and aunts now did, about Chrissie as some sort of sexual predator who had snatched Richie from a happy and satisfying marriage in the North, causing grief all round and gratification to no one but herself. Richie had been a middle-aged man, not an impressionable boy, and was, therefore, in Mark's view, even more responsible than the girl he'd left his wife for. And that girl had, up to a point, achieved a large measure of what she'd promised him. He'd sung on national television, he'd sung at the London Palladium, he'd sung in front of (minor) royalty. But he'd held back somewhere. He'd elected to come south, to set up house with her, to father babies by her, but he'd never quite completed the journey, he'd never stopped occasionally looking back over his shoulder. And because of that reluctance to commit fully, because of his always keeping the chink of an option open, Chrissie now found herself more helpless than she had probably ever been, even as a teenager, and strangely, given her experience, unqualified to find a place any longer in the only world she knew.

'You can't be her knight in shining armour,' Miriam said. 'And you mustn't patronize her. You'll just have to wait.' She'd turned her wedding ring round on her finger. 'Maybe one good thing to come out of all this is my not taking you so much for granted.'

In a roundabout way, it was his father who moved things forward. Apart from Andrew Carnegie's dictum, the other saying dear to his father's heart was 'Fortune favours the prepared mind.' Francis prided himself on having a mind open to all and any opportunity, and never to have missed a chance of being the son his father would have been proud of, the son who had been instrumental in taking the firm from its solid but small beginnings to its present size. He also never missed a chance of impressing on Mark the need to have an alert mind, a mind primed and open, and because, just now, Mark's mind was frequently preoccupied with Chrissie's situation, and the numbers of modern women who must find themselves in a similar difficulty, it seemed quite easy to come, suddenly, to an idea for a solution, while exchanging his customary few words with the receptionist on his way into work.

'Good morning, Teresa.'

She flashed him her automatic smile.

'Morning, Mr Mark.'

'Everything all right, Teresa?'

She gave a little shrug.

'As it will ever be, Mr Mark. You know how it is.'

Mark waited a moment, standing quite still, his laptop case in his hand.

'How is it?'

Teresa had pushed her spectacles up on her severely coiffed dark head. She moved them down, now, on to her nose, and gave a little whinny of laughter.

'You don't want to bother with my troubles, Mr Mark—'

Mark put his case down.

'I do. What's the matter?'

Teresa sighed. Then she looked directly at Mark through her uncompromising modern spectacles and said, 'It's my partner. He's bought a business in Canada.'

'Canada?'

'Edmonton,' Teresa said. She looked down at her desk. 'He wants us to go and live in Edmonton. *Edmonton.* I ask you.'

The kitchen table was almost covered with bottles and jars and ripped-open packets. Chrissie, wearing a plastic apron patterned with huge and improbably shiny fruit over her clothes, was methodically emptying the enormous fridge-freezer that Richie had persuaded her into buying, only eight months ago, because he said that the girls would be so thrilled to have a dispenser in the door of a fridge that would, at the touch of a button, produce ice cubes, crushed ice or chilled water.

At this moment, the fridge-freezer represented a bitter condensation of everything that Chrissie feared about the present and resented about the past. Monumental and gleaming, disgorging an apparently endless amount of part-eaten things, extravagantly inessential things, outdated things and plain rubbish – how did a packet of strawberry-flavoured jelly shoelaces ever get in there? – the fridge seemed to Chrissie nothing but a stern reproach for years of rampant folly, which in retrospect looked both repellent and inexcusable. The jars of American-imported dill pickles, of French artisan mayonnaise, of Swiss jam made from organically grown black cherries, made her feel like weeping with rage and regret. Especially as Richie, who never drank chilled water and disliked ice in his whisky, would have ignored everything in the fridge except basics like milk and butter. She looked, with a kind of disgusted despair, at the outdated jar of black-truffle sauce in her hand. What had she been doing? Richie and the girls only ever ate ketchup. Who had it all been *for*?

'Yikes,' Amy said.

She stood in the kitchen doorway, an untidy sheaf of notes on A4 paper held against her with one arm, a mug in her other hand.

Chrissie put the jar down with a bang, beside a box of eggs and a small irregular lump of something in a tired plastic wrapper.

'We are eating everything I can salvage out of this, *everything*, before I buy one more slice of bread.'

Amy advanced to the table and surveyed everything on it. She put her mug down in the chaos and picked up the lump.

'What's this?'

'Cheese?'

Amy gave a tentative squeeze.

'Too squashy.'

'Old cheese,' Chrissie said.

Amy raised her arm and threw the lump in the direction of the bin.

'Chuck.'

'Don't chuck anything,' Chrissie said, 'without showing me first.'

Amy glanced back at the table.

'This is gross—'

'Yes,' Chrissie said, 'I agree. It is gross. The possession of it, especially in current circumstances, is gross. But we are not wasting it. We can't.'

'Maybe,' Amy said unwisely, 'when I get back, it'll all be gone.'

There was an abrupt and eloquent silence. Chrissie stood by the fridge, staring inside. Amy went across the kitchen, with as much insouciance as she could manage, and switched the kettle on.

Chrissie said, 'Did you check it had water in it?'

Amy sighed. She switched the kettle off, put her papers down, carried the kettle to the sink, filled it, brought it back and switched it on again. Then she said, 'It's no good pretending I'm not going.'

Chrissie put a sliding pile of opened packets of delicatessen meats on the table.

'No danger of *that*.'

Amy waited. She looked down at her notes. Spanish quotations, her favourites underlined in red. Revision was hateful, but Spanish was, all the same, a satisfactory language to declaim out loud.

'She rang me,' Chrissie said.

Amy went back to the table to find her mug.

'Tea?'

'Did you hear me?'

'Yes. Tea?'

'No, thank you,' Chrissie said. 'She rang me to tell me that I wasn't to worry about your staying improperly in her son's flat, because you won't be, you'll be staying with her.'

Amy got a box of tea bags out of the cupboard.

'She's called Margaret. He's called Scott.'

Chrissie was silent.

'It's nothing to do with her,' Amy said.

'She thinks it is.'

'Well,' Amy said, pouring boiling water into her mug, 'don't worry, anyway. I'll do what suits me.'

'You may well not have a choice. Just as I don't seem to have.'

Amy carried her mug down the kitchen to the sink. She said, staring out into the neglected garden, 'I'm not going for them, Mum. I told you. I'm going to see where Dad grew up, I'm going to see where half of me comes from.'

'I know, Amy, I know it's what you think will—'

'I don't want to discuss it!' Amy shouted. 'I don't want to talk about it any more! I've got an exam tomorrow, and one on Thursday, and then I'm free and I'm going to Newcastle, and nothing is going to change that!'

Chrissie folded her arms and stared at the ceiling.

'Just be grateful,' Amy said, angrily but less loudly, 'just be thankful I'm not partying after, like everyone I know. Partying and talking to anyone and everyone.'

'Talking? What's wrong with that?'

'Oh my God,' Amy said witheringly. 'Oh please. D'you really think that party means party and talk means talk?'

Chrissie transferred her gaze to Amy's face.

'What does it mean then?'

Amy walked past her, carrying her mug of tea. In the doorway, she paused and said, with emphasis, 'Kissing.'

Chrissie gave a little jump. Amy said dangerously, 'So I'll be better off in Newcastle, don't you think?' and then the telephone rang. Amy waited, holding her quotations and her tea.

'Hello?' Chrissie said and then, with a smile of sudden relief, 'Mr Leverton. Mark. How—'

She paused, and then she turned her back on Amy as if the call was private, and walked slowly down the kitchen, away from her.

Amy watched. Mr Leverton only ever meant bad news, surprises of an unexpected and upsetting kind. Why was Chrissie's voice so warm, speaking to him, her body language so weirdly relieved, holding the phone as if it was a lifeline?

'Oh,' Chrissie said, her voice startled, but not displeased. 'Oh. Well, it's really kind—'

She stopped. Then, with her free hand, she untied the tapes of the plastic apron and pulled it off over her head.

'Of course I will. Yes, I'll talk to them. I'll think—'

She dropped the apron over the nearest chair back.

'I don't want,' she said, 'you to think I'm ungrateful. I'm not. I'm really grateful. It's very kind—'

She stopped again and pulled the band off her hair and shook it free.

'Thank you,' Chrissie said. 'Thank you very much. Yes, I'll think about it. I'll get back to you. Thank you.'

She took the phone away from her ear and stood there, her back to Amy, staring down the kitchen.

Amy took a hot swallow of tea, and coughed.

'*What*?' Amy said.

Robbie had built Tamsin a clothes cupboard precisely to her specifications. It filled in the space between the chimney breast (defunct) in his bedroom and the outside wall of the building, and it was fitted with sliding shelves, hanging rails and ingenious shoe trees which occupied the floor space like a row of regimented lollipops. Robbie, who preferred dark colours and matt surfaces, would have liked to paint it in a colour that blended with the brown-leather headboard of which he was so proud, but Tamsin wanted something more feminine, just as she wanted new fabrics which would ameliorate, rather than accentuate, the brown-leather headboard. The new clothes cupboard had, accordingly, been painted a pale peppermint green, and the door handles were small glass globes patterned with raised green spots. On the bed, spread out, was a set of new curtains in white, with a delicate floral design in pink and cream with green leaves.

Tamsin said she was thrilled with the cupboard. She was standing in front of it, a hand holding either open door, admiring the automatic light, the pristine interior, the long mirror Robbie had fixed inside the right-hand door. He waited for a moment, watching her reaction, allowing himself to revel in having both satisfied himself and her, and then he moved behind her, put his arms around her waist, and tucked his chin into the angle of her neck.

'No excuses now,' Robbie said.

Tamsin stiffened, very slightly. She had been planning, in a sudden, abstract kind of way, where she might put her handbags.

'What?'

'You've got your cupboard,' Robbie said. 'You can move your stuff in. No reason not to.'

Tamsin put one hand up against his face, and then took it away again.

'I love my cupboard.'

'Good.'

'It's a real *Sex and the City* closet.'

'Good.'

Tamsin put her hands on Robbie's linked arms and freed herself.

'I am going to—'

Robbie caught her arm.

'When?'

'Soon.'

Robbie let go of her, and sat on the edge of the bed.

'Tam, you've said that for months. Months. Now your house is on the market, you've got your cupboard, you're redesigning my life. What are you waiting for?'

Tamsin turned round. She looked out of the window, and then back at Robbie. She said, 'Mum's been offered a job.'

'Great!'

Tamsin began to pull her hair tighter into its ponytail.

'I don't know.'

'What don't you know?'

'It's not a very good job—'

'What is it?'

'It's a receptionist.'

Robbie waited a moment. He tried not to be distracted by the implications of having her standing there, in his bedroom, in front of the cupboard he had designed and made for her.

He said, 'But you're a receptionist.'

'Yes,' Tamsin said.

'But—'

'What would Dad think?' Tamsin said. 'What would Dad think to have Mum working for less than she's worth, as a receptionist?'

Robbie thought. His memory of Richie was of a genial, hospitable man who lived for his girls and his particular kind of music. His mother had been a fan of Richie Rossiter, and that had meant he was pretty daunted when he first went round to meet him. But in the flesh, Richie wasn't daunting. Richie was easy, unaffected and friendly. He was, if Robbie had to admit it, one of the least snobbish people Robbie had ever met, and a great deal less snobbish than his own parents, who still took an embarrassing pride in the fact that he went to work in a suit.

'It's a chain-store suit,' he'd say to his mother. 'It's not exactly Savile Row.'

'I think,' he said now to Tamsin, 'that he wouldn't give a toss.'

Tamsin folded her arms. Then she unfolded them and smoothed down her immaculate cotton sweater.

'What?' Robbie said.

Tamsin shook her head mutely.

'It may not be worth much,' Robbie said, 'but with you here, and Dilly working, it's better money than nothing. Isn't it?'

'Maybe,' Tamsin said.

'Don't you want her to work?'

'Yes—'

'Tamsin?'

'What—'

'Don't you want her to do what you do?'

'It upsets things,' Tamsin said. 'It doesn't feel right.'

Robbie reached out and took her nearest hand. He adopted the tone his father used when his mother was being unreasonable, an affectionate but slightly teasing tone.

'Hey, Tam, you're the practical one, you're the one trying to move things on—'

She didn't look at him.

'Only in the *right* way.'

'Which is?'

'Something managerial. Like she's always had. I mean, this isn't exactly aspirational, is it? She says it's all she can get right now, and any job is to be welcomed at the moment, but I think she should go on looking. I mean, is she taking this just because Mr Leverton's been kind to her?'

Robbie stood up. He took her other hand as well.

'What do your sisters think?'

Tamsin gave a little snort.

'What suits them, of course.'

Robbie waited a moment, then he dropped Tamsin's hands and put his arms around her once more. He rested his cheek against the side of her head, and his gaze on the peppermint-green cupboard, mentally filling it with Tamsin's clothes.

'Why don't you,' he said softly, 'just let them get on with it then, and come and live with me?'

Nobody had asked her about her exam. Nobody in the family spoke Spanish, she knew that, nobody in the family probably knew or cared who Lorca was, or Galdós, or Alas. When she had come back from school, in that wired, exhausted, strung-up and wrung-out state that three hours' relentless concentrating and striving causes, there'd been no one at home because Tamsin had gone straight to Robbie's from work, and Chrissie and Dilly weren't back from looking at this flat.

Nobody, either, had asked Amy if she wanted to look at the flat. She didn't, much – it was a necessary evil, she supposed, but one that could be postponed – but she would have liked to have been invited, she would have liked Chrissie to have said, 'Oh, we can easily put off going until you have finished the exams and can come with us.' But she hadn't. Instead, she had asked Dilly when her next free afternoon from college was, and had made an appointment to view accordingly, and Amy had thought, in a far-off but significant part of her mind, that a three o'clock appointment would mean that they intended to be back before she was, so that there'd be a welcome, and a commiseration or a congratulation, depending on how the exam had gone.

But there was no one. The house was empty and silent. There were no messages on the answering machine, and no contacts on Facebook that merited any attention at all. As she was ravenously hungry, Amy made too many pieces of toast, and ate them too fast, and drank an outdated bottle of 7 Up, which Chrissie said had to be consumed before she bought one other drop of any liquid but milk, and then she felt terrible and slightly sick, and dizzy with the extremes of the day, and lay across the kitchen table in a sprawl, her face against the fruit bowl.

Nobody seemed in the least surprised to find her like that when they finally came in. Chrissie and Dilly were peculiarly elated by the flat – Dilly had loved it, had seen possibilities of living in a different way entirely – and had breezed past Amy, chattering – 'Oh poor babe, was it grim, never mind, only one more to go!' – and Tamsin had come in later, looking elaborately preoccupied, and had indicated to Amy that she was extremely fortunate only to be faced by something as transitory and trivial as public examinations.

There was nothing for it, Amy decided, but her bedroom. Her flute case lay on her bed, where she had left it, but there was no urge in her to open it. There was no urge, either, to look at her laptop, or her Duffy poster, or the photograph of her father as a baby. There was no urge, oddly enough, to cry.

Amy bent and lifted her flute case to the floor. Then she lay down on her bed, and kicked her feet out until her shoes fell off on to the carpet. She stared upwards at the sloping ceiling, and instructed herself not to think about her mother, her sisters or her father.

'The future,' she said aloud. She raised her arms and twisted her fingers together. 'Think about the future.' She stopped, and held her breath for a moment.

'Newcastle,' Amy said quietly to her bedroom. 'Newcastle!'

CHAPTER SEVENTEEN

S cott was on the platform almost thirty minutes before Amy's train was due in. He had decided that he would make no move to kiss her on greeting, unless she instigated it, but all the same he had shaved, and brushed his teeth scrupulously, and buffed up the bathroom with the towel he had used after showering, and generally reassured himself that there was nothing about the flat or his person that could in any way disconcert her. At the station, he bought himself a newspaper and a bottle of water, both being entirely neutral things to occupy and accessorize himself with, and then he paced up and down the length of the platform until the London train came in suddenly, taking him by surprise, and he had to run down the length of the train to get to the standard-class section before Amy got out and had even a second to feel bewildered.

At first, he couldn't see her. There was the usual milling mass of people and bags and buggies and children, and in it no sign of Amy, and he was beginning to panic instead of searching, to ask himself what on earth he would do if she had funked it at the last minute, had got to the station and felt a wave of instinctive loyalty to and anxiety about her mother, and had simply turned and bolted back down the underground, when he saw her, standing quite still and looking about her in a way that made him ashamed he had doubted her.

She was taller than he'd remembered. She was wearing jeans and a hooded top over a T-shirt and her hair, which he'd last seen down her back, was twisted up behind her head with a cotton scarf. She had a rucksack hanging off one shoulder, and she was holding a pair of sunglasses, the earpiece of one side in her mouth, and she was standing close to the train, close to the door she'd just come out of, and was surveying the curve of the platform from side to side, looking for him, but not with any anxiety. And when she saw him, she took the sunglasses out of her mouth, and waved them, and smiled, and Scott felt an abrupt rush of pleasure and relief and shyness that almost stopped him in his tracks.

'Hello,' Amy said. She was still smiling.

'You made it—'

She didn't put out a hand or offer to kiss him. But she was definitely smiling.

'Course I did.'

'I wondered—'

'If I'd chicken?'

'Well, it's a long way—'

'No, it's not. I said I'd come, didn't I?'

'You did.' He felt he was staring.

She gestured with her sunglasses.

'Great station.'

'Yes,' he said. 'We're very proud of it.'

She stepped closer.

'I'm here,' she said.

'Yes—'

'I'm actually here!'

He relaxed suddenly. He put his hands out and took her shoulders.

'You are. And you did your exams. They're over.'

She looked right at him.

'Thanks to you, big brother—'

Then she leaned forward and kissed his cheek fleetingly. He squeezed her shoulders and let go.

'You're not officially here till Sunday—'

'OK.' She was grinning.

'You arrive Sunday morning. Can you remember that?'

'Yup.'

'Well,' he said, taking her rucksack, 'what now? Want a coffee?'

She took his arm, the one not holding her rucksack.

'Actually,' Amy said, 'just the bathroom. And mind my flute. I've got my flute in there.'

Almost the only person who'd ever slept in the guest bedroom in Percy Gardens was Scott. When she first moved in, Margaret had entertained an undefined but pleasurable idea that there would be occasional guests to enjoy the sea view from the top floor, to appreciate the carpeted en-suite bathroom with its solid heated towel rail, and the tiny room next door with its writing desk and all Scott's teenage books arranged alphabetically on cream-painted shelves. Quite who these mythical guests would be was never quite clear to her, and after she had decorated it, and hung linen-union interlined curtains at the windows, it struck her that the room would probably only ever be occupied – and infrequently at that – by Scott, who would have no taste for single beds with padded headboards, and good-quality cellular blankets and a kettle on a tray for early-morning tea. He put up with it, however, even if he left the bedclothes kicked out at the end on account of his height, and used towels on the floor, and the curtains undrawn. When he was staying, she could hear him moving about from her bedroom directly below, and she would think of the absolute contrast her guest bedroom provided with his own room in the Clavering Building, which just had a black iron bed in a room of exposed brickwork with a slate floor and a metal-framed window and steel girders across the ceiling. There weren't even, Margaret remembered, any curtains.

Her guestroom, she thought now, might be an unlikely setting for her son, but it certainly wasn't any more suitable for a teenage girl. Amy would be used to modern settings, to fresh, young surroundings, to colours and contemporary lighting and a shower. She could do her best, of course, she could put out pale towels and new soap and remove the heavy fringed bedspread from the bed she intended Amy to sleep in, but nothing could make the room look appropriate to a girl of eighteen. A modern girl of eighteen, that is. When Margaret was eighteen, she had shared a bed and a bedroom with her sister and their clothes had been hung on a row of pegs on the wall. She didn't have a wardrobe till she got married, never mind a carpet. She glanced down at Dawson, who had climbed with surprising nimbleness up to the top floor, and was now surveying the room in an assessing kind of way.

'She might be allergic to cats,' Margaret said. 'If you make her sneeze, you'll have to be shut in the kitchen.'

Dawson moved slowly across the carpet and sprang on to the bed Margaret had just made up. He sniffed the pillows. Then he turned and trampled round in a circle for a while and lowered himself into a comfortable heap of cat in the middle of the paisley quilt, closing his eyes and flattening his ears in anticipation of Margaret's telling him that he was to get up and get off that bed at once.

She didn't. She went across the room and fiddled with some china ornaments on top of the chest of drawers, and then she opened the wardrobe and looked at the padded hangers inside and then she went to the window and looked out at the early-summer sea, which was blue-grey under a grey-blue sky. Dawson opened his eyes cautiously and allowed his ears to rise discreetly again.

'D'you know,' Margaret said, and stopped.

She picked up the wooden acorn attached to the window blind, and examined it.

'D'you know,' Margaret said again, her back still to Dawson, 'I am really very nervous.'

Scott opened the door of his flat and stood back so that Amy could see right down the room.

She gazed for a while in silence, and then she took a step inside and said softly, 'Oh wow.'

Scott followed her and shut the door. He slid her rucksack off his shoulder and lowered it gently to the floor.

'This is amazing,' Amy said.

She began to walk down the length of the room very deliberately, step after step, silent in her canvas baseball boots. Scott stayed where he was, and watched her. She was looking from side to side, at the kitchen area, at the black sofa, at the bare bricks of the walls, at Scott's collection of reproduction Cartier-Bresson photographs. When she got to the piano, she stopped and put her hands on it lightly.

'This looks so cool here.'

Scott swallowed.

'D'you really think so?'

Amy nodded.

'It used to stand on a carpet. Dad hated it being on a carpet, but Mum said it had to, to insulate the noise, because of the neighbours. It looks much better on a floor.'

Scott began to move towards her.

'D'you like my view?'

Amy glanced up.

'Oh my *God*—'

'D'you remember asking me about the Tyne Bridge? That's the Tyne Bridge.'

Amy raised an arm and pointed.

'And what's that? The silver thing.'

'It's the Sage,' Scott said.

'The Sage—'

'Two concert halls, a music education centre, a children's concert hall, the home of the Northern Sinfonia. Peggy Seeger came last year.'

Amy said, 'It's like being abroad, it's so different—'

'Yes.'

She looked down at the piano.

'I suppose—'

'What?'

'I suppose this has sort of come home?'

'Except that it was probably made in America.'

She shot him a quick smile.

'You don't want me to get sentimental—'

'No, I don't.'

She looked back along the flat.

'This is so great.'

'I like it,' Scott said. 'My mother doesn't get it. Can't get it. She thinks it's barbaric to live in a place like this.'

'Let's – not talk about mothers.'

'Fine.'

'While I'm here,' Amy said, 'I don't want to wonder if I shouldn't be here.'

'I shan't remind you.'

'Where'm I sleeping?'

Scott moved behind the piano and opened his bedroom door.

'Here.'

Amy took in the sparseness, and the size of the window, and the Yamaha keyboard at the end of the bed.

She said, '*Wicked*—'

'I'm sleeping on the sofa.'

'D'you – d'you mind?'

'I like the sofa. I've often slept, unintentionally if you get me, on the sofa.'

Amy sat down on the edge of the bed and leaned backwards, spreading her hands out on the new bedlinen, still marked by the sharp creases of its packaging.

'What are we going to do?'

Scott leaned against the door jamb. He folded his arms. He had a sudden, exhilarating sense of freedom, a sense that the next few days were not, actually, going to be crippled by either the distant past or the recent past, that Amy had come north not so much for family reasons as for reasons of her own, which in turn, and wonderfully, liberated him.

'Well, he said, 'when I've shown you around a bit, I'm going to take you to a folk club.'

Amy sat up.

'A *folk* club?'

'You're in Newcastle. You're in the birthplace of the living tradition. I'm taking you to hear a girl who plays jazz, who plays folk. On her flute.'

'Oh!' Amy said, and then, again, '*Wow.*'

'Mr Harrison called,' Glenda said. She did not say that Mr Harrison's secretary had called, wanting to speak to Margaret, and when Margaret didn't ring back Mr Harrison had rung himself, as if his presence on the other end of a telephone line might conjure Margaret up by its very power.

'Oh yes,' Margaret said.

'Would you like to know why?'

'Not particularly,' Margaret said.

Glenda went on typing. There was a difference, in her view, between being rather admirably strong-minded and resistant to cajolery and, on the other hand, taking that resistance so far that you looked like a sulky adolescent. She had learned, too, that if she ignored both Margaret and Barry – two very different personalities who shared a singular capacity for pig-headedness – they would capitulate to being ignored long before she gave in out of pity. She kept an eye on Margaret, using her peripheral vision, but continued to look steadily and straight ahead at her screen.

'I can't concentrate today,' Margaret said abruptly.

Glenda let a beat fall, and then she said, 'It's that girl coming.'

'I haven't had anyone of eighteen in the house since Scott was that age. Twenty years or more. What do they eat, for heaven's sake?'

'What you give them,' Glenda said.

'Well,' Margaret said, 'it'll be Sunday lunch at the Grand Hotel. I've fixed that, with Scott. I told him, Sunday lunch and don't you wear trainers.'

'I've never been to the Grand Hotel—'

'Haven't you, dear? I'll take you on your fiftieth.'

'I had my fiftieth four years ago.'

'Sixtieth, then.'

'I may be dead by then—'

Margaret looked up.

'Don't talk rubbish.'

'She's a lucky girl,' Glenda said, 'sleeping in your guest-room, having lunch at the Grand Hotel.'

'She's Richie's daughter—'

'She can't help that.'

'Glenda,' Margaret said, 'what did Bernie Harrison want?'

Without hurry, Glenda sifted through the papers on her desk to find the note she had made of his message.

'He said he has two people he'd like you to hear, just for your opinion, one a singer, one a pianist, and he would like to invite you for dinner or cocktails or cocktails *and* dinner and he's given you a choice of five dates.'

'*Five?*'

'He said you couldn't go to the dentist on five occasions and get away with it.'

'I don't see my dentist in the evenings—'

Glenda held out the note.

'If we spoke like that, trying to be funny, to our mam, she'd say, "Get along with you, Mrs Teapot," and I never understood why.'

Margaret took the note.

'He doesn't give up, does he?'

'No.'

'On and on and on—'

'He means it.'

'Glenda,' Margaret said, 'I have nothing to offer him.'

Glenda gave a small snort.

Margaret said, 'Nothing *new*.'

'New isn't what he's after.'

'But I need it. I'm in a rut—'

Glenda said, 'Don't start that again.'

'I'll ring him tomorrow.'

'I said you'd call by close of business today.'

'And what, precisely, do you suggest that I say?'

Glenda typed a few more words. Then she said, without turning to look at Margaret, 'Why don't you ask him to lunch, too? At the Grand Hotel. Wouldn't it be easier, four of you, rather than just the three, with you fussing about Scott's footwear?'

*   *   *

282

They drove to the folk club in a taxi. Amy had assumed that Scott would have a car, but he said that there was no need for one, living in the city as he did, and the way he said it made her wonder if he could drive, and for the first time since she had arrived in Newcastle she felt shy, too shy to ask him something so personal. It was, in a way, like asking someone if they could read, especially a man, so she said nothing and climbed into the taxi with him, quelling an instinct to remark that they never used taxis at home, that either Chrissie or her sisters drove – she hated being driven by Dilly – or they used public transport.

'We're going over the river,' Scott said, 'we're going south. We're heading for Washington.'

Amy looked out of the taxi window. Newcastle looked to her as it had looked all afternoon, dramatically foreign. She hadn't expected the hills, or the grandeur of the architecture, or the size of the river, or the romance of all those bridges. Nor had she expected the energy, or the numbers of people on the streets of her own age. She felt she had been plucked out of the familiar and set down again in an extraordinary and fantastical version of the familiar – it was still England, after all, and a remarkable kind of English was still spoken – which was giving her a powerful and energizing feeling of discovery. Scott had walked her all through the centre that afternoon, up and down those steep, almost theatrical streets, past churches and St Mary's Cathedral, through Charlotte Square and Black Friars, round the Castle Keep and the Moot Hall, past Bessie Surtees House, with its innumerable medieval windows, and Earl Grey, with a lightning conductor inserted up his spine, poised on his column a hundred and thirty-five feet above the kids lounging and smoking on the sandstone steps below him. She felt dazed and thrillingly very far from home, and she was grateful to Scott for not talking to her, for just sitting beside her in the taxi and saying whatever he did say to the driver, while she looked at the river, and the sky, and then they were on a huge road heading south and she felt as she used to feel when she was a child in the back of the car, like a human parcel that had no power to do anything other than be carried somewhere and put down, at someone else's whim, precisely where she was taken and told.

The taxi pulled up outside a large modern building set in an asphalt car park. Amy had been expecting, at the least, a cellar.

'It's here?'

'Every Friday,' Scott said. He paid the driver with the lack of performance Amy remembered from her father. Why did men make so much less of handing over money, somehow, than women did? 'Home of the Keel Row Folk Club. It's an arts centre. All the folk stars come here on their tours.'

Inside, it reminded Amy of nothing so much as school. There were green walls and noticeboards and lines of upright chairs outside closed doors. Scott put a hand under her elbow and guided her out of the entrance hall into a barn-like room full of tables and chairs and noise, with a small dais at one end in front of a row of microphones on stands.

Amy looked round the room. 'I'm the youngest person here!'

'Yes,' Scott said, 'but look how many of them there are. Just look. They come every Friday.'

'They're older than *you*—'

'They know their music,' Scott said, 'just you wait. Just you wait till it gets going.'

'OK. I'll believe you.'

He smiled at her.

'Believe me.'

He threaded his way between the tables and indicated that

Amy should take a chair next to an ample woman in a patch-work waistcoat with long grey hair down her back, held off her face with Chinese combs.

The woman smiled at Amy. 'Hello, dear.'

She didn't sound Newcastle to Amy. She indicated the bottle of red wine in front of her and her companions.

'Drink, dear?'

Amy shook her head. 'I'm OK. Thank you.'

The woman glanced at Scott.

'Friday night with the boyfriend—'

'Actually,' Amy said, her voice sounding strangely distant to her, 'he's my brother.'

'Oh yes,' the woman said, laughing, 'oh *yes*. And would your brother like a drink?'

Scott said, 'I'll get myself a beer, thanks. And this one drinks Diet Coke.'

'No vodka?'

Scott leaned forward. He said, smilingly, 'She hasn't come for that. She's come for the same reason you've come. She's come for the music.'

The woman turned and looked straight at Amy, holding out her hand.

'Sorry, dear.'

Amy took her hand. It was big and warm and supple.

'It's OK.'

'D'you play?'

'The flute,' Amy said.

'The flute? The flute. The art of playing the flute is to make it sound like the human voice—'

'She knows that,' Scott said.

The woman let go of Amy's hand. Amy turned to look gratefully at Scott. He said, across her, to the woman, his voice still level and friendly, 'We shared a very musical father.'

There was a pause. Then the woman picked up her wine glass and held it up towards them.

'I think I'll just stop and start again. Good luck to you both.' She took a swallow. 'Enjoy.' Then she turned back to the man on her left.

Scott looked at Amy.

'I'll get you that Coke.'

When he had gone, Amy glanced sideways. Beyond the woman in the patchwork waistcoat was a thin man with a goatee beard, and another couple, the woman with her hair in braids threaded with coloured yarns. They were all laughing. Beyond them, at the next table, most people were laughing too, and when she looked round, from table to table across the room, the laughter seemed to be echoed. Amy thought, with amazement, that she had never seen such strange people, nor had she ever seen people having such easy fun. She touched the woman in the patchwork waistcoat nervously on one arm. The woman turned.

'I didn't,' Amy said, 'I didn't mean to be stand-offish—'

The woman smiled broadly. The man with the goatee beard leaned across her and said, in the same accent as Scott's, 'She needs keeping in her place, believe me!'

'You weren't,' the woman said. 'You were just finding your feet.' She nodded towards the stage. 'Just wait till the music starts.'

'Glad to be here,' the guitarist said.

He stood on stage in a halo of red and green lights, a lanky man in black, his hair tied back with a bandanna.

'Always glad to be here. Radio 2's Folk Club of the Year – when was it? Can't remember. Anyone here old enough to remember? Forget it. Today's my birthday. It's also my guitar's birthday. It's everyone's birthday. It's even our resident shanty man's birthday and he's planning to sing a song about a strike with all the bairns dying, just to cheer you all up. But before that I'm going to play you something. When the lads are ready, that is. Will you wait while Malc puts more gaffer tape on his accordion? Now, I wrote this tune on the ferry from Mull. Such a beautiful journey. I was on deck, the boys were in the bar. I wrote it for a friend's wedding and if it makes you want to dance I suggest you keep it to yourselves. Ready now? Ready, boys? Two, three—'

And then it began. Amy had been to concerts and gigs all her life, to Wembley and Brixton Academy and the Wigmore Hall, to jam sessions in pubs and people's back bedrooms, to theatres and hotel ballrooms to hear her father perform in his polished, relaxed, almost casual way. She had heard music of every kind, she had heard it in the company of her family, her friends and alone in her bedroom, picking over melodies as her father had urged her to do until, he said, the flute could say something for her in a better way than she could say it in words. But for all that, sitting here in an institutional arts centre surrounded by people older than her own mother, people of tastes and habits that had never, ever occurred to her before, she felt a sense of something enormous flooding through her: not exactly excitement or an exhilaration, but more a sense of relief, of recognition, of comprehension, a sense of coming home to something that she had never been able to acknowledge before as there.

The group with the guitarist played a forty-minute set. Several times, the guitarist slung his guitar sideways, and leaned into the microphone and sang. Then they left the stage and the shanty man appeared, holding a harmonica.

'It's one hundred and thirty-three years since Joe Wilson died. I'm going to sing one of his songs, in his memory. And then I'll give you Tommy Armstrong's "Durham Jail" because my father was a miner, though he never was nicked for stealing a pair of stockings, as Tommy was.'

Scott leaned towards Amy.

'OK?'

She nodded, her eyes fixed on the stage.

'Next act,' Scott whispered. 'Wait for the next act—'

'"Oh, lass, don't clash the door so,"' the shanty man sang.

'"You're young and as thoughtless as can be.

'"But your mother's turning old

'"And you know she's very bad

'"And she doesn't like to hear you clash the door."'

Scott watched Amy covertly. He'd thought she might be intrigued, might quite like it, might be curious to hear the music Richie had grown up with, the music of the mines and the ships, but he had not thought that she would love it, that she would sit enthralled while a little old man with a mouth organ sang a comic song from a nineteenth-century music hall, a lament from an oakum-picking prisoner in Durham Jail. She looked, in that cheerful, warm-hearted, unambitious room, as out of place as if she had fallen from another planet, but she was as absorbed as any of them, and when the shanty man had finished, and gone hobbling off the stage, to be replaced by a second group, two fiddlers, an accordionist and a slender girl carrying a flute, he thought she was hardly breathing.

The girl stepped up to the microphone. She was perhaps in her mid-twenties, with hair as long and dark as Amy's own, dressed in deep green, to the floor, and wearing no jewellery except for long glimmering silver chains in her ears.

'Good evening,' she said softly. Her accent was Scottish. 'We're so happy to be back. This is the twenty-ninth gig of our epic tour round England, Wales and Scotland. But we love coming here. We love coming back to the UK's home for music and musical discovery.'

She paused for the cheering, standing quiet and still and smiling. Then she bent towards the microphone again.

'Sometimes, as you may remember, I want to jazz things up a little, give them a bluesy twist. But not tonight. Tonight, you get it sweet and straight, played the way it was written.' She raised her flute and inclined her head to meet it.

'Ladies and gentleman. Brothers and sisters. "The Rose Of Allandale".'

They bought burgers on their way home, and carried the hot polystyrene boxes in the lift up to Scott's flat. The flat was dim, lit only by the summertime night glow from the city coming through the huge window, and Scott didn't switch any lights on, just let Amy walk in, and drop her bag on the floor randomly, just the way he dropped his work bag, and wander down the room, running her hand over the piano as she passed it, to stand, as he so often did, and stare out at the lights and the shining dark river far below and the great gleaming bulk of the Sage on the further shore.

She'd hardly spoken on the way home. He'd rung for a taxi while she was buying the CDs of the groups they'd heard, and she'd climbed in beside him in a silence he was perfectly happy to accommodate. In fact, he respected it, was gratified by it, and when, as they were crossing the river, almost home, and Scott had asked the driver to drop them off so that they could pick up something to eat, she had said suddenly, 'Oh, I want to be her!', he had had to restrain himself from putting his arms round in her in a heartfelt gesture of understanding and pleasure. Instead, with an effort, he'd asked her if she wanted a burger or a kebab, and when she didn't answer, when it became plain that she had hardly heard him, he almost laughed out loud.

'D'you want to eat standing there?'

She turned, very slowly.

'Where – where are you going to eat?'

He gestured.

'Where I usually do. On the sofa.'

She came away from the window.

'Will you play for me?'

'What, the piano?'

'What else?'

'Maybe,' he said. 'Maybe tomorrow. Maybe we'll both play tomorrow.'

She sat down on the sofa. He handed her a box.

'Want a plate?'

'No.'

'Good girl. Eat up. What have you had today – coffee and crisps?'

'My favourite,' Amy said.

She opened the box and looked at her burger. She sighed.

'I want to be her.'

'I know.'

'I want—'

'Wait,' Scott said, 'wait. You've work to do first.'

She glanced up.

'What work?'

'Exploring.'

She lifted the burger out and inspected it.

'What are we going to do tomorrow?'

'What are *you* going to do tomorrow.'

'What?'

'I'm sending you off,' Scott said. 'I'm sending you on a little journey of discovery.'

Amy stared at him. He winked at her.

'You'll see,' he said, and wedged his burger in his mouth.

CHAPTER EIGHTEEN

Chrissie had never felt quite at home in Sue's kitchen. It wasn't the disorder really, or the noise – the television never seemed to be switched off – but more a sense that Sue's children and Kevin were so intent upon their own robust and random lives that her presence there meant no more than if a new chair or saucepan had been added to the mix.

Sue herself seemed oblivious. The muddle of people and purposes, of washing-up and lunch boxes, of newspapers and flyers and scribbled notes, wasn't something she strove for, but rather something she simply didn't notice. She had absently moved a football boot, a magazine and an empty crisp packet from a chair in order that Chrissie could sit down, in a manner that suggested that sitting down wasn't necessarily a chair's function in the first place.

'Can I turn that off?'

'What?' Sue said. She was polishing a wine glass with a shirt lying on top of a pile in a laundry basket.

'The TV,' Chrissie said.

'Course. I've stopped hearing it. I've stopped hearing most things, especially anybody under sixteen asking for money.'

'I gave Amy twenty quid,' Chrissie said, 'and now I'm

worrying that wasn't nearly enough. A whole weekend, on twenty pounds.'

Sue put the wine glass on the table, amid the clutter.

'They'll pay for her, won't they?'

Chrissie made a face.

'That's what I was thinking when I gave her the money. They can darn well pay for her, that's what I thought. But now, I wish they weren't. I wish I'd given her more.'

Sue found a second glass, and blew on it.

'Stop thinking about her.'

'I—'

'Haven't you got enough to think about?' Sue demanded. 'Isn't there enough going on without fretting over the one child who's actually striking out?'

'In the wrong direction—'

'For *you*,' Sue said. 'Not necessarily for her. Don't you just love it that wine comes in screw-top bottles these days?'

Chrissie wandered back from turning off the television and watched Sue pouring wine into the glasses.

'I've sometimes wished, since Richie died, that I really, *really* liked alcohol. I mean, I do like it, I love a glass of wine, but I don't crave it. It would have been easier to crave something rather than just be in such a state.'

Sue held a full glass out to her.

'Tell me some good news.'

'It's sort of OK news—'

'Fine by me.'

'I took the job,' Chrissie said.

Sue let out a yelp, and clinked her glass against Chrissie's. 'Go, girlfriend!'

'It isn't amazing. In fact, it's very lowly, very lowly indeed, but it's the first one I've been offered, actually *offered*, in all these months of trying, and I suppose it might lead to something—'

'It's a *job*!'

'Yes,' Chrissie said, 'they were so nice to me. I met Mark's father, and all his uncles, and they were lovely, so welcoming.'

'You'll be so good at it—'

'I hope so. Nine-thirty to six, four weeks' paid holiday, pay-as-you-earn tax.'

'Chrissie,' Sue said, 'this is good. This is even great. This is like starting again, and do not, do not, do *not* tell me that starting again is the last thing you want to do.'

'OK,' Chrissie said.

'You're smiling.'

'I'm not—'

'You're smiling.'

'It's relief,' Chrissie said.

'I don't care what it is. You're smiling. And the flat?'

Chrissie took a sip of wine.

'If I don't sell the house—'

'You *will* sell the house.'

'I can't afford the flat on what I'll be earning.'

Sue cleared a heap of T-shirts and a pair of swimming goggles off another chair, and sat down.

She said, 'What about those girls?'

'Well, Amy—'

'I don't mean Amy. I mean Tamsin and Dilly.'

Chrissie said cautiously, 'Dilly is looking for a job—'

'Is she now.'

'And Tamsin. Well, I don't really know what's going on with Tamsin.'

'Do sit down,' Sue said.

Chrissie said, sitting, 'She keeps talking about moving in with Robbie, but she doesn't do it. He's built her an amazing cupboard, apparently, but she doesn't seem in any hurry to fill it. He's like a dog, sitting there hoping for chocolate. I thought he was so strong and masculine, and would support her the way Richie did, but she doesn't seem to want to let him any more.'

'You can't have both of them living with you—'

'I could—'

'No,' Sue said.

'There's just enough room—'

'*If* you get the flat—'

'Yes. If—'

'Still no,' Sue said. She leaned back, twiddling her wine glass round by its stem, watching it, not looking at Chrissie. 'Do you really *want* them to live with you?'

There was a pause, and then Chrissie said slowly, 'I don't know if I want to be alone.'

'Don't you?'

'No.'

'You don't know what it's like. You might love it. You might prefer it, actually, to living with two people who ought to be fending for themselves.'

Chrissie said nothing. Sue went on leaning back. Then she took a mouthful of wine and said, 'Well, Amy's having a go at it, isn't she? Amy's trying to swim without her family water wings on, isn't she? Instead of banging on about how you don't like what Amy's doing, why don't you try imitating her instead?'

Scott had given her some money. She'd felt very awkward about confessing that she'd spent the money her mother had given her on CDs at the folk club, and that her card would probably be rejected at an ATM, but he'd held some notes out to her that morning, saying, just take it, don't say anything, take it.

'But I feel awful—'

'You're family. Take it.'

'I shouldn't—'

'Yes, you should. Anyway, I want to. I want to give it to you.'

'OK,' Amy said. She glanced down at the notes in her hand. It looked as if he'd given her an awful lot. 'That's – so great. Thank you.'

'It's nothing,' Scott said. 'The hard part is now.'

'The hard part?'

'You're going to North Shields. You're going to see where Dad and my mother grew up, went to school. You're going on your own.'

Amy looked at him.

'Why aren't you coming?'

'Because I'll colour it for you. Because you've got to see it through your eyes, not mine.' He grinned. 'Don't worry. I'll tell you where to go.'

Amy said doubtfully, 'Is this a good idea?'

'Was last night a good idea?'

Her face lit up.

'Oh, *yes!*'

'Then trust me,' Scott said. 'Walk your feet off and come back and tell me. I'll be waiting for you.'

She had walked, on her own, up the steep streets to the metro station at Monument, and there, as instructed, she had bought herself a return ticket to North Shields, feeling as she did so that her very anonymity in the Saturday-morning crowds was as exciting as the adventure itself. She sat, as Scott had told her to, near the front of the train so that she could have a sense of the scene through the windows of the driver's cab, as they sped out of the glowing underground station and out on to the raised rails through Manors and Byker, past the cranes of Walker and Wallsend and out along the river shore through Hadrian Road and Howden, through Percy Main and Meadow Well, to North Shields.

On the platform, busy with people who belonged there, who knew where they were going, she said to herself, 'This is it.'

'Start with the quays,' Scott had said. 'Head for the river. Head for the quays.'

You could smell your way to the shore, almost at once. The air smelled of water, river and sea, rank and salty, and overhead there were gulls, wheeling and screaming, huge black-headed gulls with heavy beaks and solid, shining bodies. Amy headed south, staring up at the sky and the clouds and the shouting seabirds, staring about her at the street and the houses and the children, scuffing along together in packs, just as Richie must have done when he grew out of being that toddler in hand-knitted socks and bar shoes.

And then, quite abruptly, she was on a ridge high above the water, standing by a house which had plainly once been a lighthouse, looking out across the great breadth of the Tyne River, to South Shields and Jarrow, a name Amy knew because of Bede, the seventh-century monk who lived in the monastery there, whom she remembered because a history teacher had once told her class that he kept a precious store of peppercorns to make monastic food less boring. The road she was standing on was quiet, much quieter than the streets near the metro station, and the gulls seemed to be whirling higher, their cries echoing in the wind up there, the wind that was blowing in off the sea, blowing Amy's hair across her face, obscuring her vision. She caught it up in both hands, and twisted it into a rough knot behind her head, and set off down a steep and turning path to the shore.

And there was Fish Quay, as Scott had said it would be, the quayside where his grandmother and great-aunts had gutted herrings for a living. He'd said that in their day, in his mother's girlhood, the herring drifters had been packed in against the quayside several deep, but now the water lay almost empty, just a straggling line of trawlers moored alongside battered iron-roofed sheds, with the water slapping at them and long rust marks streaking their sides. Everything was shuttered, all the doors were closed, there was nobody on the street, no movement except the odd plastic bag and scrap of paper litter lifting in the wind and skittering along the surface.

She walked slowly along the quay, past the bacon grocer's with its jolly challenges painted in the window glass – 'If you aren't wearing knickers, smile!'; 'Never go to bed mad: stay up and fight!'; 'Do not enter the shop if you have no sense of humour!' – past the fish and chip shops, past the Royal National Mission to Deep Sea Fishermen, and the warehouses for Larry's Fishcakes and Blue Dolphin Seafoods, and came out at the end into the Low Lights car park, where there was a bench looking out across the wide, crinkled grey river melting into the further grey sea and, on the horizon, the silhouetted statue of Admiral Collingwood, where Scott said he and his mates used to gather after school, standing like Earl Grey high above the world below and gazing forever eastwards from his grassy mound.

She subsided on to the bench. It was wonderful there, so big and so bleak, all that sea and sky, but it was sobering too, laden with all those lives, those past lives, battling and struggling and hating the sea as much as they needed it, relied on it. Amy put her hands into her hoodie pockets and breathed deeply, in and out, in and out. This was the sort of place that last night's music had come from, it was people who'd lived and laboured here who had instinctively recorded how they were feeling, how they were thinking, in a way that could be easily remembered, could be simply passed on. She sniffed once or twice in the wind. If she shut her eyes, she could conjure up that girl last night, the girl with the flute and the lovely, light, straightforward singing voice.

If she kept them shut, she could imagine Scott as a boy down here, as a teenager in his school uniform with his tie bunched up in his blazer pocket, and not just Scott, but her father who might even – *even* – have sat on this bench, or whatever was here before this bench, and looked at the sky and the sea and the gulls, and thought and thought about music too.

She opened her eyes and tipped her head back, wriggling herself down until her body was in a straight line, shoulder to heel, the back of her head balanced on the back of the bench, and stared up at the sky. She felt taken over, bowled over, blown away by a sudden and extraordinary wave of happiness.

'Don't read anything into this,' Margaret said.

Bernie Harrison was in an armchair in her sitting room, legs crossed, very comfortable. He had a cup of coffee balanced on the arm of the chair and Dawson, stretched in his usual place along the back of the sofa, was keeping a discreet but definite eye on him.

'What would I read?' Bernie said.

He was wearing well-pressed summer trousers and brown-suede loafers, which were entirely appropriate to the dining room of the Grand Hotel at Sunday lunchtime.

'Well,' Margaret said, trying to sound unconcerned, 'this might look like a family occasion, but it isn't. I'm not, as it were, introducing you to the family.'

'Ah,' Bernie said. He smiled at her. 'You manage to put things so graciously.'

'It's better if we are all quite clear where we stand.'

'So,' Bernie said easily, 'I have been asked along to leaven an awkward social lump, have I?'

'You've been asked,' Margaret said, 'to make a four-some.'

'Not like you to be nervous, Margaret.'

'No.'

'But I'm flattered. Yes, I'm flattered. When did you last ask anyone for help?'

She didn't look at him, but she smiled.

'A while back.'

'What do we know about this child?'

Margaret sighed.

'She's eighteen, she's bright, she's musical, she's the youngest of three. She's talked a bit to Scott on the telephone but she's never been north and she's not going to like my guest bedroom.'

'Why is she in it?'

'Because,' Margaret said firmly, 'she can't possibly stay with Scott. I promised her mother.'

'Did you? You spoke to her mother?'

'I did.'

'Successfully?'

'No,' Margaret said.

Bernie turned his head.

'There's a taxi pulling up outside.'

Margaret gave a little gasp.

'Oh my God—'

'Stay there,' Bernie said.

He stood up and walked to the window, carrying his coffee cup.

'Deep breaths, Margaret. Yes, it's them. Scott, I'm sorry to tell you, looks like an off-duty footballer but the girl looks lovely. Tall and slim. Long, dark hair. A skirt, you'll be pleased to hear. What there is of it. But I can't see any luggage.' He turned and glanced at Margaret. 'I think your guest has come to stay in what she stands up in.'

Amy had never been anywhere like the dining room of the Grand Hotel. It had upholstered chairs, and ornately

299

draped curtains at the huge high windows, and the walls were decorated with long, narrow panels of stylized fruit and flowers. The carpet was very thick, patterned with medallions in russet and green, and so were the tablecloths and the napkins, which sat like small icebergs in a forest of glassware. The tablecloths even had undercloths, which went right down to the floor, which was just as well since they enabled Scott to stick his feet right out of sight so that they didn't offend his mother.

Amy wasn't quite sure what other things might offend his mother. They had, the previous afternoon when she got back from North Shields, gone shopping to buy her a skirt, and it hadn't struck either of them, till they saw Margaret's eyes on Amy's legs, that the length of the skirt might signify as much as its existence in the first place. Margaret looked OK to Amy, because she was as Amy was expecting her to be, but she also looked a bit unpredictable, as if she might suddenly object to something that had never previously occurred to anyone as a potential flashpoint. Amy thought of catching Scott's eye, and winking, but then she remembered that Margaret was Scott's mother, and therefore not an appropriate subject for complicity, and refrained.

The other man, the sort of grandfather man, was fine. He'd told Amy he was an agent, that he'd known her father as a boy and as a young man, and he mentioned several names, people he represented, whom Amy had heard of. He seemed very easy and friendly, and Amy wondered if he was a kind of boyfriend, if that was the right word when you got as old as that, and he teased Scott about his appearance and Scott, who looked perfectly normal to Amy, didn't seem to mind and just said cheerfully, 'Places like this need a bit of shaking up, Mr Harrison,' and Mr Harrison said, 'Oh for God's sake, lad. Bernie.' And Scott had laughed and shaken his head and said, 'Can't do it, sir. Sorry.'

The menu was enormous. Margaret watched Amy reading it and then she said, in a voice with far more warmth in it than it had had before, 'Choose whatever you like, pet. You must be hungry. They never give you anything but rubbish on the train.'

Scott shot Amy a warning look.

'Thank you,' Amy said politely.

'Was it a good journey?'

'Yes, thank you.'

'And was Scott on the platform to meet you?'

'Yes,' Amy said. 'Yes, he was.'

'And what,' Bernie Harrison said in a jocular voice, 'do you think of the Frozen North so far?'

Amy put her huge menu down. She turned to look straight at him.

'I think it's wonderful.'

He said, laughing, 'Well, the station's wonderful—'

'It's nice of you, dear,' Margaret said, 'but you've only seen that and Scott's flat.'

'I *love* Scott's flat,' Amy said.

'Thank you,' Scott said.

'And,' Amy said, deliberately ignoring him, and now looking straight at Margaret, 'I love North Shields and the river and the metro and the bridges.'

She stopped. There was a brief silence.

'Excuse me?' Margaret said.

'We went to a folk club on Friday,' Amy said. 'It was amazing. I – I just loved it. I loved the music. I can't stop thinking about the music. I think it's – it's so, so great. Up here.'

'You came up on *Friday*?' Margaret said.

'Yes.'

Margaret looked at Scott.

'You told me—'

'Stop it,' Bernie Harrison said.

301

'No,' Scott said to his mother, 'you wouldn't *be* told.'

'I promised your mother—'

'This isn't about my mother,' Amy said. 'It isn't about any mothers. It's about us – us *children*.'

Bernie Harrison reached out and took Margaret's nearest wrist.

'There you go—'

Amy said, 'I'm really sorry if you thought I was staying with you but I'm not. I'm staying with Scott. I've had an amazing time, the best time. I've had the best time I've had since Dad died. I really have.'

Margaret was looking at the tablecloth. Scott tried to catch Amy's eye but she was still looking at Margaret. So was Bernie Harrison.

'I don't forget,' Amy said. 'I promise I don't forget that Dad belonged to you too. To you and Scott.'

'Oh, pet,' Margaret said in a whisper.

'But I'm staying with Scott. I'm staying with Scott till I go – south again.'

With his free hand, Bernie Harrison gestured to attract the attention of the wine waiter.

'Now, young lady. Young lady who knows her own mind. I suggest we now talk about music. Don't you?'

'Did he mean that?' Amy said.

They were sitting on Scott's black sofa, Amy curled up at one end with her feet under her.

'What?'

'Mr Harrison. Did he mean that about a folk-music degree?'

'Yes.'

She was holding a mug of tea. She looked at him over the rim.

'Do you know about it?'

'Yes.'

'Why didn't you say?'

'You have to make up your own mind.'

'But—'

'I didn't know how you'd feel,' Scott said. 'I didn't know how we'd get on. I mean, all I know about being in your teens is what I knew when I was in them, but I might have got that all wrong, mightn't I, because you're a girl, not a boy. I might have thought I was helping you, which is what I wanted to do, and got that wrong too. I just had to wait, and give you time to think for yourself a bit. I couldn't push you, could I?'

'No,' Amy said gratefully.

'I didn't know what sort of music you liked, even.'

Amy smiled.

'Nor did I.'

He leaned forward.

'Want to look?'

'Look at what—'

'This music degree.'

'Yes,' she said, '*Yes.*'

He stood up and went to retrieve his laptop from the kitchen counter. He felt very tired and very, almost unsteadily, happy. It would only be later, when he was alone and stretched out on the sofa, that he could think about the day, unpick it, unravel it, marvel at it. He carried the laptop back to the sofa and sat down close to Amy, so that she could see the screen.

'OK,' he said. 'University of Newcastle. Here we go.'

She watched the screen flicker. 'You interested in taking this further?' Bernie Harrison had said at lunchtime. 'Are you serious about this?'

'There,' Scott said.

Amy leaned forward.

'Read it,' Scott said. 'Read it out loud.'

'"Newcastle University,"' Amy read, '"folk and traditional music. Bmus. Honours UCAS 4 years. Established in 2001, this is the first performance-based degree programme in folk and traditional music to be offered in England and Wales. The course explores folk music in its traditional and revived forms through practical work (composition as well as performance) and academic work."'

She stopped.

'OK?' Scott said.

'I can't believe it,' Amy said.

'Look,' Scott said, 'look. Teaching's at the university and at the Sage. Folkworks is at the Sage.'

'Folkworks?'

'It's a charity,' Scott said. 'It's an educational charity for traditional music.'

'Did – did you know about all this?'

'Yes.'

'And were you just waiting?'

'Hoping,' Scott said, 'not waiting. Other people's expectations give you a headache.'

Amy looked back at the screen.

'I love this. I *love* all this. Look at those modules, look at them, songs of struggle, songs from the US Southern states, ballads – oh *boy*,' Amy said, 'I think I'm going to cry—'

'Please try not to.'

'Happy cry—'

'Not even happy cry.'

She jumped to her feet.

'This is so *brilliant*—'

'You haven't got in yet.'

'But I will. I'll do anything. *Anything*. You cannot *imagine* how this makes me feel—'

He grinned at her.

'I can see it.'

'Wow,' Amy said. 'Wow, wow, mega wow.'

She began to spin down the room, turning like a skater, arms out, hair flying, her canvas boots thudding lightly on the bare boards. He watched her go whirling down the room, behind the piano and back again, until she came to an unsteady halt in front of him.

'Scott,' she said. She was panting slightly and her eyes were bright. 'Scott, I really, *really*, don't want to go home tomorrow.'

CHAPTER NINETEEN

It was the young couple's third visit to the house. Chrissie
had been wary of them at first, convinced that they were part
of the deceptive culture of debt-financed outward prosperity,
and that they would talk loudly about their enthusiasm and
plans for the house, and then suddenly stare at her blankly
and say they couldn't possibly afford such an asking price, as
if the fault lay with her.

The asking price had been carefully engineered by Tamsin's
Mr Mundy. He had come to see the house in person, as
Tamsin had assured Chrissie he would, and had been very
measured and deliberate, and had told Chrissie, over coffee in
the kitchen – he had deprecatingly declined the sitting room
as if to emphasize that he was merely a man of business –
that they would advertise the house at fifty thousand pounds
above the price that she should calculate on getting for it, in
order to allow for the bargaining and inevitable reduction
that were all part of the current house-buying-and-selling
market.

Chrissie had not liked Mr Mundy. She did not care for his
heaviness, nor his slightly sweaty pallor, nor his patronage,
and, most of all, she did not care for the way he was with
Tamsin, like a seedily flirtatious uncle. Tamsin, she observed,

did not respond to him in kind, but she certainly did nothing to discourage him, to the point where Chrissie made sure that, in going up the stairs to the top floor, it was she who preceded Mr Mundy, and not Tamsin.

When he left, he held her hand fractionally too long in his large, soft grasp, and said that he was very sure he could just about promise her a sale.

'Good,' Chrissie said, 'and soon, please.'

'As soon,' Mr Mundy said, still smiling, 'as it is humanly possible under current market conditions.'

Chrissie shut the door.

'What a creep—'

Tamsin remembered catching Mr Mundy with the massage-ads page of the *Ham & High* newspaper, and thought she wouldn't mention it. She said instead, 'Well, he's an estate agent, isn't he? And if anyone can sell this house, he can.'

In the first weeks of the house being on the market, there were nine viewings. One of those viewings was by a young couple with a toddler, and after two days they came again. They stood about in the rooms, behaving, as Chrissie had come to realize, with amazement, in the way that people buying houses commonly behaved, remarking – as if Chrissie had not made this house her home for the past fifteen years – on what was the matter with it, and what needed doing to make it even halfway acceptable. On that second visit, there had been so much to find fault with – outdated decor, neglected garden, absence of garage, pokiness of existing office space, tired bathrooms – that Chrissie had seen them go with a mixture of relief that she need never see them again and regret that whatever had drawn them back was not strong enough to convince them.

'I don't get it,' she said to Sue on the telephone. 'I don't want to have to sell this house but still I'm panicking that nobody will want to buy it. What's going on?'

'You're getting better.'

'I can't be—'

'You are. And they'll be back.'

'They won't. They couldn't find anything to like today—'

'They'll be back.'

And they were. They turned up, entirely insouciant, as if they had never had any intention of doing anything else.

'But,' Chrissie said, 'I really thought you didn't like it, I thought you said—'

The wife stared at her. She was dressed in a grey linen tunic over a discreet pregnant bump, and she had the toddler on her hip, and an immense soft leather bag covered in pockets and buckles slung over her shoulder.

'Oh no,' she said, 'we love it.' She looked at the toddler. 'Don't we, Jamie? We're going to make a playroom out of that room you said used to have a piano in it. For Jamie. Aren't we, Jamie?'

They offered Chrissie fifty thousand less than the asking price.

'Say no,' Tamsin said.

'I was going to. Anyway.'

'I would advise—' Mr Mundy began.

'No,' Chrissie said, 'I'll take ten off.'

'Mrs Rossiter—'

'Ten,' Chrissie said.

The young couple offered forty thousand less than the asking price.

'Fifteen,' Chrissie said.

The young couple said that they were no longer interested at that price.

'I will leave in six weeks,' Chrissie said, 'and I will take twenty thousand off the asking price.'

'Oh God, Mum,' Dilly said, 'do you know what you're doing?'

'Not really,' Chrissie said, 'but I'm going on instinct. I'm excited.'

'You're *over*excited—'

The young couple said that they would agree to exchange within two weeks and twenty-five thousand off, but that they were of course now looking at other properties.

'Done,' Chrissie said, 'done. And I've taken the job at Leverton's.'

'You can't—'

'I can.'

'She can!'

'What do *you* know,' Tamsin said to Dilly, 'you've never earned a penny in all your life.'

'I will be,' Dilly said. 'I'm looking for work now. I *will* be.'

'Playing houses,' Tamsin said scornfully, 'in that poky flat.'

'It could be a pretty flat,' Chrissie said. She was stirring Sunday-night scrambled eggs. 'I'll ring the owner in the morning. I'll tell him that the minute I've exchanged contracts on this I'll sign the lease.'

'Not before,' Tamsin said.

'I *know* not before,' Chrissie said irritably. 'Please do stop treating me like a halfwit.'

There was a fractional startled pause.

'Sorr*ee*,' Tamsin said in an offended voice.

'I've bought and sold houses before,' Chrissie said. 'I've lived on my own and earned my own living, I'll have you know. And you can't even manage to move into a flat that's being provided for you, complete with customized wardrobe.'

The landline telephone rang.

'I'll get it,' Tamsin and Dilly said in unison.

There was a small scuffle. Dilly was quicker. She twitched the handset out of its mooring and held it hard to her ear.

'Hello? Oh, hi, Ames. How goes it? How're you doing?'

There was a considerable silence. Chrissie took the egg pan off the cooker and continued to stir with elaborate concentration. Tamsin leaned against the nearest wall and folded her arms, fixing her gaze resolutely on some midpoint halfway down the kitchen. Dilly stayed where she was, listening. Then, after what seemed an unconscionable time, she said, 'Oh wow,' and, 'Jesus, Amy,' and then, 'You'd better talk to Mum. Hadn't you?'

Chrissie stopped stirring. Tamsin stood upright. Chrissie held her hand out for the phone.

'Big deal, Ames,' Dilly said into the phone, taking no notice.

Chrissie took a step closer.

'*Please*—'

'Give it to her!' Tamsin said sharply.

'They're going mad here,' Dilly said. 'Shall I pass you over?' Then she laughed. 'Countdown,' she said. 'Ready? Three, two, one, Mothah!'

She handed the telephone to Chrissie.

'And?' Tamsin demanded.

Dilly ignored her. She was watching Chrissie. Chrissie was listening intently. Then she said, 'But I want you home tomorrow. You promised you would be back tomorrow—'

'She's not *staying*?' Tamsin hissed.

'She's fallen in love with some music thing,' Dilly said, still watching Chrissie. 'Some folk-music degree, or something. Sounded a bit weird to me.'

'*Folk*-music degree?'

'She sounded completely mental about it. Newcastle University or something. Where *is* Newcastle?'

'Well, obviously I can't force you,' Chrissie said, 'but it does seem very strange, very sudden. You've only been there ten minutes—'

310

'They've brainwashed her,' Tamsin said.

'I wish somebody'd wash *your* brain,' Dilly said with spirit. 'You mightn't think you're right all the time if they did.'

'You can be such a little cow—'

'All right,' Chrissie said, 'all right. Of course I'm not going to forbid you. I couldn't forbid you, in any case. I suppose—' She stopped. Then she said with difficulty, 'I suppose I should wish you luck. Well, I do. I do wish you luck, darling. If this is what you want.'

'Oh my God,' Tamsin said, uncrossing her arms and flinging them out dramatically. 'This family is falling apart.'

Dilly went over to the cooker and prodded at the egg with a wooden spoon.

'It's all gone rubbery—'

'Yes,' Chrissie said. She sounded tired, defeated. 'Yes. Well, ring and tell me. Or text me. At least text me. Oh, and Amy? I sold the house. Yes. Yes, I think so, I think that too. OK, OK, darling. Night night.'

She took the phone away from her ear and held it, looking down at it.

'What have they done to her?' Tamsin said.

When Amy woke, it was broad daylight and the uncurtained window by the bed was full of the wide, high, cloud-streaked Northern sky. She lay there for a while, so that her mind could swim slowly to the surface, past all the events of the day before, past the lunch and the conversation, past the discoveries and the phone call home, and past – much more savouringly – the marvellous unexpected midnight hours when Scott had at last sat down at the piano and played, and she had retrieved her flute from her rucksack and joined him, and it was better than talking, better than anything, better even than playing with Dad had been, because Scott played like an equal, played as if only the music mattered and who cared who was following or leading.

It was past two in the morning before either of them thought of the time. And then Amy had discovered she was starving and they had eaten a bag of cashew nuts and some cheese slices Scott found in the fridge and shared a battered KitKat from the bottom of his work bag. Going into his bedroom, Amy had been almost overwhelmed by the need to thank him, to say that she felt rescued, guided, excited, but had not known how to do any of that without embarrassing both of them, so she had put her arms round his neck, awkwardly and in silence, and he had somehow understood, and had given her a quick, hard hug, and said, 'You're not the only one who's had a good day,' and let her go.

Then he said, 'I'll be gone in the morning, remember. It's Monday.'

'Oh—'

'I took a half-day off, Friday. Can't do more right now.'

'No, I know, I knew—'

He was tossing a pillow and an unzipped sleeping bag on to the sofa.

'Mr Harrison'll look after you. He'll show you the Sage. He knows his way round the music scene better than I do, in any case.'

Mr Harrison! Amy shot up in bed. Where was her watch? What was the time? What would happen if she kept Mr Harrison waiting?

'It was opened in 2004,' Bernie Harrison said. 'It's bigger than two football pitches and twice the height of *The Angel of the North*. And up there,' he pointed to the vast curved roof soaring high above them, 'there's six hundred-some-odd panes of glass, and each one weighs more than two baby elephants.'

312

Amy was turning slowly, head thrown back, gawping.

'I've run out of things to say—'

'I'm old enough to remember the Northern Sinfonia being founded,' Bernie said. 'It was 1958. Michael Hall. I was sixteen, same age as your—' He stopped. 'No, I suppose she isn't your anything, Margaret, is she?'

Amy retrieved her dazzled gaze from the immensity of the Sage's roof.

'Not really—'

'Your father's first wife is just your father's first wife.'

Amy swallowed.

'She – she was his only wife. He and Mum never—'

Bernie Harrison cleared his throat.

'Well, don't let it trouble you. Doesn't trouble me. You made your mark with Margaret, I can tell you.'

'I hope she wasn't upset about me not staying—'

'She's got a mind of her own and she likes to see one in other people. I've known her since she was a stroppy little object in pigtails. We grew up in a different world from now, Margaret and me. You wouldn't believe, now, our world had ever been, sometimes. It was hard, though. You can't really miss something that hard.'

Amy looked past him, along the immense shining spaces of floor, to the glass walls and the view of the river. She said a little hesitantly, 'So, the Grand Hotel—'

'Yes,' Bernie said firmly. 'She'd deny it, but that's why we like places like the Grand Hotel. We've made our mark and our brass and we like value for it. Quality.'

'Of course.'

'It may be different in London—'

'Please don't talk about London.'

Bernie glanced at her.

'Very well.'

'I've just fallen in love with all this—'

'It doesn't take half an eye to see that.'

'Everyone,' Amy said, 'has been so lovely to me.'

Bernie indicated that Amy should follow him across to the stupendous windows, to lean on the steel balustrade and look down on the river and the bridges.

He said, looking at the view, 'We've all got something to give each other.'

'I haven't,' Amy said, 'I haven't got anything. I've only just left school. I couldn't even buy my own train ticket up here.'

'You're too sharp to take me literally. It's not about the money.'

'Not having any makes you a bit helpless—'

'Are you going to let that stand in your way?'

'No,' Amy said uncertainly.

'There's ways and means. There's grants. There's charities that like giving bursaries for music. There'll be a way if you want it.'

'I want it so much—'

'Well,' Bernie said, 'we'll see. You'd have to work hard for a year, you'd have to get some experience. But if something comes of it, it'll cheer us all up, I can tell you. We've got in a bit of a rut.'

'Up here?' Amy said, incredulous, gesturing at the slim white arc of the Millennium Bridge. 'Up *here*? With all *this*?'

'We've grown up with all this,' Bernie said. 'We've watched this city come alive again. My mother worked in a sweet factory in North Shields, and I drive a Jaguar and I like a fancy place to eat. But for all that, you keep needing a new energy, you never stop looking for the next little push and shove. I'll tell you something. I've got a good business here, a solid business. *This* place – well, this place means I can think of performers I couldn't even consider ten years ago. But I still look to change, I look to improve all the time, and don't ask me who for, because I've got no children and I don't know who for, in the future, I only know it's for me, right now. And what I want right now is for Margaret to come in with me, and manage the areas of the business that she manages better than anyone. She knows the North-East entertainment business like the back of her hand. And she won't come. She goes fiddling on with that little tinpot business of hers, and she won't come.'

'Why?'

'Because,' Bernie said, 'she's stuck in a rut of her own.'

Amy put both hands on the rail and leaned back, her feet braced.

'I thought I was stuck.'

'You're never stuck at eighteen.'

'But if it's how you feel—'

Bernie Harrison glanced at her.

'Exactly. And you being young and being struck with all this made us old fogeys feel a whole lot better. Why else am I here and not in my office?'

Amy straightened up.

'Thank you very much for that.'

'I'm not doing it for you, young lady.'

'Aren't you?'

He shrugged. He was laughing.

'I never do anything without a motive. And I've got two motives this morning. One, I promised Margaret we'd all have lunch together.'

'Oh,' Amy said.

'Oh good or oh bad?'

'Oh fine,' Amy said.

'And the second thing, before we go any further, is I need to have an idea of you.'

'An idea—'

'As a musician,' Bernie said.

315

'How—'

Bernie turned. He gestured across the concourse.

'Down there,' he said, 'down one level, is the music edu-cation centre. Workshops, practice rooms, teaching rooms, recording studios. We're going down there now. I've set it up. There's a flute down there, waiting for you, and I'm going to hear you play.'

The owner of the Highgate flat was in Los Angeles.

'Oh my God,' Chrissie said, 'did I wake you?'

He did not sound quite sure.

'Not really—'

'I forgot the time difference. I'm so sorry but I quite forgot about Pacific time. I just wanted—'

'Yes?'

'I just wondered if you'd let the flat—'

'Oh no,' he said. He sounded as if he was lying down. 'No, I haven't. I was kinda waiting for you—'

'Well,' Chrissie said, 'I think it will be OK. I think – I *think* I've sold my house.'

'Good,' he said, 'good news—'

'Could you possibly wait a bit more? Could you wait two more weeks?'

'Sure,' he said, 'I can wait two weeks.' He yawned. 'I'll even be over, I think, in two weeks. I'm not sure.'

'That's so kind of you—'

'No,' he said, 'it's business. My accountant says I should let it and you seem the right kind of person to let it to. That's fine by me.'

'Thank you.'

'Call me when you know—'

'I will. I'll call you straight away—'

'And go round there. Go and see it again. The housekeeper has the keys. Help yourself.'

'Yes,' Chrissie said, 'thank you—'

'See you,' he said. He yawned again. 'From sunny California, and a view of the freeway, I send greetings and say see you in Highgate.'

Chrissie put the phone down. The call had been, despite the yawns, strangely elating. As was, to her surprise, the presence of the young couple's surveyor in the house, tapping walls and peering into cupboards in a manner that suggested he would be very, very disappointed if he found nothing amiss. Chrissie had made him tea – he'd been very specific, asking for only enough milk to cloud the tea, and one sugar – which he had left to get cold in the kitchen, but even that didn't irritate her. She was beginning, cautiously, to believe that she was feeling better. Not all the time, and not reliably, dramatically so, but she was distinctly aware that instead of believing she was at the mercy of Richie's decisions, Richie's erratic earning power and enthusiasm, Richie's fans, Richie's particular brand of sweetly expressed utter stubbornness, she was instead sensing the first stirrings of the luxury of being free to choose. She might have much – much – less money, and she would no longer own a property, but then she would no longer be in a position of dependency either, reliant upon another person for livelihood, for emotional reassurance.

The surveyor was coming down the stairs, slowly, still making notes. He'd been in the house for hours, which suggested to Chrissie not so much that he was being exhaustively, dangerously thorough, as that he had, these days, far less work coming in.

'I'm afraid your tea is cold,' Chrissie said. In the old days, she might have added, 'Shall I make you another?' Now, however, she merely smiled.

He didn't look up.

'I always drink it cold,' he said.

*   *   *

317

Tamsin, despite being at work, had been on the phone to Amy. She had rung her to tell her that they were all very upset by her behaviour, and that it was really hurtful and disloyal to behave like this, especially for Chrissie. Perhaps, Tamsin said, Amy hadn't realized what it was like for Chrissie to have to sell the house and take a pretty menial job – Chrissie, after all, Tamsin reminded Amy, was used to a professional managerial role – and it was absolutely out of order for Amy to add to all this pain by behaving with such callous disregard for anybody's feelings but her own. In fact, Amy should know that she, Tamsin, was thinking of going to live with Chrissie in the Highgate flat because it was going to be so hard, so very hard, for her to adjust without help and support.

'Have you done?' Amy demanded, when her sister paused for breath.

'For the moment. Where are you?'

'I'm sitting,' Amy said, 'with a cat on my knee.'

Tamsin gave a little snort.

'Maybe,' Amy went on, not sounding anything like as ruffled as Tamsin thought she ought to be, 'maybe Mum is doing better than you give her credit for. Maybe she quite likes choosing her life again.'

'It's not a choice,' Tamsin said, 'she *has* to do all this. And we have to help her.'

'Well,' Amy said, 'I might be helping. I might not be a burden on her. I might not be living there. More space for you—'

'You are unbelievable—'

'They take twenty-five people a year on this course. I need three Bs and grade eight, and I've got grade eight.'

'You're obsessed,' Tamsin said.

'No more than you are,' Amy said. 'It's just about some-thing different.'

'When are you deigning to come back?'

'On Friday,' Amy said, 'I told Mum. God, this cat is heavy, it's like sitting under a furry hippo or something. I've got to do the application through UCAS and all that, but I'm going into the department at the university to have a look.' She paused and then she said proudly, 'I've got an introduction.'

'I'm not asking,' Tamsin said. 'I don't want to know.'

'OK,' Amy said. 'No change there, then.'

'I want you to think about what I said—'

Amy was silent.

'Amy?'

Silence.

'*Amy*?'

Tamsin took the phone from her ear and looked at the screen. 'Call ended', it said. She gave a furious little exclamation.

'Tamsin?' Robbie said.

She looked up from her seat behind the reception desk, still frowning. She had not been expecting him.

'Robbie, not till six, you know not till six.'

He was not, to her slight surprise, smiling. He was in his work suit and looked absolutely as he usually did, but instead of regarding her with his customary expression of being alert to accommodate to her precisely current mood, he was looking, well, stern was the word that came to mind.

She said, 'Is everything OK?'

'No,' he said, 'no, it isn't. I wouldn't interrupt you at work if it was.'

She half rose.

'What's happened?'

'You probably haven't noticed,' Robbie said. He leaned over the desk a little and Tamsin felt a small clutch of real apprehension. 'In fact, if you had noticed, I wouldn't be here. I could have waited till tonight, but for once I didn't think I would. If you want to know, I'm sick of waiting.' He leaned a little further. 'Tamsin,' Robbie said, 'I'm at the end of my tether.'

A small beauty salon in Marylebone, just off the High Street, offered Dilly a job as a junior therapist for four days a week, with the expectation that she would work every other weekend. Dilly said she would think about it. She liked the look of the salon and the other girls seemed perfectly friendly, but she wasn't sure about the commitment of working at weekends, which would mean, if she only had three days a week when she wasn't working, but all her friends were, she'd be stuck in that top-floor flat alone with no one to hang out with.

The manageress of the salon had seen quite a lot of girls like Dilly. In fact she was rather tired of girls like Dilly and wasn't going to waste her breath, yet again, explaining that the current employment market was not a pick-and-choose, plenty-more-where-that-came-from scenario any more. So she looked at Dilly – pretty girl, and a deft worker – and said she should of course make up her own mind, but that the salon needed an extra girl, on the terms she had specified, immediately, and that the job would be given to the next suitable candidate who came through the door, which might be that very afternoon. She then turned away to talk to a client in a very different, animated manner, and Dilly went out into the street feeling, aggrievedly, that she hadn't in any way merited being treated like that.

She continued to feel uneasy, heading for the underground. She'd gone for the interview at her friend Breda's insistence, and everything about the salon, and the people, had been really nice. It was just the hours. It was OK, wasn't it, to decide for yourself about the hours? It wasn't right, was it, to ask someone to work part-time, and then tell them that half that part-time was going to be Saturdays and Sundays? That wasn't fair. Dilly was sure that wasn't fair. Dad had always told them that work would never satisfy them if their hearts weren't in it, and how could your heart be in something where you felt you were in some way being exploited because you were only a junior therapist, and part-time at that?

Dilly argued with herself all the way home. She texted Breda, as promised, to tell her about the interview and that she wasn't sure about the job, and Breda texted back 'MISTAKE' in capital letters, which wasn't the reaction Dilly was expecting, so she deleted the message, but the word 'mistake' clung to her mind and seemed to echo there like an insistent drumbeat. Her discomfort was increased by not being sure how Chrissie would react to her story, because there was a danger – a definite danger – that her mother might look at her as the manager of the salon had done, and Dilly wasn't at all sure that she could take that. Everything had got so unpredictable lately, and the whole Amy thing was just making it worse. The best thing to do, Dilly decided, was to hope that Chrissie would be at home alone, and that Dilly, instead of recounting the story as it had happened, could slightly readjust the narrative to conclude that Chrissie's opinion had to be sought and acted upon before Dilly could, really, either accept or decline the job offer.

But Chrissie wasn't alone. Chrissie and Tamsin were in the sitting room and Tamsin had evidently been crying. She was sniffing still, crouched in an armchair clutching a balled-up tissue. Chrissie was on the sofa, sitting rather upright, and not, to Dilly's anxious eye, looking especially sympathetic.

Dilly dropped her bag in the doorway.

'What's going on?'

Chrissie said to Tamsin, 'Do you want to tell her, or shall I?'

Tamsin said unsteadily, teasing out shreds of her tissue ball, 'It's Robbie.'

Dilly came hurriedly round the sofa and sat down next to Chrissie. She said in a horrified voice, 'He hasn't *dumped* you?'

Tamsin shook her head.

'Well then—'

'But he might!' Tamsin said in a wail.

'What d'you mean?'

Tamsin began to cry again.

'He told Tamsin,' Chrissie said, 'that he was tired of waiting for her to move in with him, and that he could only suppose that her reluctance meant she didn't really want to, so he's told her to go away and decide, and tell him finally in the morning.'

'Well,' Dilly said, abruptly conscious of her own currently single state, 'that's easy, isn't it?'

'No!' Tamsin shouted.

Dilly glanced quickly at her mother.

'I thought,' Dilly said to Tamsin, 'that you *wanted* to move in with Robbie?'

Tamsin howled, 'I *can't*, I *can't*, can I?'

'Why not?' Dilly said.

'Because of *Mum*,' Tamsin wailed, 'because of Mum and this flat and Amy – and Dad dying. And everything. I *can't.*'

Dilly swallowed.

'There's still me—'

'You haven't got a job—'

'I might have!'

'Oh God,' Tamsin said, '*might* this, *might* that. Why don't you ever *do* something?'

'Why don't *you*?' Dilly said crossly. 'Why don't you move in with Robbie?'

'Exactly,' Chrissie said.

They both turned to look at her. She had spread her hands out in her lap, and she was looking down at them.

'I wasn't sure,' Chrissie said, 'when or how I was going to say this to you. I certainly didn't plan on saying it today, but here you both are, and now seems as good a time as any.'

She paused. Tamsin sat up a little straighter, and lifted her arms, in a characteristically settling gesture, to pull her ponytail tighter through its black velvet band.

'I think the house is sold,' Chrissie said, 'and I think I'm going to take the flat. And I've definitely accepted the job, for a trial period of three months, even though I don't think of it as that, I think of it as something I'll do as well as I can until I can do something better. I get the feeling Leverton's understand that.'

The girls waited, watching her. She went on surveying her hands.

'I haven't thought what I'm going to say for very long,' Chrissie said, 'but the reason I'm talking to you is that, having had the thought, or, to be honest, having had it suggested to me, it strikes me as the right thing to do. The right way forward.'

She stopped and looked up. Tamsin and Dilly were sitting bolt upright, knees together, waiting.

'What?' Tamsin said.

'There'll always be a home for you with me,' Chrissie said, 'always. And there's one for Amy now, of course, if she wants it, which she doesn't seem to. But it's there for her, a bedroom, even if she isn't in it. But – it's different for you two, isn't it? And it's different for me now too, different in a way I never imagined, never pictured, and I can see that none of us are going to move forwards, move on from Dad dying, from life with Dad, if we just go on living round – round this kind of hollow centre, if you see what I mean, living all clinging together because that's all we know, even if it isn't doing any of us any good.'

She paused. Dilly looked anxiously at Tamsin.

'So?' Tamsin said.

'I think,' Chrissie said carefully to Tamsin, 'that you should go and live with Robbie. I think you should make Robbie your priority as you once appeared to want to because if you make *me* your priority you'll get stuck and then we won't like each other at all. Will we? And Dilly. I think you should take any job you are offered and ask about among your friends for a room in someone's flat—'

Dilly gave a little gasp.

'And discover,' Chrissie said firmly, 'the satisfaction of standing on your own two feet. I'll help you as much as I can, but I'm not suggesting you live with me for exactly the reasons I gave Tamsin. It won't be easy, but we won't get trapped in resentment, in the past, either. We are all going to try and make something of our lives and of our relationship. I don't actually think our relationship would survive living together. Do you?' She stopped again, and looked at them. She seemed suddenly to be on the edge of tears. The girls were gazing back at her, but neither of them was crying.

'And so,' Chrissie said, not at all steadily, 'I intend to live in that flat on my own after the house is sold. You'll be so welcome there, any time, but you won't be living there. You'll be living your own lives, lives where you can begin to put the past behind you, where it belongs. Elsewhere.'

CHAPTER TWENTY

Margaret had done what Scott called getting them in. She was at one of the low tables with armchairs, in the first-floor bar of the hotel overlooking the river, and she had ordered a gin and tonic for herself, and a bottle of Belgian beer for Scott, and it was very pleasant sitting there, with the early-evening sun shining on the river and the great bulk of the Baltic on the further shore with some daft modern-art slogan on a huge banner plastered to its side. Amazing what people thought they could get away with, amazing what people put up with, amazing to think of the contrasts. There was the pretentious nonsense all over the Baltic – it had just been a flour mill when Margaret was growing up – and then, at the other end of the scale, there was the old Baptist church in Tynemouth, now deconsecrated and a warren of gimcrack little shops with Mr Lee's Tattooing Parlour right under the old church window which said 'God is love' in red-and-white glass. Just thinking about it made Margaret want to snort.

'Penny for them, Mam,' Scott said, dropping into the chair opposite her.

'Oh,' she said, 'you wouldn't want to know.' She waved a hand at the Baltic. 'That rubbish, for starters—'

'He's a serious artist,' Scott said, 'and if you don't behave, I'll take you to see his video installation.'

'You will not—'

'Amy liked it,' Scott said.

Margaret's expression gentled.

'Amy—'

Scott grinned.

'She's texting, all the time.'

Margaret said, 'Dawson liked her. Even Dawson. He won't sit on just anyone's lap.'

'We've all gone a bit soft on Amy—'

'Well,' Margaret said more briskly, 'she's got work to do.'

'She'll do it.'

'She's not very practised. She's been sheltered. Over-sheltered. She thinks money's just pocket money. She doesn't know anything about money—'

'She knows enough to get Mr Harrison to give her a job.'

'Nonsense,' Margaret said.

Scott pulled out his phone, and pressed a few buttons. Then he held the phone out to his mother.

'Read that.'

Margaret leaned forward, putting on her reading glasses. She peered at the screen. She said, 'So he says there's work for her. I doubt it. He'll only have her fetching coffee.'

'She won't mind that. She'll be learning. She'll get to see his acts. She'll be performing. She can sing.'

Margaret leaned back.

'I know she can sing. It's not much of a voice yet but it's in tune—'

'Bang on the note.'

'Don't make a fool of yourself over her, pet,' Margaret said.

Scott took a swallow of his beer. He grinned at his mother.

'She's on a mission to find me a girlfriend.'

'Good luck to her.'

'I don't mind,' Scott said, 'I don't mind if she manages it—'

'What's got into you?'

Scott raised his beer bottle towards his mother.

'Same as you.'

'I'm just as I was,' Margaret said.

'No, you're not.'

'I'm—'

'Look at you,' Scott said, 'look at you. You've had something done to your hair, and that's new.'

'What's new?'

'That dress.'

'Oh,' Margaret said airily, 'this.' She looked out at the river. 'Everything I'd got suddenly looked so tired.'

'Yes.'

'Why do you say yes as if you know something I don't know?'

'Mam,' Scott said, 'I don't know anything you don't know. The difference between us is just that I admit it.'

'Admit what?'

'That I feel better. That you feel better. That we all feel better.'

'All?'

'Yes,' Scott said firmly, 'Mr Harrison too.'

Margaret took a sip of her drink.

'What has Bernie Harrison got to do with it?'

'You tell me,' Scott said.

Margaret smiled privately down into her gin and tonic.

'Why'd you ask me here?' Scott said. 'Why're you all tarted up?'

'Don't use that word to me—'

'Why, Mam?'

Margaret looked up.

'Are you in a hurry, pet?'

'No,' Scott said. 'Well, yes, actually. I'm meeting some of the lads from work.'

'And the lasses, too?' Margaret said.

Scott said, smiling, 'There's always the lasses too.'

'Ah.'

'Never mind ah. I want to know what's going on. I want to know why you asked me here.'

Margaret looked round the bar in a leisurely way, as if she was savouring something. Then she said, 'Bernie'll be here in ten minutes.'

'And? *And?*'

'I just thought,' Margaret said, 'that I'd like to tell you before I told him. That's all.'

It was late when she got home, but the night sky over the sea was dim rather than dark, and the sea was washing peacefully up against the shore below Percy Gardens. Margaret liked the sea in its summer mood, when even if it lost its temper it was only briefly, unlike the sustained furious rages of winter when she could stand at her sitting-room window and see the spray flung angrily upwards in great dramatic plumes. But in the summer, there was less sense of frustration, less of a feeling that the sea was outraged to find its wild energies curtailed by a shoreline, by the upsettingly domestic barriers of a coast road and a crescent of houses inhabited by people who thought they had the capacity to control and contain whatever was inconvenient about nature.

Margaret paid off the taxi, and walked, in her new summer shoes, to the edge of the grassy oval of grass in front of Percy Gardens, so that she could see the sea, heaving and gleaming and spilling itself, over and over, on to the stones below her. Bernie Harrison had wanted to take her somewhere impressive to celebrate, but she'd said no, they could eat there, in the brasserie of the hotel, and when he said wasn't that meant for much younger people than they were she said speak for yourself, Bernie Harrison, but I feel years younger than I did only a week ago.

Their steaks had come on rectangular wooden platters, like superior bread boards, and Bernie had found a very respectable burgundy on the wine list to drink with them, and Margaret had to hand it to him, he hadn't crowed over her once, he hadn't said, 'What kept you?' or, 'About time too,' he'd just said, over and over, that he was so pleased, so pleased, and, if he was honest, relieved too.

'Have you told Glenda?'

'Of course not. Would I tell Glenda before I told you?'

'I think,' Bernie said, reflecting on how nice it was to have chips with his steak, how nice it was to be with a woman who didn't think chips were common, 'she'll like the plan, don't you?'

'She's been on at me ever since you first suggested it.'

'Margaret,' Bernie said, putting down his knife and fork, 'Margaret. How do *you* feel?'

She glanced up at him.

'If you can't see that for yourself, Bernie Harrison,' she said, 'you need your eyes seeing to.'

He put her into a taxi in a way she found entirely acceptable, no challenges, no fake gallantry, no showing off. He'd just kissed her cheek, thanked her and said, 'We'll both sleep happier tonight,' and then slapped the roof of the taxi as if to wish her Godspeed on the journey home and somehow more than that, on a journey into something that was, of course, more of the same, but with a twist, with a new injection of vitality, a new optimism. She took several deep breaths of the sea, and then she turned and went carefully back over the rough grass to her front door, and put the key in the lock.

Dawson, with his strange, rare and precise intuition, was sitting eight feet inside the door, waiting for her. When she came in, he lifted himself to his feet and arched his back slightly and made a small, interrogatory remark.

Margaret looked at him. She remembered him as that small, battered kitten with a bloody eye and patchy fur and felt a rush of affection for him, not only for what he was and what he had overcome, but because he had by now walked so much of her path with her, had seen her out of some considerable shadows into, if not blazing sunlight, at least light-dappled shade.

'I don't see why you shouldn't,' Margaret said. 'Just this once.'

She followed him into the kitchen. He paced ahead of her, not hurrying, confident of his small victory, and, as ever, blessedly, uncomplicatedly detached.

He sat down with dignity beside his food bowl and watched her while she found a small square tin of his special-treat cat food in the cupboard and peeled back the lid, releasing a rich, savoury aroma that made him run his curling pink tongue round his whiskers.

'There,' Margaret said. 'There. You fat old bully.'

She straightened up. Dawson folded his front paws under himself, in order to bring his chin down to the level of his dish. He was purring triumphantly.

'Night-night,' Margaret said. 'Enjoy. See you in the morning.'

And then she turned to close the door and switch off the light.

Upstairs she put on the lamp by her bed, and opened the window, and drew the curtains halfway across so that there was enough space for a slice of summer dawn to fall through in the morning. Then she took off her new dress, and hung it up on a corner of her wardrobe, and put on her padded dressing gown and sat down at her dressing table to begin the rituals of the end of the day.

In front of her lay the Minton dish, waiting to receive her pearls and her earrings. It wasn't quite empty, already containing two safety pins, a pearl button, and the wedding ring she had taken off those months before and allowed, subsequently, just to lie there until it became out of familiarity no more significant than the safety pins. She picked it up now, and looked at it. It had meant so much, once, had symbolized something when the marriage was happening, and even more when it was over. It had been, for years, a talisman, a token of validation, of justification, proof that she had been, in some way that had mattered very much at the time, more than just herself.

She examined it. What a dull thing it looked now. How gladly at that moment would she have given it to Amy's mother, to that woman who'd had so many reasons, so much time, to believe that she was entitled to it. She wasn't going to think ill of Richie now, she wasn't going to waste precious energies on stacking up the case against him, nor was she going to do the same for Chrissie. Amy hadn't talked much about Chrissie except to say that she hoped she really would take this job and this flat, and start to lead her own life at last, but Margaret had had the strong sense that when Richie died he'd left his castle in London and the people it contained grievously undefended. Amy, of course, was in no place to see that yet, might not see it for years, but already she seemed to want a freedom for her mother, a wish Margaret much approved of, a wish that suggested, at the very least, that life with Richie, for all its beguiling charms, had not made allowances for much liberty in the lives around him.

She slipped the ring on to her wedding finger. It lodged itself on her second knuckle and, although it could be persuaded, with difficulty, to slide all the way down, there seemed no point in its doing so. She took it off and laid it on the dressing table. In the morning, she thought, on her way to work – she would walk to work, whatever the weather – and to tell Glenda the news about the future, she would cross the grass as she had just done, and then the road, and she would scramble down the shallow cliff slope, holding the ring, and when she got to the bottom, as a mark of respect to the past and all it represented, but also as a gesture of finality, a signal that the past was now over, she would throw the ring into the sea.